# The Assassins
# of Altis

# PRAISE FOR THE PILLARS OF REALITY SERIES

"Campbell has created an interesting world... [he] has created his characters in such a meticulous way, I could not help but develop my own feelings for both of them. I have already gotten the second book and will be listening with anticipation."

*—Audio Book Reviewer*

"I loved *The Hidden Masters of Marandur*...The intense battle and action scenes are one of the places where Campbell's writing really shines. There are a lot of urban and epic fantasy novels that make me cringe when I read their battles, but Campbell's years of military experience help him write realistic battles."

*—All Things Urban Fantasy*

"I highly recommend this to fantasy lovers, especially if you enjoy reading about young protagonists coming into their own and fighting against a stronger force than themselves. The world building has been strengthened even further giving the reader more history. Along with the characters flight from their pursuers and search for knowledge allowing us to see more of the continent the pace is constant and had me finding excuses to continue the book."

*—Not Yet Read*

"*The Dragons of Dorcastle*... is the perfect mix of steampunk and fantasy... it has set the bar to high."

*—The Arched Doorway*

# PRAISE FOR THE LOST FLEET SERIES

"It's the thrilling saga of a nearly-crushed force battling its way home from deep within enemy territory, laced with deadpan satire about modern warfare and neoliberal economics. Like Xenophon's Anabasis – with spaceships."

*–The Guardian (UK)*

"Black Jack is an excellent character, and this series is the best military SF I've read in some time."

*–Wired Magazine*

"If you're a fan of character, action, and conflict in a Military SF setting, you would probably be more than pleased by Campbell's offering."

*–Tor.com*

". . . a fun, quick read, full of action, compelling characters, and deeper issues. Exactly the type of story which attracts readers to military SF in the first place."

*–SF Signal*

"Rousing military-SF action… it should please many fans of old-fashioned hard SF. And it may be a good starting point for media SF fans looking to expand their SF reading beyond tie-in novels."

*–SciFi.com*

"Fascinating stuff … this is military SF where the military and SF parts are both done right."

*–SFX Magazine*

# PRAISE FOR THE LOST FLEET: BEYOND THE FRONTIER SERIES

"Combines the best parts of military sf and grand space opera to launch a new adventure series … sets the fleet up for plenty of exciting discoveries and escapades."

*—Publishers Weekly*

"Absorbing…neither series addicts nor newcomers will be disappointed."

*—Kirkus Reviews*

"Epic space battles, this time with aliens. Fans who enjoyed the earlier books in the Lost Fleet series will be pleased."

*—Fantasy Literature*

"I loved every minute of it. I've been with these characters through six novels and it felt like returning to an old group of friends."

*—Walker of Worlds*

"A fast-paced page turner … the search for answers will keep readers entertained for years to come."

*—SF Revu*

"Another excellent addition to one of the best military science fiction series on the market. This delivers everything fans expect from Black Jack Geary and more."

*—Monsters & Critics*

# ALSO BY JACK CAMPBELL

## THE LOST FLEET

*Dauntless*
*Fearless*
*Courageous*
*Valiant*
*Relentless*
*Victorious*

## THE LOST FLEET: BEYOND THE FRONTIER

*Dreadnaught*
*Invincible*
*Guardian*
*Steadfast*
*Leviathan*

## THE LOST STARS

*Tarnished Knight*
*Perilous Shield*
*Imperfect Sword*
*Shattered Spear*

## THE PAUL SINCLAIR SERIES

*A Just Determination*
*Burden of Proof*

*Rule of Evidence*
*Against All Enemies*

## THE ETHAN STARK SERIES

*Stark's War*
*Stark's Command*
*Stark's Crusade*

## THE PILLARS OF REALITY SERIES

*The Dragons of Dorcastle**
*The Hidden Masters of Marandur**
*The Assassins of Altis**
*The Pirates of Pacta Servanda*
*(forthcoming)*
*Books 5-6 forthcoming*

## STAND ALONE NOVELS

*The Last Full Measure*

## SHORT STORY COLLECTIONS

*Ad Astra**
*Borrowed Time**
*Swords and Saddles**

*available as a JABberwocky ebook*

# THE
# ASSASSINS
# OF ALTIS

Pillars of Reality
Book 3

# JACK CAMPBELL

JABberwocky Literary Agency, Inc.

*To*
*my son James*

*For S, as always*

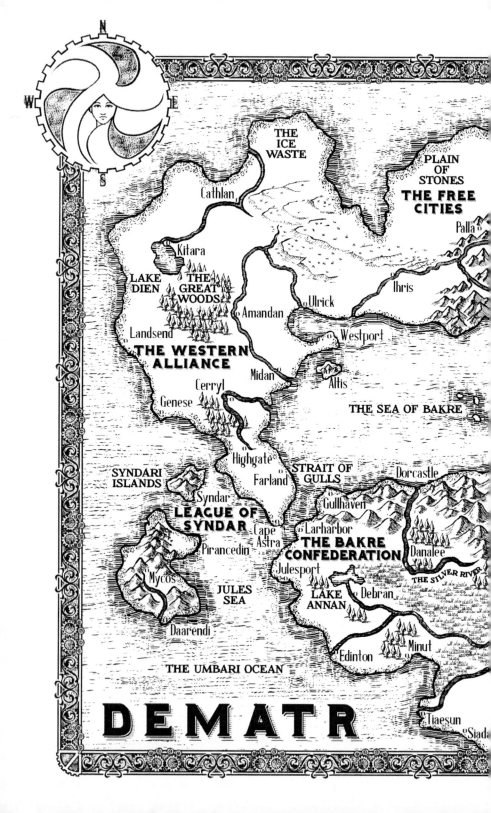

DEMATR

# ACKNOWLEDGMENTS

I remain indebted to my agents, Joshua Bilmes and Eddie Schneider, for their long standing support, ever-inspired suggestions and assistance, as well as to Krystyna Lopez and Lisa Rodgers for their work on foreign sales and print editions. Thanks also to Catherine Asaro, Robert Chase, Carolyn Ives Gilman, J.G. (Huck) Huckenpohler, Simcha Kuritzky, Michael LaViolette, Aly Parsons, Bud Sparhawk and Constance A. Warner for their suggestions, comments and recommendations.

# CHAPTER ONE

The city of Marandur had died more than one hundred and fifty years ago, when the old Imperial capital became a battlefield between rebels and legionaries. No mercy was shown. The city had been crushed between two implacable armies, its many buildings torn and shattered, and when victory was declared the legions withdrew on the orders of their Emperor, leaving the ruined city and its countless dead to disintegrate as a monument to the price of rebellion.

From that time until now, the penalty for entering Marandur had been death. From that time until now, the legions had stood guard outside the city to keep anyone from entering and anyone from leaving, for some survivors of the siege had been trapped in Marandur, their descendants forced to endure life in a city where everything had become monstrous and foreign.

But someone had entered the city not long ago, and now they were about to try to leave it. If they did not succeed, every city would soon share the fate of Marandur, and countless men, women, and children would die in the ruin of everything humans had built on the world of Dematr.

Mage Alain of Ihris stood next to a small gate set into the back wall of the University of Marandur in Marandur. Outside the ruins of the dead city awaited, along with the threat of the brutish barbarians descended from those few rebels not slain by the vengeful Imperial legions. Beyond the barbarians and the broken wall of the city, Imperial watch towers enforced the quarantine of the old Imperial capital.

If they made it past those obstacles, all that would be left to worry about would be the most powerful forces in Dematr, all of which wanted Alain and his companion either captured or dead.

Master Mechanic Mari stood only a lance length away from Alain, holding a last conversation with the masters of the University and the students Mari had worked with. She had taught Mechanic skills to common folk her Guild claimed were incapable of learning such things, not only giving away Mechanics Guild secrets but undermining the primary justification for its control of all technology. If Mari had not already been marked for arrest by the Mechanics Guild, that act alone would have condemned her.

Snow swirled lightly across a sky the gray color of the metal in the Mechanic pistol Mari always carried under her coat. Alain settled the pack on his shoulders more comfortably and checked the long knife he wore as Mari came up to him with a nervous smile. Like Alain, she wore the trousers, boots, shirt and coat of a common person, her black Mechanics jacket once again concealed in her pack, just as Alain's Mage robes were hidden within his. "Are you ready?" she asked.

"Yes." Alain started to walk toward the gate.

Mari flung out one hand to stop him and gave Alain a cross look. She turned to the scholars of the university. "My thanks again for granting us refuge when we were pursued, and for aiding me in other ways whose value I really can't exaggerate. Because you've maintained some order and civilization in the midst of a city that otherwise knows only death and decay, there may be hope for everyone."

The university students and professors all bowed toward Mari and Alain in response. "It is we who owe thanks to the both of you," replied Professor Wren, the current headmaster of the university. "You brought the first news of the outside world to us since the city was sealed off by order of Emperor Palan over a century and a half ago. You, Master Mechanic Mari, have made our heating system work again, and trained our students to keep it working. If the thanks of those declared dead by order of the Emperor mean anything, you have ours."

Mari shook her head. "I can't make any promises, but if we can figure out a way to get the current Emperor to reconsider your status, we'll try." She reached back to indicate her pack. "I'll carry your petition to the Emperor with me until I find a way to deliver it to him."

She glanced at Alain, and he read the meaning in her eyes. *Assuming that we survive getting out of Marandur. And whatever happens after that.*

"Are you sure you won't let a large force of our students escort you to the walls?" Wren asked.

Mari and Alain once again exchanged glances, then both shook their heads. "A large group would have more chance of being spotted by the barbarians," Mari explained. "If there is a fight, the Imperial sentries outside the walls will be alerted. Our best chance is to remain unnoticed by anyone."

"Very well," Wren said. "We do not know what you took from the materials we guarded for so long, but good luck in bringing them somewhere you can make use of them. The future of our world rides with you, daughter."

Alain saw Mari flinch at the title. "I'll…do my best," she said.

Professor Wren gestured to the students guarding the gate. The heavy beam holding the gate shut was lifted, and the gate shoved open just enough to let Mari and Alain through. They both slipped through the gap, the gate being immediately pulled shut behind them.

They heard the faint sound of the beam being reset behind them as they set off across a wide, open area which had once been part of a park surrounding the walls of the university. Now it was kept clear, burned and cut by the survivors inside the university to prevent any of the savages outside from approaching the walls unseen. The open area ended not far off in the ruins of the city proper, but for now they just had to slog through the dry, brown stalks of dead grass while snow continued to fall in a filmy white veil which helped conceal them as well as the devastation of the ruins ahead.

"It looks like they were right about another storm coming," Mari said in a quiet voice that would not carry far. "Too bad we couldn't wait until it hit fully before we left."

"The university's inhabitants feared snow drifts would block the gates," Alain reminded her, "and make the ruins more treacherous than usual by concealing dangerous areas. We must try to reach the city wall before the storm strikes, then use the cover of the storm to escape past the Imperial guard towers."

Alain searched the ruins ahead of them while they walked. As he and Mari had discovered after getting into the city, the barbarians had proven very good at hiding in the tumbled wreckage of their ancestors' city. "I see no warning of danger," he said to Mari.

"I wish that foresight of yours was reliable," Mari remarked, immediately afterwards giving him an apologetic look. "Sorry."

He looked at her for a moment. "It does not always provide warning. I too wish foresight was dependable. What did I do wrong earlier?"

"When? Oh, you mean when we were leaving? Alain, when you leave someone, especially people who did the things for us that those people did, the polite thing to do is to say goodbye and farewell and all that kind of thing."

"I will remember that," Alain said. Having spent most of his life inside a Mage Guild Hall being taught that other people were only shadows cast upon the illusion of the world, shadows who did not matter in any way, Alain had learned nothing of what Mari called "social skills."

"One step at a time, my Mage," Mari said. "Just treat other people like you would me." She sighed. "And do your best not to let anyone else know about the prophecy."

"Everyone already knows about the prophecy," Alain said.

"They don't know that *I'm* supposed to be the daughter of Jules that the common folk have been waiting for for centuries to overthrow the Great Guilds!" Mari scowled at the snow before them. "I don't believe it, but everyone else seems eager to. Why does everyone expect me to save the world?"

"You are not supposed to save the world alone," Alain reminded her. "The prophecy says that the daugh— says that you will unite Mechanics, Mages, and common folk into one force to change the world."

"Well, that ought to be easy enough," Mari groused. "After all, it's not like the Mechanics, the Mages, and the common folk don't all hate each other with enough passion to melt high-grade steel."

Alain puzzled over her words, though of course his expression did not reveal his confusion. Mage acolytes were taught, using the most severe forms of punishment, never to reveal emotion, and Alain retained much of that despite his time with Mari. "They all do hate each other."

She sighed heavily. "That was sarcasm again, Alain. Thank you, though, for not calling me by that name. Everyone else is going to call me the daughter, but I need you to remember that I'm Mari."

The wind was picking up, blowing the snow sideways and moaning through the ruins they had almost reached. Alain tried to smile reassuringly at Mari, a very difficult task since any kind of smile was hard for him. "You have already begun to change the world. You have a Mage following you."

"You don't count," Mari said. "You're in love with me."

"And the common folk in the university, those we just left. And the soldiers of Alexdria and General Flyn."

"Who will not last a day if the Great Guilds focus their attention on them!" Mari gestured at the blowing snow. "The longer we keep everyone else in the dark that I'm the— that person, the better. I need time, Alain. Maybe with enough time I'll even figure out why everyone wants to follow me without knowing whether I'll lead them off a cliff!" She scowled as the wind gusted. "The storm noise is going to make it harder for us to make out if those barbarians start whistling to call all of their friends after us again."

"It will also make it harder for them to hear us." Alain glanced up at the leaden sky. "The university masters do not believe that the barbarians maintain watch of the university very often, and when they do they usually watch the main gate on the other side of the university."

"I'm still not sure I believe that," Mari said.

"It is prudent not to assume our foes watch only one place, but I think what the university masters told us is likely, Mari. You saw how thin were the barbarians we encountered before we reached the university. Those creatures can barely survive in this city, and could not afford to have any of their numbers devoted to a task such as watching the university when that would not provide food."

"I hope you're right. I don't want to run into them again. But assuming they're not watching us is what we want to believe, and Professor S'san always warned me about assumptions that you want to believe. It's too easy to accept them." Mari shuddered, but not from the cold. "Alain…" Her hand went to her coat as if preparing to reach inside it, and lines of pain furrowed her brow. "I don't know if I can…"

"You do not know if you can once again use your weapon against the barbarians?" Alain asked.

"Don't!" Mari bit her lip. "I'm sorry. You sounded so emotionless when you said that, like it didn't matter."

"I am trying to put feelings into my voice again. You have said I am getting better at it."

"Yes, you are, and I have no right to accuse you of not caring." Mari swallowed, her expression miserable now. "I haven't told you, but I am really, really scared of having to draw and fire this weapon at people again. I don't want to…to…"

"Kill them." Alain said it not because he did not understand her distress, but because he thought it must be said. "It happened. Not by our choice. You were forced to defend yourself. You know what your fate would have been in the hands of the barbarians."

Mari shuddered again, more violently than the cold could account for. "I know." She took a deep breath, her expression smoothing out. "I'll handle it, Alain. I won't let you down if you need me."

"I never doubted that, my Lady Mechanic. I know how difficult those memories are for you. I have similar ones. As General Flyn told me, it is a hard thing to carry throughout a life." Alain cast about for something to divert her attention from the pain those memories brought, finally remembering something which Mari had mentioned in passing a few days ago. "I forgot to say this earlier. Happy birthday. Is that how it is said?"

Mari gave him a startled look, then laughed softly. "Oh, yeah.

I'd almost forgotten myself. I never dreamed that on my nineteenth birthday I'd be sneaking out of a ruined city on my way to try to change the world."

"With a Mage," Alain added.

"Right. I keep finding myself with you in very unpleasant circumstances." Mari smiled wryly as she said that. "But having you along makes those circumstances endurable as well as survivable." Her smile faded. "Alain, when I turned eighteen I was a Mechanic in good standing. I'd never met a Mage, and I had never questioned my loyalty to the Guild. Now I'm working against the leaders of my Guild and I've found out that I'm…that person in the prophecy. It's been quite a year." She glanced at him. "That's not even counting how many times I almost got killed in the last year."

"I have no gift for you," Alain said.

"We could always count one of those times you saved my life. You know, on your eighteenth birthday I said the same thing about not having a gift, and you said some nonsense about how my being with you was the greatest gift you could imagine."

"Yes," Alain agreed. "You told me I must be easy to please."

She gave him a sidelong glance. "You didn't have to remember that. Well, as far as I'm concerned having you with me is the greatest gift anyone could wish for, and I know you won't accuse me of being easy to please."

"Because you are difficult," Alain said.

"I never pretended otherwise, my Mage." They reached the verge of the ruins and Mari paused next to a shattered wall rearing above their heads, then pulled him close and kissed Alain, holding the kiss a long time before breaking it. "I don't know when we'll have our next chance to do that. The other thing that's happened since I was eighteen was falling in love with you, and yes, that is the greatest gift I've ever received."

She cautiously leaned against the tottering wall while they caught their breath after the fast hike across the open area. "Alain, you need to promise me something. If I die while we're trying to get out of this city or through the Imperial quarantine, you are to leave and find a place to hide your half of the banned Mechanics Guild texts. Then try to get in touch with Professor S'san or Mechanic Calu. If neither of them can be reached, try Mechanic Alli in Danalee."

He felt a deeper chill inside at the thought of Mari dying. "I will not leave you. You never leave anyone behind, and I will not leave you."

Mari gave him a thin-lipped, sad smile. "Alain, I'd never choose to leave you, either, but if I'm dead, I've already left you. The best thing you can do at that point is save yourself, because that's what I would want. If you manage to get those texts to any of my friends, there might still be a chance to change the world, a chance to stop that storm of chaos that will destroy everything. Now promise me."

Alain looked at her, fighting the emotions he still found unfamiliar and hard to control after so many years of training as a Mage to deny all feelings. The prophecy said that the daughter of Jules would overthrow the Great Guilds and change the world. It did not say that she would survive her victory. "Mari—"

Her face hardened, her voice unyielding. "*Promise me*, Alain. Promise you won't throw away your life if I'm already dead."

"If you die, then my life will mean nothing," Alain replied miserably.

"Yes, it will! If you continue what I was trying to accomplish. If you love me you will want to finish what I was trying to do. Now promise."

He finally nodded. "I promise that should you die I will try to bring these texts to safety and contact your friends."

"Good. That applies if I'm captured, too. You're not to try to rescue me."

Alain frowned at her, upset enough that the emotion showed. "I will not promise that. If you are captured, I will try to free you."

"*Alain…*"

"*No.*" He had gotten good enough at putting emotion into his words that his feelings on this must have been clear.

She gave him an aggravated glare, but must have been able to see that he would not bend on that. "Fine. Why did I get involved with a Mage?" Mari shifted her glare to the snow. "I know we'd agreed to go through the ruins because we'd be a lot harder for the barbarians to see than if we stuck to the relatively open ground along the river banks," she said in an abrupt change of the subject. "Is that still a good idea? This snow is thickening fast."

Alain squinted up at the sky again. "I think we would still be best going through the city. If this storm continues to worsen, we would catch its full fury on the exposed river banks, but in among the ruins those walls and buildings still standing will help break the worst of it."

"Unless the storm breaks them first," Mari observed acidly. As if on cue, a low rumble sounded somewhere in the distance, marking the collapse of one more long-abandoned building. "But you're probably right. Once we start moving again, let's not talk unless we absolutely have to so there's less chance of those savages hearing us."

She exhaled heavily, then kissed him again quickly. "I'm still unhappy you won't promise to leave me if I'm captured, but I don't want to go into danger mad at you. Just use your head, no matter what happens. I love you, my Mage."

"I love you, my Mechanic," Alain whispered in reply. It had taken a long time for him to be able say such a simple phrase, so alien was the concept of love to one taught the ways of Mages.

Alain followed as Mari moved cautiously among the wreckage cluttering what had once been a street through the city. Piles of debris blocked streets and other open areas, some dating to the fighting between rebels and Imperial legions a hundred and fifty years ago and some more recent, the result of slow disintegration of the ruins. Vacant buildings stood on all sides, their windows gaping on emptiness within, their walls and roofs broken in places large and small. Scattered everywhere were the remnants of ancient battle: broken and badly corroded armor and weapons and the white fragments of shattered bones from countless unburied bodies left behind after the legions withdrew. Most of the weapons were the swords, spears and crossbows used by common folk, but once in a while they glimpsed a broken Mechanic weapon like those Mari called rifles or pistols. The bone fragments, though, offered no clues as to who their owners had once been in life, whether rebels, legionaries, or helpless citizens caught in the fighting.

"I'd forgotten how very much I hate this place," Mari mumbled just loudly enough for Alain to hear, unnerved enough to break her own rule.

He was deciding whether or not to reply when a black cloud seemed to drift across the street in front of them, then vanished. Alain's hand went out to seize her shoulder while he breathed out a soft warning for silence. Mari stopped instantly, waiting while Alain peered into the gray-lit street ahead. Alain studied the area ahead of them, wishing he knew how to bring his foresight to work instead of hoping it would. But foresight was unreliable at the best of times, and now it offered no further signs. He brought his mouth close to Mari's ear. "I saw a warning of danger ahead," he murmured in a low voice. "We should go to the left or right some distance."

Mari looked in those directions, both blocked by piles of debris, and shook her head at facing two equally bad choices. Alain watched as she did an odd ritual with her finger, pointing each way several times back and forth while muttering something under her breath. Whatever she was saying ended with her finger pointing right. Mari beckoned to Alain, then began moving that way even more cautiously.

Despite the danger, Alain felt an irrational glow of satisfaction that Mari did not question his foresight. Even many Mages regarded foresight with suspicion, though in their case mainly because it required an unwelcome personal connection to anyone the foresight offered warnings about. Mechanics simply dismissed it as fortune-telling.

But not his Mechanic. Mari believed in him.

The street to the right being blocked by rubble, they had to cut through the collapsed remains of what might have been a large store. The floor inside was covered with piles of rotting debris. Mari's foot slipped and she fell sideways as some of the fragments turned under her. Alain grabbed at her arm, catching Mari just before she slid over a drop into a yawning pit which had been a basement. She stood still for a moment, then gave Alain a shaky smile. "Thanks," she whispered.

They moved on in silence for a while, out back onto the rubble-strewn street, the falling snow helping to muffle the sound of their movement at the same time as it obscured dangerous spots beneath their feet and restricted their vision to all sides. After moving right for a while, Mari paused, looking around, then came close to Alain to whisper again, her breath a welcome warmth against his cheek. "I think I know this street. If the new Imperial capital of Palandur copied this part of Marandur, then if we take that street to our left we should be turning back to the southwest, heading directly for the city walls and moving parallel to the river."

"Parallel?"

She gave him one of those looks again, the kind Mari used when he did not know something she thought everybody knew. "It's basic geometry, Alain."

"Geometry?"

"Alain, how can even a Mage possibly function without knowing any geometry?"

"Since I do not know what geometry is, I cannot answer that. I do function, though."

"Yes, you do," Mari admitted. They were very close together, the words they spoke barely audible to each other, the falling snow blocking out vision, as if they were alone inside a cocoon of white. "Parallel means…never mind. What I meant was if we go that way it will be the shortest route to the nearest section of the city walls and we won't have to worry about running into the river."

"I see. Why did you not say that before?"

Mari tensed, slapping one hand up to cover her face, then with a visible effort relaxed and lowered the hand. "Every time I start to feel superior to you I have to remind myself that you can do things I can't even explain." She pointed to the left and started off.

Alain nodded, following again as they traversed the new route, which was fairly clear until they reached a stretch where the fronts of several buildings had fallen into the street. As they struggled through the rubble, Alain heard a sudden intake of breath from Mari. Alarmed, he followed her gaze, to see that she was looking at the interior of one of the buildings which had lost its front.

Inside, the crumbling shapes of many human skeletons lay in rows, witness to ancient tragedy. Alain wondered who they had been. Citizens of the city who had taken shelter in the building only to be trapped and die, or who had been murdered by the rebels when they first took control of the city? Rebels, captured and executed by legionaries? Or legionaries, taken prisoner and killed, or perhaps badly wounded or killed in battle and taken here only to be forgotten?

Her face saddened, Mari turned away and continued moving carefully across the rubble.

It was hard to tell how much later it was that Mari stopped suddenly, crouching down. Alain went into a crouch, too, without asking why. It was strange, he thought, how good they had become at such things. Then Mari waved him up and pointed.

One of the rough paths made by the barbarians crossed their track just ahead. Alain studied it carefully, then leaned close to whisper in Mari's ear. "Someone has traveled it recently enough to trample some of the snowfall. But it was long enough ago to allow the signs of their passage to be partly obscured by more snow."

"Do we go ahead?" Mari whispered back.

"The path runs right across our route. If we do not cross it here, we will have to cross it somewhere else."

She nodded reluctantly, one hand reaching toward her jacket, then lowering again. Mari moved ahead quickly, crossing the path in a rush.

Alain stayed right behind Mari, but as he watched her, watched where his feet were going and tried to watch the ruins around them through the concealing sheets of snow, Alain also felt for the power in this area. As in most parts of Marandur, the power here was fairly weak, and without that power to augment his own Alain could not alter what Mari called "reality" and which Mages knew to be an illusion that could be manipulated. The power available would have to do, though, so Alain prepared his mind for whatever spells might be needed.

They would have to be offensive spells. Bending light around himself and Mari to hide them would not work in this storm, where the blowing snow would reveal their location anyway. Alain resigned himself to having to use superheated balls of air which he could direct to any spot he could see, a very powerful spell but one which would drain his strength rapidly. He also drew out the long Mage knife he wore under his coat.

Mari had still not taken her weapon in hand as she crept forward. She paused, looking to all sides and listening for anyone coming, then beckoned to Alain and began moving ahead as quickly as she safely could.

Alain followed, but could not avoid letting a larger than usual gap form between him and Mari. Fortune created that gap, however, as it allowed Alain to see a shape rising out of an apparently solid pile of rubble immediately after Mari had passed it. The barbarian was too close to Mari to risk a fireball, so Alain swung the hilt of his Mage knife against the back of the man's head.

Mari turned at the noise, staring at the barbarian sprawled at her feet. Then her eyes widened as they looked past Alain. He didn't see her draw out her weapon, but suddenly it was in her hand as she aimed past him. Alain dove forward as the boom of the Mechanic weapon filled the battered street and something made a loud crack in the air over him. He scrambled up beside Mari, seeing another barbarian falling backwards, staggering like a drunkard but with a spreading red stain on his chest. As the wounded man fell, more shapes rose up behind him. Mari aimed again, but even though her finger quivered on the weapon she did not fire the pistol.

"Mari?" Alain asked.

"They're not attacking," Mari said, her voice strained.

Alain studied the dark shapes cautiously. "They are small."

"Small?" Mari jerked, her expression reflecting sudden shock and horror. "Oh, Alain, they're children. Stars above, what if I had shot again?"

"We have stumbled on a village. I would not assume that it is safe to ignore the children, but we should run if we do not want to kill them."

"Where are all the other adults?" Mari's weapon quested from side to side as she searched the falling snow for signs of further attack.

"Perhaps they are waiting in ambush where we would have gone if we had not cut to the right for a while."

The shapes of the larger children were beginning to creep toward them cautiously. Mari grimaced. "Which means the other adults heard my shot and are probably racing this way right now."

# CHAPTER TWO

Without another word she spun and started running toward the walls of Marandur, her pace reckless in the snow-covered rubble. Alain followed, only occasionally pausing to look back for any pursuers. They scrambled up and down piles of debris, moving hastily through the ruins. Mari cut left, weaving between fallen buildings, and Alain followed, guessing that she was trying to confuse anyone trying to follow.

A dark, menacing shape loomed up before them, causing Mari to swing to one side with a muffled cry and aim her weapon, but then she lowered it with a gasp of relief. "It's a wrecked siege machine," she whispered to Alain. He followed her past the crumbling remains of a large Imperial ballista, its outlines vague in the snow so that it seemed almost troll-like.

The snow was coming thicker now, and the sky had darkened as the afternoon drew on. With visibility getting worse by the moment, Mari had to slow down. Alain could hear her gasping for breath, and himself felt the strain of scrambling quickly through the hazardous obstacles after a long day already spent picking their way through the ruins. They struggled through a heavily damaged area where no buildings stood at all, just higher and lower piles of ruin, leaping across occasional gaps that were all that was left of the streets which had run between the buildings.

Mari had slowed to a stumbling walk, so Alain came up beside her. "Can you keep moving, or should we seek a hiding place?"

"They're after us, Alain," she wheezed. "If we stop, they'll catch us."

"I do not hear the whistling they use to signal each other, but I agree."

"If they did whistle, at least we'd have some idea how close they are. How are you doing?" Mari asked him.

"Weary, but I can keep moving," Alain assured her.

"Same here." Mari was peering ahead. "On this side of the river, the distance from the university to the city wall shouldn't be nearly as far as we had to come when we sneaked into the city. I have no idea how much distance we've covered so far, but it shouldn't be much farther to the wall."

Alain put his arm about Mari, supporting and comforting her as they struggled through another badly damaged area. That brought hope to Alain, since they knew some of the areas of worst damage were near the walls, where the rebels had made their initial stand once the walls were breached.

"Stars above, we made it," Mari sobbed, as the high, thick stone walls which had formerly protected the city of Marandur rose out of the murkiness of the storm and the fading day. Great gaps were visible in the walls, places where Imperial siege machines, Mechanic weapons, and the spell creatures of Mages had broken the mighty stones and tumbled them inward upon the buildings they had once defended.

Mari slowed down, walking very cautiously toward the nearest break in the wall. She reached the wall and stopped completely, breathing heavily as she looked out through the jagged hole in the wall. Even through the thickly falling snow they could spot faint glows in the fields beyond: bonfires burning in front of and on the Imperial watch towers outside the city. "We have to wait here a while. It's barely dark, and even with the snow I'd prefer waiting until later to sneak through those Imperial sentries."

Alain nodded, breathing deeply himself. "We have been going very fast. I would like a chance to recover before we try getting past the legionaries. If we have need of spells, I will require my strength."

"That makes it unanimous." Mari sat down against the wall near the break, facing in toward the ruined city, her weapon cradled in both hands. She stared at it and closed her eyes. Then her expression took on a grim and reluctant determination and Mari opened her eyes again and lowered the weapon's front so it rested ready to defend them. "It's a tool," she said, as much to herself as to him. "It can be used for bad purposes, or good purposes. I have to ensure that I only use it when I must, and only for the best of reasons. I wish I didn't need it, but I do."

Alain sat down beside her, peering into the swirling snow. "Your words are wise," he told her. "I increasingly feel the same about my spells which can harm." As nervous as he was about the barbarians tracking them to this spot, he was more worried now about trying to get past the Imperial sentries. "I am assuming there will be a Mage alarm set around this part of the city as well, just as there was where we came in on the northern side."

"Yeah." Mari sat silent for a moment. "Maybe the snow and the ruins muffled the sound of the one shot I fired back there and the Imperials didn't hear it. I don't see any sign that they're more alert than usual. Do you sense any Mages anywhere near us?"

"No," Alain said. "I sense no other Mages at all."

"Why don't you sound happy about that?"

"Because there should be some trace of Mages," Alain explained. "The Imperials employ some Mages to help maintain their quarantine of Marandur. Why can I not sense any even at a distance now, as I did when we entered the city?"

She inhaled with a hiss of breath. "They're hiding themselves just like you are?"

"I believe so. It would mean they are alert and prepared. The sound of your weapon may have carried far enough to warn them something is happening in the city. We must assume there may be a Mage, or more than one, not far distant. I must be very careful about using any spells at all, or our chance of discovery will become much greater."

"Wonderful." Mari sometimes used words when she appeared to mean the exact opposite, such as now. Alain could not think of anything about this situation which he would call wonderful. "If we're lucky," she continued, "the Imperials will hole up in their watch towers during the storm. If we're unlucky, they'll increase the number of patrols just in case someone's trying to use the storm as cover to enter or leave the city. Maybe they heard enough noise from my one shot to alert the Mages, but if nothing else happens for a while they'll relax again and decide the boom was something collapsing. Once it gets dark enough, we'll find out just how alert the Imperials are tonight for people trying to sneak out of this city instead of trying to sneak into it."

"Who would be fools enough to sneak into Marandur?" Alain asked. "Who would want to enter a dead city in ruins when the Emperor has decreed that anyone doing so must die themselves?"

Mari looked over at him and grinned despite the worry he could see in her. "You're getting good at sarcasm, too. I hope I'm not creating a monster. And no, I don't mean 'creating a monster' in the same way you Mages do." She kept her voice just loud enough for Alain to hear, her eyes going back to searching the ruins for any signs of the barbarians. "But you're right. Only fools would have done it."

Mari sounded concerned and weary to Alain, so he moved a little closer, offering his shoulder, and she leaned against it with a happy sigh even though her weapon remained ready and her eyes alert. "But it was a good idea," Mari continued. "With the technology in the banned Mechanic manuscripts we found, we can really change things. If we have enough time."

"And if we can reach the island of Altis," Alain said, "and find there the tower which is spoken of in those manuscripts. It will be a long journey, filled with many hazards. You are certain we must go to Altis?"

"Yes," Mari said without any hesitation. "The notes on that page of the manuscripts said records of 'all things' are kept in that tower. That note must have been written a long time ago, but old records are exactly what we need. Unless we can learn something about the history of our world, something about how it ended up the way it is, we won't know how to fix things. We have to go to Altis and find that tower, even if it is in ruins now, and learn what we can from any surviving records. People expect me to change the world, to make it better, but I can't fix something that big unless I know how it came to be broken."

"Then we must go to Altis." Alain could feel against his back the edges of the water-tight package in his own pack which held his share of the manuscripts. Mari had shown him some of the Mechanic documents, but he had understood none of them. He did know that Mari was convinced that these texts could change the world, and that was enough for Alain.

"You're very quiet," Mari whispered to him. The snow had kept falling, and was now coating them as well the ruins. "Talk to me. It's cold and I'm scared. What are you thinking about?"

"I was thinking that none of my fellow Mages would be able to understand what I am doing," Alain admitted. "They, like me, were taught that the world we see is an illusion and that all people are but shadows on that illusion. We were told that the works of Mechanics were all tricks. They are obedient to the Mage Guild because that is drilled into us as young children. Yet here I am, having thrown off the discipline of my Guild, which seeks my death. I have decided that at least one other person is a thing of a great value, having fallen in love with that person despite my training to reject all feelings, and she moreover a Mechanic, member of a Guild which is the ancestral enemy of the Mage Guild. Other Mages would think me mad."

In the gathering gloom, Alain sensed more than saw the smile on Mari's face. "Maybe not every Mage. That old girlfriend of yours was trying to understand."

"Mage Asha was never my girlfriend. Why do you keep calling her that?"

"Because I don't believe you, my Mage," Mari said. "But that's okay. Asha felt like a good person trapped in a Mage's teachings, just like you were before I met you and, uh, 'ensnared' you. She tried to help us back at Severun. I hope she's all right."

"Yes," Alain agreed. "It would be…nice to have more friends, after so long being alone."

Mari's voice took on that slight edge it still sometimes did when talking about Asha. "Just as long as she doesn't try to get *too* friendly with you." She looked out over the dead city. "Alain, if we fail, if we can't break the grip that your Guild and my Guild have on Dematr, the whole world could end up looking like this."

"It *will* end up looking like this," Alain said. "Within a few years at most. Uncontrolled wars, breakdown of the governments of the common folk, mobs, rioting, the same anarchy that has riven what once was the country of Tiae in the south. The efforts of our former Guilds to control the bedlam will only magnify the chaos, until the Guilds are swept away along with all else."

"Unless…" Mari drew in a deep breath. "Unless the daughter of Jules stops it by overthrowing the Great Guilds first. Alain, why is it me? Jules died centuries ago. Who knows how many women descended from her have lived since then? And I don't even believe that she's actually my ancestor. Why me? Why now?"

"I do not know for certain," Alain said. "I would say that it must be now, because no more time remains. And I would say it must be you, because there is no one else who could do it."

"Neither of those conclusions is particularly comforting," Mari grumbled.

They sat quietly then for a while, listening for trouble, watching for danger, as the darkness grew heavier along with the snowfall. The wind had calmed, and aside from the gentle hiss of the falling snow, nothing moved or made a noise. But Alain distrusted that sense of peace, wondering what moved silently beyond their very short range of vision.

Some pieces of rubble rattled not too far away, a tiny avalanche of debris that brought both Mari and Alain to full alertness. The heavily falling snow made it hard to tell exactly where the noise had come from. Mari stood up very slowly and carefully, trying not to make a sound, snow cascading from her as she rose. Alain waited until she was ready, then he did the same, snow showering off his body with a soft murmur. *Perhaps it was just the nearest ruins shifting as they decay. Perhaps.* A scraping sound came from somewhere close by, as if something had rubbed up against something else. *But I do not believe it.*

Alain put his mouth to Mari's ear, speaking as quietly as he could. "They are out there. I am sure of it. We must go now."

She nodded wordlessly, then lifted one foot, moved it slowly to the side, brought it down with great care, then slid a little ways along the wall. Alain followed, his eyes and ears straining for any more signs of their pursuers. A fight now would surely alert the Imperial watch towers.

Another rattle not far away. Alain thought it might have come from their left. Mari kept moving as soundlessly as possible, easing right with her back against the wall, almost to the nearest gap now where the wall had been breached long ago.

Alain clearly heard a foot come down in the snow, then the rasping of breath from more than one man. *They are almost on top of us.* He reached for Mari's arm and pushed her toward the break in the wall, knowing that only speed could save them now.

Mari jumped, grabbing the edge of a huge, broken stone to steady herself, then vanishing around the corner. Alain leaped after her, hearing the rush of feet and the rattle of debris as their pursuers also abandoned any attempt at stealth. He made the corner, rounding it into the break just as hands grabbed at him. Alain lunged forward and down into the opening in the wall, trying to break the grip and found himself staring up at Mari, who had her Mechanic weapon in her hand and was swinging it like a club instead of firing it. He heard the thud of the weapon's impact against something, then the hands on him let go and Mari was pulling Alain up and along. The ancient wall was thick here near its base. They had to skid across broken, massive stones slick with snow, not knowing in the murk how much farther they had to go. Then they suddenly dropped into darkness.

Alain had only a moment to feel the fear of the fall before they landed in a snow drift which had piled up on the outside of the walls. He and Mari staggered out of the drift, not knowing whether their foes would try to chase them beyond the city walls. They had not gone more than a short distance before they heard the unmistakable thumps of more bodies landing in the snow drift behind them.

"We're trapped between two enemies," Mari gasped. "If we move too slowly those barbarians will catch us, and if we run at the Imperial line they'll see us or we'll trip that Mage alarm you warned me about and—"

"That is what we must do," Alain said as the answer came to him. "We must distract the Imperials, and we have to deal with the barbarians. Or let each side take care of the other for us."

"What do you—?" Mari got it, her words sounding with sudden enthusiasm. "Use our two problems to cancel each other out? That's some brilliant math for someone who doesn't know geometry, my Mage."

Alain pulled Mari close. "Hold tight to my cloak. Use both hands. And come along as fast as possible."

Alain went straight ahead, walking as quickly as he could in the snow with Mari at his back. They could hear the sound of others behind them. Then Alain spotted the drifting strands which indicated a Mage alarm. Instead of trying to move the strands aside, Alain walked through them.

He walked a little farther, then paused as he felt a presence not too far distant. "There is a Mage near," he breathed into Mari's ear. He heard her muffled curse. "Release me, walk near, and drop flat and motionless when I say to."

He felt her nod, then Mari was coming along beside him, her face grim. She knew he could not cast a spell now without the other Mage knowing and quickly finding him. But with the snow so heavy and the night aiding them, perhaps they would need no more invisibility.

Alain sensed the Mage coming closer. He or she would be moving with Imperial soldiers, thereby providing a rough picture of where the legionaries were. Then Alain heard the rustling sounds of someone forging through the snow behind them. He dropped, pulling Mari flat as well, and hurriedly brushed snow over her back and his own as best he could, waiting while the snow fell on them.

Someone blundered past them from behind. Alain did not dare move his head much, but he caught a glimpse of shaggy hair and a shapeless mass of rotting old garments before the barbarian moved on a little more without spotting Alain or Mari.

Moments later Alain heard noise from in front and saw the glow of torches through the snowfall. "Stay very still," he murmured to Mari, his lips touching her ear. Already the snow had laid a thin, concealing layer over them both.

A long line of Imperial soldiers came tramping through the snow, one legionary in five holding a flaring torch aloft and the others with drawn swords. A second line came into view behind them almost immediately, these legionaries bearing crossbows. A yell of alarm sounded and the barbarian Alain had seen earlier came floundering through the snow, trying to make it back to the city. Alain heard the thump of crossbows firing, and the barbarian staggered, standing and swaying for a moment before falling face down in the snow less than a lance length from Alain, a crossbow bolt protruding from his back.

The Imperial soldiers were close enough together to have made it impossible for someone to get past them without being seen, but there were gaps between each legionary, and the soldiers were searching for foes on their feet, not expecting anyone to be concealed under the snow. Alain watched the legionaries coming, tensing in case he had to act, but the mound of snow forming over him and Mari as the heavy snow continued caused the closest legionaries to veer to either side to avoid the apparent drift. There were cries behind and to the side, then shouted orders. The Imperials broke into a trot, chasing the barbarians back to the city, intent on killing every one that they could. Legionaries searching for fleeing enemies before them paid little attention to the snow beneath as they swept past to either side of Alain and Mari, one so close his foot almost brushed against Alain.

Alain waited just a little longer, then staggered up, pulling Mari with him. "Now we walk."

Her voice was chattering with cold. "Walk? Toward the Imperial watch towers?"

"Yes. The illusion we wish to create is that we are part of the legionary force. We are hard to see in the darkness and the snow, and we do not resemble the barbarians. Walk as if we belong here, Mari."

"You're the Mage." Mari walked along with him, trudging through the snow but trying to look like she was in no hurry as she matched Alain's pace. "Where's that other one?"

"Not too far distant. I cannot tell if he seeks me."

"Then link arms with me so we look like one of us is supporting the other."

Alain did not ask why, putting his arm about her as they struggled through the snow toward the Imperial watch towers and the large fires burning between them.

The air grew brighter as they neared the Imperial beacons, Mari and Alain aiming between them as if walking toward a watch tower. Behind them, occasional shouts and metal-on-metal clangs told of combat, the barbarians and the Imperials busy with each other. Dim shapes materialized off to their left. "Hey!" someone called from what appeared to be a small group of legionaries. "You guys get nicked?"

Alain had held his breath at the first hail, but he suddenly understood Mari's idea. In the limited visibility, the soldiers had guessed he and Mari were other soldiers returning from the small battle against the barbarians. But their retreat might have raised suspicions if it had not also appeared that one of them had been injured.

Mari called out a reply, her voice taking on a slightly different accent. "Yeah."

"How many of them did you get so far?"

Mari did not hesitate before replying. "Ten that I know of."

"Ha! Hope there's some left for us! That'll teach the dead to try to leave that pile of broken garbage. The healer's in the tower you're heading for."

"Thanks." The shapes of the Imperial soldiers dimmed and then vanished in the snow as the legionaries dashed toward the sound of fighting.

Mari changed their path to angle away from the tower, heading straight out from the city.

"Why did you sound different?" Alain asked as they struggled through the snow.

"My accent?" Mari said. "That legionnaire had a Centin accent. I learned about different Imperial accents from listening to commons when I was at the Mechanics Guild Academy in Palandur. I answered him back trying to sound like I was from Centin, too, because the Empire builds its legions with men and women from the same areas."

They drew even with the towers, then began to leave them behind. Alain started to relax slightly, then felt his Mage senses tingle with sudden warning. He reached over, grabbed Mari and pulled her down flat into the snow once more. She lay next to him, not moving, waiting to find out why he had acted. Moments passed, the snow falling down to coat them once more with white. Alain could feel the cold biting into him, worse this time, but stayed motionless, his hand still on Mari to urge her to do the same.

Several more shapes came walking out of the storm, their outlines hard to make out as the snow swirled past. Alain could see the helmet plume of a high-ranking Imperial officer. Then he made out the unmistakable shape of Mage robes on one of the other figures. The group trudged past, not speaking among themselves, but just as they were starting to fade into the storm again the Mage stopped.

The Mage turned, peering in the direction of Alain and Mari. Alain did not dare make any preparations for a spell, since that would betray them instantly, but he heard Mari's hand slide under her jacket to grasp her weapon.

The Imperial officer said something which Alain could not make out, the tones outwardly respectful but betraying the revulsion which commons felt toward Mages. The other Mage did not respond for a long moment. Then the Mage started walking again, not toward Alain but away, vanishing into the storm-driven gloom along with the soldiers.

Alain began breathing once more. He waited a few moments longer, then urged Mari up again.

Mari was shivering badly as she dusted packed snow off of her front. "I r-really h-hate th-this," she whispered through chattering teeth. "D-did that M-mage s-sense you?"

"I do not know. We must put distance between ourselves and this place in case that Mage returns." Alain ached to use his powers to warm the air around her, but doing so would instantly tell the other Mage where he was, so instead he took Mari's arm again and together they walked steadily away from the line of watch towers. The flaming lights of the towers dimmed and then vanished in the storm, and no more noise of battle could be heard as they struggled through the deepening snow.

They crested a small rise and began going down the other side, then both stumbled into a small ditch lying across their path. Alain bent to look. "It is the side of a road."

"A road." Mari shook her head. "We can't risk running into anyone on the road, not this close to Marandur."

"No. They would surely arrest us on suspicion even if they did not kill us on sight." Veering sharply to the left, they headed away from the road, staggering occasionally as they hit a deeper drift of snow. "We have been going hard since early this morning," Alain managed to say, wondering whether he was supporting Mari or if she was supporting him as they trudged onward. "We need to rest."

"Not until we find cover," Mari got out between rapid, shallow breaths.

They went onward, Alain feeling exhausted and knowing that Mari was at least as tired. He looked back occasionally, still seeing no sign of pursuit, and noting with relief that their tracks were being filled in by the still-falling snow.

More shapes reared up out of the gloom, causing Mari and Alain to stagger with alarm. "Trees," Mari said in a worn-out voice.

"If there is even a small group of trees here we can hide among them, allowing the snow to cover our tracks this far."

"But we're not that far from the city," Mari insisted, her voice slurring with fatigue.

"Mari, if we keep walking, we will keep leaving traces of our movement. And we must rest."

"All right," she mumbled. They moved in among the trees, not able to make out the full extent of the woods in the limited visibility. It was a fair-sized grove, though. Mari came to a stop, swaying on her feet, where two trees growing close to each other had formed a natural break against the weather. Pulling their blankets out of their packs, they wrapped themselves up together, sharing the blankets and their warmth. Mari buried her head next to Alain, her breathing now deep and slightly ragged. "We made it. I think."

"I think so, too." Alain rested his own head near hers, enjoying the warmth of her breath. "But I am afraid tomorrow has come. Your birthday must be over now."

"You forgot a cake for me, didn't you? And you invited legionaries and barbarians to the party."

"Regretfully, yes." He waited a moment, then heard how even her breathing had become and realized Mari had fallen asleep. Alain stayed awake a little while longer, trying to listen for any sign of danger, but soon passed out from fatigue as well.

He awoke with the sun high in the sky to the distinctive sound of axes thunking into wood. Raising his head cautiously and staring around, Alain could tell the wood cutting wasn't going on anywhere close by, even though the sound carried clearly in the clean, cold air. The snow had stopped, but the sky was still gray with leaden clouds. Mari was blinking awake beside him. "What is it?" she asked.

"I will check." Disturbing the blankets as little as possible, Alain crept cautiously toward the sounds. Using the cover of the trees to screen himself as much as possible, he got fairly close before he managed to spot the woodcutting crew working away. But almost as soon as he saw them, a loud voice ordered the cutters to stop.

Gliding slightly closer, Alain could see an Imperial officer berating the man in charge of the woodcutters. The man was arguing back, his hands and arms moving in the exaggerated motions of vehement debate. Alain listened for a little while, then eased back into the woods and returned to Mari. "Woodcutters made the noise, but they were stopped by an Imperial officer who claims they are cutting too close to

Marandur. The leader of the woodcutters is arguing that this patch of woods is outside of the Emperor's ban and has been cut for ages. I saw a bribe pass to the officer, so the matter is probably resolved."

Mari nodded wearily, running one hand through her hair in a futile attempt to comb it into decent order. "Not our problem, then?"

"Yes and no. The officer asked if the woodcutters had seen anyone heading away from the city. He reminded them of the reward for turning in anyone who tries to leave Marandur."

She grimaced. "Then they know or suspect that we made it out."

"The snow may not have completely obscured some of our tracks before they were found, especially near the city walls where the legionaries were searching intensely," Alain replied. "Perhaps they think it was some of the barbarians. But it is not impossible that the Mage we saw was able to sense a trace of my presence. My Guild is still seeking my death, so that Mage may have been warned to watch for me even though the Mage Guild did not realize that we were in Marandur."

"So at a minimum, the Imperials are looking for a couple of refugees from Marandur. And your Guild might be hot on our heels, too." Mari blew out a long breath. "You really know how to make a girl feel great first thing in the morning, Alain. Remind me not to ask you how I look right now. Stop. I'm not asking you to tell me that." She paused, thinking. "We need to get moving again. Get far enough from Marandur that we can blend in with the people in the countryside. I know Palandur from my time at the Mechanics Guild training academy there. But I didn't spend much time worrying about anything outside the city gates, especially anything this far away."

"I know nothing of the area at all."

Mari winced as she moved, pulling her pack around to dig out the map she had brought with her all the way from the Bakre Confederation. She studied it for a little while, then shook her head. "I can't tell how far we've gotten or where we need to go next. But we need to get moving."

"Yes. Which way?"

She frowned again, then looked up at the sun. "South. It's not directly away from Marandur, but it should take us to some secondary roads running to Palandur. There'll be plenty of traffic on those roads, even in the winter, and we'll just be two more travelers."

Alain thought about the pristine stretches of snow outside the small patch of woods they occupied. "How do we avoid leaving a clear trail for the Imperials to follow?"

Mari didn't say anything for a while. "I have no idea," she finally said. "There are no other tracks out there? Nothing we could use to cover our own?"

"There are the tracks made by the lumber wagon and its horses."

She made a helpless gesture. "We'll have to use those. Which means we have to wait here at least until the wagon leaves." Mari's expression brightened. "That might actually work out. I've seen how the Imperials handle trying to catch someone. They set up checkpoints and send out patrols, gradually expanding the search."

"This helps us how?" Alain asked.

Mari drew a circle in the snow before her, then another larger one around it, then an even bigger one around that. "It helps us because the Imperials assume their prey is running at the best pace it can manage. Therefore as they expand their perimeter their checkpoints have to cover wider areas. While we wait here, the checkpoints and patrols will think we're doing the sensible thing and running like crazy, so they'll keep searching areas we haven't gone to. By the time we start out tonight, the Imperials will have searched this whole area and already declared it clear."

Alain considered the diagrams, nodded, then asked a question. "But what if they find us while they are searching this area?"

"That is the one weak point in the plan. We'll have to keep an eye out for search parties and react as best we can." Mari glanced around. "We should have a much better chance of evading searchers in these woods than out in the open, so it's the option we've got. Can you still sense that Mage?"

"Yes, but he is not close."

"Let's hope he stays distant." Mari settled back against the twin trees again, wincing. "I am so cold, and so tired, and so hungry, and so thirsty. Can Mages make food or wine?"

"How could Mages do that?" Alain asked, startled by the question.

"They make dragons."

"That is different."

Mari gave him one of her narrow-eyed looks, then pulled the blanket up over her head. "Don't bother me until nightfall unless you see Imperials or find food."

"I have food in my pack. The university sent some extra with us. Your pack was already loaded with your tools, so they—" Alain stopped speaking as Mari yanked the blanket down and glared at him. "Had I not mentioned that before?"

"No," she replied in her dangerous voice. "You had not mentioned that. So you have more food?"

"Yes."

"What about drink?"

"Just water."

"When were you planning on telling me about that? Before or after I collapsed from hunger and thirst?"

Alain paused to think, deciding not to answer that last question directly. "I was trained not to think about physical discomforts like food and drink, so I do not always feel such things as you do."

Her anger subsided as quickly as it had arisen. "Sorry. I know your acolyte training was very rough."

"Perhaps we should eat now."

"Perhaps we should," Mari muttered.

He got out the food, which while sparse still represented a generous gift from the university, whose inhabitants were always on lean diets. Mari let him back under the blankets, so that even though it was still icy cold outside they were able to share their warmth. "I'm sorry I've been in a bad mood," she finally mumbled again in apology. "We're both under a lot of pressure, and we're both suffering from the cold and all the walking in the snow we've had to do. I don't have any right to act like I'm the only one suffering. How are you doing?"

"It could be much worse," Alain said.

"Yeah. And it probably will be," Mari said. "Can I ask what is probably a silly question about Mage stuff?"

"Of course," Alain said. "I know many of my questions about Mechanic things sound odd to you."

"Fair enough," Mari said. "Why can't Mages make food if they can create something like a Dragon? Why can't you imagine into existence a steak or a roast chicken?"

"It would not be worth the effort expended," Alain said. "The amount of strength and power required to create such a thing would exceed whatever benefit the food would give."

"Wow," Mari said. "That actually makes sense to me."

"But it does not matter," Alain continued, "because there would be no benefit to it. What Mages create is an imitation. Dragons, trolls, and other spell creatures do not live, they imitate living creatures. They bleed, but it is not blood. They have muscles and other flesh, but it is not actual meat."

"What does it taste like?" Mari asked, staring at him, her expression both fascinated and revolted.

"I have not tasted it," Alain said. "An elder once told my group of acolytes that it is like eating dirt or dust."

She made a gagging expression as if she had actually tasted some. "All of a sudden I am very grateful for any other form of food. Go ahead and try to sleep some more. I'm a little restless, so I'll stay awake and keep an eye on things."

It was about noon, and the thunking of the crew cutting wood had not yet let up, when Alain awoke to Mari cautioning him to silence. It was not hard to understand why, since he could faintly hear the tramp of many feet in the snow. Mari crept out to check, then came hastening back. "About a cohort of legionaries, spread out in a search line, walking across country and heading this way."

# CHAPTER THREE

No Mage could create a spell using only his or her own strength. Mages needed to draw on the power they could feel in whatever location they were—power whose source remained unknown and which varied unpredictably in magnitude from area to area. Some places held so little power that Mages would have to exhaust themselves to create even a minor spell, while others were rich in that resource—though whenever power was drawn on by a Mage it would lower the amount in that area until it slowly renewed. Alain, accustomed to having Mari unable to grasp any aspect of the Mage arts, had been surprised when she understood that. "Like a battery, which can be stronger or weaker and can be recharged," she had said, an example which Alain had not understood but apparently satisfied the mind of a Mechanic.

Now Alain felt for the power in the area around him, sensing how much was available here as only Mages could. "We could run, but only across the open fields. We would be seen easily, if only by the footprints we made in the fresh snow. If we stay here, there is enough power available to me to sustain a concealment spell for some time."

Mari grimaced, but did not dispute his words. "You can hide us without that other Mage spotting you doing it?"

He concentrated on the Mage he still sensed on the edge of his awareness, far distant from here. "For a while, yes. By the time the Mage helping with the quarantine could tell these Imperials that another Mage was active here, the legionaries should have long since left." Alain studied their surroundings. "They will look up in the trees and around the trunks."

Mari pointed to a jagged stump which only came up to her waist. "So we go there, where we couldn't possibly hide?"

"Not without a Mage."

It still took some work to get everything back inside their packs, muddle any trace that they had been sitting next to the trees, and then find a spot right next to the stump where they could stand with the smallest chance of having a legionary blunder into them. Mari ended up backed against the stump, her arms once again around Alain from behind, he pressing back and looking in the direction from which the cohort of legionaries was approaching. "You really are enjoying this, aren't you?" Mari whispered. "I think you could make me invisible even if I wasn't glued to you like this."

"No, I could not," Alain said. "But it is pleasant."

She did not reply, because they heard commands being called. The woodcutters on the other side of the trees did not hear the approaching legionaries and kept up their racket, so Alain had to watch carefully, unable to count on knowing how close the legionaries were before they got close enough to see him and Mari. "I will start the spell. Stay very still and very quiet."

"No problem," she muttered back.

Common folk believed that Mages changed real objects. Mechanics considered Mages to be fakes who claimed to be able to do impossible things. Neither was correct. Alain's training had focused on enabling him to realize that nothing was real, that the world he saw around him was just an illusion. And if all was illusion, then with enough strength and power and concentration other illusions could be temporarily placed over the existing illusions. The illusion of a wall could have the illusion of an opening placed on it.

The illusion of light, traveling in straight lines, could be altered so that the light curved around a Mage, concealing him or her.

Alain bent light so that no one could see either him or Mari, only the broken truck behind them. They stood silently as the legionaries began coming into view. Alain, concentrating on maintaining the spell as the line of Imperial soldiers slogged wearily into the woods, wondered if the distant Mage had picked up the small spell yet.

A centurion walked with the legionaries, barking out orders.

"Check every tree. Check the branches, check behind it, then check the branches again."

Most of the legionaries carried swords, and several had crossbows. None carried any of the Mechanic weapons that Mari called rifles, but that was small comfort. The legionaries displayed little enthusiasm for their task, and from their weary expressions and tired movements Alain guessed the legionaries had been up and searching since last night. But under the eyes of their centurion they did as instructed, checking every tree carefully.

None of them came near the stump to search, but Alain had to breathe as silently as possible when the centurion came to stand near it, glaring around at his troops. "Pick it up, boys and girls! We've got a lot more territory to cover today until we find them, and when we do find them we can rest. We'll also have the Emperor's favor for offing those who tried to leave Marandur."

One of the legionaries grumbled loudly enough for Alain, and the centurion, to hear. "Whoever it was flew away, and they didn't do it on any Mage Roc."

"You got something to say, Juren?" the centurion demanded.

"All I'm saying," the Imperial soldier complained, "is that whatever got out of Marandur left footprints like a person's, but then those footprints disappeared. It's like they flew away. And there's only one… person…what could have done that."

Another legionary nodded. "There's been funny stuff heard in the city lately, like something was stirring. It's been her city for a long time. Maybe she decided to leave."

The centurion walked over to the nearest offending legionary and shoved him backwards with a stiff-armed blow. "You think the officers would be happy to hear you saying that, Juren? What about you, Hsien? You want to go tell some of them what you just said to me?"

"No, Centurion," the legionaries mumbled.

"Get it out of your heads. All of you. Anyone mentions her again, they get five lashes. If I hear her name, it'll be ten lashes. Got that?"

The legionaries called out hasty acknowledgments. "Now move on. Check the rest of these woods."

Alain risked taking a deep breath as the soldiers moved onward, but neither he nor Mari moved until the legionaries had vanished from sight in the direction of the woodcutters. Though they were only partially concealed by the stump at their backs from any legionary of who might come back this way, Alain took the risk of dropping his spell. But it was too late. He had already sensed a response from that far-off other Mage.

The sound of axes halted. They could hear the voice of the centurion, barely audible as he interrogated the woodcutters.

"Was he talking about me?" Mari breathed into Alain's ear. "The daughter? Why would they think I can fly?"

"I do not know." Alain was also puzzled. "They were afraid of this 'her' the legionary spoke of. I have not seen that reaction among commons speaking of the daughter of Jules. But I do not know who this other woman could be that they fear."

"That one soldier said they shouldn't say her name," Mari noted. "Why wouldn't they say my name if they knew it? Has the Emperor banned any mention of the daughter of Jules?"

Alain made a small, uncertain gesture. "I do not think the Imperials regard the daughter legend as something to be suppressed. But they also said Marandur has been this woman's city for a long time. How could that be you? How could that be the daughter?"

"And why would legionaries be afraid of me?" Mari wondered.

"Perhaps they have heard of what happens to dragons foolish enough to attack you," Alain replied.

"Oh, gosh, you are so funny, Mage. Can you tell how amused I am?"

Alain tried not to wince as her grip on him tightened. "Since we are speaking of things to be concerned about, I should tell you that the presence of the other Mage vanished very quickly a few moments ago. He must have sensed the spell I used and is now working harder to conceal himself."

"Let's hope those legionaries get out of here fast."

Alain remained prepared to hide them from sight for a little longer, then as the legionaries showed no sign of backtracking he focused on hiding his presence from the other Mage again.

Mari looked up at the sky, where the clouds were beginning to show signs of parting. "It's well past noon, and it sounds like these legionaries are chasing off the woodcutters. Maybe we'll be able to leave once the legionaries have moved off, too."

"The sooner the better," Alain agreed.

Worried about the other Mage, he and Mari moved to the far side of the woods as soon as it seemed safe. The edge of the woods gave way to a long shallow slope of rolling, snow-covered grassland running all the way to the horizon. A churned path marked where the woodcutter wagon and horses had come and gone, the wagon itself already well away from the woods but still visible though distant. The legionaries, still spread out in a long search line, were trudging in the wagon's wake.

Mari and Alain had to wait until the sun was well down in the sky and the last legionary had vanished behind one of the rises before they bolted from cover, moving as quickly as they could through the snow already disturbed by the horse-drawn wagon so their own tracks would be lost in the muddle.

After going a good way down the path, they came to a trail running north and south at almost right angles to their movement and already showing signs of some traffic since the snowfall. Mari grinned for the first time that day, leading Alain southward down the trail and away from the searching legionaries. But once the sun set, traveling over the uneven, snow-covered track became more difficult. By midnight, her legs rubbery with weariness, Mari slipped and almost fell before Alain caught her. "Maybe we should stop and rest," she murmured as if even the task of talking in a normal voice required too much effort.

Alain urged her onward. "We are out in the open, too exposed to anyone searching for us. More legionaries may come along this way. Once daylight comes again, we must be concerned about Mages searching for us."

"You can tell when Mages are coming," Mari grumbled.

"If the Mage rides a Roc, such a warning would come too late to be of use."

"Do you always have to be right?" Mari complained, but settled her pack again and kept trudging alongside Alain.

It was still a while before dawn when scattered farms began appearing on either side of what had widened to become a small road. Alain kept them going, worried that the closest farms to Marandur would be obvious places for anyone to search, and though Mari obviously wanted to stop she kept walking with the same stubborn refusal to quit that she so often revealed to Alain.

The sky was beginning to show traces of dawn's light when Alain saw an abandoned barn off the road, its roof half fallen in and two walls sagging drunkenly. He turned Mari toward it and they staggered into the small shelter the structure still provided. Mari dropped to the floor, not even bothering to remove her pack. Alain hesitated, swaying on his feet, then managed to kneel and get Mari's pack off as well as his own before lying down next to her and falling into exhausted sleep.

By the time he awoke, most of the day was gone. Mari made numerous tiny noises of pain as she sat up, and even Alain, toughened as he was by his years of acolyte training, wanted to wince as stiff muscles protested any further use. Mari pulled out the last of the food from Marandur. "It's appropriate we eat this inside a ruin, I guess."

A chill wind picked up as they left the barn late that afternoon, blowing snow over the landscape and making their journey much more miserable but also quickly concealing any signs of traffic on the road, including their own. Evening wasn't far off when their small road intersected a larger one ambling through the plains. Mari studied the road, brushing back snow from its surface. "This road has been used a fair amount since the snowfall. Wagons, horses, mules, not many people on foot. That's what we'd expect in farm country."

"I see no sign of Imperial searchers," Alain said, "but if they were small cavalry detachments I do not think their signs would stand out on this road."

"That's probably right," Mari agreed. "We're a long way away from...you-know-where. Let's make sure from now on we act like normal citizens out for a walk. Nothing to hide, and nothing to fear from any Imperial authorities." Mari patted the pocket in her backpack in which she kept their false Imperial identification papers.

They spent a few hours following the road to the west as the sun set. The sky was now clear of clouds, and the stars and a brilliant moon provided good light. Then the road joined with a larger highway which showed signs of even more use.

Alain guessed that it was about midnight when they reached a major, paved road, which even at this late hour had occasional traffic. An inn with a coach stop sat nearby, its lights promising food, warmth and comfort. Mari reached over and hugged Alain with one arm. "We made it, my Mage. We made it."

"We are still far from Altis," Alain pointed out, bringing his own arm around her.

"You didn't need to tell me that. I'll worry about Altis tomorrow. For tonight, all I want is a warm meal, a warm bed, and you beside me in that bed."

"I want that, too," Alain said. Tired as he was, he could not help noticing how good she felt as he held her with one arm.

"Good." Mari gave him an amused look. "Watch your hand. Get it higher. Not that high. You know where my waist is. In case you're wondering, we're still keeping our clothes on once we get into that bed."

"I did not mean to touch you in the wrong places," Alain said.

"The problem, my Mage, is that they're the right places, and your touch felt way too good. That's why we're keeping our clothes on."

❖ ❖ ❖

Mari yawned as she watched the walls of Palandur grow steadily nearer through the windows of the coach. After all the walking they had done through wind and weather she had felt justified in paying for seats on a coach, even though that was a bit of a luxury for two people on the run with no way of knowing when they would get more money or how. But she still had a decent amount of cash from what she had brought with her and from the money which General Flyn's troops had insisted she take.

Mari still felt guilty over that last source of money, which supposedly had been in exchange for a horse. In truth the soldiers had given generously because they believed her to be the long-foretold daughter of Jules. Mari had thought the idea ridiculous, and still could not believe it.

But Alain had seen it. One of the Mage elders who was different from most of the others had told him what his vision meant: that Mari was that daughter, and that he must protect her because the world would fall into ruin if she failed.

*No pressure*, Mari thought for about the thousandth time.

The time they had spent in ruined, dead Marandur felt almost like a dream now, or rather like a strange nightmare which contrasted with the simple normality of the world around them. Common folk attending to routine errands and travel, a horse-drawn passenger coach, a quiet countryside unmarred by ruins, and the walls of a living city growing rapidly nearer. If not for the watertight package in her backpack containing texts of technology long forbidden by the Mechanics Guild, Mari might have questioned whether she ever had actually been in Marandur.

The coach lurched to a halt, the doors opened, and all of the passengers stumbled out, stiff from the hard, cramped seating. Waiting for them were an even half-dozen of the Empire's internal police, seated behind a table which was obviously a regular fixture at the coach stop. The Imperial citizens lined up without question. Mari pretended to need to retie her boot laces while she watched the first few citizens get questioned. Seeing that the police weren't searching any packages, she beckoned to Alain and they joined the line as if they, too, were used to this sort of thing even though as a Mechanic and a Mage they had never been bothered by the demands placed on common folk within the Empire.

When they finally reached the head of the line, Mari handed over the two sets of forged Imperial identification papers she had acquired months ago before going to find Alain. The Imperial officer studied the papers with a frown. "Two of you together?"

Mari nodded. "Yes. We're students at the university in Palandur."

"I can read," the officer replied, pointing to Mari's papers. "Why were university students traveling outside Palandur?"

She might not have been bothered by Imperial checkpoints in the past, but Mari had been required to answer plenty of similar questions by Senior Mechanics and other supervisors, especially when she was an apprentice. She put on the same outwardly respectful attitude as she answered. "We wanted to try hiking in the winter."

"Pretty stupid if you ask me, walking around outside in the winter." The other officers grinned at their comrade's comment.

"It was pretty cold. We won't do it again," Mari agreed, trying to appear meek.

"Where did you go?"

"A lot of it was cross-country. We went through Sinda, and stayed one night at the inn at Kolis."

"Northeast of here, eh?" The officer handed Mari back her papers. "Did you see any other hikers? Coming down from the north? Maybe some in very old clothes or rags? Two of them?"

"Old clothes?" Mari asked as if totally puzzled by the question. "Like beggars?"

"Yes. They could've been men or women."

Mari shook her head. "No. We didn't see anyone like that on the road."

Another officer spoke up. "Or it could have been a young woman, very good-looking, dark hair, with or without a young man. She might have been wearing a Mechanics jacket."

"A Mechanic?" Mari put disdain into her voice. "No, we didn't see any of them and I'm glad of it."

"I didn't say she was a Mechanic, citizen. I said she might have been wearing one of their jackets." His gaze shifted to Alain. "She's someone you might have noticed, young man. Any attractive women like that catch your eye?"

Alain shook his head in denial.

Mari didn't have to feign unhappiness at the question. "He's got a girl."

The officer grinned at her reaction. "How about Mages? Maybe one, traveling with a common girl?"

"No." Mari pretended revulsion this time. "Why would a common girl——? Ewww."

The officer nodded, smiling knowingly. "Some girls like that sort of thing. Are you sure you didn't see anything? There's a reward. A big one."

"We could use a big reward," Mari admitted. "But I didn't see anyone."

"What about tracks in the snow?"

She couldn't very well deny seeing those. There were tracks everywhere. "We did see some tracks."

"Where at?" the officer asked, his eyes brightening. "North of Kolis?"

"Yes. In the fields there." If she denied that, and such tracks had been reported already, it could unravel her entire story.

"Which way were the tracks headed? What kind where they? Boots?"

Mari shook her head, looking regretful. "We couldn't tell. They were just big tracks in the snow and there had been some melting."

"One or two sets of tracks?"

Pausing as if trying to remember, when in fact she was trying to recall how much she and Alain had walked side by side instead of one behind the other, Mari finally nodded. "Two. I'm pretty sure there were two."

The officer regarded her for a moment, then smiled briefly. "Thank you, citizen. The Emperor appreciates your assistance." Pulling out a silver coin, he tossed it to Mari.

She caught it with a delighted grin, then she and Alain walked toward the gates of Palandur. Alain looked around to see if anyone was close, then spoke in a quiet voice. "And I thought I was a good liar."

"It's for a good cause," Mari said. "They think whoever got out of Marandur was most likely two of the barbarians. No one would ever mistake you and me for two of them. Of course those other questions mean they have some idea that a rogue Mechanic and Mage might be in the area, though if they keep searching for a 'very good-looking' girl they won't look twice at me. I figured it didn't hurt to throw them off the track." Mari gave him a sidelong glance. "Do you think they've heard about you and me meeting up in the Northern Ramparts? It sounded like it."

"It did." Alain paused. "It is never wise to assume that someone in authority has told you everything they know."

Mari felt her self-satisfaction ebbing away. "What do you mean?"

"The Mage who was with the Imperial guards around Marandur. He or she surely knew I was not one of the barbarians. That could be why the officers asked about a Mage."

"Yes, but— Yes. Couriers on horseback would have been here days ago. Maybe the questions about the barbarians are just cover for them asking about you and me?"

"It is very possible," Alain said. "If you had betrayed knowledge of why the Imperials were asking about someone in rags, those officers would not have let us depart."

"Fortunately, I thought of that before I answered. But if they've heard something about us, why are they searching for a 'very good-looking' woman?" Mari wondered.

"I believe that you are very good-looking," Alain said.

"Yes, but you're crazy," Mari retorted. "Those Imperial officers and whoever tipped them off aren't in love with me. If it was Asha they were after, I could understand that description, but no one who saw Asha could think she was dark-haired. Those soldiers in the Northern Ramparts could have passed around that I have dark hair, but they saw enough of me to know I wasn't beautiful."

Alain shook his head. "Illusions can take many forms."

"Oh, even you admit that anyone calling me beautiful would be seeing an illusion?"

"No. But perhaps to the soldiers with General Flyn, the one who had saved them, the one they thought to be a certain special person, would appear attractive for those reasons as well as for her appearance."

"Hmmm. Stranger things have happened, I guess. At least if the Imperials are looking for some beauty they won't focus on me." Mari looked around casually. "However, if you judged those officers correctly, they might have someone following us anyway, just because we sort of match what they're looking for."

"Yes. What will happen if they check with the university to see if we are enrolled there?"

"We'll be in trouble. If they find us again." Mari walked on a few more steps, then pretended to have a problem with one of her boots. Turning as she knelt on one knee, Mari fumbled with the laces again as she swept her gaze across the people behind them. Standing up, she nodded to Alain as they started walking once more. "One of the officers is behind us. Not close, but he was there, just sort of strolling along."

"Why would he do this?"

Mari glanced at Alain to see if he meant the question seriously. "He's following us to see where we go."

"But if you wish to find a Mage in a city, another Mage can try to do so using his or her Mage senses."

She sighed. "Alain, the rest of the people in the world don't work that way. They can't sense people at a distance, so they do things like following them without being noticed. We need to lose this cop so the Imperials don't know where we are."

"Lose him?"

"Throw him off our track."

"Oh, like a military force seeking to conceal its movements from enemy scouts." Alain studied the street ahead. "I recommend we look for this university and 'lose' him near there. It will match our story."

"All right. I think I remember how to get to the area." Mari looked up at the massive east gate in the walls around Palandur, feeling an odd sensation. "Alain, I left this city several months ago, the youngest person ever to qualify as a Master Mechanic in the history of my Guild, not knowing that the Guild's Senior Mechanics had already decided to set me up for kidnapping and murder by the scum who run the city of Ringhmon. It feels so strange coming back here now, with everything looking the same, and yet everything is different."

"Are you different?" Alain asked.

She looked at him, surprised by the question, then thought about it. "Am I different? I've been through a lot. I've fallen in love. So much of what I was taught to believe I now know to be a lie. I've been told I'm... someone. Does that make me different?"

"When I sense you near me," Alain said slowly, "your presence burns brighter than before, but it is still the same, just brighter."

"My presence." Every once in a while her Mage would say something totally strange like that. "I thought you could only sense other Mages."

"I can sense you as well," Alain said as if that was unremarkable.

"That thread thing, you mean," Mari said.

"Yes, that thread which connects us, but also you. You are very bright and warm, like a fire."

That felt kind of nice, Mari thought. Also kind of weird, though. A male Mechanic would have said something like that to her as a form of exaggerated flattery, but Mari had no doubt that Alain meant literally what he said, that she was somehow a fire to his Mage senses. "Do I get...warmer...when I'm angry?"

Alain shook his head. "No. There are times when your brightness becomes more intense, but that happens when you are thinking hard on something."

"Really? So you're actually admiring my mind?" Mari laughed out loud with delight at the idea, drawing looks from the nearest commons on the street.

Mari gazed at the buildings around them as she and Alain went through the gate. She had known Palandur, but now she knew Marandur as well, and the similarities between the dead city and living one were disconcerting enough to drive the laughter from her. At some moments everything felt unreal, as if what Alain had said the Mages believed really was the way things were, and she was walking through some kind of illusion in which dead city and living city were both here at the same place and time. Mari reached out to grip Alain's hand, comforted by that solid presence. "I'm pretty sure I know the way to the university from here. It's near enough to the Mechanics Guild Academy that I saw it a few times."

Mari began edging to the south, trying to remember the layout of the Imperial capital. She found another pretext to search the crowds behind them, confirming that the Imperial police officer was still sauntering along within eyesight. "He's definitely staying with us."

There were a good number of Mechanics in Palandur, swaggering down the streets with commons giving way as expected of them, so no one thought it unusual for Mari and Alain to avoid those Mechanics by wide margins. Mari tried to discreetly study them to see if she recognized any, but wasn't able to tell through the crowds and the distance she had to put between herself and the Mechanics for safety's sake. "There are probably Mechanics here who would help me," she muttered to Alain, "but the academy is full of others who would turn me in without a second thought."

"Are we going to that Mechanic Academy?" Alain asked.

"No. I don't dare go near it, and isn't that ironic for a girl who was one of the stars of the academy several months ago?"

Mages were here, too, in relatively large numbers, moving silently among the commons like wraiths avoided with fear and loathing. Alain seemed unconcerned about being recognized by any of them in his common clothing, and Mari recalled him once saying that no Mage would bother looking at a common.

When they reached the area of the university, Mari's relief at finding it was submerged in a moment of shock and recognition. "Alain, I was right. When the Imperials built Palandur they copied

Marandur. The university here is identical to the one in Marandur. Or rather identical to what the university in Marandur looked like before the city was destroyed." There was the same open stretch of land separating the walls of the university from the city around it, here a well-maintained park with clipped grass and trimmed trees ending in a brick wall standing about the height of two people. But the gate they could see in the wall stood wide open and no sentries stood guard over the students and other citizens wandering in and out. The city buildings facing the wall across the open area were bright, clean and tall, instead of the crumbling ruins which had menaced the university in Marandur, and crowds of people went about their business under the gaze of assorted Imperial police and officials.

Alain was looking around, too. "It is strange to see here how the other place once was."

"Isn't it?" Mari looked up, seeing the buildings rising above the top of the wall and easily picking out the mirror images of the offices where she had spoken to the masters of the university in Marandur, the structure where she and Alain had been given rooms, and the top of the big building which contained the steam boiler which provided heat to the university buildings. "It's like seeing a very old person you knew who has suddenly become young again. It really brings home what was lost. I hated that city, the way it felt haunted, but now I just feel like crying over the waste of it all. We...Alain, we have to stop that from happening here, and in other cities." She took a deep breath. "But we can't gawk at this or we'll be noticed. How should we lose this cop who's following us?"

Alain indicated an area where buildings housing sellers of food and drink had attracted a large gathering of students and other city dwellers. "We go there, enter a crowded place, and try to mislead the officer when we leave."

"And maybe we'll get something to eat while we're at it? All right."

Mari aimed for a bar which appeared to defy the laws of physics by having more people inside than could actually fit. Once inside, she slid sideways instead of moving toward the counter, pulling Alain with her as she hugged the wall. Mari caught glimpses of the officer as he entered, shook his head, then faded back out the door. "So much for that idea. He's going to wait outside and pick us up when we leave." She scanned the crowd. "But this is Palandur. Imperial codes say that any business has to have two exits. Where is the other one?"

Tugging Alain along with her, Mari wedged herself through the crowd, unable to spot the fire exit. "Hey!" another girl protested as Mari accidentally bumped her. "Wait your turn!"

"We're just trying to find the other exit," Mari said, hoping a real local would know.

"Why?"

"Uh…this guy…he's not my boyfriend…and there's someone outside and…you know."

The girl grinned. "Yeah, I know. Guys get possessive. The back door is through there, past that set of shelves. Make sure you go left when you leave or you'll end up back on the same street as the front entrance."

"Thanks!"

Mari edged in that direction until they reached the shelves, finding a door with a faded "emergencies only" sign painted next to it. Judging by the wear and tear on the door it had been used fairly frequently for "emergencies."

The alley outside featured the usual stacks of trash and garbage, leaving a path leading both left and right. Mari took Alain left until they reached another street occupied by many pedestrians. "And, that, my Mage, is how people who aren't Mages hide themselves from other people."

Alain nodded. "You created the illusion of one deceiving her friend."

"Yeah. It was kind of embarrassing," Mari admitted. "I've never actually done that. I mean, cheat on a boyfriend."

"You have had boyfriends?"

"I…hey, what kind of question is that?" She smiled at him. "In every way that matters, there was no one before you. Now that we've lost that Imperial, we need to leave the city as soon as we can, through the west gate. There are horse-drawn trolleys everywhere, so we'll grab one and—" She stopped speaking. Alain was staring at her. "What does that look mean? This better not be about that boyfriend thing."

"It is not," he said. "When you mentioned the west gate of the city. Great peril awaits us there now."

Mari grimaced. Alain's foresight. "All right, then, maybe if we take the south gate—" Alain's alarm grew visibly. "That too? How about the north gate? Back to the east gate? Are you saying that there's great peril awaiting us at every gate out of this city?"

Alain nodded. "Very great peril. Someone watches for us to leave the city. In the time since we entered, something has happened."

She took a deep breath, calming herself as she thought. "Did the other Mages sense that you're here?"

"I am confident that they did not. If my presence could be detected, the Mages in Palandur would not be watching the gates. They would be coming to attack me."

"All right. That's a good point. But we can't stay here. We have to get out of this city."

Alain shook his head, his face grim enough for Mari to see the emotion. "I agree, but we cannot leave today. Mari, I have never seen such a dark warning from my foresight. It warns not just of peril but of death. We should not have come to Palandur, I think. This city is a trap."

# CHAPTER FOUR

Mari resisted the urge to punch the nearest wall in frustration. "I wish your foresight had told us that before we got here. It's not like we had much choice. Every road in this region converges on Palandur, and the Imperials insist on everyone passing through the city security checks. Is there any hope that the threat will be less tomorrow?"

"It may be. I do not know."

She stood looking around indecisively. "There are two other ways out of the city. We can try a boat or ship down the river—"

Alain shook his head. "Great danger."

"—or we can take a train." Mari paused, but this time Alain only looked concerned. "No warnings from your foresight about that?"

"No. But Mechanic trains worry me for other reasons."

"I know. Alain, someday we'll take a trip on a train and actually get where we're going without being attacked or blown up or something. Why wouldn't the Mages here be watching the train station?"

He thought about that before answering. "Even though some Mage Guild elders know I used a Mechanic train at least once, on the occasion when they sent a Roc to attack us, it is likely that here they simply did not think of the Mechanic trains when considering ways to leave the city. They have guarded all the ways in which they believe that a Mage would leave the city and do not realize there is another way available to me."

Mari grimaced, brushing back her hair. "It never hurts to have an opponent with blind spots, but I don't want to try the train here unless we absolutely have to. There are way too many Mechanics in Palandur who can recognize me and could easily be passing through the station. It wouldn't be as dangerous as fighting our way out past Mages, but it wouldn't be safe, either."

"Perhaps one night in Palandur would not be too dangerous, compared to the risks of leaving."

"Yeah," Mari agreed. "I was thinking the same thing. Palandur is a big city, full of people, and with lots of places to disappear. We can go to ground and stay quiet. We spend the night here in one of the cheap hostels where we can get a room, no questions asked, then see how bad things look tomorrow."

Alain looked past her, his gaze slightly unfocused. "All I can tell from my foresight is that your plan does not make things worse," he finally said.

"Gee, thanks."

"You are welcome." He hesitated. "Was that your sarcasm?"

Despite everything, Mari couldn't help smiling. "Yes. And a plan that doesn't make things worse is probably the best we can hope for."

Alain didn't try to smile back. "I should have foreseen the danger of coming here."

"Your foresight is unreliable, Alain," Mari replied. "That's not your fault. I think we should be grateful it kicked in when it did, before we got to one of those gates." That seemed to make Alain feel better, so she kissed him, which made her feel better.

Mari led the way again, heading for a low-rent part of Palandur where she knew cheap hostels would abound. It wasn't an area which Mechanics normally frequented, but she had heard some male Mechanics at the academy boasting about brief but memorable stays in the hostel rooms there with some of the many courtesans who plied their trade in Palandur. By the time noon had come and gone, they were dropping their packs onto the dusty floor of a tiny room on the third floor. The smirking desk clerk had asked whether they wanted to pay for the night or for a much shorter period of time. Mari, with an angry look she couldn't suppress, had paid for the night.

Alain sat down on the thin mattress of the bed which dominated the room. "It should be very hard to find us here, even if we have to stay longer than one night."

Mari sighed, looking around the shabby room. "Yeah. Maybe. Though the idea of spending more than one night in this kind of accommodation is less than appealing. I still want to leave this city as soon as possible. There are way too many dangers here. My Guild's headquarters. Your Guild's headquarters. The Imperial police. All the instructors and other Mechanics I knew in my days at the Mechanic Academy. The sooner we're headed for Landfall, the better."

Alain nodded in agreement. "We can try again tomorrow."

Mari pulled out of her pack the remnants of the food they had bought on the road. As she did so, her eyes fell upon the petition from the university in Marandur. Mari had a brief fantasy of carrying the petition to the Emperor, of the Emperor realizing the injustice being done to the survivors trapped inside the university, ordering it corrected, and then offering aid to Mari in her own efforts. That fantasy dissolved into an image of the Imperial Center for Truth, the place where prisoners were sent to confess whatever "truth" Imperial authorities wanted to hear. As a Mechanic, Mari had exchanged horror stories about the place with other Mechanics, safe in the knowledge that she would never face Imperial torture designed to produce confessions. Now that assurance of protection from the Imperials had vanished along with a lot of other certainties.

Nor did she think the Emperor was very likely to be a reliable or trustworthy ally, even assuming he didn't immediately sell her to the Mechanics Guild in exchange for some small advantage. The rulers of the common people on Dematr, regardless of whether they were elected by the people or occupied a mighty throne like that of the Empire, actually served the whims and demands of the Mechanics Guild and the Mage Guild. No government, no city or country, could survive if either Guild withheld its services and granted special support to the enemies of that government or country. The support of one of the Great Guilds could also be bought, of course, as long as the price was high enough and the goal sought did not conflict with the aims of the Guilds. The Mage Guild and the Mechanics Guild had a long history of hatred and conflict between them, but they were effectively allies in keeping the common folk slaves to the desires of the Guilds.

The common folk had long chafed under their servitude to the Great Guilds. Mari knew she would find many allies among the commons, but the Great Guilds could not have maintained their power for centuries without the aid of common allies who would sell out their fellows for power or money. She could not afford to trust everyone, and especially not anyone near the Emperor. There were plenty of stories about Imperial politics, and none of them inspired confidence in the Imperial court.

Mari carefully resettled the petition in her pack, knowing that it could not be delivered at this time without ensuring her own painful death.

"Is something wrong?" Alain asked.

"We need more to eat," Mari replied, not wanting to talk about depressing things at the moment. "Listen, the Imperial cops and your Guild are looking for two people, right? As far as I know, my Guild has no idea I'm around here, and we're in a part of Palandur where Mechanics rarely come during the day. Senior Mechanics wouldn't expect any Mechanic to stay in a place like this, so they shouldn't be looking here even if they suspect I'm in Palandur. If any Mechanics do show up I'll be able to spot them easily by their jackets and stay out of sight. We need food and a few other things. Why don't I go alone to the nearest market area and pick stuff up?" Alain eyed her, his face completely impassive. She knew what that meant by now. He was worried and withdrawing into his Mage persona because he couldn't show his concern. But at least this time his foresight wasn't setting off any alarms. "Alain, I'm a big girl. I'll be all right. It won't take long."

"I could go instead and run this risk," Alain volunteered.

Mari came close and hugged him. "My love, you can do incredible things and think of stuff I never could, but you still have very little grasp of money and you don't know how to bargain. An outdoor market isn't like a storefront business where the prices are set and posted up front. In time I'll teach you enough about those things that you can get by. Right now you'd be cheated by the merchants and maybe get robbed as well, even if the nearest Imperial cops didn't get suspicious of you. I can handle this. I won't be that far off."

He nodded slowly. "If you think it should be done this way."

"Just stay safe here. You can watch our packs and keep them safe. If anything happens to me—"

"I will come looking for you." Alain's voice was calm, unemotional, and unyielding.

Mari gazed at him and knew argument would be futile. She felt both aggravation and a strong sense of reassurance. "All right."

She rattled down the cheap stairs, hoping to get her errands done quickly. As worried as she was about being caught herself, Mari felt even worse at the idea of Alain being caught if he tried to rescue her.

The nearest market square was easy to find, with sellers shouting out the virtues of their wares and a steady stream of people entering and leaving the area Mari lounged against a building for a while, studying the scene and watching for anyone who might be watching for her. Nothing unusual caught her eye, just the normal mix of common people going about their business, children darting among the crowd while stressed-out parents tried to rein them in, a few young couples clinging to each other, older folks sitting as they played cards or talked. To one side a street band played string instruments, their regulation street performer license posted nearby just in case any of the ubiquitous Imperial police wandered past.

Mari sighed as she took it all in. After everything she and Alain had been through in the last several months, the peaceful and familiar scene felt comforting as well as dreamlike.

But those thoughts led her back to Marandur, and for a moment Mari saw not this market square in Palandur crowded with life, but one of the ruined squares in Marandur, surrounded by crumbling, dead buildings and choked with rubble, rusting weapons and armor, and the splintered bones of the uncounted men, women and children who had died long before.

She blinked to clear her eyes of the vision and the tears it threatened to bring. *Alain and I might have struggled our way through the square in Marandur which was the counterpart of this one. Everything here in Palandur seems so unchanging, like it was always here and always will be. But that's an illusion. It will vanish, replaced by death and emptiness, and it will vanish soon if I can't figure out how to do something that no one on Dematr has ever managed. Even the Empire will descend into the same chaos as Tiae if the grip of the Great Guilds isn't lifted from this world, and all cities will become like Marandur.*

Sometimes the whole prophecy and daughter thing feels overwhelming. Sometimes? Every time I think about it. But Alain is right. We can't give up and we can't afford to fail.

Swallowing and then breathing deeply to regain her composure, Mari dove into the crowd of customers, trying to lose herself in her shopping tasks.

She felt more secure in the crowded marketplace. Without her Mechanics jacket on she was just one more person in the mass of commoners. Surely her and Alain's enemies would have an impossible problem trying to find one of them in such a place. Mari went from seller to seller, picking up some necessary travel supplies, lingering for a while over a jewelry display. She found herself looking at pairs of matching rings. Promise rings. *Do I want to marry him? That other vision said it will happen.* Might *happen. There are no certainties, as my Mage keeps telling me. The stars above know that I could do a lot worse. Did I ever think I'd be looking at promise rings and thinking of a Mage?*

*What am I waiting for, anyway? He loves me. He's risked his life for me so many times already that I can't keep count. He trusts me. He respects me. He's never failed me. And I love him. I have no trouble at all imagining myself with him. Mentally and physically. But he's respecting my wishes to wait. What else do I want in a partner? What else could I possibly ask for? He's already proposed to me. Why not say yes and promise myself to him?*

And then someday Alain and I can have a daughter, and she can grow up until she's about eight years old and go off to the Mechanics Guild schools and we can cut her completely out of our lives without a single letter of explanation or a single word of goodbye or any sign at all that her mother and father knew they were ripping out a little girl's heart

Mari shuddered, biting her lip so hard she tasted blood, blinking away tears born of old anger and sorrow. *You're over that. Remember? So what if your mother and father cut all ties after you went to the Mechanics Guild schools? You're grown up now. You're too strong to let that get to you. They can't hurt you any more.*

Why? Why couldn't they have sent one letter?

I won't be like that. I could never do that to my child.

I don't care what my mother did. I'm not her.

I could never hate her. Not even now. Doesn't that mean I'm different?

But Mother never showed any signs of being like that. None I can remember. How do I know I won't turn into that?

*Face it, this isn't about Alain. It's about my worries about me. Until I resolve those fears, I'll never know if I'm somebody who might be willing to cast her own daughter aside without a single look back.*

Shaking her head in anguish and confusion over her feelings, Mari composed herself, then went to the food stalls to buy some provisions for the night's meal and the journey to Landfall. She had just paid for the last and bent down to pick up her bags of purchases when a soft, emotionless voice sounded next to her.

"Mechanic Mari."

Mari froze, her heart hammering in her chest, then slowly looked up to meet the gaze of a pair of beautiful blue eyes. The eyes were set in an even more beautiful face framed by long blond hair, all of it mostly hidden within the cowl of a Mage's robes. "Asha." Then her shock subsided enough for Mari's manners to come back to her. "Mage Asha. Sorry, Lady Mage."

"I need to speak with Mage Alain." Asha pulled her cowl a little higher to better hide her face and hair, but even with her Mage attempts to keep emotion from her voice, Mari could hear a faint note of urgency. Being around Alain had made her much more sensitive to subtle signs of emotion. "Is Mage Alain still safe?" Asha asked.

"As safe as I am. Which is to say, not nearly enough." The crowds around them were all edging away, putting distance between themselves and the Mage. A few spared pitying glances for Mari. A pair of Imperial police on a corner were looking in another direction as if unaware of anything going on. Everyone watching thought Mari was a common like them whom a Mage had decided to hijack as a personal servant or to torture or for some other reason inexplicable to normal people. None of them were crazy enough to try to interfere, because no one in his or her right mind invited the attention of Mages. "Let's pretend you've told me to come with you," Mari said. "Go to your right, out of the market and down that street with the tavern on the corner. I'll follow looking meek and terrified."

Asha's face offered no clue as to whether she thought that was a wise plan or not. She nodded with no visible emotion, then turned and began walking, while Mari hastened to pick up her packages and follow, not entirely feigning worry since a lot of people were watching her now and that was the last thing she had wanted.

A woman at a stall she passed called out in a low voice. "Is there anyone we should tell of you?"

Mari shook her head. "I'll be all right. She just wants some of the food I bought."

"Blasted Mages. Take care, girl!"

Once far enough down the road which Mari had indicated, she called quietly to Asha. "The hostel is to our left, about three blocks. If you turn at that next corner we can make a few more turns along the way to see if anyone is following." Mari took a moment to be glad that Asha had kept her eye-catching beauty concealed behind her robes and cowl. That would have attracted an extra measure of attention.

Mari directed Asha through some more turns, even doubling back at one point to ensure no one was shadowing them. Unfortunately, with so many people on the street at this time of day she couldn't be certain that no one had followed, but it seemed unlikely. Asha followed Mari's directions without comment or protest, her expression when Mari could see it unreadable. Finally, Mari brought them to the hostel and ducked inside. Fortunately, the desk clerk was momentarily busy with other customers, two men with two courtesans who were falling out of the tops of their dresses. The eyes of the desk clerk and the two men were locked onto the cleavage of the courtesans, and the courtesans kept their own eyes on the wallets of the two men, so no one noticed Mari lead a Mage up the shaky stairs.

She rapped softly. "It's Mari." A moment later Alain opened the door. Mari was fleetingly surprised that Alain didn't seem startled to see Asha.

"I sensed you approaching," Alain told Mari, "and that Mage Asha was with you, though Mage Asha conceals herself well."

He was doing it again: reverting to that expressionless, emotionless Mage voice and face. Already unsettled by Asha finding her, Mari glared at him as she shut and locked the door. "Act human, blast you. I've put a lot of work into getting you to show feelings and I don't want to see that go to waste."

Alain, startled, nodded before turning to Asha. "Mage Asha, I am happy to see you."

Asha raised one eyebrow the tiniest amount. "Happy?" she asked without feeling.

"Yes, Mage Asha. You are my friend."

"You still think of me as friend?" Asha gave Mari a glance from those gorgeous eyes.

Mari fervently hoped that Asha couldn't sense all of her feelings right now.

Asha nodded at Alain. "I have been trying to remember what 'friend' meant. Helping is involved. Helping with no obligation."

"Like you did at Severun," Mari said. "Warning Alain and misleading those other Mages. We've both been worried about you since then." It felt good to say that, because it was true, and because her pangs of jealousy still bothered Mari.

"Worried?" Asha asked. "Is that what I have sensed in myself when I think of Mage Alain and you?" She looked full on at Mari. "Do you still say that you…love Mage Alain?"

"Yes."

"Do you already carry his child?"

Mari felt her face getting hot. "Excuse me?"

"My questions discomfort you? Why is this?"

Mari took a deep breath, remembering her attempts to explain privacy to Alain. "Why don't we all sit down?" She and Alain sat on the edge of the bed while Asha took the room's one chair. "No, I do not carry Alain's child. That has to wait, even if I decide to do that."

"You do not want Alain's child?"

Mari's face got hotter. "Yes, I do. Maybe. I don't know." She wasn't even completely ready to discuss that with Alain, let alone with another woman she hardly knew. "But not now."

"You are not happy because of my question." Asha blinked at Mari, then looked at Alain. "What are the words?"

"I am sorry," Alain said.

She nodded and turned to Mari once more. "I…am…sorry. I… try to understand how you see him, even though I am still attempting to be aware of such feelings once more. But I know that you think of him very much."

"How do you know that?" Mari asked, not certain that she should be asking, but curious that a Mage would say such a thing.

"When you think of Mage Alain," Asha explained dispassionately, "your self blazes clearly to my senses even across great distances. This is how I found Mage Alain, knowing that you would be with him."

Mari suddenly realized that what she had felt before was not embarrassment. Not compared to what she felt now. "You can tell when I'm thinking about Alain?"

For his part, Alain had developed an anxious expression at Mari's reaction. "This is an unusual thing, Mage Asha."

"I had never heard of it from other Mages," Asha replied without emotion. "Yet even now Mechanic Mari's presence flares before me very brightly. She must be thinking of you."

"Oh, yes," Mari said, struggling to keep her voice under control. "I'm thinking about Alain right now, yes, I am. Can you tell what I am thinking, Alain?"

"You…are unhappy."

"Yes, Alain, I am unhappy. I thought you told me that Mages can't read minds." Mari's words came out sounding only partly strangled with emotion.

"They cannot," Alain said quickly. "I do not know what this thing is which Asha can see from you."

"She knows what I'm thinking about you! Do you have any idea what some of the things I've— Oh, blazes," Mari gasped, wondering if anyone could possibly feel this humiliated.

Asha was watching Mari with visible curiosity. "You are not happy to know another can sense your thoughts of Alain?"

"Happy," Mari said with all of the restraint she could manage, "is not quite the right word."

Watching Mari and looking more alarmed by the moment, Alain leaned toward Asha. "This thing you sense from Mari, it is like that from a Mage?"

"Yes," Asha agreed. "Like when a Mage casts a spell. The presence is clear, even though it is different from that of a Mage."

"Then," Alain said, choosing his words carefully as he looked at Mari, "Asha does not know what you are thinking of me. She only knows *that* you are thinking of me."

Mari glared at him suspiciously. "Just that? Nothing else? No… details? No…pictures?"

"Pictures of what?" Alain asked.

"Nothing! Not a blasted thing! Now answer the question!"

Alain, looking like he had the time they faced a dragon in Dorcastle, turned back to Asha. "Do you see any pictures?"

"No." Asha switched her gaze from Alain to Mari and back again, betraying no reaction at all. "What pictures should I be seeing? Perhaps if I focus on attempting to see such pictures—"

"NO!" Mari paused to get control of herself. "Please do not, Mage Asha."

Asha suddenly revealed a tiny measure of understanding. "You are concerned that I may be seeing your imagined manifestations of physical desire for Mage Alain."

Mari stared at Asha. Mari's face was so hot now that it felt like it was on fire. With nowhere to hide, she buried her face in her hands, wishing with all her might that a hole would appear beneath her and allow her to fall deep into the Earth.

"Master Mechanic Mari." Asha's voice was very low, and very close. The female Mage must be kneeling beside her. "I saw nothing. I will see nothing. Yet I have done something to cause you to conceal yourself. I do not know what should be done now."

That probably was the closest a Mage could come to an apology. In fact, it was a remarkable act for a Mage. Mari concentrated fiercely on what Asha had said and managed to lower her hands enough to see Asha. "Can you imagine how I feel right now?"

Asha stared back blankly. "How…you…feel? You?"

"Me."

"Shadows…feel?" Asha looked over to Alain for confirmation and must have received some. "But it is usual to imagine having physical relations with others. Why does this distress you?"

Mari shook her head. "We really need to talk, Mage Asha."

"We are talking."

"No. Alone. Without Alain here."

"Why?" Those beautiful blue eyes in that beautiful face looked back at Mari with no trace of feeling or understanding. "Is this a secret from Mage Alain?"

"No." Mari forced her hands back into her lap, though she still couldn't look toward Alain. "It's just…some things are very private. Not to be shared."

"Like Guild secrets?"

"Um…yes. Sort of. But just for each person. Personal secrets."

Mage Asha was thinking so hard that a slight furrow appeared on her brow. "Why does it matter what others know? They are but shadows."

"It matters," Alain said. "I still do not know why, but it does matter. Mari calls it having social skills. I have never before heard of a Mage being able to track someone who is not a Mage, except for the thread I sense that connects Mari with me."

"A thread?" Asha asked, her Mage tones making her sound uninterested in the answer.

"It does not exist, but it does exist, running invisibly between us. I do not know what it is. Could you sense Mari even more strongly than I do?"

"I do not know," Asha said. "I asked careful questions of elders, but saw their suspicions rise quickly and could gain no answers. It seems some tie exists between me and Mechanic Mari now. As the feelings I cannot admit to have become stronger inside—a sense of…wanting to…share…life, of not being the only real thing in a world of illusion populated by shadows—I am able to sense her more strongly."

Mari buried her face in both hands again. "Just one big happy threesome," she mumbled. "Alain, we need to talk."

"We are talk—"

"*Alone!* Do you Mages always have to do that?"

His hand touched her shoulder very gently, so Mari lowered her hands and glared at him as Alain spoke with great care. "There is no other for me but you."

"Me and my blazing bonfire of love, you mean?" Mari glanced over at Asha, who to Mari's surprise was betraying discomfort and confusion. "Mage Asha? Is something wrong?"

"Mechanic Mari," Asha said, "it is hard to explain. I have…a brother and a sister. I saw them when I left Ihris. They saw me. I could say nothing, show nothing. I was taught they…mean nothing. They showed…what other shadows reveal when they look upon Mages." Asha paused for a long moment. "I saw their expressions, and I told myself they did not matter, but I lied. Then I met you, and for the first time since I left the Guild Hall as a Mage, for the first time since I became an acolyte, someone looked at me and…and…smiled. No one smiles on a Mage, Mechanic Mari. I had not known how much I missed seeing a smile when another looked upon me, shadow or not."

Mari's embarrassment vanished as the female Mage's words hit home. She reached to grasp Asha's hands, barely noticing the shock in the female Mage at being touched. "Call me Mari, Mage Asha. That's why you feel a connection to me? Because I smiled at you? I thought you didn't care. You didn't react at all."

Asha gazed into Mari's eyes. "We are taught, in many ways, harsh ways, never to show what we think, what we feel."

"I know." This close, Mari had no trouble seeing the scars on Asha's hands and face, the same sort that Alain bore, the marks of the discipline that Mage Guild acolytes suffered. Some of the scars were so old that Asha must have been just a little girl when they did some of those things to her.

Asha looked down at Mari's hands holding hers, but she didn't try to withdraw them, instead seeming oddly vulnerable to Mari. *She wants me to like her,* Mari realized. *She's been alone for years, since she was a little girl, and now she's trying to find herself again. Asha sees what has happened with Alain and she wants the same for herself, but she doesn't even know how to ask. Instead of being envious of Alain, she's been helping him. And I've been jealous and angry and suspicious of this woman.* "Mage Asha, please say you will still be my friend."

Asha stared at Mari for a long time, then nodded. "I would be… happy…if that were so." Her mouth twitched, as if it were attempting to remember how to smile. "I have been trying, since I met you and Alain. Trying to remember." She looked at Alain. "I have an uncle who is a Mage also."

He nodded to her, Alain's eyes distant with some memory. "You once spoke of him."

"So long ago, it seems." Asha looked into a corner for a moment, then refocused on Alain. "He and I have talked a little. He… remembers, too, I think, but is not ready. I am not certain."

Asha took a long, slow breath. "I am remiss. I think of myself when there is much to warn you of. Alain, I must tell you of the danger here in Palandur."

"You know of this danger?" Alain asked. "I know only that my foresight warns of great peril at all gates from the city."

"Then your foresight spoke well. When I arrived at the Mage Guild Hall in Palandur this noon, I was told that one of the Mages there had also received foresight, seeing that sometime this day Mage Alain would leave this city."

"This Mage knew me?"

"Yes." Asha said. "Mage Niaro, who as an acolyte envied your early success."

"I remember Niaro," Alain said in the emotionless way of a Mage, giving Mari no clue as to what he felt about that other Mage.

"The envy of Mage Niaro perhaps provided the connection needed to see your future actions," Asha continued. "The Mage Guild Hall sent every Mage available to watch the gates and the waterfront, but there was some concern because Niaro had seen himself in the vision. I do not know what this means."

"It means he saw something that might happen, not something that will happen," Mari explained, then realized that she, a Mechanic, had just had the gall to enlighten a Mage about foresight. "Alain told me about that."

But Asha took Mari's knowledge in stride. "That explains it. Alain's foresight warned him not to leave, so the vision of Niaro did not take place. The elders believe that you must be in the city, though, and I understand this certainty now, for only if you were here could Niaro's vision have had any chance of happening. However, Niaro himself is mistrusted, for the elders see the emotion which ties him to you, and they care little for foresight."

"Will the Mages remain on guard tomorrow?" Alain asked.

"I was told to be ready to help guard the gates this night. They will watch for days beyond this one, I think." She nodded to Alain. "Your ability to hide yourself from other Mages is very strong now. Even I could not have found you as I did before. Only Mechanic Mari led me to you."

"Then we will be safe in this city," Alain said. "We can wait until the Mages tire—"

"Hold on," Mari cautioned. "Mages aren't the only ones looking for us, remember? The Imperials want us, and the Mechanics Guild wants me."

Asha studied Mari. "Why do they seek you? The Mage Guild elders say that Alain may be with one he knew before, that he must die before he betrays the Guild to this woman, who may be the daughter spoken of in the prophecy made long ago."

"They know of this?" Alain asked. "They know that Mari is the daughter?"

"Yes," Asha said. "I do not know how, but I did learn more of the prophecy. It was made by a Mage who encountered the one called Jules in centuries past. He did not know who she was when he saw her, and it took many years before the Guild discovered the identity of the woman."

Mari slapped her forehead. "That's why Jules had time to hide her children among other commons."

Asha's eyes went back to Mari. "You are that one? The daughter?"

"I…" Mari stared at the floor. "Maybe."

"She is," Alain said. "I had a vision which revealed it."

"Some other Mage must have had a vision of her as well," Asha said. "Her time comes, and more feel her presence. The Mage Guild will kill Mari as soon as it can."

"I will not let them kill her," Alain said. "Did they elders tell the Mages here of the storm?"

Asha shook her head slightly.

"Many Mages have seen this," Alain explained. "A storm approaches swiftly, born of the anger and frustration of the commons you and I were taught to see as shadows. They have lived in chains too long. The commons will rise, losing all reason in a frenzy of destruction, striking at each other and at the Mage Guild and the Mechanics Guild, destroying everything."

"This will happen?" Asha asked, her expression still completely impassive.

"Only the daughter can prevent it," Alain said.

"Can even the daughter do so much? Many already seek her death."

"We know this," Alain said. "She must succeed—"

"Hello!" Mari burst out. "I'm sitting right here! How can so many people be wanting to kill me and you two be ignoring me?"

"Your own Guild seeks your death as well?" Asha asked without apparent emotion. "Why?"

Mari waved one hand with mock flippancy. "Oh, associating with a Mage, betraying Guild secrets, treason, the daughter thing... Professor S'san told me that my Guild wants to take me alive so they can question me, but I have no doubt what they'll do when they're done asking questions."

"The Mage elders wonder if the Mechanics Guild seeks to use the daughter against the Mages," Asha said. "I sense in many elders and Mages a disbelief. They know of the prophecy, and they know that this Mechanic is foreseen to be the one who fulfills the prophecy, but they do not accept that this may happen, because Mari is a Mechanic. The elders will not accept that a Mechanic could triumph over the Mage Guild, which is too powerful and has wisdom on its side. How could any Mechanic prevail against Mages?"

"Their own illusions blind them. The Guild will not act with its full force?" Alain asked.

"I do not think so, not until the daughter has more fully revealed herself."

"Revealed herself?" Mari asked. "Revealed herself?" With every word spoken the conversation was getting harder for her to listen to.

"Openly proclaim who you are," Mage Asha said.

"Not going to happen," Mari said.

"But it must," Alain said.

"No." Mari glowered at him. "I will find whatever answers that tower on Altis holds. I will use the banned Mechanics Guild technology to change this world. I will do everything I can to stop that chaos storm. And I will do my best to stay alive while doing all of that. But I will not stand up in front of the world and say *look at how special I am, everybody!*"

Alain looked at Asha. Asha looked back. "She is a Mechanic?"

"She is," Alain confirmed.

"All Mechanics believe they are special." Asha looked seriously perplexed, which meant even an average person might have seen it in her expression. "Even the Mage Guild says that Mari is special, not like the other shadows. But she does not?"

"No. Mari often denies—"

"Will you two stop talking as if I'm not here?" Mari demanded. "Exactly what have I done that is so special?"

"You have slain two dragons," Alain said. "Few ever slay even one."

"You have helped Mage Alain to find a new wisdom," Asha said. "And perhaps you shall show me that path as well."

"You have a general sworn to your service," Alain added. "As well as at least two other Mechanics, the one named Calu and your elder S'san. And a Mage who follows you."

"Two Mages," Asha said.

"You have entered and escaped from Marandur," Alain said. "And you told me you were the youngest ever to become a full Mechanic and the youngest ever to become a Master Mechanic."

Mari stared at them. "All right. That...might...sound...a little... special. But that doesn't make me better than anyone else. I just have a...bigger job to do. A much bigger job. And to answer the earlier question more specifically, the last thing I need to do is give the Empire any more reasons to get their hands on me and Alain. So, no revealing."

Asha studied Mari for a few moments before speaking again. "Why does the Empire already seek you? Is it because of the prophecy again?"

"I hope not," Mari said. "Unless your Guild told them, they shouldn't know."

"The Mage Guild does not want to give hope to the shadows it treats as nothing," Asha said.

"However," Mari said, reluctant to admit the truth, "Alain and I both are under death sentences from the Empire. Because we went to Marandur." She whispered it, not wanting to risk being overheard.

"Marandur. Mage Alain spoke of this," Asha said. "Why?"

"There was something important there," Mari said. "It's hard to explain to a Mage, because you do things so differently from Mechanics. Basically, I think the Mechanics Guild doesn't believe in the prophecy of the daughter either, because the Senior Mechanics who run it can't conceive that anyone could overcome the Mechanics Guild. The same as you said the Mage elders are thinking. And the Senior Mechanics are right that defeating them would be impossible if I only had access to the same tools that they have. But I found—that is, Alain and I found—ways to build new Mechanic tools. Tools that will give us a chance to defeat the Mechanics Guild."

"Tools?" Asha asked.

"They are like Mage spells," Alain explained.

"No," Mari said. "Tools aren't spells. Tools are how we make spells. Did I just say that? It's a good thing Professor S'san didn't hear me. Anyway, it's things like semi-automatic rifles, assembly lines, better far-talkers, food preservation, medical equipment, better steam propulsion systems. That kind of thing." Asha was staring back at her blankly. "Better weapons, better ways to make them, better ways to talk over long distances, better ways to do everything."

Mari frowned as she thought about her last statement. "That's not true. Even with the new Mechanic knowledge I found, all of the technology in those forbidden texts, I couldn't do what Mages do."

"Wisdom from a Mechanic," Asha murmured. "She is special," Asha told Alain.

"Yes," Alain agreed. "She is."

"You're doing it again," Mari said. "I'm still here and part of this conversation. Alain is special, too, you know," she added.

"Mage Alain." Asha looked at him, her eyes revealing some deep emotion. "I learned something more concerning you. By what elders have told me, and by what they did not say, I have learned that Mage

Alain was to be humiliated by failure on his first contract. If he also died, that would have been a matter of welcome to the elders."

"Do you mean Alain was set up, too?" Mari demanded. "The Mage Guild knew he was going to run into serious trouble?"

"The elders at Ringhmon knew more of the plans of the shadows there than they revealed to Mage Alain," Asha continued. "They were not surprised that the caravan he guarded was attacked, nor that the attack was so powerful as to be beyond any Mage's ability to counter. They did not expect him to survive, believing that either in the attack or afterwards, alone in the waste, he would die."

Mari stared at Asha, aghast, but Alain simply nodded, his expression perfectly calm. She could see him withdrawing a bit into his Mage state to deal with the ugly news.

"This explains much," Alain said tonelessly. "I wondered why the elders in Ringhmon were unconcerned with the fate of the caravan but acted much distressed over my arrival. All of their questions centered on the Mechanic who had accompanied me in escaping the ambush and the desert waste."

"Just so," Asha said. "She had not been anticipated. This also I learned, Mage Alain. Your suspicions regarding the attack in Imperial territory were correct. The plan was again that you should fail in your task, and this time surely die in the process. Your fate would not be left to the efforts of commons or chance. Some Mages would be ordered to ensure you did not escape, and if possible the common military force that you accompanied would be eliminated completely, leaving no witnesses and ensuring the magnitude of your failure would be as great as possible."

"I had wondered why so many Mages were in the force that attacked the Alexdrian soldiers, and how those Mages could have known so surely where I and the Alexdrians would be," Alain said. "If not for Mari's arrival, I would surely have 'failed' again just as the elders planned. But I was ordered to the Free Cities from Dorcastle. Do you say the plan had already been decided upon at that time?"

"Yes, Mage Alain, your fate had already been decided before you left Dorcastle." Asha paused. "I was able to learn much because the elders themselves are asking many questions, and in the questions asked, answers can be found. The elders do not understand how you escaped the dragon in the north. They know no single Mage could have defeated that spell creature, nor any force of commons." Her eyes went to Mari. "The elders do not even consider the possibility that one of the toys of the Mechanics could have accounted for the dragon."

Mari, stunned by what she had been hearing, managed to nod. "They're partly right. If my friend Alli hadn't designed those special weapons, I couldn't have nailed that dragon."

Alain had let some puzzlement show. "Could you learn why this decision was made, Mage Asha? To humiliate me and see my death before ever I met Mari? I had assumed my errors after coming to know Mari had led to the decision that I must be eliminated as a threat to the Guild."

"I cannot be certain," Asha said. "But the elders do now openly declare you to be in error, ensnared by the wiles of a seductive young female Mechanic whose charms you could not resist."

"Oh, give me a break!" Mari burst out. "Just who is this irresistible, seductive young female Mechanic?"

"You have ensnared me," Alain pointed out.

Not in the mood for joking about that, Mari glared at him so strongly that Alain visibly flinched. "Any time you want to be free of my snare all you have to do is ask, Mage Alain. Did you learn anything else, Asha?"

"Yes," Asha replied. "Mage Alain, you are not the youngest ever to have been declared a Mage. A century ago, one was declared a Mage at the age of sixteen. She died before she became seventeen, in a failed contract. The records say she had neither the experience nor the skills of a Mage, despite having been declared so by several elders at the Mage Hall in Cathlan. Forty years before that, one gained Mage status at twelve. He died at the age of thirteen, also on a failed contract, and also because of a lack of skills and experience, the records say. I suspect that the records lie. I found records of a few other young Mages who did not die, but failed in major tasks and were returned to acolyte status."

"That's an interesting and disturbing pattern," Mari agreed.

"Why?" Alain asked. "Why must young Mages die, Mage Asha? Could you learn that?"

"No one admitted to deliberately seeking the elimination or discrediting of those judged too young. You know what we were taught: that skill and wisdom alone determine whether one can be a Mage. No physical issue such as age should have any bearing on the matter, for all is illusion," Asha explained. "Instead, I was told, sometimes those given Mage status are unwilling to accept guidance from their elders and thus lack sufficient wisdom. Sometimes they have yet to become themselves, their nature still in flux. Sometimes they are more prone to feelings, lacking enough self-control."

"How could those arguments be aimed at me or other young Mages?" Alain asked.

"Focus not on the illusion of the words but on what they conceal," Asha advised. "Turn those points about and you see what the elders reject. Who questions the wisdom of elders, Mage Alain? The young. Who changes the most in a short time as they age? The young. Who feels the changes of the body the most strongly as it grows, making self-control indeed more difficult? The young. Unpredictable. Questioning. Prey to the emotions given extra strength by the changes in their bodies." Asha shook her head. "You, like other Mages deemed too young, were judged too likely to err, too likely to seek new answers, too likely to challenge the elders. And this is what you have done, though perhaps that only happened under the force of the elders' attempts to eliminate you."

"Self-fulfilling prophecies," Mari said, seeing both Mages turn questioning looks upon her. "That's a saying for when you create the conditions that make a prediction come true. Your elders said that young Mages would fail, and then set them up to fail. Your elders believed that Alain would deviate from what they call wisdom, and they forced him into circumstances in which he did just that. So they were correct, because they did things to make themselves be correct."

Alain nodded to Mari. "Wisdom which justifies itself."

"But why not just admit those concerns?" Mari asked. "Why not say you need a certain level of maturity before you can be a Mage, whether it's true or not? My Guild has done that, setting experience requirements in place that mean in the future no one else can be promoted as fast as I was, regardless of how well they master Mechanic arts."

This time Alain shook his head. "The elders cannot admit such a thing. As Asha said, a fundamental aspect of the wisdom they teach is that the physical is irrelevant. Nothing is real."

"Wow," Mari commented. "We've gone days without you saying nothing is real, and I haven't missed it at all."

"But it is so by the wisdom Mages are taught," Alain said. "If nothing is real, to say that the physical body in fact creates conditions which prevent anyone from being a Mage would be to undermine much of what they teach."

"As Mage Alain said in Severun," Asha added, "the wisdom we were taught is lacking. The elders should examine where the errors lie and make changes, but instead they cling to what they know."

Mari couldn't help a short, sardonic laugh. "Just like what Professor S'san and I talked about with the Senior Mechanics who control the Mechanics Guild. Different wisdom, but the same refusal to contemplate changes."

"Mari," Alain said with a visibly surprised look, "the reasons Mage Asha gives for my elders moving against me are in part the same reasons your professor gave for your Guild's hostility to you. There also we see similarities."

"You're right." Mari sat back, trying to think. "Do you remember one of the first things we talked about after we met? How your elders and my Senior Mechanics seemed to have a lot in common? I wonder if every group of managers who becomes used to being in charge, who is dedicated to nothing more than keeping things the same and themselves in power, ends up acting in the same ways even if they use different justifications? They don't want anyone questioning their decisions or their authority." Something else occurred to her then. "Questions. Asha, you must have asked a lot of questions to find out all of this. You took some serious risks."

"I have attracted the attention and disapproval of the elders," Asha said, the lack of feeling in her voice providing no clue as to how she felt about that. "However, I have attracted such attention and disapproval before."

"You have?"

Alain gestured toward Asha. "I have told you, Mari, that Mage Asha could never appear other than attractive."

Mari stared at Asha. "You actually got in trouble because you were beautiful? Seriously?"

"My appearance," Asha said, "must surely be my fault, must surely reveal a lack of wisdom."

"What were you supposed to do about it?"

Asha's shoulders twitched very slightly in what might have been a Mage shrug. "I could have shorn my hair, scarred and damaged my skin, broken things to make them heal in misshapen ways—"

"No!" Mari burst out, horrified. "That would be so wrong. Hurting yourself that way? Maiming yourself? Please don't ever do that."

Asha gazed at Mari for a long moment before replying. "I have been hurt before, Mari. It is nothing. But to harm my features would have served no purpose. To strike at my appearance would have been proof that I took note of it, and would have condemned me in the eyes of the elders just as much as how I look now."

"No matter what you did, you'd be wrong?" Mari asked. "You know, back when Alain and I first met, I was really surprised that a Mage and I could have something in common. Now I'm learning that a female Mage and I have something in common, too. I'm glad you never hurt yourself. I'm sorry I freaked out earlier. I know I'm a little weird at times and I'm sorry. I just…" Mari hesitated, her voice sinking to a whisper. "I love you so much, Alain. I don't want you to be hurt. Especially not because of me. And sometimes thinking about that makes it hard to handle everything else. I've got a world to save, but it wouldn't mean anything if I lost you."

"It must be difficult to see others as real instead of as shadows," Asha said.

"It is difficult," Alain agreed. "There is much pain to be found in such seeing. But there is also much joy."

"Joy?"

"You will know it when you feel it," he assured her. "I begin to suspect that none are shadows, but all are real for good or ill."

Asha nodded, her eyes intent. "I will think on this, and look upon the shadows who cross my path. Do your powers diminish yet, Mage Alain?"

"My powers grow, Mage Asha, even as my love for Mari grows."

Mari felt her face getting warmer again, but this time her blush came along with a smile.

"Your powers do not just remain as they were? They still grow?" Asha's astonishment was clear to Mari.

"There is no doubt. I was able to test them in Marandur, and was forced to use them there to a greater extent than ever before. I am more powerful now."

"Then you do learn a different wisdom, and perhaps a better one as well, Mage Alain. Perhaps the elders were right to fear you." Asha looked around. "It is not safe that I stay here. The Guild Hall will expect me back to help watch the gates for your departure, Alain. If I can, I will tell you when it is safe to leave this city."

Mari leaned forward, touching Asha again on the hand, pleased and surprised when Asha did not recoil. "You don't have to keep risking yourself for us."

"Is that not what a friend does?"

"Yes." Mari smiled. "And you are a friend. But friends also worry, and hope that their own friends are safe. Please be careful, Asha."

"Please?"

"It means I'm asking you if you'll do something, not telling you."

"I see. Please. I will remember this word, but not use it around

Mages." Asha stood up, bringing her hood up around her head, then turned to go without another word.

Mari waited until she had left, then rose and locked the door again. "You could have said goodbye, Alain."

"It did not occur to me when speaking with another Mage," Alain admitted.

"Then next time I'll remind you. Did Asha really suffer a lot more from the elders because she's beautiful?"

"She did," Alain said, his eyes once more getting the distant gaze of someone looking into their memories. "Asha was often berated as an acolyte for being too attractive. Some thought that meant she was too closely tied to the false world of appearances. This caused her distress, which was reason for more attacks on her by the elders for showing emotion. I know that as an acolyte Asha considered her appearance a true burden, and it was."

"But you helped her at least once, right?"

"Only once," Alain said. "The punishment was severe enough to dissuade me from trying any further, and I could see in Asha that she would avoid being helped again so as to protect me from more such punishment." He paused, dredging up a memory. "I remember that once Asha did speak of changing her appearance. An elder spoke with her, and later that same elder told us that any attempt to damage Asha's appearance would show a greater flaw than her beauty."

"An elder convinced her not to mutilate herself?"

"Yes." Alain shook his head. "Did that elder act out of kindness? I had never suspected such before, but today I wonder."

Mari stared out the grimy window of their room. "I guess even the Mage Guild has some elders who care about people."

"Perhaps. One elder I spoke with in Dorcastle cared about me, the one who told me what my vision meant, and that you were the daughter. She cautioned me to tell no one else and to protect you. How many Mages have kept hidden the feelings they were supposed to have forgotten? I had thought myself alone in that, but there may be many Mages who have remained silent, who keep their feelings concealed, but who would welcome a different path." Alain gave an impression of subdued distress. "The wisdom the Mage Guild now teaches requires a very difficult path, one with much hardship."

"Alain, I've seen the marks it left on you. It must have been horrible."

"It was what it was," Alain replied in a low voice. "Acolytes learned to deal with it. We had no choice."

"I couldn't have done it."

He gave her his most serious look. "Yes, you could have. But I am glad that you did not have to endure what Mage Asha and I did."

Mari looked out the window again. "As hard as things are, I guess we can be thankful that they weren't worse. We've made it this far, and even though I feel at times like it's us against the world, we've got friends like Asha. Oh, stars above, I forgot that I went out for food. You're probably really hungry. Let's get something to eat from what I bought in the market and pack up the rest just in case we have to leave in a hurry."

Their involuntary day in Palandur drew to a slow close, Mari watching the shadows shift as the sun fell lower in the sky. By the time the sun set, she was restless and nervous. "Hopefully, the way will be clear to escape this city-sized trap in the morning. Maybe the Mages will give up quickly."

"Mages can be very patient," Alain said.

That made her laugh briefly. "I should know that by now. They'll wait, you think?"

"Perhaps for several days. If they believe I am in the city," Alain added, "they may search for me inside it as well. Do you think we should take watches tonight?"

Mari gave another worried glance out the dirty window. "Yeah, I do. I can't sleep right now, so you go ahead. I'll wake you about midnight." Mari didn't bother lighting the candle on the room's small, rickety table. She sat near the grimy window, staring out at the night sky barely visible between other buildings. For a while, there were lights outside, torches illuminating the fronts of a few taverns, but as the evening wore on those were extinguished and the night grew darker. Early in the night, too, there was constant traffic on the hostel's stairs, the creaking and clattering easy to hear as courtesans and their customers went to and from rooms. Mari tried not to listen to the sounds coming from the rooms next to hers and Alain's, and eventually those quieted along with the dwindling of the noise from the stairs.

She wondered what the next day would bring. Some danger, if the past was any guide.

Despite her nerves, the long day after many long hard days wore on her, and Mari began to get drowsy as the hostel and the streets outside grew silent. Her head kept sagging, her eyes closing, mind fuzzy with fatigue.

The headache came out of nowhere, dispelling sleep as Mari winced at a sudden stab of pain. She came to full alertness as another stab, more painful than the first, made her head throb. Mari pressed her hands against the sides of her head, trying to guess the cause of the pain. She rarely had headaches, making this one even more bizarre. A third stab hit, more intense yet.

Mari bent over, screwing her eyes shut against the last blast of pain. She waited, bracing herself for another shock.

But no more stabs came. Mari cautiously straightened up again, trying to find any trace of unusual pain in her head and finding none. She looked around, judging from the silence outside and inside the hostel that it must be close to midnight.

Wood creaked somewhere, a tiny sound that she probably wouldn't have noticed when drowsy. Now, fully alert, Mari perceived it clearly in the stillness that otherwise enveloped the hostel. Mari held her breath, listening as intently as she could. Leather mattress supports squeaked in one of the adjacent rooms. Someone in that room muttered something that could barely be heard through the thin walls.

Wood creaked again. The staircase. Who would be so careful coming up it? Those who had used it earlier in the night had clumped up or down without caring who they bothered. But now someone was trying not to make any noise.

Trying to sneak up stairs.

Trying to get up here without anyone hearing them.

She got up, trembling with the need to move both as quickly and as quietly as possible. Reaching for Alain, she shook him awake. Alain stared at her as Mari held a finger to her lips to signify the need for silence, then pantomimed danger. Alain rolled out of the bed, the rustling of the sheet sounding huge in the night. He pulled on his boots and reached for his pack. Mari did the same, blessing their habit of sleeping fully clothed in case of emergency.

Another soft sound, from the short hallway outside of their room. A footstep, perhaps. Someone was approaching very cautiously.

Mari edged to the window to peer out and down. Imperial building regulations called for a fire escape ladder out there, but there was no telling what shape that ladder was in. She gestured to Alain that they should go through the window. He nodded.

The door to their room exploded.

# CHAPTER FIVE

Fragments of wood pelted the bed where Alain had been lying, then incredibly bright strands of lightning ripped through the doorway and into the bed, flaying the mattress and igniting everything that could burn.

Mari kicked out at the window frame, popping it straight out of the wall while after-images of the lightning danced in her eyes. She heard a sharp explosion and looked back to see the area just beyond the shattered doorway erupt into flames. Alain turned away from the destruction. "My fire spell may slow them down. Go, Mari!"

She hesitated. "You're coming too, right?"

"When I can—"

"Now! Or I stay, too!"

Alain looked ready to argue, then nodded. Mari pulled herself through the small window opening and out onto a tiny landing, which swayed precariously under her. She grabbed at the ladder fastened to the side of the building while Alain came through after her. As Alain left the room, lightning flared again, filling the place where they had been and almost knocking Alain off the landing. Mari got a hand on his arm and held him until he could grab the ladder, then started clambering down as fast as she dared.

She let go to drop the last several feet into the alley their room had overlooked, rolling to break the fall and coming up with her pistol in her hand. A robed figure appeared nearby and raised one hand, a long Mage knife gleaming in the dim light. Mari, knowing the Mage wasn't Asha because he or she was too short, aimed for the center of the figure and fired, her shot illuminating the alley with a flash of light. In that momentary brightness she could see that the robed figure was also heavier than Asha. The Mage grunted with pain and was knocked to the ground by her shot, the knife falling to one side. Mari took three quick steps to stand over the fallen Mage, who was writhing on the ground. Mari pointed her pistol at the Mage's head, seeing expressionless eyes looking back at her from the rounded face of an older man.

*Kill him!* her nerves screamed. *He's a Mage! He could still be very dangerous!*

But the wounded Mage did not move, did not betray any of the signs she was familiar with in Alain of preparing to cast a spell. Mari lowered her pistol, then yanked a cloth from one of her pockets and knelt to jam it over the Mage's wound, where blood was welling out to soak the Mage's robes. "Hold that tight over the wound until a healer can see you and you may be all right," Mari whispered, then jumped back and to her feet, looking for Alain.

Instead of Alain, Mari stared at another figure which had appeared at the opening to the alley. It looked vaguely human-shaped, but was taller and much broader than any human Mari could imagine.

The noise of feet hitting the surface of the alley sounded close by, and Mari spun as she brought up her weapon, finding her pistol pointed at Alain's nose.

He looked at the pistol and shook his head. "You keep doing that," Alain said, then reached out and pulled her back as more lightning rippled down from above, lashing the alley and blowing apart some nearby crates of trash.

Mari looked up, seeing a robed figure on the landing of their former room, his or her shape outlined by the fires burning behind. Aiming carefully almost straight up, using both hands to steady the pistol, she fired twice. The sound of the shots filled the night, sounding huge after the silence which had once enveloped this part of the city.

At least one of the shots apparently hit, as the lightning Mage fell backwards and out of sight into the room. "I think I got him. Or her."

A guttural roar sounded from the head of the alley. Mari twisted to look that way. The thing there was now lumbering down the alley toward her, its weight making the ground shake.

Alain spoke with what Mari considered remarkable calmness. "It is a troll."

She fired at it, the light from her shot this time revealing a crude being which looked like a half-formed attempt to make a creature in the form of a human, but one that towered over her and was so wide it almost filled the alley. The creature didn't even react to Mari's shot, nor from the next two bullets she carefully aimed and fired directly into it. Once again the sound of her shots echoed thunderously through the once-sleeping city, streets now stirring around them as the din of Mechanic and Mage weaponry filled the air and fire spread in the hostel above.

Alain raised his right hand, the air glowing above his palm, and a moment later the creature facing them howled as the fireball appeared in its face. The troll reeled back, pawing at itself.

Alain's hand came down on Mari's shoulder. "We must run," he said. "Neither of us can kill a troll."

"I was reaching the same conclusion," Mari gasped, spinning around to look at the other end of the alley. Piles of trash were heaped against a fence that was about as tall as Alain. "We can't run past the thing. Come on. This way."

The Mage whom Mari had shot had crawled to one side to avoid the troll as it looked for Mari and Alain through still-dazzled eyes. The wounded Mage silently watched as she and Alain bolted down the alley toward the fence.

"I will need a moment to gather strength to create a hole," Alain gasped.

"What? Just go over it!" Mari shoved Alain forward and then up as he scrambled clumsily to get over the fence. She followed, cursing the weight of her pack and hearing the troll coming on behind them again. Alain helped her over the fence as he got to his feet on the other side.

"I never thought of going over a wall instead of through it," Alain confessed.

"Mages," Mari grumbled. She staggered as her feet hit the ground, then shoved Alain onward toward an opening visible a short distance ahead, giving way onto another street. The once-quiet night was now filled with the noise of crackling flames. Shouts and screams came from the hostel and surrounding buildings, and the sound of ringing bells from near and far called the fire wardens of Palandur to action. On top of that came the deep thud of gongs calling the city guard to the site of the battle. "We'll talk about different ways to get past walls later."

They had almost reached the end of the alley when three robed figures appeared before them, two in the act of drawing and brandishing the long knives of Mages. They must have surprised this group, leaving the Mages unable to concentrate on spells. With too little time to aim and fire, Mari ducked under a swinging blade and then smashed her pistol barrel against the nearest Mage's temple. That Mage fell heavily to one side.

By the time Mari turned to help Alain, his opponent was down as well. Mari brought her pistol to bear on the third Mage, who had made no move to attack.

"Wait," Alain cautioned, going past Mari to stand directly before the third Mage. "It is Asha." He held up Asha's hands so that Mari could see they were bound together and tied to a cord about her waist.

"She was a prisoner?" Mari rushed over as Alain used his knife to sever the cords around Asha's wrists. Close up, Mari could see the blindfold across Asha's eyes, which had been concealed from easy view by the cowl of her Mage robes.

Her hands free, Asha lowered her hood and pulled off the blindfold. "The elders were able to detect my presence far better than I expected. While remaining out of sight, some of them tracked me to your room. That is how they found you. I was confronted when I returned to the Guild Hall and forced to accompany the Mages attacking you. Though they thought me helpless with my vision blocked, I attempted to warn you by using my strange tie to Mari."

"You what?" Mari said. "I didn't— Those headaches? Something you did caused those headaches?"

"She does not lie," Alain said.

"Alain, she was tied up and blindfolded! I know she's not lying! Come on, sister, we need to get out of this city and you're coming with us!"

"No." Asha looked back the way that Mari and Alain had come. "I must stay. There is one who requires my...my...help."

The fence behind them splintered, the troll staggering into sight as it looked around for Mari and Alain. "Asha, we're being chased by a troll!" Mari cried.

"It will seek you, not me, as long as I conceal myself."

"Mage Asha," Alain said, "the Guild sees you as an enemy now. You are in danger. The elders would have ordered your death as soon as Mari and I were dead. If we now leave you alone—"

Asha shook her head. "I will not be alone. I cannot leave now. One needs me. Go. I will find you again, no matter where you are."

The troll had seen them and was now stalking forward.

Mari hesitated. "Alain, can you hide us the same way—"

"No. The troll can sense us by other means since we are its prey."

"I can find you, Mari. Just think of Alain." Asha reached out to touch Mari's hand. "Go now."

Alain still wavered, visible emotions flashing across his face. Mari reached out and grabbed his arm. "We have to do as she wants, Alain! Run! That thing is right behind us!"

They ran, the troll's frustrated roar echoing behind them, Mari's hand locked onto Alain's as she ran all out down the street, legs pumping as fast as she could drive them.

"Weapon," Alain gasped.

Mari realized that she was still holding her pistol in one hand and hurriedly holstered it . It wouldn't do for the Imperials to see her carrying that when they came charging in to restore order. The glow of the fire was continuing to spread, lighting up the sky, and increasing numbers of people were flooding into the streets as they left the hostel and surrounding buildings that had caught fire from blown sparks. The clanging of fire bells could be heard in all directions, growing rapidly louder as the fire wardens converged on the increasing conflagration. Mari heard the troll again, then saw it stomp into the street and stare around, coming after them with its shambling gait. She was just thinking how fortunate it was that trolls moved a lot slower than dragons when a squad of the city guard showed up.

"Halt!" one of the Imperials yelled at Mari.

"Troll!" she yelled back, gesturing wildly.

The city guards stumbled to a stop as they saw the troll, not making any attempt to stop Mari and Alain as they tore through the ranks of the guards. Mari heard orders being shouted and the thump of crossbows firing, but didn't look back, instead taking the next corner at the best speed she could.

Alain was gasping for breath beside her. "Should we not help?"

"Against that?" Mari wheezed. "Besides, if we did, the Imperials would just kill us, too, once the troll was dead."

Another group of Imperial police dashed onto the street, spreading out to form a line. "Halt!" their leader shouted, pointing at Mari.

She skidded to a stop, trying to decide whether or not to try bluffing her way through again or to just threaten them with her pistol. Before Mari could reach a decision, a crowd of commons erupted from the entrance of the building next to her and rushed the thin line of Imperial guards.

The Imperials closed ranks to support each other and swung their hardwood clubs with practiced skill. The first citizens to reach them fell with bleeding heads or broken arms, their screams adding to the tumult.

Mari yanked Alain back into motion, swinging around the fight as more citizens piled onto the street. "We don't want to get stuck in that mess," she gasped to Alain.

Alain nodded wordlessly, trying to keep up with her until Mari had to slow down again, her lungs and her legs burning. But she kept heading away from where flames were leaping higher into the sky and the bedlam of battle rose behind them. "That is not our fault," she got out between attempts to breathe.

Despite her urgency, Mari stumbled to a halt and stared behind them as an inarticulate cry of rage filled the night. It was as if the roar of the troll had been hugely amplified. It wasn't the troll, though, but rather a sound rising from thousands of human throats, giving vent to wordless rage and frustration.

It frightened her worse than the troll had.

This time it was Alain who urged her back into motion. "Where are we going?" Alain got out as he also struggled for breath.

"The train station. We can't risk the gates or the water with the Mages watching those ways, so we're taking the blasted train." She had to pause and inhale deeply several times. "It's too blasted dangerous to stay in this city with the Mages out to kill us both. There's a risk I'll be recognized, but at least we won't run into any trolls at the train station."

"Assuming the Imperials kill this one before it finds us again." They reeled to a halt as what looked like half a cohort of Imperial legionaries hauling a ballista came at quick-step down the street with a mounted officer urging them on. "But it seems the Imperials will make every effort to finish the creature," Alain added as they crossed the street in the wake of the legionaries. "Enough hits from a siege machine will stagger even a troll."

Behind those legionaries came the rest of the cohort, expressions grim. Mari wondered if they were going to battle the troll, or the mob of Imperial citizens.

Mari held onto Alain as she led the way, zigzagging through the streets while trying to keep a bearing on the Mechanic train station, looking back occasionally where the glow of the fires lit the night and echoes of fighting still resounded.

❀   ❀   ❀

The waiting area for common folk at the Mechanic train station was uncomfortable at the best of times. Mari had sent Alain to buy two tickets to Landfall after coaching him on exactly what to say and how much money to give the apprentice occupying the ticket window. The Mage, who could walk through walls, foresee the future, and create heat out of nothing, had come back visibly proud of having successfully handled something that complicated.

They sat on hard, narrow seats in one corner of the waiting area, heads lowered as if they were sleeping while awaiting the departure of their train, which also served to keep Mari's face partly concealed. As the morning wore on, more and more Imperial citizens waiting for the same train took seats, too, providing more cover for Mari when the occasional Mechanic sauntered through. Fortunately, as usual, the Mechanics made a point of ignoring the commons. Mari, who had often been annoyed when some of the Mechanics she was with flaunted such attitudes, now felt only gratitude for the arrogance which helped render her invisible.

"Will the Mechanic train run?" Mari heard one Imperial woman ask another. "The city council has closed the gates."

"The Mechanics are not affected by the city council's actions." The second woman had the look of a high-ranking Imperial bureaucrat, her suit and accessories as precisely arranged and selected as if it were a uniform. "They will do what they want."

"Arrogant and uncivilized," the first woman complained. "What happened in the Gorgan District, anyway?"

Mari strained her ears to listen to the reply.

"Officially, no one is saying anything," the Imperial bureaucrat replied. "But I've heard from those who've seen all the reports that it was an all-out fight between a large group of Mechanics and a large group of Mages. An absolute, pitched battle with Mechanic weapons and Mage spells ravaging the entire district. Four buildings were totally destroyed and several others damaged."

"You're not serious!" the first woman gasped. "In the heart of Palandur?"

"Gorgan isn't exactly the heart of Palandur," the second woman replied dryly. "Some of the buildings that burned should have been torn down years ago. Still, it's pretty frightening, isn't it? The city guard couldn't handle it all, so they actually called out part of the city legion to deal with it. Some sort of Mage monster had to be destroyed. Imagine being caught in the middle of that. The fires still haven't been completely extinguished."

Mari sniffed cautiously, hoping no scent of smoke still clung to her, and tried to suppress a guilty feeling. *It's not my fault that buildings I'm in keep getting burned down. Well, the one in Ringhmon was my fault. But not these.*

"What about the rioting?" the first woman asked.

"What rioting?"

The first woman paused, as if uncertain what to make of that question. "In Gorgan. There are rumors that hundreds have been injured, large numbers of stores and homes destroyed—"

"Imperial citizens do not riot," the Imperial official said in a tone of voice that both warned and reprimanded. "Anything that happened in Gorgan involved Mages and Mechanics and no one else."

Mari could almost hear the first woman gulp nervously before speaking again. "Of course. You're right. Surely the Emperor's not going to tolerate that behavior from the Great Guilds?" she said, hastily changing the subject back to the first topic. "Even from Mechanics and Mages?"

The second woman lowered her voice dramatically, but Mari could still hear. "He is reportedly very, very unhappy and has expressed that to the heads of both of the Great Guilds."

"It's about time! Those Mechanics think they're better than the Emperor himself, I'm sure!"

The woman was in fact right about that, Mari thought to herself. But Mari wasn't going to say that out loud. She leaned back and looked at Alain. "I guess we were the large group of Mechanics," she murmured.

"I will try not to take offense at being mistaken for a Mechanic." Alain gave her a glance. "What happened with the Mage you fought in the alley before I came down?"

Mari bit her lip, looking at the floor. "I shot him. I had to. He had a knife and he looked like he was getting ready to make a spell. But after I shot him he just lay there, hurt. I gave him something to control the bleeding and told him what to do. He should be all right if a healer gives him antibiotics."

"In the middle of a battle you paused to give mercy to an enemy?"

"Yeah. I know. It wasn't very smart." She inhaled deeply, feeling the rawness in her throat from last night's exertions. "But that's who I am."

"I am happy that you did that," Alain said.

Despite her disquiet, Mari tried to bend a smile his way. "A Mage approving of an act of mercy? What's the world coming to?"

"Perhaps something better, if the one who will bring the new day wields mercy as well as a weapon," Alain said. "What of the other you shot at? Your weapon struck the lightning Mage?"

"I think so," Mari said. "Either that or I scared the blazes out of that Mage."

"The loss of that one would cause me no grief," Alain admitted. "Especially if it was the same Mage who tried to kill me during the ambush of the Alexdrians on the northern plains. Asha did not lie to us."

"You told me that at the time and I never doubted it. I hated leaving her behind. Did you get any look at all as we ran, to see what happened to her?"

Alain nodded. "As we began running, Mage Asha vanished from sight using the concealment spell. That would have made her presence obvious to other Mages, but hidden her from the troll since it had not fixed on her. She probably held the spell only until safely past the troll."

"I wish we could have done that," Mari said. "Do you have any idea who needed her help?"

"No. Perhaps the Mage you shot, though I do not know why that would concern her." Alain paused. "It is all right to be concerned about Asha?"

"Alain!" Mari stared at him. "You really felt that you needed to ask that? I must have been awful."

"It is just that you have sometimes seemed unhappy when speaking of Asha—"

"Because I was being stupid! And jealous! There, I said it. I admit another one of my flaws." Mari grasped Alain's hand tightly. "Of course you can be concerned for Asha's safety. Is there a thread between you and her?"

"No," Alain said. "That is only between us."

Despite her resolve not to be jealous of Asha any more, Mari still felt a flash of relief to hear that. "I hope she's all right, Alain. Should we wait somewhere for her?"

"That would be too dangerous, since we have no idea how long we must wait. Mari, what did Asha mean when you spoke of her warning you?"

"She gave me a headache," Mari replied shortly, feeling oddly reluctant to discuss it.

"She made your head hurt?"

"That's what headache means, doesn't it?"

"Yes." Alain was looking at her with a wondering expression. "Asha was able to use her link to you in this way? That is remarkable."

"I'm glad you think so," Mari said. "Personally, grateful as I am for her warning, I am less than thrilled that any other woman can reach into my head because I'm in love with you. Even Asha."

"This still bothers you?"

"Of course it bothers me." Mari looked away, unable to watch him as she kept speaking. "Yes, I was half-dreaming about you just before the headache hit. I guess my bonfire of adoration for you was hot enough that Asha could toast some marshmallows on my brain. That's what jerked me into full alertness so I heard those Mages coming up the stairs."

"It saved us?" Alain asked. "Why are you unhappy when you speak of it?"

"Because I'm not comfortable with knowing that every time I think of you I am transmitting passionate signals to the entire world!" Mari hissed. "Why is that hard to understand?"

"Transmitting?"

"Sending out messages!" Mari leaned back, looking up at the ceiling. "Do you have any idea how embarrassing it is to have someone able to tell every time I'm thinking about you? 'Oh, there she goes again. I wonder if she's in bed with him right now. Or maybe they're just kissing.'"

"Or planning to change the world," Alain said.

"I'm sure that's the first thing that comes to Asha's mind."

"But she would only try to sense you when she is trying to find you," Alain offered. "It is an effort, Mari, like any other spell. It tires her, requires power, and cannot be sustained for long periods. She will only do it when she is trying to locate us, and then for short lengths of time."

"Really? You're sure?"

"Yes."

"Then why doesn't my transmitter of love tire me out? Asha made it sound like I'm broadcasting to everyone and everything on Dematr, which, I have to tell you, doesn't make me happy. How many people besides Asha are listening in while I light up the world with thoughts of you?"

Alain started to answer, stopped, then spoke slowly. "It is not the same thing. Certainly no one can read your actual thoughts."

"You said that before, and that had better be true."

"Asha has a tie to you. You now serve to assist her in finding me when you increase the intensity of your feelings. I am not sure how to explain it right."

Mari stared at him. "Increase the intensity? I'm an amplifier as well as a transmitter?"

"A what and a what?"

"I'm an amplifier and a transmitter," Mari repeated. She gazed upward. "I don't believe this is happening to me."

"Do you really think about me that often?" Alain asked.

"That's none of your business!"

"It is not?"

"No! What I think about you and when I think about you is my business! I wonder if there is any way to ground out my signal?"

"What?" Looking confused, Alain tried one last attempt at reassurance. "Mari, I would advise that you not worry about it."

That did it. "Of course you wouldn't worry about it! You're not transmitting your lust to the world! And if you were, you'd be happy, because you're a man!"

Alain nodded quickly, his expression wary, and changed the subject. "The rioting must have become worse after we escaped the area."

"Yeah." Mari closed her eyes briefly, trying to calm herself once more, then opened them to look at him. "I know what you're thinking. I'm not blaming myself for that. It was as though the citizens there were a bomb waiting to go off, and the Mage attack just acted as a spark to make them explode. Do you have any idea why?"

"They were very angry," Alain said, thinking. "They appeared to have no goal but fighting and destruction."

"That's what I saw, too. What would make people act like that?"

Alain kept his eyes on her. "I saw a few acolytes act in a similar way during my training. Pushed too far, unable to continue to live as they were, but believing they had no chance of becoming Mages, they erupted into violence against any Mage and elder within reach. Those acolytes were quickly killed, of course."

Mari nodded, feeling sick inside. "They didn't have any hope. Nothing to make them think things would ever get better. No reason any more to restrain their worst impulses."

"The leading edge of the storm," Alain murmured. "Perhaps if someone gave the commons hope, it would help them."

"How can anyone give them hope that things will get better? That things will ever change for them?" Mari suddenly understood, and looked down at the floor, trying to avoid coming to the only possible conclusion. "You mean, if someone…revealed herself."

"Yes."

She stared at the vague patterns in the flooring, her stomach knotting at the idea. "All right. I will think about it. But not until after we find that tower on Altis. It must have been kept secret for a reason, and I don't want too much attention on me from the commons until we've found any answers that place holds."

Alain did not reply, but she sensed his approval and agreement. Unhappy, Mari settled back again to wait. The train was supposed to leave in about an hour, so they had a little while left to wait before they would be allowed to board the passenger cars.

Another train rolled into the station, a freight from the south by what Mari could see of it. She stared at the sky, willing the sun to rise faster. "I'm going to see how they're doing at getting our train ready."

"I do not think that you should," Alain said. "It is not wise to walk around this place when your fellow Mechanics might recognize you."

"I can keep my head down. It'll only be for a few moments. I'm going to go crazy if I have to keep sitting here." Before Alain could object again, Mari stood up and walked quickly to where she could view the train which was being prepared to go to Landfall, trying to judge how close it was to boarding passengers. Mechanics moved around it, working on the cars and the steam locomotive which would pull the train. Despite her resolve not to linger in this spot, Mari stared at the locomotive, remembering happy times spent maintaining and operating locomotives during her training. Feeling depressed, Mari finally turned back towards Alain.

And found herself facing a portly, middle-aged man in a Mechanics jacket. The man stopped in mid-stride, staring at her, his broad mustache seeming to bristle. She stared back, knowing that he had recognized her. "Professor T'mos. Good morning." It had been less than a year since she had seen him last, but it felt like a lifetime had passed.

T'mos nodded, frowning just as he had the many times he had discussed Mari's behavior with her when she was a student at the academy. "Good morning, Master Mechanic Mari."

She feared that he would immediately sound an alarm, but instead the professor tilted his head to one side to beckon Mari to stand near the wall. "I did not expect to meet you here."

Mari smiled as if unconcerned. "All roads lead to Palandur." She could see out of the corner of her eye that Alain was watching them without seeming to watch them. Mari studied Professor T'mos, trying to figure out his attitude toward her. They had been on good terms when she had been at the Mechanics Guild Academy, Mari thought, but only on a student/professor basis. T'mos had devoted considerable time to counseling her on proper ways for Mechanics to act. All in all, his attention to her had been a little suffocating, but Mari had liked him enough as a teacher to tolerate that.

Professor T'mos nodded again, his mouth working as he thought. "Have you come to Palandur to report to Guild Headquarters?" he finally asked.

"I wasn't planning on that, no."

"Maybe I should be clearer." T'mos took on the same attitude she remembered so clearly; the wise, mature professor speaking to the inexperienced young student. "You're in a lot of trouble, young lady. Surely you know that?" Mari nodded. "There is an arrest order out. Running isn't the answer. The Guild will catch you eventually if you try to do that. Whatever you did, you still need to trust in the Guild's mercy."

Mari shook her head. "Professor T'mos, the Guild's mercy in my case consisted of setting me up on my first contract to get kidnapped and killed by commons. You must have heard of that."

"Rumors, Mari. Surely you don't believe the sort of nonsense that commons speak against the Guild."

"Some very experienced Mechanics confirmed that it happened that way, Professor." Well, one had, anyway, but Professor S'san was worth a hundred regular Mechanics in Mari's estimation.

"Politics," T'mos snorted. "The Guild would never harm any Mechanic, and you shouldn't listen to those who claim otherwise. I don't know who you've talked to, but that's what got S'san. She was forced to retire for meddling in politics, Mari. You need to rethink anything she taught you unless you want to end up sidelined yourself, which would be a great shame given your potential."

Mari felt her temper rising, which had always been a problem during T'mos' lectures to her. The difference now was that Mari didn't try as hard to keep her temper in check. "Never harm a Mechanic? The Guild ordered me to go unescorted to Tiae. You know what Tiae is like now. Total anarchy. I'd have been enslaved or, if I was lucky, simply killed."

"The Guild must've had a good reason for ordering you to Tiae," T'mos assured her. "Unescorted? That wouldn't happen. There would have been an escort."

"No, Professor, I confirmed that there would be no escort even though I was assured one would be there."

"Hmm." Professor T'mos shook his head, then changed the subject slightly. "Analyze that, Mari, and you'll see the flaws in your concerns. What possible reason do you think the Guild would've had to send you on a suicide contract?"

Mari spoke quietly, but kept her voice firm. "I had learned about those who call themselves the Order, those who aren't of our Guild but have the skills of Mechanics. I knew Mages could actually do things beyond our understanding. Not tricks, but actual temporary changes to reality. Even though I'd promised to stay quiet, those things were apparently enough to condemn me in the eyes of the Guild's Senior Mechanics. That and some belief of theirs that I would threaten their control of the Guild someday."

T'mos made an irritated gesture. "The so-called Order is a tiny bunch of tinkers who'd be lucky to fix a broken pot. The Mages are very good frauds, though, and I'm not surprised they fooled even you given your lack of experience. But Mari, I know much more than you. What you say you thought you knew wasn't true. Why would the Guild have tried to silence you for that? And frankly, whoever told you that the Guild feared your abilities as a leader when you're still this young is a fool. The Guild encourages good leaders."

Mari had always been unhappy with being talked down to, but willing to tolerate it. After all, Mari had been inexperienced, her instructors were indeed the best in their fields, and her knowledge of the world had been second-hand, since she had been kept within Mechanics schools since being forced to leave her family at a young age.

But she wasn't that inexperienced girl any more and she had seen a great deal of the world in the last several months. "Professor T'mos, how can you tell me something that you know isn't true? Do you honestly believe that the Mechanics Guild is right to deny truth solely so that it can maintain its hold on power? Aren't you alarmed by the way the technology used by the Guild is deteriorating, regressing as we lose the ability to make and do certain things because anything that might be considered innovation or change is prohibited? You're a smart Mechanic. Surely you can see that the road the Guild is following is a dead end."

T'mos smiled sadly. "Mari. Always the questioning one, aren't you? If there are things you think you know, then you need to lay them out before the Guild so—"

"I did." Mari spread her hands. "And I was put under a Guild interdict and sent into great danger."

"No." T'mos displayed an annoyance at being interrupted that Mari recognized. He always had treated her like a child of his, hadn't he? "You're under an arrest order because you didn't listen, because you jumped without thinking. How many times did we discuss your impulsiveness? And now here you are! You and whoever it is you're traveling with." He glanced around, studying the other people in the waiting area.

So the Guild now knew or suspected that she had a traveling companion, but still didn't know who it was. Mari, sensitized to spotting subtle emotions by being with Alain, thought she detected another layer of aggravation beneath the professor's annoyance. Maybe, as Professor S'san had suggested, T'mos really had once thought that he and she would end up together as something much more than professor and student, though still authority figure and obedient follower. The thought made her stomach clench with sudden nausea. "The Guild thinks that I'm traveling with someone?" Mari asked, hoping to learn more of whatever the Guild knew and get T'mos' attention back on her.

Professor T'mos shook his head and sighed with disappointment. She recognized that, too, and was ready when T'mos tried his next approach. "The Guild knows a great deal more than you give it credit for, Mari. You're a Mechanic. Descended from those who came from the stars themselves. So am I. This other Mechanic...I *assume* he's a Mechanic..."

Mari knew she was probably flushing in anger a bit at T'mos' tone, but it wouldn't be hard to make the professor think that her reaction reflected embarrassment. "You don't think that I'd take up with a common, do you?"

"Of course not, Mari," T'mos said, smugness tingeing his words. He apparently thought that he had tricked her into confirming something. "This Mechanic, whoever he is...?"

"I'd rather not say."

"All right, Mari, but he doesn't have your best interests at heart."

"He...seemed all right," Mari suggested.

"Can't you trust me more than some romantic fling you've picked up? Is he behind this? Is he driving it? Controlling you? Listen, the Guild can protect you. We're your true comrades. Turn yourself in, young lady. For your own sake."

Mari pretended to think about it. T'mos appeared to believe that his old manipulations would get through to Mari, as if she hadn't changed in the least since leaving the academy. *Is he "controlling" me? Does T'mos believe that I can't think or act on my own? All right, then. Perhaps I need to give my old professor another illusion to play with so Alain and I can get out of Palandur in one piece.* "Professor," she whispered, "I am worried. I never meant things to go this far."

T'mos smiled encouragingly. "It's not too late. Trust me."

"I will." Recalling the old saying about lying like a Mage, Mari looked around with a nervousness she didn't have to feign. "I'm meeting someone here. He's supposed to arrive this afternoon. I'm staying at one of the old hostels in the Devjin District. Tonight I'll get him to come with me to Empress Tesa Square. We'll go to the café facing the fountain of the Empress. You know the one."

T'mos nodded, easily recognizing the name of an area in Palandur near the academy where Mechanics often went for food or drink. "The Rakesh café?"

"Yes! I won't let…my friend… know what's going on, but I'll bring him so you can talk to him, too."

The professor nodded again, his lips curving into an approving and confident smile. "And you'll be ready to turn yourself in?"

"I don't know," Mari temporized. "Why don't you come alone and talk to both of us? Is that all right, Professor?" For a moment, she worried that she had overdone the innocent young student act, but T'mos apparently didn't think that she was acting.

"Of course, Mari," T'mos said soothingly. "Of course. I'll come, we'll talk with this man you're traveling with, and we'll get things resolved, eh? But you must ensure he comes along with you. I want the chance to reason with him as well."

Mari nodded, looking at his eyes and seeing, just as she had expected, that Professor T'mos planned on arriving in Empress Tesa Square with an army of Mechanics at his back, intending to scoop her up along with "this man." "That's a good plan. I'm so glad you've helped me think this through."

Surely Professor T'mos couldn't believe that she was that naïve. But T'mos merely smiled with benign approval, showing no sign of doubting her apparent lack of sophistication.

"Now, please, Professor," Mari said, "you must go. If he sees you when he gets here, he might get suspicious and may not agree to go to Empress Tesa Square."

"That's what we will do then." T'mos reached out to grasp her upper arm, holding on and squeezing lightly with every sign of affection. "I've missed you, Mari. I'll do what I can to straighten out this mess, and maybe we can work together again. That assistant teaching position is still available."

Mari managed to fake another smile as her guts knotted again. "Wouldn't that be wonderful?"

T'mos nodded a final time, and with a knowing wink started away, but then turned back, causing Mari to catch her breath for fear that he had seen through her. "Empress Tesa Square, the Rakesh café, tonight," T'mos said. "What time?"

"Three hours after sunset."

"That's fairly late, but I'll be there." With another wink, T'mos left. Mari watched him go, wondering why she had never noticed before that the professor strutted when he walked.

She waited a little while, knowing that Alain was still discreetly watching, then slowly walked toward the door the professor had used, gazing out at the increasing number of people rushing to and fro, yawning and reluctant, as the work day and workers woke to life. T'mos was barely visible down the street, striding along with no sign of special haste, apparently confident that Mari would do as she had said. Mari studied the entire area, but could find no indication of other watchers, though she could see a wide plume of smoke still rising in the direction of the Gorgan District.

Finally going back to the bench, she sat down next to Alain without looking at him. "That was an old professor of mine," she murmured. "You have permission to say, 'I told you it wasn't wise to go over there, darling.'"

"I told you it was not wise to go over there, darling," Alain repeated tonelessly.

"You're right, dear." Mari sighed heavily.

"The meeting did not seem to go well on your side," Alain spoke softly to her. "But this old teacher of yours departed looking very satisfied."

"Right. He thinks I'm going to hand myself over to the Mechanics Guild on a silver platter tonight"

"He does not think you are leaving?" asked Alain an uncharacteristic amount of surprise noticeable in his voice. "Even though you are here where the Mechanic trains leave?"

"No, he doesn't." Mari looked toward the door by which Professor T'mos had left. "I told him I was waiting for someone to arrive, and he wants to catch that someone even more than he does me. I guess he couldn't conceive that I'd be clever enough to lie to him. It's strange, Alain. When I met Professor S'san again she was everything I remembered, and she treated me like someone she respected who had grown since I'd last seen her. But Professor T'mos turned out to be a bit different from what I'd remembered, and he acted like I was still a snot-nosed youth trying to figure out which end of a hammer to use. It's funny how sometimes the world turns out to be like we expect and other times totally different."

"It is all just an illusion," Alain assured her. "This Professor T'mos sees the shadow of you he wishes to see, even though it is not you."

"Sometimes I wish I believed it was just different illusions," Mari said. "That nothing is real. When things seem really bad, believing that must be comforting."

"Sometimes," Alain said. "Other times it makes you question why you should try. If nothing is real, then what difference does anything you do make?"

Mari smiled and looked at him. "You've made a very big difference for me. You've never let me down, and I think of you more often than I probably should because it usually makes me happy to do so. Hello, Asha," she called softly to the air, feeling a little giddy after her narrow escape from T'mos. "I'm transmitting again! How's the bonfire?"

Alain looked baffled once more. "You find that amusing now?"

"Yeah."

"But a short time ago you were very upset by it."

Mari nodded. "Yes. What's your point?"

"Then you have decided this transmitting is humorous?" Alain asked, relieved.

"No," Mari informed him. "Next time it comes up I might be upset again."

Alain sat quiet for a while before speaking slowly. "So any time this transmitting comes up you might find it amusing, or you might find it upsetting?"

"Yeah."

"How am I supposed to know in advance whether you will laugh or get angry when the subject comes up?" Alain asked.

"You can't." Mari gave him a barely apologetic look. "Sorry."

"I see." Alain nodded, bewilderment showing in his eyes.

"I said I was sorry. That's just the way it is."

Alain scratched his head, then gave her one of his small smiles. "Then I will just think of it as another adventure."

"That's the spirit." An apprentice came through the room, calling out that boarding was now permitted for the train to Landfall. "Thank the stars. What a time we've had here. I feel better about leaving Palandur than I did about leaving…that other city." Stars above, she had almost said Marandur out loud. Mari shook her head, wondering if her carelessness was going to get both of them killed.

Despite Mari's fears, they managed to board the train without anyone recognizing her, partly by keeping Alain between her and any Mechanic who passed by. She waited with increasing nervousness after they sat down in one of the coaches intended for common passengers, worrying that T'mos would tell some other Mechanics of her presence at the station.

But apparently she had judged him rightly as wanting to ensure that her "friend" was captured as well. The train pulled out of Palundur on time and was soon rolling uneventfully through the gentle countryside of the central Empire. The only problem was that Alain sat by her side, unusually tense, looking around constantly for danger. "Relax," Mari told him for at least the tenth time. "I admit our earlier train trips have included some unfortunate events, but nothing is going to go wrong this time."

"The Mage Guild in Palandur—" Alain began.

"Is still trying to sort out what happened last night and whether or not that troll tore you into tiny pieces and stomped on them. You still haven't sensed any other Mages nearby, right?"

"I did not last night, either," Alain said, peering suspiciously out the window at a distant speck in the sky. "I do not think that is a Roc, but I will keep an eye on it."

"Fine. Enjoy yourself." Mari settled back, trying to relax. The city of Landfall was a long way off, but the train made excellent time over the even terrain. After the adventures of the previous night, Mari found herself dozing off, waking once after sleeping for some time, and then insisting that Alain get some rest while she stayed alert. "Yes, I promise to watch for Rocs."

Mari glanced at the setting sun as the express train finally slowed again to pick up passengers and cargo at the big station where the roads from Centin in the north and Alfarin to the south joined with the road between Palandur and Landfall. Alain had awakened when the train stopped. She grinned at him. "I can't help wishing I could see the expression on Professor T'mos' face when he realizes I'm not going to show up in Empress Tesa Square. Though I think he's going to be more disappointed at not getting his hands on you."

Alain frowned at her. "You said something like that before. Why would this old teacher of yours have any feelings against me?"

"It's a long story, and to be perfectly honest it sort of makes me sick to my stomach to think about it now, so if you don't mind I'll fill you in at some future time."

The stop was long enough to make Mari have to fight off fidgeting. They were so close now to getting out of the Empire. So close to avoiding the death sentence mandated for anyone who entered the forbidden city of Marandur, and so close to embarking for Altis to search for the mysterious tower that might hold a lot of answers that she needed to have.

An alert would go out once she didn't show up in Empress Tesa Square, transmitted through the big far-talkers in the Mechanics Guild Halls. But it would be a few more hours before that happened, and by then they should be much closer to Landfall. "We'll have to figure out how to leave this train before it reaches the station in Landfall," Mari murmured to Alain. "My Guild will have sent out word by then that I might be aboard. The train will have to slow down a lot when it reaches the outskirts of Landfall, though, so we should have plenty of chances to jump off."

His gaze on her was intense. "Jump off? As we did last time?"

"Well, no," Mari said. "That time the train was going a lot faster and we had to fall farther and we couldn't see what we were jumping into. This time should be a lot easier."

A few new passengers came into their carriage and took seats nearby as the train finally lurched back into motion, gathering speed slowly. "What were all those cops doing?" one asked another.

The question was met with a shrug. "Checking all the people getting off. Another security alert, I suppose. A lot of the police got on the train, too, did you see? In the first passenger carriage. I guess they're looking for someone again. An escaped convict, maybe."

The first man spoke in a lower voice. "I heard the police are looking for two people who left Marandur. There's been legionaries and police all over the roads back east of here."

"Really? Anyone fool enough to go to Marandur gets what they deserve."

"Well, some folk say whoever came out originally went in a very long time ago." The man lowered his voice as he whispered to the other.

Mari turned to Alain. "Imperial police are on the train. They're in the front cars and moving back, looking for us."

He nodded, looking out the window beside him. "I heard."

"Any ideas?" she asked.

"Not at the moment."

The train kept gathering speed. Mari gazed bleakly through the window at the landscape rushing by, then ahead to where the Imperial police were undoubtedly methodically checking every passenger before moving back to the next passenger carriage. She had seen Imperial officers conducting searches and knew just how efficient they could be. Their packs would be searched, and what was in them would ensure that she and Alain were recognized and arrested. "Hiding won't work and fighting would be hopeless. We could overcome the cops on the train, maybe, but hundreds of others would converge on wherever the train stopped."

"Yes," Alain agreed.

"That only leaves one alternative."

"I was afraid that you would say that."

# CHAPTER SIX

Alain waited for Mari to explain exactly what she was going to do, thinking as he waited that it had indeed been a mistake to try traveling on a Mechanic train again. Night had fallen completely, so that once they had left the lights at the Mechanic train station the inside of this coach had become as dark as the outside.

Mari leaned back and whispered in Alain's ear. "Time to go."

That was a bit worrisome, given the speed with which the land outside was rolling by.

Straightening herself up, Mari spoke in a tired but nonchalant voice just loud enough to carry a bit. "I think there are more seats in the next carriage, so we can lie down to sleep. Do you mind moving?"

Alain stood, pulling Mari's pack down from the shelves that ran over their heads, then his own pack as well. "We can attempt it."

She led the way out the rear door of their car and onto a small platform that led to the similar platform on the front of the next car on the train. Walking across the small gap between the platforms would bring them to a door leading into the front of the next car. Instead of proceeding to the door, though, Mari went to the railings on the side and looked out and over, squinting her eyes against the wind created by the motion of the train. Leaning back again, she made a helpless gesture. "I can't see far enough ahead in the dark to spot any good places to land, and we don't dare wait to jump anyway."

"Jump? You said when we next jumped from a train it would be moving slowly and we would be able to see where we would land."

"Yes," Mari said. "That was the plan, but we had to change the plan. We're going to jump now. Why did you think we came out here?"

"I was following you."

"Well, follow me when I jump." With a worried expression now, Mari hooked her leg over the railing, then brought the other leg across, holding on with both hands, her back to the railing and her feet on the narrow edge of the platform beyond the railing.

Since there wasn't enough room on this platform for him to join her, Alain stepped across to the next car's platform, then also stepped over the railing and hung on, balancing on the edge as the metal lines that Mari called rails rushed by below them and the wind buffeted them. Even over the rush of the wind he could hear the chugging roar of the Mechanic creature called a locomotive which pulled this train.

Alain stared down at the ground, which was moving past as fast as a horse could run. "Is this safe?"

"No!" Mari said. "Of course it's not safe! But we don't have any other choice! After you hit the ground, don't get up for a little while. We want to make sure no one from the train sees us."

"What if I cannot get up at all?" Alain asked.

"Try to fall softly!" Mari ordered. He was still staring at her, trying to figure out if she was really serious, when Mari reached out and latched onto Alain's hand. "We'll jump on the count of three! One… two…three!" She jumped, pulling Alain along.

He landed awkwardly, losing his grip on Mari, falling, sliding down a slight embankment and rolling over several times before eventually skidding to a halt. The last car of the Mechanic train rolled past as he lay there, the lights and noise of the entire train vanishing into the night. Dizzy and aching, Alain sat up and looked for Mari, wincing as new bruises announced their presence.

Mari lay a short distance away. He felt a moment of fear, then relief as she got her arms under her and tried to stand up, hopping slightly as her right leg seemed unwilling to bear her weight. "Ouch," she announced.

Alain got to his feet and moved to help, flinching as his own foot protested. Just a sprain, he hoped, and not something broken. "Are you all right, Mari?"

She lowered her right leg gingerly, her face showing pain. "I think so. Walking isn't going to be any fun for a while." Mari gazed in the direction the train had gone. "If anyone had noticed us jumping, the train would have already braked and started back this way. Looks like we got away. Now we just have to find another way to get to Landfall."

"Will we have to ride one of the trains again?" Alain hoped that he did not sound too aggrieved.

She looked at him, then started laughing. "You poor man. Have you ever asked yourself what you did to deserve getting stuck with me?"

"I simply consider myself to be very fortunate."

Mari grinned, her teeth white against the darkness of the night. "Just keep telling yourself that, my love. No, I won't make you ride a train again. At least, not anytime soon. They really are too dangerous now that we know the Imperials are checking them all for suspicious pairs of young men and women, and by the time we could try to board another one my Guild would have sent warnings out that I was traveling as a common." Her smile faded. "Can you see anything around here?"

Alain peered around, searching the darkness and seeing nothing manmade in the night-shadowed landscape but for the metal lines the train rode on. "Nothing."

"Then that means we start walking to Landfall. We're most of the way there from Palandur." Mari took a step and gritted her teeth. "That's going to hurt for a while, but I can manage it. How about you?"

"About the same. Do we walk all the way?"

"I hope not." Mari pointed in the direction they had been traveling. "Sooner or later we'll have a chance to bum a ride on a wagon. Or maybe we'll find a coach station and be able to ride at least part of the way. That reminds me." Sitting down, she rummaged in her pack, finally surfacing with a small sheaf of papers. "Our new identities."

Alain studied the papers. "You had two sets of false Imperial identification papers for us?"

Mari grinned. "I'm a Mechanic. I like to have spares handy in case I need them. And I have a nasty suspicion that the names on those other identity papers are now on the Imperial police's arrest list." She stood up again, adjusting her pack. "We're a step-brother and -sister from Emdin now. Any ideas why we're going to Landfall, if anyone asks?"

"Seafood?" Alain suggested.

"That sounds good to me. We're off to see the big city, Landfall the Ancient, and enjoy the sea while the crowds are small at the tail end of winter and before we have to get the crops in when spring comes." Mari gave him a questioning look. "That is when crops are planted, right?"

"As best I recall. It has been a long time since I was a boy on my family's ranch"

"You need to tell me more about that while we walk, if you don't mind. I'd like to know more about your childhood." She tested her right leg. "That's not as bad. Ready?"

"Will not the Imperials be looking for us here if they suspect we left the train?" Alain asked.

"Yeah. That's why we're going to walk way over to the left until we find a road going in the same direction."

"Across the fields. In the dark."

Mari gave him one of those narrow-eyed looks. "Do you have a better idea?"

"I was hoping you had a better one."

"Nope. We've only got one choice." She paused, thinking, as Alain waited. "There's a common theme running through our lives these days, isn't there?"

"I thought so."

She shrugged, and again he could see the gleam of her smile in the night. "We can either let it terrify us or we can start seeing the humor in it, I guess."

"At least there are no trolls tonight."

"Exactly. Mage, it's sometimes frightening just how much you and

I are truly made for each other." Smiling and limping, they started across the fields, searching for a road heading for Landfall.

The first night was in some ways the hardest, walking overland with minor injuries from their leap off of the Mechanic train. Alain was able to make the night pass a little faster by telling Mari some of the things he remembered from his parent's ranch in the days before the Mages came to take him when Alain was five years old. Many of the memories he had suppressed while training to be a Mage. Now it was bittersweet to recall his parents, who had died while Alain was still a Mage acolyte. It made him feel better to share with Mari, though.

Alain tried to draw out Mari a little about her own girlhood in the city of Caer Lyn before being taken by the Mechanics, but once again Mari refused to talk about that, insisting that it was past and completely forgotten, almost yelling at Alain when he mentioned her mother. "I don't care about her!" Mari said with a sad scowl that contradicted her words.

It was well past midnight before they literally stumbled onto a minor road going west. Already worn out from the events in Palandur the previous evening and day, Mari was almost asleep on her feet and Alain in not much better shape. They found a place just off the road where a few trees offered shelter and fell asleep in each other's arms despite the cold.

The next morning, Mari stood looking around morosely. "I've been thinking. This isn't like a little while back when we traveled south to Severun and then Marandur. Back then your Guild, my Guild and the Order were looking for us, but the Imperials weren't. Now they are. I have a nasty feeling that any form of public transportation is going to be too risky to use."

Alain, still seated, nodded and looked up at the sky. "We will have to pursue other methods, including avoiding the main road west."

"Right. Do you know anything about sneaking through a country-side? I'm sort of making this up as I go along."

"Yes, I do." Alain forced himself to his feet, wincing as sore muscles protested. He took an odd pleasure in the look of surprise on Mari's face. "Because I can cast fire, the Mage Guild intended that many of my contracts would be to common military forces. As a result, I received some training in military matters, including how scouts operate. I have also seen the use of scouts on a few occasions."

"What do scouts do, exactly?" Mari asked.

"They seek to travel and see all about them without themselves being seen."

"Ah." Mari grinned. "That sounds like just what we need. What do we do first?"

Alain thought about it, making sure he remembered important details. "We are on a less-traveled road already. If the enemy—that is, the Imperial security forces—are actively searching for us, they will have checkpoints at intersections of roads."

"Oh, sure." Mari nodded, then couldn't stop a yawn born of too little sleep. "Excuse me. That makes sense. They can't cover everywhere, but occupying intersections offers the best chance of intercepting anyone using the roads. We just have to keep our eyes out for intersections and avoid them without being obvious about it."

"It would be best to avoid roads altogether," Alain cautioned, "but that would make our journey much harder, and since this land is divided into many farms we would have to deal with many fences and many landowners who would question our presence."

"Much harder and a lot more time," Mari agreed. "We'll stay with minor roads, hitching or paying for rides when we can, and walking when we can't."

❀ ❀ ❀

It took over a week of hiking and occasional rides in passing wagons. Every time they approached an intersection Mari discreetly pulled out her far-seer and scouted ahead, allowing them to spot Imperial checkpoints early enough to evade them without being seen themselves.

Unfortunately, that usually meant avoiding riding on wagons, since dodging checkpoints would arouse the suspicion of drivers. By the time they sighted Landfall, Mari was wondering how much longer her boots would hold out.

Mari timed their arrival at the Imperial checkpoint outside the south gate to coincide with a rush of travelers. The officer they met eyed their new identification papers briefly, shoved them back at Mari and gestured to the next traveler.

Not far inside the city gate a small park beckoned, with few people in it at this time of the day. Mari sat down on a badly weathered stone bench under an ancient tree, pulling off her boots to rub her feet. "Ow, ow, ow. I am so tired of hiking."

Alain sat down next to her, nodding wearily.

Mari leaned back, closing her eyes. "I suppose I should be grateful. All of this walking must be doing wonders for me. I'll bet my legs must look great." She glanced over at Alain and grinned. "Not to mention my rear end. Am I still distracting when you watch me walk from behind?"

"Very distracting," Alain said. "I will be happy to evaluate your legs, if you wish."

"I bet you would. You'll see them someday, Mage, and a lot more besides." Mari stretched, thinking happily of the upcoming sea voyage, on which any walking would be limited to going around the deck. "I'm probably looking forward to that day more than you are."

"I doubt it."

She laughed. "All right. We won't have any trouble finding the waterfront. I vaguely remember it from a few years ago when I came here from…my first Guild Hall."

"In Caer Lyn," Alain said.

"Yes," Mari replied, hoping the sudden frost in her tones got through to Alain. She stood up abruptly, her good mood vanished. "We should go check the sailing schedules."

Alain's voice held a sigh of resignation. "All right."

Her disposition lightened a bit on the way, partly because she felt guilty for snapping at Alain and partly because she was finally getting a chance to see a bit more of Landfall the Ancient, supposedly the oldest of cities. Many of the buildings showed ample signs of age in the weathering of their stone or in their old designs. Many of the trees were very old as well, with wide trunks, gnarled bark and expansive spreads of branches. The streets of Landfall were wide and straight, a perfect grid varying only occasionally to accommodate terrain or some special building.

Special buildings such as the Mechanics Guild Hall. Mari saw it in the distance, where the Guild Hall rose next to the same river that flowed downstream from Marandur and Palandur, and felt the same mix of yearning and anger at the thought of what she had lost and the lies she had been told.

Alain stayed silent the entire way. Though he never talked as much as Mari did, she had slowly learned to sense different qualities in his silence. Sometimes it was the quiet of someone lost in his own thoughts, an intriguing silence, and sometimes Alain would be wordlessly enjoying her presence, which was a nice silence. But this silence loomed like a fortress in which the gate had been sealed, as Alain drew into himself because he thought he had been wronged.

Upset as she had been, Mari had to admit that those times when he sealed the gate it was usually because she had given him good cause. Stubborn as she could be, Mari knew that she had been wrong to snap at him this time. "I'm sorry," Mari finally muttered.

He nodded, but still said nothing.

"You know how I feel about that," Mari continued. "You shouldn't have brought it up."

Alain looked over at her. "I said the name of a city."

"Yes, but—" She glowered at the worn cobblestones beneath their feet. "I don't think you can understand."

"I understand that you avoid thinking about and confronting your past."

"What makes you an expert at dealing with the past?" Mari whispered savagely.

"I have stood at the graves of my parents."

It was odd how painfully such an impassive statement could lash at her. Mari grimaced. "All right. You have a point. I can only guess how hard that must have been for you. It's different for me."

"Would you feel better if your parents too were in their graves?"

That was as harsh a thing as Alain had ever said to her. Mari fought to control her anger. "No. I admitted that you have a point. Please drop it."

"We always drop it, yet always it stays with us and between us."

She stopped walking so abruptly that Alain took another step before he caught himself and came back. Mari stared at the ground, not really seeing the cobblestones now. "Maybe this was all a mistake. You and me."

"Do you believe that?" he asked, and once again she could easily sense the emotion in his words.

Mari thought about possible responses, about more ways to hurt Alain, and then got a grip on herself. "No. Not really. I was trying to attack you so I could avoid facing things I don't want to face. I can't forget the past, Alain."

"I would never ask you to do so. But will you let the past destroy the present?"

She exhaled slowly, dimly aware of annoyed pedestrians going around her and Alain where the two of them stood still on the sidewalk. An image of Marandur came to Mari, and it took her a moment to realize why. "Is that what I'm doing? Building a wall around the ruins of my childhood and maintaining those ruins as some kind of horrible monument to my suffering? Alain, please stick with me. I know something has to change. I don't know how, yet. Please…don't go."

His voice finally relented. "I will never go."

Mari took a deep breath, smiled at him, then took his hand as they started walking again. "I don't deserve you."

"If you did not deserve me," Alain said, "then destiny would not have brought us together."

"I'm sure. Maybe destiny wanted to punish you." Feeling better, Mari spent the rest of the walk to the docks trying to relax.

Unfortunately, once they got there a series of talks with agents selling tickets on outbound ships kept producing the same result. "It will be three days before a ship leaves directly to Altis," Mari said with disgust. "I do not want to spend three days here, worrying about various people who are looking for us."

"One night in Palandur was almost too many," Alain agreed.

Mari studied the boards where sailings and ships were posted, finally shaking her head. "There's only one thing to do. Yes, again, we've only got one good choice. There's a passenger ferry leaving about noon for Caer Lyn. From there we can surely get a ship heading straight for Altis without having to wait much, if at all."

"You have not been back?"

"Not since I left the Guild Hall there." But she knew what he was really asking. Had she ever gone home again. "No. Once I became a Mechanic, I guess my parents decided there was no place for me to go back to." It came out not in anger, as she knew it usually did, but sadly.

He nodded, not pressing it this time.

"But getting on the ferry means getting past the Imperial customs checkpoints." Mari looked around, an idea coming to her. "They're looking for two people traveling together. If we buy two tickets for two separate compartments, and then go through customs separately and board separately, that might ensure that the Imperials don't take any special notice of us. Once out of Landfall, we'll be clear of the Imperials and not have to worry about them anymore." She frowned as Alain shook his head. "What? The Sharr Isles are independent."

"They are called independent," Alain explained. "To a Mechanic such as you, the real status of the Sharr Isles would not matter, but the independence of the Sharr Isles is purely at the sufferance of the Empire and maintained by the Great Guilds. It serves the Empire's interests to have so-called independent islands to funnel trade to and from the west. Even then, only the supremacy of the Great Guilds and their insistence that the Imperial borders expand no farther has kept the Empire from claiming the islands. The Sharr Isles take no step without Imperial approval, and do whatever the Empire commands. In exchange they gain the right to call themselves free and are defended by the Empire's formidable military."

"Great," Mari groused. "So even in Caer Lyn we'll have to worry about the long arm of the Empire. Well, we'll cross that bridge when we come to it."

"What bridge is that?"

One moment he was explaining geo-politics and history to her, and the next he was confused by something simple and everyday. Mari closed her eyes, took a deep breath, then looked at Alain. "That is a figure of speech. It means we will deal with that situation when we encounter that situation."

He nodded back, his expression serious.

"The ferry is the *Sun Runner*," Mari continued. "Let's go get the tickets. I'll go first, with you in line behind me, and you can just copy what you see me say and do. All right?"

The plan worked without any problem, though the length of the line to get past Imperial customs and border control worried Mari when she saw how close it was getting to the *Sun Runner*'s sailing time. The line moved slowly, everyone waiting with the stolid acceptance of official inconvenience that marked life in a state such as the Empire. When Mari finally reached an official, that woman eyed Mari's papers with disinterest. "Traveling alone?"

"Yes." An Imperial customs official just wasn't as intimidating as a troll.

"Purpose of travel?"

"I spent a few years in Caer Lyn as a child." Alain had taught her that lying by telling a misleading truth was far less likely to be apparent to any questioner than telling a complete fabrication.

"Emdin," the officer commented. "You came straight from there?"

"Yes," Mari replied. "Through Alfarin."

"Have you been north or east of Alfarin?" the officer pressed.

That called for a flat-out lie. "No. I went from Emdin to Alfarin and then here." Mari tried to look and sound like a rustic girl who didn't have much experience in the wider world. "Should I have gone another way?"

"No," the officer replied, sighing in the manner of someone tired of dealing with the public. "Did you see any unusual travelers? A pair of them, one an uncommonly attractive young woman with dark hair, the other a young man? They might have been claiming to be students at the university in Palandur."

"I saw many other travelers, but none that seemed unusual," Mari said, wondering again at why the Imperials seemed focused on an "uncommonly attractive" young woman. "I didn't meet anyone who looked like that."

The officer glanced at Mari's pack. "Are you carrying any contraband?"

"No." Not by Imperial definitions, anyway. It was the Mechanics Guild which had banned the ancient texts in Mari's pack, manuscripts which the Imperials didn't even know existed.

"Pass." The official handed back Mari's papers and gestured her onward.

Mari went up the gangway onto the *Sun Runner* and leaned on a rail, looking down at the pier where Alain was just reaching another Imperial official to be interviewed. She wasn't too worried about how well Alain would handle that. The ability of Mages to lie without any sign of misgiving or deception was legendary.

Sure enough, after a very brief interview Alain was waved onward and came up the gangway. He glanced at Mari, then once aboard took a place at the rail nowhere near her but still within eyesight.

It wasn't too much later that whistles sounded and sailors began taking in the gangway and the lines holding the *Sun Runner* to the shore. Commands were shouted from the high quarterdeck at the stern of the ferry where the ship's wheel rested. More sailors ran up into the rigging and along the spars, and soon sails unfurled on the masts above the ship, shining white against the blue sky. Mari felt the ferry lurch beneath her as the sails caught the wind. The *Sun Runner* swung out away from the pier and into the harbor, then began gliding across the water toward the harbor entrance.

Mari watched the city of Landfall and the territory of the Empire slowly recede, thinking about when she had entered the Empire with Alain months ago and far to the north from the mountains of the Northern Ramparts. *We made it. Through the heart of the Empire, through the forbidden city of Marandur itself, and out through the Empire's oldest and largest port.*

*Maybe Alain and I can actually sleep in peace tonight, without keeping one eye open for danger. I've forgotten how that feels.*

Several commons were talking in low voices nearby, just loudly enough for Mari to catch the conversation. She had been trying to ignore them, but then Mari heard something about Jules and listened closer.

"She was seen in the Northern Ramparts," a woman insisted. "Just a few months ago. The daughter of Jules. Wearing a Mechanics jacket, she slew a dragon single-handed to save some commons, wouldn't take any payment, and healed a dozen badly injured soldiers with the touch of her hand."

"Nobody wearing a Mechanics jacket would care about commons," a man grumbled.

"*She* did, but she didn't act like a Mechanic except that she fixed all of their Mechanic weapons, too. And then," the woman added, "a Mage showed up and swore allegiance to her and they went off together. People saw it. Some say she's on her way to see the Emperor, to ask him to let her lead the legions against the Great Guilds."

Mari pressed the palm of one hand against her forehead, closing her eyes to try to block out this latest development. *Blasted soldiers. I save their lives and this is the thanks I get, them telling everybody who I am!*

Stars above. I thought "who I am." Not "who people think I am." Am I starting to accept it? Am I starting to believe that I really am the daughter? I don't want to be her. I don't want that responsibility. But…she's needed.

Caught in the internal discomfort of her thoughts, Mari barely noticed the second man shaking his head, but when he started speaking his words immediately caught her attention again.

"I don't doubt she's trying to get to the Emperor," the man said in a low voice. "I'm sure she wants back in the palace again, after all these centuries."

"What?" the woman asked in anxious tones. "What do you mean?"

"You've heard of Mara, haven't you?" the second man whispered. "Consort to the first emperor, Maran himself? So incredibly beautiful, they say she bewitched Maran and almost ran the Empire for a time."

The first man nodded. "I heard about that. She never wanted to get old, so she made a deal with the Mages to keep herself young forever. But it's just a story, isn't it?"

"Some say it is, some say it isn't."

"How could even the Mages keep someone young forever?" the woman asked.

"I don't know," the second man said. "It must be pretty hard, or pretty terrible, but she had the entire Imperial treasury to pay them off, and Maran's hand backing her." The man lowered his voice so much that Mari had to strain to hear it. Not that she wanted to hear it, but her curiosity was too strong by this point. "She doesn't age, because she's not really alive and not really dead. Mara drinks blood, they say, to keep herself looking young, the blood of young men. She has no trouble seducing them to their deaths because Mara is still as beautiful as she was when Maran reigned. And after all these centuries she knows more magic than any Mage. They say the Emperor Palan himself sealed her into a tomb in the old Imperial capital when the city was destroyed, but there are reliable stories that somebody or something came out of Marandur recently. You must have seen how the police have been extra vigilant lately, checking anyone traveling. Word is they're looking for whoever left Marandur, where Mara has been imprisoned in her lair for more than a century. Someone woke her up. Someone freed her. She's come out now. That's what's trying to get to the Emperor and back in the palace again. Mara the Undying."

A hush fell over the three commons, while Mari stared at the waves, aghast.

"But," the woman finally asked, "what if she really is the daughter of Jules and not Mara?"

"Believe what you like, but if I meet her I'm going to be looking to see if her teeth have sharp points," the second man said.

"I'm not so young anymore," the first man remarked, "so I guess she wouldn't want my blood, and I'm not a citizen of the Empire, so it doesn't matter to me whether she's Mara or the daughter of Jules, as long as she does in the Great Guilds."

"That's easy for you to say," the second man muttered.

The small group wandered off past Mari, who stayed leaning on the rail, hoping her expression didn't show how appalled she was. *I thought it was bad enough being the daughter of Jules. But that's a lot better than having people think I'm an undead, vain, blood-drinking seducer of emperors and young men.*

At least it explains why the Imperials keep asking about a very good-looking dark-haired young woman. They actually think Mara might have been the one who left Marandur? Granted, if any place would be a suitable lair for the undead it would be Marandur. I suppose the only good thing about that rumor is that no one is likely to recognize me from it. Incredibly beautiful? That's about as true as the sharp teeth.

Though now she felt an irrational urge to find a mirror and check how her teeth looked.

Mara the Undying. Stars above. I'll take being the daughter of Jules any day over that.

Alain blinked against the late afternoon sun as he looked forward along the deck, then aft. The *Sun Runner* was sailing slightly south of west to reach Caer Lyn, with an easy breeze filling her sails and a pleasant sea sending gentle swells to meet her. They had been at sea for a while now, the Imperial coast had long since vanished beneath the horizon, and even though he and Mari had been on the alert for anyone watching them, no one seemed to be paying them any particular attention.

But Mari had insisted on waiting to go to their cabins. "If anyone on the *Sun Runner* is pursuing us, I want to see them before they find out which cabin we're staying in tonight. Who knows how many Imperial agents are aboard this ship. We can't afford to be trapped in a room."

He had recognized the wisdom of that, and so had waited while Mari joined him for periods and then left, to see if anyone followed her. After what had happened in Palandur, that sort of concern was only prudent. "There are no Mages aboard as far as I can tell," he had told Mari, which was one thing to be glad of. But he was tired of hauling his pack around, tired of standing at the rail, and was looking forward to tonight, when he and Mari would be catching up on their sleep in an actual bed in one of their cabins.

That was all they would be doing in that bed, of course. Alain remembered Mari joking about how her legs looked, and tried to think about something else.

"Hey." Mari came toward him after her last attempt to check for anyone following her, yawning again. "I can't wait to find one of our cabins and take off this pack. I'm thinking if anyone aboard was after us, they would have betrayed themselves somehow by now. Still no foresight warning?"

"No, but you know that does not mean danger does not exist."

"It's something, though." Mari yawned hugely this time. "Stars above, I'm tired. It's been a long trip from you-know-where. We should turn in soon. Do you know some people always sleep at night and stay awake during the day? I think they're called normal."

"How boring," Alain responded. "They probably also never get attacked by trolls or dragons."

"I haven't decided which I like least. Dragons are definitely faster, though. I prefer enemies I have a chance to run away from." Mari leaned on the railing with her arm touching Alain's, sighing happily. "Do you realize how long we spent inside the Empire? It's great to at least feel free again. And aside from Asha, whom I'm doubtless transmitting to at this very moment, we shouldn't have to worry about anyone from our Guilds locating us until we reach Caer Lyn."

"Asha will not tell any elder where we are. She is in as much danger from the elders now as are we. But even if there are no agents on this ship, the Imperials in port will be checking people arriving at Caer Lyn," Alain cautioned.

"We'll just do the same thing we did when we got on the ship. Once we're both off this ship, we'll find a ship headed for Altis and get right on it. I don't want to spend an instant longer in Caer Lyn than we have to. For safety."

"For safety," Alain repeated in a neutral voice. He knew she was not being honest with herself, and she knew she was not being honest with herself, but Alain thought that he had pushed her enough on that for now. He wondered if Mari would feel any differently when she actually saw once again the city she had once called home.

"You know," Mari added thoughtfully, "we really need to plan things out more instead of just rushing into them. Develop a nice, detailed plan and then carry it out, just like we did when we got on this ship. We should try to do that every time from now on."

Alain was about to reply when he heard whistles sounding and looked up. Sailors were rushing into the rigging again, and soon the motion of the *Sun Runner* altered, the gentle rolling turning into a slow wallow as the sails were furled overhead and the ship glided to a stop. Mari stared at Alain, then at the empty sea before them, then back at the deck house blocking their view of the other side of the ship. Together, they rushed to the nearest passage across the deck.

Alain caught up with Mari as she came to the rail on the other side of the ship. Mari did not say anything, just pointed, face rigid. Another ship had approached, a ship with only short, stubby masts and no sails visible. A stream of pale smoke rose from a huge tube rising out of the center of the strange ship, which was almost completely made of metal. On the front of the other ship, something which looked like a very large version of the Mechanic weapons Alain had seen was mounted on the deck and pointing at their own ship. A pair of large boats were already in the water, being rowed over toward the ship Alain and Mari were on, the dark jackets of the Mechanics crowding the boats easily visible.

# CHAPTER SEVEN

The Mechanics Guild," Mari breathed. "That's one of their steam-powered ships. There are hardly any of those left working any more, but they're so much faster than sailing ships that they must have caught the *Sun Runner* easily. How did they know I was on board this ship? How did they know to intercept this ship?"

"What do we do?" Alain asked.

"We can't jump off like we did the train." Mari rubbed her forehead, her face frantic. "Our only chance is to try to hide somewhere below deck."

Mari turned, starting to fight her way through the crowds of passengers boiling out onto the deck to point and stare and wonder what had led the Mechanics Guild to stop this ship. Alain stayed close to her, frustrated by the slow progress they were making. The crowd on deck had become so dense that it was hard to move at all even though ahead of him Mari was shoving hard.

Suddenly a group of Mechanics wedged their way between Alain and Mari, using the butts of their weapons to strike at anyone in their way. Alain had to stagger back a half-step to avoid having one of the weapons strike him, then found himself separated from Mari. He lunged forward, disregarding the cries of anger from commons he was pushing aside. Alain made it through a knot of commons, then maybe a lance length farther, and suddenly found himself at the edge of a small area of deck cleared of commons.

He stopped, gazing at the scene within that area.

Mari was standing still, facing several Mechanics. Two had Mechanic weapons pointed at her. One middle-aged male Mechanic reached forward and roughly jerked back Mari's coat, checking the area under her shoulder. "Not carrying the pistol today, Mari?" he demanded.

"It's in my pack," Mari answered. "Honored Senior Mechanic," she added in the kind of voice which Alain had learned meant sarcasm.

The Senior Mechanic's hand rose, but he stopped before hitting Mari. "Where's your friend?"

"I have no friends," Mari replied in a voice now emotionless.

"That's probably the only thing you're going to say that I'll agree with," the Senior Mechanic noted coldly. "But the Guild knows that you were traveling with someone. Where is he?"

Mari shrugged. "I don't know."

"Answer me! Is he on this ship?"

Alain could see Mari's mocking smile. "We split up a while ago. Doesn't the Guild know that?"

Another Mechanic took Mari's pack. "Should I search it?"

"No!" the Senior Mechanic barked. "Don't look in there. It will be searched later, by authorized Senior Mechanics only."

Alain could see the resentment in the other Mechanic at the Senior Mechanic's haughty tone, but he stood obediently holding Mari's pack.

At a gesture from the Senior Mechanic, a female Mechanic stepped forward and patted her hands all over Mari's clothing, then stepped back. "No concealed weapons," she reported.

"Good. Get her to the ship." The Senior Mechanic led the way as the others grabbed Mari and pushed her along, the commons splitting to leave a free path for the Mechanics.

Alain watched, shoving his way through the crowd to keep the Mechanics in sight, trying to figure out what to do. In this dense a crowd, invisibility would be a hindrance, not an aid. Simply attacking the group of Mechanics around Mari would do no good. His heat might just as easily harm Mari as her captors, his knife was no match for their weapons, and even if he somehow triumphed without hurting Mari, the metal Mechanic ship with its big weapon would still remain.

But he became aware of a rumbling noise from the crowd of passengers, slowly rising in volume as more and more commons joined in. It took Alain a few moments to make sense of the words, then the intensity of the noise rose again and he heard them clearly. "It's the daughter!"

"The Mechanics have the daughter of Jules!"

"They're taking the daughter!"

The different cries merged into a welter of shouts in which only the words "daughter" and "Jules" were clear, but that was enough. As Alain watched with growing concern, the crowd surged forward toward the Mechanics, the commons yelling and seizing anything that might serve as improvised weapons.

The Mechanics had heard the shouts, too, and were backing along the rail in a tight group, their weapons pointed outward. Alain could see the growing fear in their eyes, the sort of alarm which could lead to panic and then the use of the Mechanic weapons. Even though the crowd of commons far outnumbered the Mechanics, Alain had seen what Mechanic weapons could do. Mari had told him that these were called "lever-action repeating rifles," and while he did not know the meaning of that, those same weapons had wiped out a caravan which Alain had tried to protect. Alain knew that something had to be done, but he hesitated because his training as a Mage had told him nothing about how people thought. Alain had no idea how to stop the crowd before a massacre occurred.

Then he heard Mari yelling over the sound of the crowd. "No! Stop!" Her face appeared as Mari shoved her way to the front of the frightened Mechanics despite having her arms held behind her. "They've got rifles, blast you! If you try to charge them a lot of you will die!"

The Senior Mechanic in charge of the boarding party looked nervously from Mari to the crowd. "Listen to her!" the Senior Mechanic shouted.

Mari bent an angry look on the Senior Mechanic, then faced the crowd again. "Back off. Please. For your own sakes."

A common stepped forward slightly from the crowd, an older man with short-cut hair and a face red with fury. "We're willing to die for you, Daughter."

"I don't want anybody dying for me!" Mari yelled back. "It's senseless. Even if you overcome these Mechanics and free me, that still leaves that ship out there. It can shell this ship and sink it, then make sure no life boat or life raft stays afloat. You would all die. Please, let them take me."

"We can't let the Mechanics destroy our only chance for freedom!" a woman cried, her voice torn between anguish and fury.

"Don't die in vain!" Mari called back. "As long as I live, that chance remains."

Perhaps inspired by Mari's words, the Senior Mechanic drew his pistol and put the small end against Mari's head. "Rush us and I blow her brains out! Do you hear me?"

Alain had to restrain himself from launching a spell at the Senior Mechanic. He did not know enough about how the Mechanic weapons worked to be sure he could kill the Senior Mechanic before he killed Mari, and an attack on the Mechanic leader would surely produce an immediate reaction which would turn into the massacre which Mari feared.

Mari's face had gone rigid. The crowd had become suddenly silent, so Alain could hear what Mari said to the other Mechanics. "The Senior Mechanics would order your death as easily as they ordered mine, as easily as this one put a gun to my head."

"Shut up!" The Senior Mechanic glared at the crowd of commons. "We are going to the ladder down to our boats. She is going in the first boat, and she'll have weapons pointed at her head the entire way. Try anything and she'll die."

The commons stood glowering as the Mechanics began backing toward the ladder, the weapon of their leader staying pressed tightly against Mari's head. As Mari's arms were being freed for the climb down she caught a glimpse of Alain in the crowd and he saw Mari mouth the words "I love you," then after a brief pause one more forceful, unspoken word. "Go!" A moment later she was being shoved down the ladder and out of sight.

Alain ignored Mari's command, but as he tried to think of a plan to save her he heard the volume of anger in the commons rising again. At least this time he knew how to halt them, by following what Mari had done. "Do not," he called. "She asked you not to die now."

Eyes turned to him, one of the nearest commons giving Alain a challenging look. "How do you know she means it?"

"Because I am her friend," Alain replied. "Listen to Lady Mari. Another time will come."

"Lady Mari?" another common said. "I heard the Mechanics call her Mari."

"That was the name she used," a woman called. "In the Northern Ramparts! You're really her friend?"

"I saw him with her earlier," another woman said. "Side by side along the railing. They were talking."

"If you're really her friend then you know that we have to do something," another common insisted, her eyes blazing. "We can't let them just take her!"

Alain looked across the water toward the metal monster which was the Mechanic ship. Mari was already climbing down the access ladder on this ship into a boat which would leave at any moment. The Senior Mechanic had followed, leaving another Mechanic in charge of those still on deck. Little time remained to act, and while he was on this ship he could not help Mari. *I need to get over to that strange ship with her. I cannot get over there on my own.* An idea finally came to him. *But perhaps I can convince these Mechanics to take me there. They are looking for a friend of Mari's. I will create an illusion that will give them what they seek.* "I will do something, convincing them to take me to that ship. If the rest of you wish to help her, then listen to what she said and trust that we will find a way to escape. Another day will come."

"What can you do alone?" the most belligerent common demanded.

"I am her friend," Alain repeated. He could tell that wasn't enough. Too many of the commons were beginning to turn back to face the

Mechanics, their expressions fixed with anger and determination. "I have traveled far with her. We have been through great perils together."

Another common stared at Alain. "She was traveling with a Mage. The people who saw her up north said she was traveling with a Mage."

Everyone nearby froze, their startled eyes on Alain. He hesitated only a moment, knowing that he had to keep these commons from rioting against the Mechanics, and to do that he had to convince them that he could do something they could not. Alain nodded once, then for a moment let his expression go into the emotionless state of a Mage. "I am her friend and her Mage and I will help her," Alain said in a very low voice, letting his tones take on the impassive tones of a Mage. "Did you not know that of the prophecy? The daughter will unite Mages, Mechanics, and the common folk into one force which will overthrow the Great Guilds and free the world. Wait for her, as she commanded. Her day will soon come."

Even though commons sometimes tried to mimic the emotionless expression and voice of a Mage, none of them could drive feeling from their face or tone as a Mage could. Convinced by Alain's demonstration, the commons made way for him, their expressions ranging from disbelief to amazement, but visible above all on their faces was a dawning and joyous hope. One man began crying, tears running down his face as he whispered the same words over and over. "She's really come. She's really come…"

The other commons shushed the man, blocking him from being seen and heard by the Mechanics.

Alain relaxed to let some emotion show again, then stepped out of the crowd. The weapons of the Mechanics still on deck instantly swung to point at him. Alain held up his hands as he had seen Mari do. "You were looking for Mari's friend," he said, trying to mimic the arrogant tones of a Mechanic.

One of the Mechanics beckoned Alain closer. "That's you?"

Alain came closer, lowering his voice so that only the Mechanics could hear it over the growing murmuring from the crowd of commons behind Alain. "That is me," he confirmed, trying to put a sneer into it such as the member of the Order had used at Pandin. He thought it came out sounding pretty good, or rather bad.

The Mechanic flushed with anger and raised his weapon. "Watch how you talk to your betters, common."

"I am not a common," Alain replied in the exact same tones.

Sudden interest flared in the Mechanic's eyes. "Another Mechanic, eh? They thought Mari had one with her. Prove it! What's your specialty and where are you from?"

He had to convince them. Alain kept trying to mimic the manner of the member of the Order as he answered, using information he had heard while traveling with Mari during their journey south to Marandur. "Umburan. That is where I used to work." Specialty. What did that mean again? Alain used the name for one of Mari's Mechanic devices. "Far-talkers. My specialty is far-talkers." The biggest lies he had ever told, and no one he knew was here to see how well he had done it. What a shame.

"In Umburan?" the Mechanic pressed with skepticism Alain could easily see.

He needed something to make the illusion complete. Details. Those mattered in forming an illusion. Mechanic Calu had told Mari something which she had then told Alain. That might provide the detail needed right now. "Yes. Umburan," Alain replied. "The big far-talker there could not be fixed."

"He's right," another Mechanic said to the first. "Umburan was down for a long time. Besides, who knows about far-talkers except Mechanics? If he was a common he wouldn't have heard of them."

"All right, then." The Mechanic grinned unpleasantly. The crowd of commons had gone silent, listening intently to what Alain and the Mechanics were saying. "Dumb enough to join Mari but smart enough to throw yourself on the mercy of the Guild now, huh?"

Perhaps one of these Mechanics was like Calu. "You should listen to Master Mechanic Mari. She was betrayed by her own Guild when she—"

"Shut up! None of us want to hear any treason. And for your

information, it's just Mari now. Her Guild title has been revoked by order of the Guild Master."

Alain felt anger, balanced by a calm confidence he could not understand. It allowed him to maintain the cool arrogance he wanted to project. "She remains a Master Mechanic beyond any ability of anyone to deny her that status."

He could hear the commons behind him muttering, passing along what they had heard and commenting on it. "The daughter used to be a Mechanic, too, but she's revolted against them to help us."

"Just like Jules worked for the Empire before she struck out on her own for freedom."

"A Mechanic, and she told us not to risk helping her so we wouldn't be hurt. She *is* the daughter."

And one worried voice in low tones. "But maybe she's Mara."

That statement was followed by grumbles about Imperials, then the Mechanics were gesturing to Alain. As he took the final steps to reach them, he could no longer make out the murmuring among the commons.

Alain's pack was pulled off, then another Mechanic seized his arms and pulled him toward the access ladder. "Wait, you idiot," the first Mechanic growled. "Search him!"

Having a Mechanic, or any stranger, run hands over him was hard for Alain to endure. As a Mage he had been taught to avoid human contact, and his time with Mari had only dented that teaching, not overcome it. He managed to stand still, even when the Mechanic doing the search paused, then reached inside Alain's coat to surface with the long Mage knife. "Where the blazes did you get this?" he demanded of Alain.

"I got it from a Mage," Alain said, which was exactly what had happened. He had been presented with the knife by a fellow Mage on the day Alain had been granted Mage status.

"You took it off a Mage?" The Mechanic grinned as he stuck the knife into one of the outside pockets on Alain's pack. "You and that Mari have more guts than you do common sense. Did you kill the Mage?"

"He was still alive when I took it from him."

"No way!"

"Stop talking to the guy and get him into the boat!" the first Mechanic ordered.

The man who had searched Alain went down first. Alain turned to descend, seeing that the boat carrying Mari was halfway to the Mechanic ship. In her common coat she was easy to spot among the black jackets of the Mechanics, and she seemed very alone. But not for long. He would soon be with her on that ship.

He hoped he had done the right thing.

As Alain began to descend, facing the crowd again, he saw the commons watching him. Always before, commons who had known he was a Mage had given him looks of fear and of disgust. But these commons looked at him with hope. It staggered Alain for a moment. Then he nodded to them, feeling a strange surge of strength within him before the Mechanics ordered him to descend.

Reaching the bottom of the ladder and dropping into the second boat, the Mechanic in the lead gestured Alain to a seat in the center as they waited for the rest of the Mechanics to come down the ladder. "What did you guys do, anyway?" he whispered to Alain.

What should he say to a Mechanic? "We learned things that the leaders of the Mechanics Guild did not want anyone to know. This was after the leaders of the Guild tried to have Mari killed because they feared she might someday be a threat to their authority. That happened at Ringhmon."

The Mechanic stared at Alain with worried eyes, then shook his head in warning to Alain not to say anything else as more Mechanics climbed down into the boat. The Mechanic leading this group came last, moving down the ladder quickly as the rest kept their weapons pointed upward toward the commons rushing forward to line the rail and look down at them. Some of the commons still carried the objects that they had seized to use as improvised weapons, but even though the menace in their postures and expressions was impossible to miss the commons all watched silently.

"Get us back to the ship," the lead Mechanic ordered, untying the line securing the boat to the ladder as the other Mechanics got busy putting oars in the water. "Blasted crazy commons. Mari must have been stirring them up already. She'll get us all killed."

Alain shook his head. "Mari wants no one to be hurt. You heard her tell the commons not to attack you. All she wants is to fix things. She would still be loyal to the Mechanics Guild if she had not been threatened with death by its leaders while faithfully trying to carry out the orders of her Guild."

"I told you to shut up!" The lead Mechanic stuck the end of his weapon close to Alain's face. "You try to rouse up any more trouble and I'll put a bullet between your teeth."

At times like this, Alain's Mage training was particularly useful. He gazed back at the Mechanic without any sign of worry or concern, and eventually the Mechanic had to lower his weapon with an angry grunt. Some of the other Mechanics grinned in admiration, and Alain realized that they had been impressed by his impassivity in the face of the threat. He nodded calmly to them, wondering if any of these Mechanics were like Mari's friends, Mechanic Calu and Mechanic Alli.

As the boat came around, the setting sun glared into Alain's eyes. He sat silently as the boat he was in crossed the distance between the ships, seeing the boat ahead carrying Mari reach the Mechanic ship. He saw her climb up the ladder, the Mechanic behind her holding one of the long weapons pressed against her. As she reached the top of the ladder, Mari was shoved out of his sight and into the metal hull of the ship. Alain watched, hoping that he would soon see Mari again.

As soon as his own boat was tied to the Mechanic ship, Mechanics pushed Alain to the wood and rope ladder going up the metal side of the Mechanic ship. He went up as fast as possible, on the chance that Mari might still be near the ladder, but he saw no sign of her when he reached the deck. Mechanics there grabbed him and used their weapons to prod him along the deck, through an entry with a metal hatch, and through more hatches and passageways and down steep metal stairways until he was thoroughly lost. The interior of the metal ship was well lit by glass globes that glowed with a steady, bright light, another Mechanic trick which his elders had once assured Alain did not actually work.

Reaching an open hatch giving access to a very small room, Alain's escort used blows from their weapons to propel him inside hard enough that he fell. His escorts then slammed the hatch, leaving Alain in total darkness. He heard a metallic rasping which he assumed was a lock being fastened on the outside of the hatch.

Alain rolled to a sitting position, wondering how many new bruises he had picked up today, where his pack had been taken, and most importantly where Mari was now. He tried to remember if there had been another locked hatch located next to the one he had been shoved through. It seemed reasonable that the prisoners would be confined near each other, especially since the Mechanics who had taken them into captivity did not think either of them could walk through a metal wall.

Not that he could walk through many walls out on the sea. The power here was very limited, as it always was on the water, though the reasons for that remained unknown to Mage elders. But he still felt the aftereffects of that strange burst of power as the commons had looked at him, and now as the motion of the ship changed to mark it moving ahead, Alain could feel new power becoming available as the ship traveled across the sea. He had felt something like that on the Mechanic train, moving so rapidly that the flow of power was always renewed by reaching new supplies of it. It was strange to think that a Mechanic creation could thus benefit the work of a Mage. In this case, it might be what allowed him to rescue Mari.

Alain calmed himself, reaching out his mind to sense Mari's presence. The thread he had first sensed between them in Ringhmon was strong again, leading unerringly to one side. From the strength of the thread and the intensity of Mari's presence at the other end, she must be very close. Unable to see anything in the total darkness of his cell, Alain crawled over a rough and uneven surface made up of big ropes coiled on the deck until he reached a barrier. Alain rapped the metal wall, listening for a response.

After a moment there was a knock back.

Her presence had flared when he knocked, so it must be her on the other side. Alain sat back, thinking. Getting through a Mechanic metal wall should not be any different from getting through any other wall. Nothing was real, every wall and everything else being just illusions born of his mind. As the wall was imaginary, he would imagine an opening in it, creating and maintaining the illusion upon an illusion with the help of the power the world held here.

The spell posed an unexpected problem, though. How did he imagine a hole in a wall when he could not see the wall? His elders had always taught that a Mage must be viewing what should be changed. Alain frowned at where the wall should be, trying to think of a way around that.

He had not yet felt all the way to the side. He had not seen any wall there. Could he imagine that where he had not felt there was no wall?

The effort was unexpectedly difficult, like a physical act done in an unfamiliar way, as if he were trying to walk on his hands rather than his feet. But Alain felt the power flow, felt his strength ebb dangerously, then reached out to where the hole should be.

It was there. Alain felt the edges, then dodged through and caromed right into someone else in the total darkness on this side of the wall. They both fell with muttered grunts, then Alain felt two hands lock on his throat. "Who are you and where did you come from?" Mari hissed.

It wasn't easy to talk with Mari's hands clamped on his windpipe, but Alain managed to get out one half-strangled word. "Alain."

"What?" Mari's hands loosened, then let go of his neck to run over his face and upper body as if trying to see him by touch. "Alain? It's you?"

"Yes." Alain coughed, massaging his neck. "That hurt."

"Sorry. I thought I was alone in this little compartment and then— How the blazes did you get here?"

"I turned myself in," Alain explained, reaching carefully to touch her. "I could not leave you alone, so I came to find you in your cell when you were imprisoned. It is a kind of tradition with us, is it not?"

"You big idiot. I love you, but you shouldn't have gotten yourself stuck on this ship." Her voice was despairing. "Escaping from this ship will be almost impossible."

"I had to come help you."

"No, you didn't! I told you to go and stay safe! I don't want you in this kind of danger on my account." Mari's hands found his face again, then her lips came against his. "Stars above, I'm glad you're here."

Alain wondered if his voice reflected his confusion. "Are you happy or angry that I am here?"

"Both. You shouldn't have done it."

"You would do the same for me."

"That's not the point!" Mari insisted.

"It was the only way to rescue you," Alain pointed out.

"I'm not rescued, Alain. We're just in the same cell again, only this time you can't—" Mari suddenly stopped talking. When her voice came again, it held hope. "You can. You got in here. Where were you locked up?"

"In a similar room next to this one."

Mari stayed silent for a moment, then sighed. "I'm pretty sure there's a guard out there. We can't just open the door, even if I could see where the lock was, so we can't get out like we did in Ringhmon. And the inside of a Mechanics Guild ship will have a lot of Mechanics walking around, so we'd be spotted pretty quick. Why did they bring you here, Alain?"

"I told you. I informed them that I was the friend of yours they were seeking."

"But if they thought you were a common who had been accompanying me, why didn't they just shoot you on the spot? Surely you didn't tell them you're a Mage?"

"I lied to them. I told them I was a Mechanic."

He could hear her disbelief. "You were able to pass as a Mechanic? Alain, that's one of the scariest things I've ever heard."

"You are a good teacher," Alain said.

"I'm not supposed to be teaching you to be a Mechanic!"

"I could not help learning how to act like one," Alain admitted. "You have been teaching me how to show feelings again, and you are the person I look to most often as an example of how to do that."

"I take back what I said earlier," Mari replied. "*That* is the scariest thing I ever heard. You are not to become just like me. Understood?"

"No one else could be just like you," Alain said.

"That had better be a compliment, but even if it isn't I have to admit you're probably right. You came in behind me. How long is it until sunset?"

"It will be dark soon," Alain told her. "I assume night is the best time to make whatever escape we attempt?"

"It should be," Mari agreed, "but I have no idea how to escape. We need to deal with the guard outside the hatch here, then we'll have to find my pack—"

"Our packs."

"Find our packs. Right. We can't leave those texts behind. Then after we recover our packs we need to do something to keep this ship from chasing us and then we need to escape off of the ship. That's a pretty tall order."

Alain shrugged before realizing she would not see the gesture in the total darkness of the room. "It should not be any harder than escaping from Marandur."

Mari laughed softly. "I can't decide if you're getting confident or crazy as a result of hanging around with me. Listen, maybe—" She stopped speaking as the thud of feet sounded outside the door to the room they both now occupied and the rasping of metal announced a lock being unfastened. "Oh, no. Can you—"

"Stay silent," Alain cautioned. He groped his way to the side, then stood up and waited for a moment until the hatch began swinging open. Alain called upon his arts to hide himself, bending the flow of light so that it wrapped around him rather than striking him, hoping he would have the personal strength to hold the spell and that the power in the areas the ship was sailing through would be great enough to help support it.

Mari had come to her feet as well and was doing her best to look defiant, despite having to shield her eyes from the light. Two Mechanics entered and pulled her out, not even bothering to look around. Alain followed as closely as he dared, trying not to make any noise, but the heavy footfalls of the Mechanics covered the sounds of his own movements anyway.

A third Mechanic standing outside the hatch stared impassively at Mari as she passed, and two more Mechanics fell in as extra guards. The sentry moved to close the hatch. Alain dodged quickly, but the hatch struck his leg briefly and painfully before closing. The sentry blinked at the hatch, swinging it out and closed again, then shrugged before closing it a final time. "What about the other one?" he asked.

"Later," one of the Mechanics replied. "The captain wants to see them one at a time. Stay here and stay on guard."

"Yeah, yeah." The sentry leaned against the hatch to Mari's prison, looking unhappy with the continuation of his duty.

The other four Mechanics put Mari between them, the two at the rear prodding her along with their weapons, unaware of Alain following close behind. They walked along short hallways and took stairs upward, climbing into the higher levels above the main deck. Alain caught glimpses of the outside through infrequent small, circular windows, seeing that the sun had almost set and night was coming on quickly. Their small procession passed other Mechanics, who always stood aside. Those Mechanics averted their eyes from Mari with expressions that were trying to conceal emotions, but to Alain's practiced eye hinted at feelings from curiosity to sympathy to fear to hostility.

He concentrated on maintaining his spell, grateful for how the ship's motion kept supplying new reserves of power. *And I know for certain that there are no other Mages anywhere near, so I need not worry about revealing myself to them.*

They finally reached a short passageway where one of the escorts knocked on a door labeled CAPTAIN, then opened it and led the way in. Alain barely managed to squeeze in as well before the door was closed, finding he had precious little space to stand without touching any of the Mechanics. Fortunately, the four Mechanics had herded Mari to stand in front of a desk where a middle-aged woman Mechanic sat, leaving room for Alain to stand back against a wall. Alain barely managed to avoid a small cry of satisfaction as he spotted both his and Mari's packs sitting in one corner of the room.

The woman Mechanic at the desk gazed at Mari with obvious dislike. "Former Master Mechanic Mari, now only Mari. Even the Guild makes mistakes sometimes, and you're the biggest mistake in quite a while. I've never looked upon a traitor before."

Mari stared steadily back. "Try looking in a mirror."

"How dare you—"

"You're betraying everything, every Mechanic, everyone—!" Mari was yelling, when the woman made a gesture and one of Mari's guards used his weapon as a club, jamming the wide end against Mari's side and causing her to choke off her words with a gasp of pain. Alain noticed that the other three guards looked uncomfortable at the abuse but did not protest it.

"You'll stay silent unless you're answering my questions," the woman Mechanic said in a harsh voice. "Why did you go to Marandur?"

Mari straightened up with some difficulty, then shrugged. "It seemed like a good place to hide. No one would look for me there."

"Then why did you leave?"

"Because I couldn't stand it anymore. The place is haunted."

"Did you go to the Mechanics Guild Headquarters in Marandur?"

"I went to what was left of it," Mari said scornfully. "Just a big pile of rubble and rusted-out equipment. There wasn't anything there that I could use."

"You should have had the brains to know that before you went to Marandur. Where were you going on that ship?"

Mari seemed indifferent as she answered. "West."

"Why?" the woman asked with barely concealed anger.

"For my health. I thought I'd visit the hot springs on Syndar."

"Liar." The woman pointed to a map on one wall. "That ship was going to the Sharr Isles. Where your family lives."

This time Mari's eyes sparked with real resentment that Alain had no trouble spotting. He was sure the Mechanics in the room could easily see it as well. "So what?" Mari spat out.

"I didn't think you were going to them," the woman replied with a cruel smile, "but it never hurts to check."

Looking from Mari to the older woman, a thought occurred to Alain. The Mage Guild had tried to sever him from his family by convincing him that his family did not matter. Not as people, and not as mother and father. The teaching left Mages looking only to the Guild for what life they had. From what Mari had said, the Mechanics Guild thought little of commons and yet had never ordered her to stay away from her family. She had broken contact with her family because the family had broken contact with her.

Or, rather, Mari had been convinced that her family had broken contact with her, leaving her nowhere else to turn but her Guild. Had Mari's Guild used its own tactics to sever the family ties of those from common origins? And if they had, how could he get Mari to listen to the possibility when she refused ever to talk about her family?

But that would have to wait. There were more critical things to deal with right now.

"Who is this other Mechanic you were traveling with?" the woman demanded.

Mari made a contemptuous noise. "A lovestruck fool who I used to help me. He's harmless."

"We'll see what he has to say about that."

Alain tensed, wondering if Mari would betray knowing that he was aboard, but she was quick-witted enough to frown at the captain's words. "I left him—" Mari began.

"On that ship. He turned himself in." The captain smiled unpleasantly. "We'll see how much loyalty he has to a traitor."

"He doesn't know anything," Mari insisted.

The captain shook her head. "Why would I believe a word you say? I'm glad you're not wearing the jacket you've disgraced. Just in case you're planning on sleeping easily for the next few days, let me tell you what's going to happen to you. You're to be returned to Guild headquarters in Palandur. Hooded and in chains, with a gag in your mouth, so you can't corrupt any other Mechanics. If you cooperate and answer every question put to you truthfully, you may be allowed to spend the rest of your miserable, traitorous life in a tiny cell in Longfalls. If there's any question about your truthfulness, you'll be turned over to the Empire to answer for your visit to Marandur. I'm sure the Emperor will want to make a special example of you, one involving an extended and painful death." The female Mechanic gave every sign of enjoying reciting the terrible future intended for Mari. "Are there any questions?"

Mari nodded. "Two questions. The first is, do you actually think that I'm stupid enough to believe that the Guild will still let me live when it has already tried to kill me more than once? The second is, how do you live with yourself, Senior Mechanic?"

The woman flushed with anger and gestured again. Alain had difficulty restraining himself as the same guard once again bludgeoned Mari with his weapon. "Take her out of here," the captain ordered, "and make sure she falls down a few ladders on the way back to her cell. Maybe that will bang a little sense into her. Then bring the other one."

"Yes, Senior Mechanic," the leader of the guards said with the eagerness of the type of follower who wanted to impress any superior, then as Alain slid to the side the Mechanics yanked open the door and dragged Mari out between them.

Once again he had to move fast, and once more his foot caught in the door as one of the Mechanics tried to close it. That Mechanic shoved the door harder, shrugging as it closed without hindrance the second time.

Mari had noticed, though, her eyes widening briefly before she carefully schooled her expression to reveal nothing but an apparent stoic acceptance of her fate.

They reached the first of the stairs down, and the Mechanic in charge moved to trip Mari and tumble her down them, but one of the other Mechanics stepped in the way. "She could break some bones going down that."

"So? You heard the captain."

"We're not Mages who torture people for fun. This girl is...she used to be a Mechanic."

The first Mechanic glared at his companion. "You're disobeying orders?"

"Get them in writing," the second Mechanic insisted. "If you think those orders are all right, get them in writing and show them to me."

"The captain's going to hear about this, Kalif."

The other Mechanic wavered, then shook his head. "The Guild wouldn't allow someone to be treated like that. Now let's get her back to her cell."

"Sure." The first Mechanic stepped back, glowering. "I'll let you explain things to the captain when we get back with this one's friend, and you can ask the captain for her orders in writing."

Alain tried to relax. He had nearly leaped at the Mechanics when Mari seemed threatened with serious harm. Now, as Alain followed the Mechanics back toward the places where he and Mari had been imprisoned, he measured his remaining strength, trying to decide what to do. Once they reached the improvised cells, Mari would surely be locked up again—and then the room where Alain was supposed to be confined would be opened. He was already tired from the effort of holding the concealment spell and could not see how his usual weapon, the fireball, would be able to defeat these Mechanics without also harming Mari and causing enough noise to bring more Mechanics running.

If only he had another weapon, a weapon which did not require his rapidly diminishing spell strength to employ. But his knife had been taken from him, and would have little effect against the Mechanic weapons even if he had it.

The Mechanic weapons.

Alain took a long look at the Mechanic weapons the guards were carrying. *Impossible. I cannot use them, even if I am pretending to be a Mechanic.*

Do I have to know how to use them? An illusion. They already see me as another Mechanic. If I hold one of those weapons, they will see the illusion of another Mechanic ready to employ it. If the illusion is strong enough, they will act as if it is real.

They came down a last stairway and walked up to the sentry, the guards almost ready to shove Mari back into her cell. Alain dropped his concealment spell and slammed his elbow into the side of the Mechanic who was farthest back, while reaching with his other hand and grabbing the Mechanic's rifle, wresting it free from the surprised and staggered Mechanic. As the Mechanic who Alain had attacked reeled into his companions, Alain tried to hold the weapon just as he had seen Mechanics do it. He was certain that he had the right end pointed at them, and his hands should be in about the right places, but that was the extent of his knowledge when it came to using a Mechanic weapon.

By the time the other Mechanics turned to look, Alain had the weapon pointing at them. "Do not move," Alain said in the most menacing voice he could manage, copied from the tones of the Senior Mechanic. "Make no sound."

# CHAPTER EIGHT

Mari wasted a precious second gaping at Alain. Not because she was surprised by his sudden appearance; she had seen the door catch on something and knew it meant that Alain was close by. What stunned her was seeing the Mage holding a Mechanic rifle as if he intended using it. Fortunately, the other Mechanics were a lot more shocked by Alain's appearing out of nowhere than she was, giving Mari time to recover and hastily seize another rifle from the unresisting hands of a second Mechanic. Stepping back, Mari leveled the rifle at her former guards. "The rest of you set down your weapons slowly. Don't make any noise. I know the Guild intends to kill me, so I've got nothing to lose by killing you all."

The Mechanic who had hit her with his rifle shook his head. "You can't get away, you idiot. You're on a ship at sea."

"Then there's no sense in you dying trying to stop me, is there?" Mari answered coolly.

Mechanic Kalif was staring at Alain. "How did you get out of your cell?" He turned an accusing gaze on the sentry, who mimed bafflement.

Alain answered calmly, though not as impassively as a Mage would have. "There are things the Mechanics Guild does not know." Mari could see from the sweat on his brow that Alain had been working hard to stay concealed.

Kalif turned his eyes to Mari. "How do we know you won't kill us as anyway as soon as we put down our weapons?"

"Because I never hurt anyone unless I'm forced to," Mari said.

"That's not what we were told."

Mari's laugh mixed sadness with derision. "I can't take the time to explain how many lies you've been told, not just about me but about everything. I won't let the Guild torture and kill me just because I learned things that the Guild doesn't want any Mechanic to know. Now put down your weapons and raise your hands, or my companion will start shooting." It was quite a bluff, considering that Alain probably didn't even know how to fire a weapon. Mari didn't dare look, but she suspected that Alain didn't have a finger on the trigger of the rifle he was holding.

Fortunately, the other Mechanics didn't focus on that detail. Kalif lowered his rifle to the floor cautiously, as did the others. Mari indicated the cell she had occupied. "All of you, in there."

"You can't get away!" the guard who had bludgeoned her repeated angrily.

"I'm really tired of people like you trying to tell me what I can and can't do." Mari used her thumb to pull back the hammer on the rifle, then raised it to aim at his face. "And I'm even more tired of people like you who are willing to hurt others just because someone else tells them to. Get in there. I won't repeat myself a third time."

He went in hastily, followed by the other former guards and the former sentry, the tiny compartment barely holding all of them. Mari looked at Mechanic Kalif as he turned to face her. "Thank you. I know this isn't a nice way to repay your humanity, but thank you."

"Mari," Kalif said, "the Guild won't really torture and kill you. They're trying to play games with your mind is all. Give it up. You can trust the Guild."

"I believed the same thing once," Mari said. "Until the Guild set me up to be killed. There are other Mechanics who know about that, who know it's true. Maybe you can find some of them. Now, you and you," she said, pointing to two of the other Mechanics. "Take off your jackets and toss them out here." Both Mechanics hesitated, glaring at her. "Alain."

Alain obligingly stepped forward, raising the weapon a little awkwardly, and spoke in tones that mimicked the Senior Mechanics Mari had dealt with earlier. "Do as you are told!"

The two Mechanics yanked off their jackets and threw them out the hatch to land at Mari's feet.

"Close the hatch, Alain." Mari kept her rifle aimed at the five Mechanics until the hatch swung shut, then immediately grabbed its handle and twisted it down before pushing the lock closed.

Only then did she turn back to Alain. "Stars above, you're a sight for sore eyes, my Mage." She kissed him very quickly. "How long were you with us?"

"All the way. The woman has our packs."

"I saw. We need to pay her another visit. She's expecting you already." Mari indicated the bigger jacket. "Would it bother you to wear that?"

"Not at all. It is just part of the illusion."

"Right." Mari hastily put on the other jacket. "We need to look like we belong here. I couldn't believe it when I saw you holding one of these rifles. When did you learn how to use one?"

"I do not know how to use one."

"I was afraid of that. Please, very carefully, give me the one you're holding. Don't press or push anything." Mari took the rifle from Alain gingerly, breathing a sigh of relief once it was out of his hands. "Very good bluff, my Mage."

"Did you want me to shoot them? I do not know how to do that."

"No, I didn't want you to shoot them. That was a bluff, too." Mari opened the lock on the room which had held Alain, putting all but two of the rifles she had taken into it and swinging the hatch shut again. "All right, I'm going to set the safety on this rifle and give it back to you. There isn't a round loaded and the safety is on, so as long as you just carry it and point it and don't move anything on it, the rifle shouldn't go off. See this lever thing on the bottom? That needs to be swung down and then back up to load a round, so if you don't move the loading lever, then the rifle can't fire."

Alain was watching her, frowning in concentration. "Lever?"

Of course a Mage wouldn't know what a lever was. "Never mind. Just don't move anything on the rifle. And don't point it at anyone!

Unless I tell you to. We're going to walk back to the captain's cabin as if we're on official business. If anybody tries to talk to us, let me answer."

"All right. But I can talk like a Mechanic. What is an idiot?"

Mari grinned. "Someone like a Senior Mechanic. You really do have the arrogant voice down. Where did you learn it?"

"I…have observed Mechanics."

"I'm the Mechanic you've spent almost all of your time with—" Mari paused. "Do I do that?"

"Very rarely, and never to me since first we met. Mari, the Mechanics on this ship are far more likely to recognize you than they are to recognize me."

She blew out an exasperated breath. "You're right. You take the lead. Do you remember the way to the captain's cabin?"

"I believe so."

"Same here. Hopefully one or the other of us will remember all the details." Mari took a long, calming breath, then tried to look relaxed and casual. "Let's go."

There were fewer Mechanics in the passages of the ship now that the normal work day had ended, and they paid little attention to what appeared to be two of their fellows. Mari tried to unobtrusively avert her face whenever they passed other Mechanics, or use Alain to shield herself from being seen directly. It felt very odd to be walking behind Alain while he was wearing a Mechanics jacket. He didn't look half bad in the jacket, though. He actually looked pretty good. Really good, Mari thought.

Alain was even mimicking the exaggerated self-confidence and swagger of a Mechanic. She knew he wasn't copying her. She never had been able to get the swagger thing down, thinking that she looked ridiculous whenever she tried.

Mari ducked her head again, pretending to examine her rifle, as they passed two more Mechanics who were talking together. They paid no attention to Mari and Alain.

They finally reached the captain's quarters, Mari breathing a sigh of relief that they hadn't gotten lost on the way. Pausing a short distance away from the door, Mari looked at Alain, speaking very quietly. "There's three things we have to do before we can try to escape. We have to get our packs back, which means dealing with that witch of a captain, then we have to disable the ship's far-talker so they can't tell anyone that we've escaped, and then we have to somehow sabotage the main propulsion system so the ship can't chase us down. Only after all that can we try to steal a boat."

"We cannot steal a boat unnoticed?" Alain asked.

"No. Too much noise, and the lookouts could easily see us."

"How will we do all these things? What is the plan?"

"The plan?" Mari hesitated. "We don't really have a plan. We'll have to improvise."

"Improvise?"

"That means making things up as you go along," Mari explained.

"But you told me earlier today that we need to have a plan before we begin anything complicated," Alain objected.

"Yes, I did, but— Fine. Our plan is to improvise."

"But you said that means not having a plan."

Mari glared at him. "If our plan is to improvise, then that means our plan is to not have a plan. Can we get on with it now?"

With a slightly baffled expression, Alain nodded in agreement.

Mari readied her weapon, walked the rest of the way to the captain's door and knocked the same way the guard had before. Hearing a muffled order to enter, Mari opened the door and pointed her weapon at the Senior Mechanic in one smooth motion. "Hi, Captain. I decided to come back." The Senior Mechanic made an abortive motion toward one side of her desk, halting when Mari cocked her rifle. "Go ahead and go for your pistol. I'd love an excuse to put a bullet in you."

Alain came in after Mari, closing the door and then going directly to their packs while the captain stared at them with glittering hostility. "The packs have not been opened," he told Mari. Next to one of them he found his Mage knife, and concealed that under his coat once more, grateful to have something other than the long Mechanic weapon.

Mari smiled at the captain. "Are there orders from Palandur that even you can't look inside my pack? I wonder what Guild headquarters thinks I've got in there? The truth? That seems to be what they're most scared of. It doesn't matter, though. People will learn the truth no matter what the Guild does."

"What doesn't matter is whatever you try to do," the woman spat. "You'll die a traitor's death."

"I don't think so," Mari stated in a soft voice that nonetheless carried something menacing that made Alain turn to stare her. "And if I do, I consider being a traitor to the likes of you to be an honor. Though I do appreciate your confirming that the Guild intended seeing me dead after getting whatever information it could from me. Turn around."

The Senior Mechanic shook head slowly. "No. You'll have to kill me to my face, and I know you don't have the courage to do that."

Mari laughed softly. "You're not nearly as ugly as the dragons I've faced, honored Senior Mechanic. Well, maybe you are as ugly as the troll, but did it ever occur to you that I'm not interested in killing people if I don't have to?" She stepped closer to the desk, nerved herself, then quickly swung the butt of her rifle so it struck the woman on the temple. The captain fell sideways, sprawling on the deck. "Make sure she's out," Mari asked Alain, suppressing a sick feeling at having clubbed another person unconscious.

Alain checked, then nodded. "Shall we tie her up?"

"Yeah." Mari looked around. "We're on a ship. Why can't I see any rope?"

"How about this?" Alain asked. "It is slick and not too thick, but it looks like rope."

"That'll do." Mari picked up the intercom wire and yanked. It didn't give, so Mari stuck her rifle barrel behind it and twisted until the wire broke with a snapping noise. Then she handed the free length to Alain. "It's actually wire. Make sure it's not too tight."

"Wire? You mean metal? But it bends like stiff rope and feels like cloth?"

"Yeah. The cloth is insulation, and no, I don't have time to explain what insulation is. Do you remember how to tie knots?"

"Not very well," Alain admitted.

Mari grabbed the wire from him, then pulled the captain's wrists behind her back and tied the wire around them, making sure the wire was over the sleeves of the captain's jacket so it wouldn't cut off the blood to her hands. The other end of the wire was still attached firmly to the wall. She then pulled open drawers in the captain's bureau, using a spare shirt to tie the captain's legs together. Mari stuffed a handkerchief she found into the captain's mouth as a gag. "That's the best we can do. Let's— Wait. One more thing."

Yanking open the captain's desk drawers, Mari found a pistol. "Same size cartridges as mine," she explained to Alain, getting a blank look in exchange. Mari grabbed the entire box of cartridges and stuffed it in a pocket of the jacket she was wearing. Given what the Mechanics Guild charged for a single round of ammunition, she might just as well have pocketed a sack full of gold.

"Now, we need to find this ship's far-talker. It'll be somewhere up high." Mari led the way out into the passageway, their movements a little harder now with the big packs on, then out onto an open upper deck area where the sea breeze gusted between parts of the metal ship's superstructure. The sun had completely set, leaving the upper parts of the ship in darkness interrupted only by the stars above and the navigation lights on the mast of the ship. There was no sign of the passenger ship *Sun Runner*, which had apparently been set free to continue its interrupted voyage while the Mechanic ship turned back toward Landfall.

Another Mechanic came by, alone, and Mari waylaid him. "How do I get to the far-talker from here?"

The Mechanic provided the directions, then peered at Mari. "Are you new on board? Got a boyfriend?"

"Yes and yes," Mari replied.

"Every girl on this ship is taken," the other Mechanic grumbled good-naturedly, then headed off about his business.

Mari watched him go, then sighed with relief. "I didn't want to have to club down another Mechanic. Come on." The directions they had been given lay along the outside of the ship's superstructure, so they had to move carefully with only starlight to mark their path. It wasn't very far, but Mari was getting increasingly nervous by the time they reached the hatch with a sign identifying it as the place where the ship's long-distance far-talker was kept. The longer she and Alain had to spend taking out the far-talker and the propulsion plant, the greater the chance of their being discovered or alarms being sounded. Mari rapped a brisk knock on the hatch, opened it without waiting for a reply, and quickly entered the far-talker room.

As she had expected, the far-talker was being watched at this hour by an apprentice. Mari gritted her teeth, then brought her rifle to bear on the girl. "Apprentice, I strongly recommend that you don't move or make any noise while my friend here ties you up." The girl sat frozen with fear while Alain used more wires to bind her.

Mari laid down her weapon and shut off the main power switch to the far-talker, then started pulling open access panels. Then she just stared at the rows of vacuum tubes gleaming in their sockets, and the ranks of circuit boards with their brightly-banded resistors. "I can't do it," she whispered to Alain.

"Do what?" he asked, coming close.

"Break this stuff. Stars above, Alain, I've spent my life learning how to fix this gear, how to treat it with respect and keep it working. Do you know how much artistry goes into those tubes and circuit boards? They're all hand-made. It's…it's beautiful."

"But it must be broken?"

"Yes," she whispered again.

Alain looked at the butt of his rifle, then at Mari. "Is there anything else you must do in here?"

"Um, I need to check the message log to see if they've reported my capture and see if any special orders have come in regarding me."

"Do that," Alain said.

With another sick feeling inside, Mari walked over to a desk near the bound apprentice. As she opened the message log, Mari heard the sound of breaking glass and snapping boards. She had to pause, breathing deeply to calm herself, then nerved herself enough to glance back and see Alain energetically pounding his rifle butt into the openings beneath the access panels.

Shuddering at the destruction, Mari quickly scanned the message log. *There's the report of my capture, then right after that the report about Alain. A far-talker specialist from Umburan? How did he convince them of that? And here I've got him smashing this far-talker. But no orders received back yet. I guess the Guild Masters in Palandur are too busy celebrating my capture.* She glanced over at the apprentice. "I'm sorry. I really am. I'm not doing any of this because I want to. Please remember that we didn't harm you. We're going to put a gag in your mouth, but if you breathe calmly you won't have any trouble."

"Are you Master Mechanic Mari?" the apprentice asked hesitantly.

Here it came, a young Mechanic trainee already terrified of her because of the lies her Guild had told. Mari nodded. "Yes."

To Mari's shock, the apprentice turned pleading eyes on her. "Take me with you."

"What?"

"Please. I want to join you. Whatever you're doing."

Mari had to think for a moment before answering. She had never expected to receive such a request from someone she didn't even know. "Listen, it's too dangerous. My friend and I have very little chance of getting off of this ship alive. Stay here and you'll be all right. Come with us and you'll probably die very soon or be captured and treated as a traitor."

The apprentice shook her head. "But—"

"There'll be another time. Somehow. Please don't risk yourself now."

She nodded to Mari. "How will we find you?"

*We?* Mari stared again. "There are still some things I need to do, but after that I'll find a way to let the right people know."

"And we'll be able to build anything we want? The Guild won't be able to tell us not to anymore? The Senior Mechanics won't be able to do anything they want?"

"That's what I hope for."

The apprentice nodded. "Put the gag in my mouth. Good luck, Master Mechanic Mari. You've got a lot of friends."

"I do? More than I realized, it seems. But I've also got a lot of enemies, and I don't want people like you hurt by those enemies. Good luck to you, Apprentice…?"

"Madoka."

"I'll be seeing you, Apprentice Madoka." Mari gently placed the gag in the apprentice's mouth, then stepped back and nodded farewell. Then she grabbed Alain and rushed from the room.

Closing that door behind her, Mari paused again for a moment. "Now the engine room. That's the last thing we need to do. We need to take out the boiler."

"The boiler?" Alain asked, his eyes showing a most unmage-like level of alarm. "You are going to destroy a boiler? Like the one in Dorcastle?"

Mari glared at him. "No. Not like that. Why is it whenever I talk about a boiler you think I intend exploding it?"

"That has been my experience."

"I am a Mechanic! I am trained to fix things! I only break things under the direst necessity!" Mari paused. "Like now. But I won't blow up this boiler. That would kill a lot of the crew. I have to disable it some other way. Come on."

Alain followed Mari as she hurried back down the ladder. "It's going to be low inside the ship," she told him. After taking some more turns and ladders down, they ran into another lone Mechanic, who gazed at them in surprise.

"The captain has told us to take these packs down to a place near the boiler," Alain said, surprising Mari.

"You mean the armory?"

"Yes," Alain agreed with a readiness that awed Mari. She suspected that he had no idea what an armory was, but Alain still acted completely self-assured.

"You took a wrong turn, then. It's quicker if you go back to port, two ladders down and then you'll see it just aft."

"Thank you," Alain said, then paused just long enough for Mari to nudge him to the left as the other Mechanic went about his business.

Sure enough, when they reached the bottom of the second ladder Mari could feel the heat from the boiler room and easily found the hatch leading into it. She put her hand on the lever to open the hatch, looking back at Alain. "There'll be more than one person tending the boiler even at night. I need to handle this one. Stay back and follow my lead."

She could tell Alain was shocked when they entered. What would a Mage think of this, a world made entirely of Mechanic creations? Heat pulsed through the boiler room. Tubes of various sizes led everywhere, snaking around the room like a forest of straight, curved and bent vines which had overgrown the room and then somehow been turned to metal. In the center, the huge squat metal cylinder that was the boiler radiated the heat which filled the air and brought sweat springing out on their skin.

Mari walked toward the boiler as it rumbled with the fires and steam within, for the first time really understanding why Alain thought of boilers as a sort of creature like a Mage dragon. She held her weapon casually, as if not planning to use it.

Another Mechanic sat near the boiler, his face flushed with the heat, staring glumly at various dials and other objects in the age-old attitude of someone standing a boring and routine watch.

This watch wouldn't be either boring or routine, though. "I have a message from the captain," Mari explained as the Mechanic turned to look at her. She had to speak a little loudly to be heard over the growl of the broiler and the hum of the vent fans driving air. "I need all the Mechanics on duty here to listen to it."

"Sure." The Mechanic looked backwards and yelled. "Hey, Yon and Gayl, we got a message from the captain!"

A few moments later the other two Mechanics came walking up from different directions, both wearing clothes marked by sweat. One was a girl not much older than Mari and the other a man who seemed close to the captain's age.

Mari waited until the three were all together, then brought her rifle to bear on them. "I'm sorry to report that the prisoner has escaped and is threatening to shoot anyone who makes any noise. Which one of these lines is the fuel feed for the boiler?"

The three Mechanics stared at her, but none of them spoke. "All right, have it your way." She gestured to Alain. "Keep them covered." Alain gazed back, his expression controlled but betraying confusion to her since she knew him well. "That means point your weapon at them," Mari hissed in a low whisper.

"But you told me not to—"

"Until now! Point it at them now!"

He nodded, somewhat clumsily pointing his rifle in the direction of the three Mechanics, none of whom seemed to doubt Alain's capability to use the weapon. Mari bent down, studying the labeling on the many pipes running by. Fortunately, the labels were as standardized as everything else the Mechanics Guild maintained. She quickly spotted the right pipe by the color and its code. The pipe was down low, just above the deck gratings and about as big around as her finger.

Now what? She needed to break this in a way that couldn't be easily or quickly fixed, yet not threaten the lives of every other Mechanic on this ship. Mari beckoned to Alain, then pointed to the pipe. "That's the fuel line feeding the boiler. Can you make part of it disappear?"

Alain studied it for a moment. "How much?"

"Just a little. Like so," she indicated with spread finger and thumb.

"There is little power available. I can only do this once."

"That's all we need. But wait a moment." The fact that Alain was a Mage remained unknown to the Mechanics Guild so far, and maybe it should stay that way a little longer. Mari faced the other Mechanics. "Turn around. I won't hurt you if you turn around." The three Mechanics exchanged frightened glances, then first one and then the other two turned and faced away from her. "Now, Alain."

"Very well." Mari saw Alain take on a look of concentration, and a section of the pipe vanished. Thick fuel oil started gushing from one end of the gap, its strong smell immediately obvious.

Mari stood back and kicked hard several times, forcing one end of the pipe at the gap out of alignment. "Okay."

Alain relaxed and the missing segment returned, though since Mari had kicked the end of the pipe away the restored segment now no longer matched up and the fuel continued to splash out, covering a spreading area of the deck and dripping down into the bilges. "You're very handy to have around when I need to break something," she commented. "All right," Mari called to the three other Mechanics, "we're are leaving now." She gestured with the weapon. "Out."

Mari went last, her head beginning to ache from the fumes of the fuel oil still pouring from the pipe. The lights around them started dimming and one of the Mechanics made an abortive move back. Mari stopped him with a threatening move of her weapon. "No fuel's going to the boiler, so it's losing steam pressure fast," she explained to Alain. "The fires will go out in a very short while. Then the steam pressure will totally fall off and the electricity will fail as well as the propulsion."

He nodded, then shook his head.

*Oh, right. He doesn't even know what a lever is and I'm explaining a steam plant's operation to him.* "But that's not enough. We need to start a fire."

"Fire?" Alain looked doubtful, and she noticed that he seemed to be drawn and tired. "I have done a great deal since coming aboard."

"I'm sorry. It's important."

He sighed. "You always say that, and I always find a way. Where?"

"The liquid. It will burn, but it has a high flashpoint. That means it needs a lot of heat to get it burning."

"I will do what I can." The three captive Mechanics were just outside the hatch, unable to see what Alain was doing. Mari stood in the hatch watching them but keeping one worried eye on Alain as well.

Alain held his hand before him, palm up, looking at it. The air above his hand began to glow noticeably as the lights of the ship dimmed more. Alain looked back into the boiler room toward the pool of liquid beneath the broken pipe, and the glowing air above his hand vanished.

Flame fountained out in a frightening blast that drove Alain, Mari and the three other Mechanics away from the open hatch. Mari glared at the three captives. "Get out of here! Run!" They stared at her, then turned and bolted.

Alain stared as well. "Is that wise?"

"What was I supposed to do?" Mari growled. "Leave them in the fire? Walk around holding three Mechanics at gunpoint? Tie them up and maybe let them burn or drown? I will not kill if I don't absolutely have to!" She paused, remembering something. "Blast. Come on."

Mari led them back at a run to the place where she and Alain had been imprisoned, their journey complicated when the lighting on the ship went out and only a few replacement lights sprang on to provide dim illumination. "Battery-powered emergency lamps," Mari explained, looking back and seeing that Alain had his *whatever-you-say* expression on, meaning he understood nothing but was willing to accept that she did. Amid her fears she felt a surge of real joy at his trust in her, trust that meant all the more since he had plenty of grounds for knowing she wasn't perfect by any means.

But she also noticed that Alain was visibly struggling to keep up with her, gasping for breath as he followed. Despite her urgency, Mari slowed down some.

Along with the lights, the fans providing air through the ship had now died, leaving an eerie silence in their wake punctuated by growing numbers of alarmed cries from members of the crew and the sound of feet thundering on the metal decks as Mechanics dashed to and fro in hopes of discovering the problem. Mari, seeing Alain faltering more, stepped back to help him keep moving. "They can shut off the fuel and get that fire out, but by the time they do that we should be off this ship," she explained, trying to cover her growing fear with talking. "The boiler room will be badly damaged. They won't be able to get steam up again for quite a while."

Finally reaching the place where they had been confined, Mari stopped at the locked hatch, unfastened the lock, then lifted the handle and yanked the hatch open. The five Mechanics inside stared back. "I won't leave anyone locked in a room on a ship that might sink," Mari announced. "But if any of you come after me I'll blow your heads off. Understood?" Without waiting for a reply she grabbed Alain again and ran for the closest ladder at the best pace which Alain could manage.

Reaching the next level up, Mari hesitated, looking in each possible direction, then ran up another ladder, thinking that would take her to the main deck level. Alain leaned on her, struggling up the steep steps, as the tumult grew around them. The ship's crew dashed around and past them, staggering as the ship rolled drunkenly in the seas, its last traces of headway lost without the propulsion system working anymore.

"We are still improvising?" Alain asked.

"That's the plan, yes," Mari assured him. "We're going to improvise our way off of this ship." She saw an open hatch with the darkness of night visible through it and dodged that way.

Out on deck there were Mechanics rushing around in singles and small groups. In their stolen jackets and the darkness, Mari and Alain blended in without notice. "Follow me." There were life rafts fastened nearby, but they were small and lacked sails. Drifting helplessly on a small platform wouldn't save them. With Alain still leaning on her, Mari ran toward the stern, where she could see lifeboat davits rising from the deck.

Skidding to a halt at the first boat, she bent to read the instructions, blessing the Mechanics Guild's obsession with spelling out written procedures. "Just as I thought I remembered. It's a gravity release system."

"A what?"

"It doesn't need any power," Mari explained. Yanking off her pack, she tossed it in the boat. "Put your pack in there, too." Then she hurled the weapons they had stolen into the boat as well.

As Alain threw his pack into the lifeboat, Mari pulled out heavy pins that had held the lowering mechanism locked, then threw herself against a big lever. Alain added his own strength and the lever swung over with a dull, metallic thunk.

The davits sagged outward, taking the boat out over the water, and the lines holding the lifeboat close to the davits began unreeling, the boat freefalling to land in the sea with a tremendous splash. Mari yanked off her stolen jacket and dropped it on the deck, gesturing to Alain to do the same.

"Hey, what's going on?" A Senior Mechanic was staring at them, the same man who had led the group that had captured Mari. "Why are you lowering a lifeboat? I didn't hear anything about abandoning ship."

"We're lightening the ship," Mari yelled back. "Getting rid of excess weight. Captain's orders."

"That's ridiculous! Who told you—? Hey! You're—!"

Mari crouched slightly, spun, and kicked out, catching the Senior Mechanic in the gut and knocking him backwards. Straightening, Mari grabbed Alain's hand. "Jump!" she whispered urgently.

Alain, bless the Mage, didn't ask any questions, but went over the rail with her. The side of the ship rushed past as they hurtled downward, the drop briefly terrifying, then they hit the water and went at least a lance length underwater. Mari fought her way back to the surface, spluttering and trying to swim toward the lifeboat bobbing in the water nearby, the weight of her boots and her clothing trying to drag her back down.

For several heart-stopping moments Mari wondered if she would make it, then made a desperate lunge and closed one hand over the rail of the boat. Alain reached it at the same time she did and they helped each other in. Mari rolled onto the bottom of the boat, coming up against their packs and staring upward, where she could see the silhouette of the Mechanic who had been questioning them visible against the ship's rail. The Senior Mechanic was pointing toward them and yelling. "Get the sail set, Alain. We've got to get out of here."

The Mage stared helplessly at the mast mechanism.

"Sorry, I keep expecting you to do everything," Mari gasped as she elbowed him aside, swinging up the small mast and locking it, then yanking at the lines holding the sail bound tightly to the mast. Her hands shivered with cold and water dripped off her clothing and hair in steady streams, but Mari tried to ignore those distractions. The sail came free, flapping for a moment before billowing out. "I'll trim it. You get to the tiller and steer us out of here."

"Tiller?"

"That stick thing at the back! Move it from side to side and the boat will turn. Hurry!"

As Alain threw himself to the back of the boat and awkwardly grabbed the tiller there came the unmistakable boom of a rifle shot, followed immediately by the flat, hard slap of a bullet hitting the water nearby. The lifeboat swung around, wallowing in a way that ironically made it harder for someone to aim at, then steadied, the sail now taut and the boat oh-so-slowly gaining speed away from the looming mass of the Mechanic Guild ship.

More shots rang out and tiny geysers erupted around the lifeboat. Mari grabbed one of the rifles she had thrown in the boat, then looked upward and back at the Mechanics shooting at her, knowing that she couldn't fire back when some of her targets might be Mechanics like Kalif or Apprentice Madoka. Instead, she pointed her weapon nearly straight up and fired several shots, pumping the lever awkwardly with the rifle held that way, hoping the sound of the shots would frighten the Mechanics aiming at her and praying a lucky hit wouldn't strike her or Alain. A *plonk* marked a hit on the boat, wood splintering under the impact. "What of the big Mechanic weapon?" Alain called. "The one on the front of the ship?"

"With power out on the ship they'll have to train and load it manually. Hopefully they'll be too busy with the fire to think of that until we're too far away." On the heels of her words, as if mocking them, a deep boom came from the direction of the ship, causing Mari's heart to stutter with fear.

# CHAPTER NINE

Mari waited for the roar of a heavy shell headed their way, frozen with dread of what even a near-miss would do to the frail wooden lifeboat. But then she realized that there hadn't been any muzzle flash from the big gun and saw the dark shape of the Mechanic ship alter as it listed to one side. "Something blew up on that ship." The ship listed more. "They're flooding. Alain, they're flooding the boiler room to put out the fire before it destroys the ship."

"Will that sink them?"

"If I remember right, the idea is to take in enough water to put out the fire but not enough to sink yourself." A few more shots rang out in a ragged volley and Mari heard bullets snapping by overhead. "We're almost out of range."

"They cannot pursue?" His voice had calmed, she realized, as her own tone had grown less worried, but Alain still sounded exhausted.

"No, they can't follow us. That boiler room is out of order for a long time. I'd stake my Mechanics jacket on it." She yanked open the lifeboat's tiny emergency locker and checked the compass. "Which direction are we going, anyway? Let me see. East? Alain, you're taking us back toward the Empire!"

"You told me to get away from the Mechanic ship as fast as possible," he complained.

"Oh, yeah. All right, let's go out a little farther until they've lost sight of us, then do a wide turn and head west. As long as we go west it should be impossible to miss the Sharr Isles since they've got some good mountainous heights." She laughed, giddy with relief. "This'll actually work out. We've escaped and the ship saw us heading back toward the Empire so maybe they'll warn the Guild to look for us there. But we'll still get to Caer Lyn and take a ship out of there to Altis."

She could see Alain nod. "Our plan worked," he said.

"Our plan?"

"The plan not to use a plan."

"Oh, that plan. Are you being sarcastic, my Mage?"

"Perhaps," Alain said.

"How long have you been planning to say that?"

"I just made it up."

Mari couldn't quite suppress another laugh. "All right, just for that, you can keep steering for a while, even though I'm happy to hear you making a joke." Mari settled herself in the bow, trembling as reaction to recent events set in. She was torn between total tiredness and the residue of the fear which had been driving her. "It's been another long day, hasn't it? Once we're on course we can tie that tiller to keep us going straight and maybe both get some sleep. It's got to be several hours' sailing time to the vicinity of the Sharr Isles."

She saw Alain drooping over the tiller. "You went beyond your limit again to do what I asked, didn't you?"

He raised his head and nodded. "It was necessary."

"It's still amazing what you can do, and that you keep finding the strength to do it." Mari moved cautiously to sit next to Alain, uncertain of the stability of this boat, then held him tightly. "Have I told you today that I love you?"

"When you were being taken off the *Sun Runner*," Alain said.

"I was afraid that would be the last time I could say it to you." She took a deep breath. "Get a little sleep, Alain. You earned it. I'll keep on eye on things for a while."

He didn't answer, and when she looked over at him Mari saw that his eyes were already shut.

She braced him against her, held the tiller, and looked up at the stars.

❧ ❧ ❧

Mari blinked up at the darkness, wondering where she was. She looked to one side and Alain was there, lying right next to her, smiling at her. She smiled back, reaching for him. His hands were on her body, touching everywhere, and it was feeling very, very good and—

The door crashed open. Men and women came storming in, their faces shadowed but their Mechanics jackets a clear sign of their identities. The Mechanics were leveling weapons at her, demanding that she raise her arms high, and stars above she was naked in front of all of them and—

Mari jerked into wakefulness, staring at the bow of the boat , her breath coming rapidly, heart pounding in her chest. She must have fallen asleep next to Alain. The gentle rolling motion of the lifeboat hadn't changed, providing a strange contrast to the violent action of her nightmare. Its sail was still drawing a good breeze.

Alain was stirring next to her, sitting up. Mari tried to pretend that she was still asleep, but it didn't do any good. "You had another bad dream," Alain said in a soft voice.

"After what we've been through, that shouldn't be any surprise," Mari mumbled.

"I believe these dreams have less to do with recent history than with things you will not speak of."

There he went again. Bringing up her family. "Not a good time, Alain."

"It is never a good time. Some nights you awaken in my arms, distressed, unhappy, and yet you will not ever speak of what haunts your dreams."

Mari had been leaning against Alain. Now she sat up straighter, looking directly ahead. "You know why I have nightmares sometimes. It's happened ever since I had to shoot those barbarians in Marandur."

"Those nightmares are different," Alain said. "You react differently in them. There is another reason you have nightmares."

"Who made you such an expert on me?" Mari turned her most intimidating look on Alain. "This is my problem. I'll figure it out. I'll deal with it."

"You are not alone."

She almost snapped at him once more in response, then realized the statement had more than one meaning. By closing him out of her problems, she was closing him out of her life.

Mari took a few long, slow breaths. "It's…guilt, I guess. And that's probably because of my mother. It's got to be her fault."

"You blame your mother for your nightmares?"

"Why not? That's what mothers are for. Daughters blame them for their problems."

"Why does this stand between us?" Alain asked.

That took several more breaths, while Mari nerved herself enough to answer. "Because I want you so bad. Physically, I mean, as well as loving you. And I know I must feel guilty about that. Because having sex is how you have children, even if you're taking measures not to have children, and if we have children…"

He waited, not saying anything.

"If we have children," Mari said in a whisper, "I might do to them what my mother did to me." She shuddered as the words finally left her, closing her eyes against the world around her.

Alain's arm came around her, gently offering reassurance. "You do miss them."

"No, I don't! If I wasn't good enough for them, then they're not good enough for me!"

"Anger will only—"

"*I'm not getting angry!*"

There was a moment of silence before Alain spoke again with the tone of a man walking into a pit full of lions. "Since neither one of us is angry, may I mention something?"

This was going too far, too fast. Why couldn't he just leave it alone? "As long as it has absolutely nothing to do with my parents, sure."

"May I speak of mine?"

Mari glared down at the bottom of the boat. "All right," she grumbled.

"The last words I heard my mother say were 'remember us.'" Alain said. "I never could forget those words or my parents, and I feel certain that my parents never forgot me."

Tears mingled with her rage this time. "That makes me feel so much better, hearing about how your parents never forgot you." It came out sounding vicious, making Mari feel even worse.

"Mari, you gave me back the ability to feel, to stop denying my emotions. Why do you fight so hard to deny your own feelings?"

She just stared downward. "She abandoned me, Alain. Her own daughter, forgotten, tossed aside. My mother did that, and her blood flows in me." Mari raised her gaze, meeting Alain's eyes. "I can't imagine ever doing that to a child of mine, but my mother did it, and her blood is in me, and so maybe someday I would. And I will not risk that, Alain. As long as there is any chance that I might cast a child of mine aside because I inherited such a dark legacy, then I will not have a child. Why is it so hard for you to understand how horrible that is for me to think about?"

"Because you have never told me of it," he said.

Mari pretended to be concentrating on moving the tiller so that the boat was on just the right course. "All right, you have a point there," she finally admitted. "But now you know, and I hope you will respect that this is not something to do with you. It's me. I have to get through what happened."

Alain nodded, his voice calm. "What do you believe happened, Mari?"

"With my parents? I don't believe anything. I know." Her voice was shaking with anger. "I went off to the Mechanics Guild and I never got a single letter from them. Not one, not ever. For a few years I kept hoping they would least send something on my birthday, but no, nothing, nothing at all, and I wrote so many letters to them, Alain, so many letters, and I was still a little girl and I poured my heart into those letters and I begged them to please write and they never did." The tears were coming again, blast it. Mari watched them fall into the bottom of the boat and mingle with the small puddles of sea water there.

"You know that they never wrote?"

"I checked. For years I checked often with the retired Mechanic who served as the mail clerk for the Guild Hall, and he never had anything for me!" Mari had been only ten years old the last time she had asked about mail from her parents, but she could still see his face, the old man kindly and regretful. *Commons are like that. They get jealous. They cut you off. I'm really sorry, Mari. But you have the Guild now.*

"Mari," Alain said in a soft voice that barely carried, "did he tell you that no letters had been received, or that he had none for you?"

"What difference does it make how he said it?"

"Do you remember speaking with your friend Mechanic Calu about the letters he sent from the Guild Hall in Caer Lyn to you at the Mechanics Guild Academy, and the ones you sent to him and Mechanic Alli? At least some of those letters did not arrive, even though they were sent between Mechanics. Does this happen often?"

"No! I've never heard of any Mechanic complaining about it. I'm guessing now that I was being watched closer than I thought even then and that the Guild's Senior Mechanics must have been intercepting some of my mail to see if I was being treasonous. But that's not—" Something registered then, something too terrible to confront. "No. Oh, no, no, no."

"My Guild never made any secret that we were to cut all ties to our parents," Alain continued. "They taught us to believe our parents were nothing. The elders did this openly, because our training as Mages was believed to require it and because it ensured our loyalty to the Mage Guild. As I watched the Senior Mechanic on that ship taunt you, it came to me that your Guild took a different path, convincing you to deny your parents by making you believe that your parents had denied you. You know for a fact that some letters you sent were never delivered, and some sent to you were never received. This between Mechanics. What of letters to and from commons?" He paused, then spoke gently. "Your Guild elders lied to you about so much. I believe they lied about that as well."

Mari was staring at him, feeling the tears streaming down her face again, but not in anger. No, what she was feeling now was a sense of dismay so deep it threatened to swallow her. "They lied to me and who knows how many others. We were just kids. We had no idea someone would do something like that. They cut us off from our families, and let us believe it was our families' fault."

"I think this may have happened, yes, Mari," Alain said, his voice soft.

"No!" It was more a howl of despair than a word, and Mari hurled herself against Alain to clasp him and cry in great, trembling sobs. "Then my parents didn't leave me. They never got my letters, did they? The Guild just burned their letters, probably, and told me, and told my friends, that our parents hated us now, and we believed them, and we believed that the Guild was the only family we had. Oh, no." She couldn't stop crying, wracked with more pain than she had ever let out, and Alain held her, saying nothing else for a long time.

Eventually Mari subsided to shivering, then finally was able to speak again, her voice sounding as lost as the place in her heart. "Gone. They're gone. And it's my fault for believing the lies of my Guild."

"They are not gone," Alain said.

"Yes, they are. How can I ever face them now? They never heard from me when I was an apprentice. I've been able to visit them for years and I never tried, never did anything. They must think I'm an awful Mechanic who looks down on them and wants to pretend they never existed. I can't possibly ever face them." Mari buried her face in Alain's chest. "Why did you have to tell me this? It hurt less before, because at least I could blame them."

"It is not too late."

"Yes, it is!"

"It is too late for me to see my parents," Alain continued, and Mari winced. "They are dead. You still have a chance to make it right."

"Alain," Mari whispered, "I can't. I'm not strong enough, I'm not brave enough. I can't go there."

"You are not alone."

This time it meant another thing, and she pulled back a little to stare up at him.

Alain nodded to her. "You do not need to be strong enough alone. You have a friend who will help you."

"Would you really? But, Alain, even then—"

"I will be beside you."

"What if they find out that you're a Mage and they hate you?"

"If you are reassured that they love you, whatever they think of me would be a small thing."

Mari's despair was replaced by fear mingled with wonder. "Maybe I can, if you're there with me. Maybe." Mari looked out across the water, to the west where Caer Lyn lay, trying to grasp everything that had just happened. "My mother didn't abandon me."

"No."

"I don't have that in my blood."

"No."

"I could be a good mother, if we're ever blessed with children. Maybe. At least I can try my best." She turned her head to look directly at Alain. "Do you still want to get married?"

The clearest smile she had ever seen on him illuminated Alain's face. On an average person, it would have been a small bend of the lips, but from someone trained as a Mage it was amazing. "Yes."

Mari kissed him long and deeply, having to pause afterwards to catch her breath. "Then I've made up my mind. I'm going to promise myself to you. I tell you that right now. We'll be married. I can't believe it took me this long to be willing to say that. I can't remember where or when it happened, but at some point I stopped being able to imagine life without you in it. And though I don't know why you like me so much, and I don't know what I've ever done to deserve your love, you've shown that you love me more than I ever thought anyone could. So I'm proposing to you now even though you proposed to me back in that inn west of Umburan. I want you to know that I want this as much as you do. Nobody and nothing will ever separate us."

When Alain finally spoke, his voice was rough with more emotion than she had ever heard from him before. "I will never leave you. I wondered if your fears were about me, if my being a Mage was still something you could not overcome, or if you found other things about me wanting."

"Stars above, Alain, you're perfect. Except for little things. I looked for flaws, believe me. I wanted to run when I realized I was falling in love with you. But I guess this destiny of yours had its little joke with us."

"I hope you retain this illusion about my perfection," Alain said. "And I will remain certain that you are indeed perfect. Except for little things."

"I think there's a few big things, but we just resolved the biggest. You do realize that I'm getting the better deal, don't you?" said Mari, fighting back tears again.

"On that we must continue to disagree." Alain looked behind them, toward the east. "It will be dawn soon. Shall we watch the sun rise together, on this first day of a new day for us?"

She sat next to him, gazing eastward where the sky was beginning to show the tint of dawn, half afraid this was a dream as well. "Right now I don't care if I never bring a new day to the world. This new day for us is enough."

"That may be out of our hands," Alain suggested.

"We could always give up, but I guess you and I aren't the kind of people who give up. It does scare me, Alain, that..." She braced herself, then said it. "That I am the daughter of Jules. That I actually have a chance to overthrow the Great Guilds. Because there are so many things that could go wrong, and so many people could be hurt. I don't know if you heard what that apprentice in the far-talker room on the ship said, but apparently there are Mechanics who are starting to believe things about me, too. It's just crazy."

He smiled at her again. "You are more than you think you are."

"Says the man who thinks I'm more beautiful than Asha," Mari replied, "who herself must be getting burned by the intensity of my bonfire right now."

"You are more beautiful than Asha," Alain began to protest.

"And you are delusional. Sometimes I wonder if you believe that I'm just one more imaginary thing in a world you believe to be an illusion, and you're thinking you can change me just like you can change other things."

He sounded puzzled by her statement. "What would I want to change about you?"

"How long a list do you want?"

Alain actually laughed for a moment, for only the second time since she had met him. "I am afraid my fate is to love you as you are."

She grinned. "Another word for fate is doom, you know. Or destiny. Should we invite destiny to our wedding?"

The sun peeked up over the horizon in a sliver of dazzling brightness as Alain answered. For the moment, there was no hint of a storm threatening. "I have a feeling that destiny will be there whether we invite it or not."

✤ ✤ ✤

The rays of the rising sun brought light to the sky and shone on the peaks of mountains rising from the sea ahead of them. Mari used the sight of those mountains to adjust the course of their boat, her eyes sometimes distant as if she were trying to recall old memories.

Alain knew that feeling well enough. *Strange how, given the differences in our lives before we met, so many things are similar between us even if the reasons are not the same.* He watched her, thinking that Mari looked more relaxed than he had ever seen her.

At one point she gave him a half smile, eyes sad. "There are some walls I need to knock down before we get to the island. I've been building them for about ten years, so they're pretty strong." Mari paused as if gathering resolve, then spoke hesitantly. "Alain, what would you have done if your parents had lived and you'd gone back to them, and they'd rejected you like you said your grandmother did? You don't have to tell me, if it's too hard to think about, but I guess I'd like to know how you might have dealt with that."

"I am not that good with people," Alain said, his own reluctance probably obvious to Mari. The idea of that happening—of his parents rejecting him as his grandmother had—hurt a great deal even to think about. "I have too little experience with expressing feelings."

"You're a lot better than you think you are, Alain." She forced another smile at him. "Can you try to imagine what you might have done? Please?"

Alain nodded to her. "I…think I would have told them that I had done as they wished, that even though I had become a Mage, I had remembered them. I would have told them that even though they rejected me now, I would always remember them."

He had to pause then to control the feelings which rushed back upon him. "If they had spoken to me as my grandmother did…it… would have been very hard. But I would have known they still lived, and they would have known I had not forgotten them." Alain met Mari's eyes. "It would have been easier than learning that they were dead."

Mari reached to touch his hand. "I'm sorry I made you think about that. You're so right that I'm lucky to have the chance to fix this. If they do reject me…well, I'll know I tried, and they'll know I tried, despite everything." She relaxed for a while after that.

But Mari grew tense again as the shore of the island rose over the horizon, the sand shining white under the morning sun. "Two things, Alain. No, three things. We can't bring the rifles with us. There's no way to hide them in our packs, and commons do not just walk around with rifles. I hate to leave them, if for no other reason than that they're worth a great deal of money if we could sell them, but that might attract my Guild's attention. Also, I can't bring us in to the port. I've tried steering more that way, or what I think is that way, but I don't know enough about sailing to get the boat to go in that direction. And while we have good reason to assume that our Guilds and the Imperials will take a while to figure out we might have gone to the island anyway after escaping from the Mechanic ship, we can't linger here. I want to be away before nightfall if we can manage it."

"What of the other thing?" Alain asked. "Are you still resolved?"

Mari took a deep breath before answering. "Yes, we will make every effort to see my family. I have no idea where my mother and father work. We'll have to go by my old house, and hope they still live there, and that one or both of them are home. And it may be that you have to physically drag me to the door of that house, Alain."

The wind drove the lifeboat ahead quickly as Mari aimed for a stretch of sand backed by dense growth with no signs of human presence. They ran the lifeboat onto a narrow beach before the sun had risen far in the sky, splashing ashore through the surf onto soft sand, then with difficulty pulling the weight of the boat a bit farther up onto the beach. Mari gazed back at the boat, her expression thoughtful. "What do you think our chances are of hiding it?"

Alain considered the large object. "Burying it would take a long time. It is too heavy for us to haul into the brush ahead, and covering it with brush on the beach would only make it more obvious. It is painted white, so at least it does not stand out too clearly against the sand."

"We could set it on fire. I can't see any sign of people nearby, and it shouldn't generate much smoke."

Alain looked out to sea. "Is there any chance the Mechanic ship we damaged will see it and come here?"

Mari grinned in a wicked way as she considered his question.

He had seen that expression before, when she was watching the smoke rising from the ruins of the Ringhmon City Hall. Alain realized that Mari looked unusually attractive when she was contemplating the results of major sabotage she had committed against people trying to imprison her. That probably ought to concern him, but it did not.

"No, there's no chance of that," Mari finally said. "As far as we could tell before we lost sight of it, the ship didn't sink. That ship is very valuable, so there is no way the Mechanics aboard would abandon it unless they had no alternative. But that boiler isn't going to be working for quite a while. I'm guessing that, being Mechanics, they rigged some sails on their masts and are painstakingly making their way either here or back to Landfall. Most likely Landfall, since they last saw us headed that way and the Mechanic repair facilities are probably a lot better there. With the big far-talker on the ship out of order, they'll be dependent on their hand-held far-talkers, which means they'll have to get close to shore to tell anyone what happened. So, short answer, there's no way that ship could be close enough to see any smoke."

"In that case, I agree that we should burn the boat. Sooner or later someone will find the remains, but it will take time to identify them and by then we will be long off the island."

"Sounds good to me." Mari pulled her pack out of the boat while Alain got his, then she hefted both Mechanic rifles, looking resigned. With a grimace, she took one by the front, whirled it around in a wide swing and hurled the weapon out into the surf. A moment later the second weapon followed it, disappearing with a splash into the incoming waves. "Let me spare you extra effort for once, especially since a spell might alert other Mages that you're on this island." She gathered some dry wood, pulled down the sail and bundled it on the bottom of the boat, then used her Mechanic fire-starting device, clicking it so that sparks flew onto the wood and the sail. Alain watched, fascinated, still unable to understand how the thing Mari called a flint worked to create sparks. In a short time a fire was rising in the center of the boat, the flames pale in the bright sunlight and only a thin thread of weak smoke rising into the sky.

"Good bye, little boat," Mari said in a guilty voice. "Thanks for getting us safely here, and sorry we had to do this."

Alain gave her a surprised look. "You speak as if the boat is alive."

"Well, maybe it is in some way. Maybe it's just a Mechanic thing, but we tend to think of what we create as having some sort of life." Seeming embarrassed, Mari hoisted her pack, then turned and led the way through the undergrowth on the far side of the beach. "Unless things have changed a lot, there should be a coastal road running just inland from here. We should be able to catch a ride into Caer Lyn proper pretty quick."

"They will not wonder who we are, out here with these packs?" Alain asked.

"No. Our clothes have dried. We'll tell them we're students from the college in Caer Lyn who were backpacking through the upcountry. I think students did that when I was young, because I recall my mother talking about it a few times."

"Your mother worked at this college?"

"I guess maybe she did. When you're eight years old, you don't really notice all that much about your parents."

Mari's prediction proved to be accurate. They reached the road within a very short time and not long afterwards waved down a horse-drawn wagon heading south toward the city. "How far are we from Caer Lyn?" Mari asked.

The driver scrunched up his face in thought. "Not too far. We'll be there well before noon. Looks like you two have had kind of a rough time. Been out a while?"

"Um, yeah," Mari agreed, accepting Alain's hand up into the back of the wagon.

Alain sat down among the parcels in the back. "There should be time for the visit."

Mari nodded, her expression tense. "If I try to change my mind, don't let me."

"I have promised to drag you to your parents' house."

"You might have some trouble doing that, but I'll try not to fight you too hard."

He thought she needed something to lighten her mood. A joke? Alain tried one. "As long as you leave no new scars on me."

That earned him a startled look, then a sad look, then some puzzlement. "Why did you say that? Every time I see your scars I think of what they did to you when you were learning to be a Mage."

"I thought it would…relax you," Alain said.

"Oh. Um…all right." She gave him a smile that was obviously forced and then lay back, gazing up at the sky.

He decided it would be wiser not to attempt any more jokes.

It was just short of noon when the wagon dropped them in Caer Lyn. Mari spoke with the driver briefly, then came back to Alain as the wagon drove off. "He gave me directions to…where we need to go. It's not far, so we have time." Linking her arm in his, she started off down the street, breathing slowly, her tension radiating so clearly that Alain could feel it. After walking for a while, they reached a winding street that wove its way down a low hill, the roadway lined with narrow two-story houses set side-by-side, every house presenting brightly colored doors to the world. "It's a custom in the Sharr isles," Mari explained, her voice too fast and too high in pitch. "They paint the doors bright colors, for luck and…and…other things. This is the street we want. About halfway down. The…the door was green. I remember how pretty it was."

As they walked down the slope, Mari began dragging back, her steps slowing, but Alain held her arm in his and kept her moving. Looking over at her, Alain could see Mari's eyes darting about as if trying to spot landmarks from a memory dimmed by too many years away. "I was only eight when the Mechanics took me from here," Mari murmured as if she had never told Alain before. "I can still see my parents in my memory, though, standing in our doorway as I was taken away. I could never forget that."

They reached a short walk ending at a vivid green door to a modest, two-story town home standing wedged between its neighbors. Mari came to a total halt, staring at the door, her arm shaking in his, her face rigid. "Mari?" Alain asked, thinking that she looked as upset as she had when he had told her she was the daughter.

Mari glanced at him with a jerky movement of her head, then breathed deeply and slowly in an obvious attempt to calm herself. Alain began walking and after an initial resistance Mari followed, her arm clamped on his now. Reaching the door, Alain let go of Mari's arm, then gestured toward the door. "I am here, but this is your moment. I am beside you, but you must do this." Since his Mage training led him to be impassive in the face of stress without always realizing it, Alain made sure he showed a smile to reassure her.

Mari stood there for another moment, looking as nervous as Alain had ever seen her, even counting the time a dragon had been chasing them in Dorcastle. She reached a decision, pulling off her commons coat, then diving down into her pack to haul out her Mechanics jacket and put it on. Settling the jacket on her, squaring her shoulders and brushing back her hair with both hands, Mari took one more deep breath and then rapped firmly on the emerald-green door, the sound of the knocks echoing down the quiet street.

Several moments passed before a middle-aged woman opened the door, her eyes taking in the dark Mechanics jacket and then lowering their gaze respectfully. Looking at her, Alain could see the tension in this woman, too, though hers was a barely repressed hostility. He could also see the ways in which Mari resembled her, not least in the raven-black hair which on the older woman now showed streaks of gray. "Yes, Lady Mechanic?" the woman said in a formal and cold voice which also betrayed to the Mage enormous resentment and anger.

Mari was unable to speak for a moment, visibly trembling and blinking rapidly. She swallowed, then got out one word in a whisper. "Mommy?"

# CHAPTER TEN

Alain heard the little-girl sound in Mari's voice, her use of the child's term for her mother, and knew that an eight-year-old girl was finally speaking again to the mother she had lost more than a decade before.

The woman froze, then drew in a ragged breath. She looked up, hope warring with disbelief in her expression, finally gazing directly at Mari's face. "Mari? Is it really you?"

"Mommy!" Mari gasped again. She threw her arms around the woman, who after only a moment's hesitation gripped Mari with equal fervor, sudden tears wetting her face as Mari managed to speak a few more words. "Oh, Mommy, I'm so sorry."

Seeing tears running down Mari's own cheeks, Alain took a step away. His work was done and he thought this was what Mari would call a private moment. "I will keep watch outside while you—"

"You'll do nothing of the kind!" Mari interrupted through her tears, taking one hand away from her mother long enough to drag Alain back. "You'll come inside and share this joyous moment you caused to happen!"

*Joyous?* Alain wondered, seeing the amount of tears flowing from both women. But he yielded to Mari's grasp, coming along as her mother led the way inside.

Once the door was closed, the two women stood looking at each other. Mari's mother reached out one hand to touch her daughter's face. "It's been so long."

Mari's face twisted in misery. "They lied to me. I was too young to know what they were doing. I thought you didn't care. I never got any letters. You never got any of my letters, did you?"

"You sent letters?" Her mother's eyes spilled tears again. "I knew it. I knew you must have tried to send letters. For ten years I have believed that and now I know I was right."

"How can you ever forgive me?" Mari whispered. "I didn't know what they had done, but I should have tried to talk to you before now. I am so, so sorry, Mommy."

"Did you think I couldn't forgive my own daughter? Even if you had been at fault?" Mari's mother wiped tears from her face with both hands. "And I believe you that you weren't at fault, that you didn't know what they had done."

"I thought horrible things about you. I thought…I thought…" Mari shook her head, quivering with sobs. "I'm so sorry."

"Come sit down, Mari." A smile lit her mother's face. "How long have I dreamed of saying that again? And here you are at last."

Mari and her mother walked a short distance to the left into a front room with a couch and chairs. Alain followed, even though he felt at the moment as if he were using his invisibility spell, so thoroughly were the two women focused on each other.

Mari and her mother sat close to each other, their knees almost touching. Mari took a shuddering breath. "Can you really forgive me?"

"Of course I can, Mari." Her mother sighed. "Just to be able to say your name and not feel an ache of loss is so wonderful. I see you are a Mechanic now, and I know you can't spend much time with common folk, but—"

"No!" Mari leaned forward, her face working with emotion. "You're my family. I was lied to and deceived into thinking the Guild was my family, but now I know how terrible a lie that all was, and I will never reject you again." Mari wiped her nose. "I must look like a mess. I'm sorry. We had a very difficult trip here, what with fighting the Mages and their troll in Palandur and then having to jump off the train and evade Imperial patrols and police, and then my Guild captured us and we had to just about sink the ship to escape and steal a lifeboat to get to this island."

Her mother just stared at Mari, then shook her head. "It seems we have even more catching up to do than I had expected. Wait. We." She finally looked at Alain. "My manners. I'm Eirene, Mari's mother. But you already know that, don't you?"

Alain inclined his head toward her. "I am Alain. Alain of Ihris."

Mari leaned in toward him and held Alain's arm. "I wouldn't be here if not for Alain. He's the one who realized that my Guild had deceived me about you, and he gave me the strength to come here despite my fears. And...well, he's also saved my life a few times. I mean, literally, he's saved my life."

Eirene turned a wondering look on Alain. "How can I ever repay you?"

Mari laughed. "That's one of the first things I said to him, too. Oh, Mommy...Mother. I need to call you Mother. Is that all right? There's been so much I need to tell you about."

"The journey here seems to have had enough to talk about for days," her mother replied. "Mages? Trolls?"

"One troll," Alain said.

"I knew Mages hated Mechanics, but I didn't know they still attacked them." Eirene frowned. "But you also said your Guild captured you. Are you in trouble with your Guild?"

Mari bent her head. "You might say that."

"But you're a Mechanic."

Alain spoke again. "A Master Mechanic. The youngest one in the history of her Guild."

Eirene's face lit with pride. "That's my girl. But why would your Guild—?"

"Mother, I am not exaggerating in the least when I say that if I told you why my Guild is angry with me, if I told you the things I have learned, it could result in your own death." Mari clenched her fists, staring at the floor. "It's not my Guild now."

Her mother reached out to clasp one of Mari's fists in her own hand. "Whatever has happened, you are family. Your father will be so happy to see you again. He won't get home until sunset, but—"

Mari gave her mother an anguished look. "We can't wait that long. Not nearly that long. It would be far too dangerous for you."

"It's that bad?" Eirene asked. "It's fortunate that I wasn't teaching today, if your visit must be short. But if the danger is so great, maybe we shouldn't tell Kath about this."

"Kath?"

"Your little sister. Kath was born the year after you were taken from us. I was already carrying her when you were taken, though I didn't know it yet."

"My little sister?" Mari seemed ready to cry again. "I have a little sister? I never knew…where is she?"

"At schooling. She should be home soon. But if it's so dangerous…"

Mari turned a pleading look on Alain. "It would be all right to see her, wouldn't it?"

"I believe so," Alain answered. He had his doubts about the wisdom of bringing Mari's newfound little sister in on the secret of their visit, but Mari obviously wanted very badly to see her.

Eirene sighed again, heavily this time. "Mari, you need to know that Kath doesn't think much of her big sister. Kath believes you abandoned us. She has taken that very hard."

"I don't blame her for that." Mari shuddered with anger. "I'm going to change things, Mother. I don't know all of the details yet, but once I get some more data I'm going to make some decisions and change things so no more little girls or boys get torn from their families. Not ever again. The Great Guilds will not be allowed to continue that, or a lot of other things. I'm going to stop them."

Her mother's face reflected amazement. "Stop the Great Guilds? Mari, you sound like the daughter of—" The door slammed open.

Mari was on her feet and had her pistol out in a heartbeat, leveling the weapon at the door.

Alain had stood, his right hand before him, already preparing to draw power for a spell, his left hand gripping the Mage knife he had drawn from beneath his jacket.

A young girl stared back at them.

Eirene got up slowly, her hands out in a calming gesture. "Kath, please close the door. Don't say anything. It's all right. Just close the door quietly."

The girl's stare went to her mother. Then she nodded, turned with slow movements and closed the door softly.

Mari, looking embarrassed, had returned her weapon to its place under her jacket. Alain relaxed himself, returning the Mage knife to its sheath under his coat, then stood waiting.

"Kath, come here," Eirene said gently. "Do you know who this is, Kath?" she asked, gesturing toward Mari.

The girl stared at Mari and her face hardened, going from anxiety to anger. "No. She's just some Mechanic."

"This is your big sister, Kath. This is Mari."

"I don't have a big sister!"

Mari took a step forward, her face working again with emotion. "Kath—"

"Don't you say my name!" Kath yelled furiously. "You have no right! Not after what you did!"

Eirene came forward, too, her voice soothing. "Kath, please listen—"

"Listen? Mother, I've spent my entire life watching how sad it made you whenever anyone mentioned her, or whenever you thought about her. I've spent my whole life listening to how sad you and Father were whenever you talked about it. This…this…Lady Mechanic hurt you! How can you even let her in our house?"

Mari tried again. "Kath, I didn't know—"

"I thought Mechanics knew everything! Well, you don't! There's a lot you don't know, and when the daughter of Jules gets to Caer Lyn I hope she—"

"Kath!" Eirene's voice cut across the room like the crack of a whip and Kath finally subsided, looking worriedly at her mother. "You know you are never to speak of such things, you know how dangerous it is to talk about them, especially in front of a Mech—" She bit off the last word. "I'm sorry, Mari."

"No," Mari replied. "You're right. Saying that in front of a Mechanic, another Mechanic that is, would be very dangerous. Please, Kath, listen to your mother…" Mari gave Eirene a stunned look. "I mean, listen to our mother. I don't want you to be hurt."

"Then why—" Kath began, anger rising again.

"Quiet, young lady!" Eirene ordered. "You will listen now. Mari was eight years old when she was taken from us, just a little girl younger than you, and that Guild lied to her and deceived her and made her believe that we had cut her off. They kept all of our letters from her and they kept all of her letters from us. Mari has spent ten years believing that we wanted nothing to do with her. We are not the only ones who were hurt."

Kath stared at Mari again. "You still could have tried."

Mari nodded. "You're right. And I should I have tried. But I was too scared," she said in a small voice. "Too scared of what I might find if I came here. If it hadn't had been for Alain…" She gestured toward him and smiled.

Off balance, Kath focused on Alain. "Who is he? Another Mechanic?"

It was Eirene's turn to be uncertain. "I don't know if he is or not. Mari and I were so busy talking to each other that I didn't ask about her friend. I suppose he is another—"

Alain bowed slightly toward Eirene. "I am not a Mechanic."

"Oh," Kath said. "So you're her servant? The great and wonderful Lady Mechanic can't go anywhere without a servant to attend to her."

"I am servant to no one." Alain looked at Mari and saw her flinch, then nod reluctantly. "I am a Mage."

The room went totally silent, Eirene and Kath gaping at Alain. He could feel no other Mages anywhere nearby, so Alain risked a tiny spell, creating a very small ball of heat and then on a whim pointing his finger at a candle on the table next to Kath as he directed the ball of heat to be there. The wick of the candle burst into flame and Kath flinched back, staring at the candle as if it were a snake preparing to strike.

Mari took a quick step toward Alain, seizing his arm. "Mother, it's true that Alain is a Mage, but he is not—"

"A Mage?" Eirene asked, her voice dazed and dismayed.

"He's not like other Mages, Mother!" Mari cried desperately. "He is honest, he is brave, and he is kind. I know this. I would be dead by now if not for him. I told you that. The first time we met he saved my life."

Alain looked over at Mari. "I recall that you saved my life first."

"Fine! We saved each other. The point is, Mother, this is a very good man. This is the most wonderful man I ever met, and he treats me with all of the respect and concern I could ever ask for. Please get to know him before you judge him."

"Mari," her mother said, "the way you're talking about him. It almost sounds as if—"

Mari's grip on Alain's arm tightened. "I love him. He loves me. We haven't exchanged promises yet, but we're engaged to be wed."

Eirene's eyes widened, then she didn't so much sit down as fall into the nearest chair. "A Mage?" she whispered. "You want to marry a Mage, Mari?"

"He's different, Mother! Please get to know him, please trust me," Mari pleaded.

Kath had finally taken some steps forward, gazing at Alain. "You don't look like other Mages."

Alain bowed to her. "I am not like other Mages. Mari has given me back my feelings, and my life."

"Do you really love Mari?" Kath asked.

"Yes, I do."

"Isn't your Guild mad about that?"

Alain nodded. "My Guild seeks my death."

"Oh, wow." Kath looked at Mari. "What about your Guild? Aren't the other Mechanics upset?"

"Yes, Kath," Mari said dejectedly. "The Mechanics Guild is very unhappy with me. They're trying to capture me. We narrowly escaped them on our way here."

A big smile slowly spread across Kath's face. "You're on the run. Fleeing from your Guild because the man you love is a Mage. The two of you are giving up everything for each other! How incredibly romantic!"

Mari stared at her little sister in disbelief. "It is?"

"Oh, of course it is! You have to make sure they don't stop you from marrying the man you love! I'll bet you'll get married in some hidden place deep in the Great Woods! Or maybe far Daarendi! Fleeing lovers go there all the time."

Mari was laughing and Alain felt himself smiling, noticing Eirene watching him with wonderment. Mari looked from her mother and then back to her sister. "I haven't really thought about where we'd get married, Kath. We just got engaged a short while ago."

"The important thing is not to get caught," Kath cautioned.

"I will remember that, Kath," Mari replied, her lips quivering as she suppressed another laugh.

"What if they catch you? Can you defend yourself? You pointed something at me when I came in. Was it a Mechanic weapon?"

"Yes, Kath." Mari smiled at Alain, then brought out the weapon slowly. "Would you like to hold it?"

"Mari!" Eirene cried. "Those are deadly!"

"It's all right, Mother. I'll unload it. It will be perfectly safe." As Mari's mother watched anxiously, Mari drew the weapon, did something that Alain had never been able to figure out which caused part of it to fall into her hand, pulled back the top and peered into it, then gave the weapon to Kath. "It's called a pistol. A semi-automatic, clip-fed pistol. You won't see many like this. Most Mechanic pistols are revolvers. Don't worry. It can't fire. I took the bullets out."

Kath held the weapon awkwardly. "It can kill people?"

Mari flinched, then nodded, biting her lip. "Yes, Kath, it can kill people when it's loaded."

"Have you killed anyone with it?"

"Kath—!" her mother began.

But Mari gestured to her mother. "It's all right. Yes, Kath, I have."

Mari's voice was weighed down with sorrow. "I had to. I hope you never have to." Kath swung her arm, pointing the weapon at Alain. "Wait, Sister! Never point a weapon at someone unless you wish to harm them, and I hope you never wish to harm Alain."

Kath lowered her hand and stared at Alain. "You're really a Mage? Have you ever rescued Mari from a dragon?"

Alain shook his head. "It was the other way around. Mari rescued me from a dragon. In the Northern Ramparts, after my battle with an Imperial legion."

"You fought Imperial legions?" Kath asked, awed. "And Mari killed a dragon?"

Mari made a dismissive gesture. "It wasn't all that big a dragon."

"It was huge," Alain corrected her. "The largest I have ever seen, and you killed it with one blow from your weapon."

Kath stared down at the pistol in her hand with a dumbfounded expression.

"I didn't kill it with that," Mari assured her, gently retrieving the weapon. She put the smaller part back into the handle, pulled the top of the weapon backwards and let it slide forward again, pushed something on the side of the weapon, then returned it beneath her jacket. Only then did Mari notice how her mother and little sister had been watching her. "What?"

Eirene smiled. "You really are a Mechanic. Just watching you do that, I felt so proud of my little girl."

"She is not a little girl," Kath insisted. "She's older than me, and I am not a little girl, either."

"You tell her, Kath," Mari said with a grin. "Anyway, I didn't use my pistol to kill the dragon. It's too small to hurt a dragon."

"As we discovered at Dorcastle," Alain agreed. "You had to slay that dragon using another Mechanic creation."

"Right, but *we* killed that dragon, Alain." Mari noticed Kath staring at her again.

"My big sister has killed two dragons?" Kath asked.

"So far," Alain answered, earning himself a narrow-eyed look from Mari.

"Alain," Mari said, "you'll have my family thinking I'm dangerous."

"You are dangerous," Alain said. "You told me so yourself, and so did my Guild elders, though I think they failed to understand just how dangerous you can be."

Mari shook her head and laughed.

Her mother gave Alain a questioning look. "I have never before seen a Mage smile, and now you not only do that, but you seem to have just made a joke."

"He's different, Mother," Mari said once more.

Kath reached up tentatively for Mari's hand. "Would you like to see my room?" Mari nodded and was instantly tugged along into another part of the house, leaving Alain and Eirene standing alone.

"Sir Mage," Eirene began.

Alain held up one hand to halt her. "To the mother of Mari, as to her friends, I am Alain."

"I'm glad you're not wearing your robes… Alain." Eirene shook her head. "This is all hard enough to accept as it is. I didn't think that Mages liked other people."

"Mages are taught that other people do not exist, that they are only shadows who merit no interest or concern." Alain nodded his head in the direction which Mari and Kath had gone. "I met Mari, and it became clearer and clearer to me that other people were real, and that she was real, and that feelings should be accepted, not rejected. What I told Kath is what happened. Mari gave me back my life."

Eirene watched Alain closely as he spoke. "She's certainly done something. I've seen Mages converse, and it's very strange because they seem so inhuman. But you're far from that."

"It has been difficult to relearn how to show feelings, to accept feelings. Mari sometimes calls me a long-term project."

This time Eirene laughed. "Every man fits that description. I'm sorry I was so taken aback, but I hope you understand. There's been so much in such a short time. It's so wonderful that Mari is back with us, and that she's grown into such a splendid woman, don't you agree?"

"There is no other woman like her," Alain said, earning himself a smile from Mari's mother. "But Mari was right when she said that we cannot stay long. Mari did not wish to alarm Kath, but her Guild does seek her and wants to bring about her death. My Guild seeks to kill both of us, as do the Imperials."

"Given the sentiments that Mari expressed, I'm proud but not surprised that the Mechanics Guild is unhappy with her. The Mages and the Imperials also want to kill her and you?" Mari's mother took a deep breath. "There have been a lot of rumors lately among the common folk, stories claiming that someone like no one else has appeared. You heard Kath, what she started to say. Have you heard of the daughter of Jules, Alain?"

Alain hoped his Mage training successfully hid his reaction to the question. "I have heard of the prophecy."

"The rumors say a young woman has been seen, in the Northern Ramparts, one who has the heart of a common person, the soul of a hero, and the skills of a Mechanic, and who is traveling with a Mage." Mari's mother speared Alain with her gaze. "That's an odd coincidence, isn't it? A Mechanic traveling with a Mage. Who would have expected two such pairs in the world at the same time, and both of them not long ago in the Northern Ramparts, especially since no such pair has ever before been seen?"

"It is amazing," Alain agreed in as noncommittal a voice as he could manage.

"And the rumors say this woman slew a dragon with one blow. They also say the woman was called Mari, something that struck me as a painful coincidence when I heard it. Moreover, a ship came in late yesterday from Landfall, with the passengers claiming that Mechanics had captured the daughter of Jules and taken her to their ship. They also named her Lady Mari and said she was a Mechanic." Mari's mother looked away, closing her eyes and showing distress. "I cannot imagine how you escaped. You have tried to spare my feelings as well. Mari must be in incredible danger."

"As are you," Alain said in a low voice. "If either of the Great Guilds should suspect that she has reconciled with you and once again cares for you, then you will be their next target. You must keep this hidden, must not let anyone know that Mari once again accepts you and you accept her."

"That is wise advice." Mari's mother let out a long, slow sigh. "You are protecting her?"

"I will die before I let harm befall her."

She looked at Alain again and smiled slightly. "I believe you. Is Mari actually going to try to overthrow the Great Guilds?"

Alain struggled for an answer he could tell her. "I cannot speak of that."

"I know that Mari is my daughter, Sir Mage. But according to legend the children of Jules were scattered and hidden after her death to protect them from the Great Guilds, because already the rumor was spreading about her daughter. Now no one knows who carries the blood of Jules. Do you believe it is Mari?"

Alain stared at the floor, unable to think what else he could say. "I am bound not to speak on this matter."

"Why not? Something to do with your Guild?"

"I have made a promise. Not to my Guild."

Eirene studied him, then smiled in a tight-lipped way. "I see. A promise to Mari?"

"I am not even certain I can confirm that," Alain said, "without being called to account."

"Oh. Mari has a temper?"

"In the same way that the sea has water, yes."

Eirene grinned. "She got her temper from me, you know."

"I would not wish to offend either of you, then."

This time Mari's mother laughed. "Oh, yes. Now that I'm over the shock and have had a chance to speak with you, I think Mari did choose well. You are a very different Mage." The levity died. "But I won't put you in the position of being torn between my questions and your promise to her, even if it seems I will be your mother-in-law someday."

Alain felt one more small smile form. "Her temper is not all that Mari got from you, it seems."

"You are good, aren't you? And another smile for a moment. I wish I could meet your— You spoke of the memory of your parents. Are they dead?"

"Yes." Here, surrounded by another family, that should have hurt more, but instead it seemed to make the past easier to bear. "Both my mother and my father died six years ago, at the hands of raiders from the shores of the Bright Sea. I have seen their graves and I know this did happen." He paused, then blurted out, "I was not there when they needed me."

Eirene eyed him, then nodded in sympathy. "Sir Mage—"

"You must call me Alain."

"I'm sorry, Alain. You're about Mari's age, I guess. Yes? So, six years ago you would have been twelve? And you'd been taken by the Mages just as Mari was taken by the Mechanics, locked up in their Guild Hall? Alain, you may be powerful now, but six years ago you could have done nothing."

"I could have tried."

"Alain, listen to a mother." He met her eyes, and Eirene nodded again. "Your mother would far rather that you lived, instead of that you died trying to defend her and your father without hope of saving them. Your father would feel that way, too, I think. You could have done nothing then. But now you are strong, and you may be doing something very great. I know I would be proud of you, and glad that you lived."

He stared downward again, then forced out the words. "But I am a Mage."

"You have a Mage's powers," she replied softly. "You may call yourself a Mage and you may have been trained as a Mage. But you are not a Mage when it comes to your heart. That much is already very clear to me. Now you are a man who I believe will make my daughter a good husband, and that is something any man could take pride in. If your parents can somehow see you now, they will be happy with you. I do believe this."

Alain squeezed his eyes shut tight to hold back tears, then nodded.

"It is odd how destiny works. I brought Mari here so that she might find peace with her past, and I too have found something of that here."

"Would it be all right if I touched you, Alain? I have heard how Mages are…"

He nodded silently.

Mari's mother came closer and held Alain for a moment. He had to force himself to relax at the contact, feeling a different kind of peace from that which he felt in Mari's arms. "Keep my daughter safe, Alain," Eirene murmured. "She's going to need someone like you beside her, and if you need a mother still, I will always have enough room in my heart for someone who loves her."

"Thank you."

"She taught a Mage to say thank you?" Mari's mother laughed as she stepped back. "What a girl I have."

A short time later, Mari and Kath returned. Kath was wearing the Mechanics jacket now, the overlarge garment hanging on her smaller frame in a way that Alain found to be oddly touching. "Are you two getting along?" Mari asked in outwardly light tones, but Alain could sense the worry beneath them.

"If I wasn't married to your father, I'd try to steal Alain from you," her mother teased. Then Eirene's expression saddened as she caught sight of Kath in the jacket. "Dearest, I know that's meant well, but…"

"I'm sorry." Mari hastily took back the jacket. "I know how you must feel about my having been taken by the Guild."

"I couldn't bear to have Kath taken as well. There's been more than one nightmare about that in the years since you left." Her mother gazed at Mari. "When were you going to tell me about the daughter of Jules thing?"

Mari stopped moving, then her expression turned furious as she glared at Alain. "You told her?"

"No," Alain denied.

"I guessed," Mari's mother added. "Your man here did his best not even to let me know that I'd gotten warm. He still won't tell me anything because of a promise he made to someone."

"He told you about the promise, then," Mari grumbled, her anger shading into stubbornness.

"I had to pry that out of him, too. Let him tell me, Mari."

"No! It's not safe! The less you know—" Mari's face reddened. "The less you know, the more danger you might be in. I've been so angry at Senior Mechanics for hiding the truth, and here I am trying to keep the truth from my own family." She looked from her mother to her little sister, then exhaled in frustration. "Fine. Tell her."

"I have seen that Mari will bring a new day to this world," Alain said. "I have seen that she is the daughter of the prophecy. A great storm approaches which will endanger all of this world, but she can stop it."

Mari's mother sat down again, breathing deeply. "I still see you as my little eight-year-old, Mari. But you're grown, with a man of your own, and it seems your fate is to be the person this world has long awaited."

"Mother." Mari knelt by her mother, her face anguished. "Please. I'm your daughter."

"You'll always be my daughter," her mother agreed, once again touching Mari's face gently. "But perhaps Jules is back there in our ancestry as well."

"Mother, I know that must be true, but I really cannot deal with that. I'm just me. I'm trying to fix things. And I will, if I can." Mari lowered her head. "I didn't ask for this. I don't want it. But I have to try. I have to succeed."

Kath came up beside them, her mouth still open in surprise. "Mari? You're the daughter of Jules? Oh, my stars. My big sister is the daughter."

Eirene spoke harshly. "And that is the very last time you will say that, Kath. To anyone. If you do, it may mean the death not only of you, but of me and your father as well. Many powerful people do not want the daughter to succeed. They will kill her if they can, and anyone else who they think is helping her." Kath gazed wide-eyed at her mother, horrified. "Not one word, Kath. Not to anyone."

"If I caused harm to come to you," Mari said, "I couldn't endure that. Please listen to Mother, Kath. Mother, sooner or later Mechanics will come here, trying to find out whether I've contacted you. You have to pretend you never heard from me, that as far as you're concerned I'm no longer part of this family. Give them their own lie back to them and they'll believe it."

"I will, Mari." Eirene let fury show. "I won't have trouble seeming to be angry when they ask about you. Those other Mechanics may think that I'm enraged at the thought of you, but I'll be aiming it at them."

Alain nodded. "Do the same if Mages ask of Mari or me. Mages can tell when a common person lies. But if you form the lie right, they can be misled. Tell them you hate Mechanics and would not help them. Tell them you have not seen a Mage, and think of what you said about me, that I am not any longer what they would consider a Mage."

Mari's mother listened intently. "We can do that. Right, Kath? And of course your father will be able to say that he never saw you and not be lying at all."

"Mother," Mari said helplessly. "I don't want to leave. Not ever again. But every moment we are here is a mortal danger to you."

Eirene stood, reaching to rest her hand on Alain's arm. "I know you must go, but remember that we're now your family too, Alain. Assuming that Mari doesn't change her mind about marrying you, but women in this family tend to be a bit stubborn when they've decided upon something, as you may have noticed."

He looked down at her hand, feeling something fill him as if he were drawing on power. The sensation staggered Alain for a moment. Then he smiled at Mari's mother. "Mari has brought me many things, but I did not expect this. Thank you."

Mari grinned as she hugged her mother. "Now I have to marry him, don't I?" Her smile went away. "Take Alain's advice. If anybody asks you what my plans are, you can honestly say that you don't know. Oh, stars above, if only Father had been here. But Alain is right, we need to be gone as quickly as possible."

Eirene glanced at Alain and sighed. "I wish your father could have met Alain. A Mage in the family may be a hard sell for your father, Mari. Kath and I will work on him, though."

"Father really doesn't like Mages," Kath agreed. "You should hear him."

"Wait here, Mari and Alain, and say your goodbyes to Kath," Mari's mother instructed. "I'll be right back." She dashed off deeper into the house.

Mari turned to Kath. "Hey, little sis. You take good care of Mother and Father for me, all right?"

"Yes, Lady Mechanic." Kath smiled. "I'm glad you came back."

"Thank you. I only wish I had done it years ago. I'm very glad to know I have a sister, and I'm very glad she's you."

"Are you still really a Mechanic, Mari?"

She thought about that before answering. "Yes. I'm a Mechanic in terms of what I know and what I can do. I'm still proud of that. But I'm not a Mechanic in the other ways, thinking that I'm better than anyone else and that I can do anything I want to other people."

"Good." Kath smiled at Alain, too. "Can you teach me Mage things someday?"

"It is very difficult," Alain said. "Perhaps someday we can try."

Eirene came back into the room and shoved a bag at Mari. "Here. Take this, you two. We didn't have much in the way of prepared food handy, but what we did have is yours. Wherever you're going, I'm sure you'll need food. You'll be able to find drink, I trust. Oh, and there were some cookies which Kath hadn't eaten yet, so I put those in, too. Sorry, Kath."

"Cookies?" Mari's face crumpled up at the word, and she looked like she was about to cry again. "It's been…so long."

"Too long," Eirene agreed, tearing up as well. "I know you have to go, but don't let's wait another ten years before we see you again, young lady."

Mari hastily changed out her coat again, concealing the Mechanics jacket in her bag, then checked her weapon. "Kath, remember you have to lie about seeing us and about still hating me. You have to help protect Mother, Father and yourself."

"And not one word about you being…you know who." Kath nodded and gave Alain a serious look. "Take care of my big sister. Mari is depending on you."

Despite his growing sense of urgency, Alain took a moment to bow to her. "I will do my best to follow your advice, Lady Kath."

Kath bowed back to him. She gestured to Mari, then leaned up to whisper something to her.

Mari nodded back quickly, then faced her mother, visibly bracing herself. "Mother, there's a chance we'll never see each other again. I may not live long enough for that. Know that I will be thinking of you as long as I live, and that I never stopped loving you, even though for far too long I tried to pretend to myself that I had."

Eirene reached out to give Mari another embrace. "My hopes and my love go with you, dearest Mari. I'd be lying like a Mage—sorry, Alain—I'd be an awful liar if I said I wasn't worried, but I'm also very proud. Be careful. Alain, take care of my little girl, and help her do what she must do."

"I will," Alain promised as Mari's mother led the way to the back door.

"You're going to the harbor?" Eirene asked. "Head south along the alley a little way until you reach the access going east, then take the road where it comes out and follow that to the southeast."

"All right." Mari hesitated. "Alain? What's wrong?"

He looked out toward the front of the house. "I sense a warning. There is some danger in that direction."

"Mages?"

"I do not sense other Mages."

Mari turned a stricken look on her mother. "Mechanics. Coming here already."

# CHAPTER ELEVEN

Mari hesitated, her expression filled with dismay, for what seemed to Alain to be a long time even though he knew it was actually only for a few moments. "Alain, how bad is it?"

He frowned, trying to gain a better sense of the danger. "It does not feel as bad as what we have seen in the past. More as if…it were something that *may* be."

"If we're here when the Mechanics show up?" Mari said. "Mother, we're heading out fast. Remember my advice, say you haven't seen us, and everything should be fine. We'll be watching until we know you're safe." She grabbed her mother one more time, holding her tight, then tore herself away. "Come on, Alain."

"Be safe," Eirene called, then turned to Kath. "Get in the bath."

"What?" Kath protested.

"If those Mechanics come here, and you're in the bath, they won't think we've just had guests of any kind. Get moving, young lady."

Alain nodded in farewell to Mari's mother and protesting little sister, then followed Mari as she hastened up the alley. "You said we will watch?" he asked.

"There's a place." Mari gazed at him intently, but Alain did not think she was really seeing him, instead focusing on her memories. "If it's still there. This way." She turned into another narrow way, concealing her pistol under her coat and moving briskly but not so fast as to arouse notice.

Alain followed a short distance behind, watching for anyone who might be watching Mari as she turned west, then north again, the streets and alleys climbing enough that the slope wore at his pace. Finally she cut south before pausing where a short street came to an end. Catching up with Mari as she crouched behind bushes bordering the barrier halting further travel, Alain saw that they were positioned some distance from the front door of Mari's old home but could clearly see it down the slope.

She brought out the Mechanic device Mari called a far-seer, placing it to her eyes. "I'd hide here sometimes," she whispered to Alain. "When I was little. I'd play spy with my friends and pretend Mother was an enemy I'd been assigned to watch."

She swung her head and the far-seer slightly, looking up the street. "Carriage. Two Mechanics. Only two? I can't see any rifles."

Alain could not make out details at this distance, but he could see the open coach carrying the Mechanics halt outside the bright green door. Both of the Mechanics got out, the driver remaining in his seat to control the horses.

Mari tensed. "I recognize one of the Mechanics. Master Mechanic Samal. I know him. He's a decent man. Why did it have to be Samal?"

"Perhaps that is a good thing," Alain said.

Samal and the other Mechanic walked up to the green door and knocked, the sound carrying up to Mari and Alain.

After a short period which served to increase their tension, the door opened and Alain saw Mari's mother in the same posture with which she had first greeted Mari. Outwardly respectful—but also clearly resentful.

"If only I could hear them," Mari muttered fiercely. "They haven't manhandled Mother yet, though."

Alain could see Mari's mother shaking her head, saying something he couldn't make out except for the angry tones in which she spoke. The Mechanic with Samal rudely gestured Mari's mother aside and the two Mechanics entered.

The pause this time was longer. Mari jerked as a sudden high-pitched cry came through the open door of the house.

"That is not your mother," Alain said.

"No. It has to be Kath. They'd better not—"

The two Mechanics came out the door, laughing to each other.

Another shout came from the house, this one clearly young, feminine and outraged.

To Alain's surprise, Mari started shaking with suppressed laughter. "Kath. Mother told her to get in the bath, remember? Those Mechanics must have gone in to make sure we weren't hiding in there."

"Kath sounds upset."

"Upset? Alain, don't ever walk in on a girl near Kath's age while she's taking a bath. Upset does not begin to measure the reaction you'll get." Mari had relaxed, grinning at the scene through the bushes screening them from view. "Mother did it just right. She must have told them she hadn't seen me and didn't ever want to see me, and then Kath provided a great distraction when they searched the house."

The Mechanics were getting into their carriage. The one Mari had called Master Mechanic Samal was speaking sharply to the one beside him. "I wonder who that is with Samal?" Mari murmured, the far-seer still to her eyes. "I don't recognize him, but I get the feeling that he told Samal to do this."

"Perhaps now that other is discredited in his eyes," Alain said.

"I think so. Samal looks annoyed, and he wasn't easy to annoy. Believe me, when we were apprentices we tried."

"It worries me sometimes when you speak of the things you did as an apprentice," Alain whispered back to her.

Her grin widened even though Mari's gaze remained on the Mechanic carriage which had surged into motion, the clop of the horses' hooves echoing from surrounding buildings. "If you only knew the whole truth, dear Mage, you might not be so eager to promise yourself to me." Mari finally looked away from her far-seer for a moment, her eyes on his. "Did that go as well for you and my mother as I thought it did?"

"I had a strange feeling in your home, Mari," he said.

"Strange? Um… it's understandable that you felt a bit awkward."

"No, not that." Alain tried to put his thoughts into words. "When you and Kath reconciled, when your mother offered me a place in your family, I felt…I felt as if I were in a place where much power was concentrated."

Mari frowned at him. "You mean Mage power, the stuff you draw on to do those spells? My family house is located where a lot of that is available?"

"No." Alain shook his head, frustrated. "I cannot explain it because I do not understand it. It was if the people there added to the power I might be able to draw upon. This should not be possible, and I am not sure I could have used that power. It was, as I said, strange."

She watched him intently for a while. "Let me know if you ever figure it out. You could have knocked me over with your little finger when my mother said it was your family, too. Isn't she wonderful?"

"I see where you get it from," Alain said.

Mari gave a pained laugh as the carriage of Mechanics turned down another street and was lost to sight. "Still delusional, I see. Wasn't Kath great? Far Daarendi! Could you believe it?"

"I would prefer Daarendi to a hidden place deep in the Great Wood," Alain confided.

"I remember when I was that age. The romantic fantasies I wove!"

"Would you tell me some of them?"

"No! They'd be far too embarrassing now. Ridiculous stuff. You know, meeting some impossibly wonderful man and then we'd go off and have adventures together."

"That does not sound so ridiculous," Alain observed.

Her smile slowly grew as she looked at him. "No. Maybe it's not."

❖ ❖ ❖

Alain felt no further hint of warning, and the attitude of the Mechanics as they left Mari's family home had betrayed no trace of peril, but Alain and Mari kept walking along the road as fast as they could without attracting much attention, hoping to get a ship out of Caer Lyn before the day was out. They saw a few other Mechanics passing on the streets, but none nearby and none showing signs of alertness or alarm. Whatever had caused the Mechanics to visit Mari's family home had not resulted in any further activity.

"A routine check," Mari speculated. "Maybe they hadn't heard that I'd been captured by that ship and were following earlier orders to see if I had contacted my family."

After that, Mari seemed preoccupied during the walk toward the area near the docks where the sailing schedules would be posted and tickets available for purchase. For his part, Alain worried about the ship on which he and Mari had originally set out for Caer Lyn. Mari's mother had said the *Sun Runner* had arrived here late yesterday evening, and many commons on that ship had seen Mari. It was one more complication, one more set of people who they would hopefully avoid running into before they got out of this city.

But despite his internal concerns Alain couldn't help noticing the way Mari kept giving him looks out of the corners of her eyes. Sometimes the looks seemed appraising, sometimes happy, sometimes worried. "Is something wrong?" Alain finally asked.

Mari looked startled. "Wrong? No. I was just thinking."

"Is it anything I can help with?"

"Maybe." She was looking ahead, biting her lower lip.

"Is it something dangerous that concerns you? Should I be worried?"

Mari took a moment to answer. "No, it's not some danger. The streets feel very calm." She paused. "So as for whether you should worry, that would depend upon what sort of things worry you."

"I have no idea what that means."

"I'm just thinking about things! There's something I have to decide." Mari looked up at the afternoon sun. "And I think I need to decide soon. Those Mechanics who came to my old home really centered me on the issue of not knowing what each new moment will bring. Will we even live to reach Altis? What if my Guild intercepts whatever ship we get out of here?"

"I am concerned about that as well."

She hesitated before speaking again. "Alain, I want you to be completely honest with me. You told me that when I was transmitting about you Asha couldn't actually read my thoughts, she just knew I was thinking about you but couldn't tell any more than that. Is that really true?"

Having hoped that Mari had somehow miraculously forgotten the issue of Asha being able to detect her when Mari was thinking of him, Alain was not thrilled by the question, but he nodded firmly. "That is true. She knows only that I am the subject of your thoughts. She cannot tell what those thoughts are. No one can."

"Not even you?" Mari asked with a half-smile. "Can she...tell what we're doing when I'm thinking about you?"

"Asha?" Alain puzzled over the question. "No. She said she could not, and I do not see how she could. At this moment, for example, she could not tell that we were walking. Why do you ask?"

"It's just something that I needed to know." Mari fell silent again.

Alain gave it up, walking quietly alongside her and gazing ahead for any Mechanics as he also cautiously felt for signs of Mages nearby. Some other Mages were here, but none of them were bothering to hide their presence, a good sign that Alain's own arrival in Caer Lyn remained unnoticed. Once he spotted the black jackets of more Mechanics in the distance, the Mechanics in a small group and not acting as if they were alarmed at all.

By the time they actually reached the area near the waterfront, the afternoon was far gone. Mari led them to the wall boards on which sailing schedules were posted, hastily studying the list. "There. The *White Wing*. That's the one we need. It sails on the tide, which isn't that long off, but it gives us enough time." She hesitated. "Just enough time, maybe. Can you get us tickets while I take care of something else?"

Alain nodded. "I have bought tickets before, so I can do the same here, but what—?"

"One cabin!" Mari called, already heading off up the street at high speed. "Make it a good one if we can afford it, and make sure it's private!"

"But—"

"One cabin!" By that time Mari was far enough away that Alain gave it up and went to the agent to purchase the tickets.

The *White Wing* proved to have a few cabins left. Alain looked at the costs, regretting once again that Mage training paid little attention to such practical issues as how to handle money. Mages could stay or go anywhere they wanted since no one dared refuse them, but such extortion would draw far too much attention to him right now even if he hadn't developed a most unmagelike conscience. Now, without Mari on hand, Alain was not certain how much he should pay.

The agent noticed him hesitating, and smiled encouragingly. "You want the *White Wing*? Tell you what, since she's about to sail and needs to fill those cabins, I'll give a good deal on one." He named a price, then looked expectantly at Alain.

Alain tried to look like he was considering the offer, while wondering if it was actually a good price. "That is for two?"

"If you're sharing a bed."

"Yes." There was something else Mari had said was important. "It is private?"

"Absolutely!" the agent beamed, then winked at him.

What did that mean? But at least Alain was certain this man did not conceal ill-will, just a false sort of friendship probably aimed at convincing Alain to buy what the man sold. "All right." Alain nodded to the agent, then counted out money slowly enough to watch the agent and know when there was enough.

"You'd best not waste any time getting to the landing," the agent advised. "There have been some rumors about the harbor being closed soon."

Alain stepped back out onto the street and looked around for Mari, feeling a pang of worry when she was not immediately visible. But a moment later she came into view up the street, beckoning him. "Hurry!" she called.

"But the ship—"

"I know! Come on!"

Shaking his head, Alain trotted to join her, only to have his hand grabbed as Mari urged him along faster. "In here." He found himself in a plain office-type room, facing a disinterested-looking woman seated at an unadorned desk. Mari seized a piece of paper on the desk and thrust it at him along with a pen. "Sign this right here."

Alain looked at the indicated place. "What is this?"

"Just sign!"

They had been in plenty of situations before where one of them had to trust in and immediately follow the instructions of the other. Alain awkwardly scrawled his signature, wondering if anyone else would actually be able to read it. Penmanship had not been a major concern of Mage training. As soon as Alain finished, Mari scooped up the document and passed it to the woman at the desk along with several coins.

The woman glanced at the paper, counted the coins, then looked at Mari as she recited in a bored voice. "Do you make this promise of your own free will, with no thought of deceit or reservation?"

Mari nodded. "Yes."

The woman looked at Alain. "You?" she asked in the same bored tone.

Alain stared at her, then at Mari who was nodding vigorously at him. "Uh, yes."

The woman signed the paper, picked up a stamp and slammed it down on the document, slammed the stamp down on another document which she handed to Mari, then without looking at them spoke again in her jaded, monotone voice. "Congratulations on behalf of the people and city of Caer Lyn. May your lives be filled with the joy of this day." She tossed the first document into a file nearby. "And now we're closed, so please do any celebrating outside."

Mari took Alain's hand again, pulling him out and back down the street toward the docks as she stuffed the paper she had been given into one of her coat pockets.

"Mari," Alain asked, "what is that paper? What just happened in there?"

She looked back at the place they had left, her expression shifting, walking so fast that Alain had trouble keeping up. "In there?"

"Yes. In there. What did I sign and what did we just do?"

Mari's face worked with indecision. "We, um, we…"

"Mari?"

"We got married," Mari forced out quickly, not looking at him.

"What?" Alain asked.

"We got married," she repeated. "You said you wanted to. You proposed to me back at that inn west of Umburan."

"Yes, but—"

"And I said yes last night and gave you my proposal, too, and you accepted that. So we got married."

Alain stared at her. "I had expected a marriage to be a little different."

Mari nodded, smiling brightly but still looking straight ahead as she kept walking fast. "I know wedding customs in Ihris probably aren't the same as they are here."

"Mari, I know nothing of customs for marriages in Ihris or anywhere else, but I had thought that no matter where a marriage occurred, the man would know when it is taking place."

"Well, I admit that is usually done." Mari glanced very quickly and anxiously at Alain, then down at the ground as they walked. "It was just a civil ceremony. I'm nineteen and you're eighteen so it's perfectly legal and will be recognized anywhere, though of course we won't be telling people our true names. We did use them on the marriage document but without our Guild titles it'll just be one more piece of filed-away paperwork that our Guilds will never locate. We can do something bigger and more formal later if you want. Invite guests. That sort of thing."

"That is hardly the point, Mari. Such an important event, such an important decision—"

"We did have a guest, you know," she added, still keeping her eyes averted. "You said destiny would be there, and I know it was. It felt very special for me. I felt very special."

"I was simply confused and doing what I was told," Alain replied.

"From what I've heard, that's not all that unusual for men at weddings." Mari stopped abruptly, turning to face him, looking directly at Alain with a pleading expression. "We only had a few moments. They were closing. There wasn't time to explain. You said you wanted to marry me."

"I do." Alain rubbed his forehead, trying to absorb what had happened. "I mean, I did. I just did not expect it now."

Mari took a deep breath, closing her eyes, apprehension in her expression and her voice. "Alain, you and I have cheated death a number of times already. In some cases only luck saved us. There are plenty of powerful enemies still trying to kill us. Our luck could run out any day. Any moment. We talked about that." She opened her eyes to look directly into his, her face suddenly calm. "I realized something after we left my family's house. If I die tomorrow or next month or even today before the sun sinks any more in that sky, I want it to be as your promised partner in this life."

"I…" It finally sank in. For only the second time in his life, the first being while the caravan he was protecting was being blown apart around him, Alain felt completely unable to think. "I…"

"I know it was selfish of me. I should have given you a chance to say if you wanted it that way, too."

It was just so hard to grasp. Alain's mind stayed stuck. He could not speak.

Her face started to crumple up in sorrow. "You didn't really want me, did you? You're unhappy."

The thought of her tears somehow got his brain moving. "Mari, I am very happy. We will be together always now?"

She nodded, wiping at her eyes. "Mostly, at least. I hope."

"Then this is the most wonderful as well as the most unforeseen day of my life. But at the moment I am also very, very overcome with feelings. I do love you, I do want you, but I cannot find any other words right now."

Mari gave him an unsteady look. "Then you're not mad at me?"

"I do wish I had known what was going on."

"She only stayed as long as she did because I bribed her!"

Alain laughed. For a moment, every day of his life as an acolyte and a Mage, detached from all other people, seemed like a long, bad dream from which he had only just been awakened. "You told me you are impulsive. I should have taken the warning and been prepared for something like this."

"Exactly," Mari agreed, grinning. "You should have expected this. I don't know why I should have to explain it." She tugged at him again, getting them back into motion toward the docks.

Mari leaned in to kiss his cheek as they walked rapidly toward the docks. "I'm so happy. Even though there are still lots of people trying to capture or kill us. You're going to be happy, too. I just know it."

"I am already happy," Alain protested. "Completely overwhelmed and very surprised, but happy."

She put her mouth near his ear and whispered. "Don't you remember the night you'd never forget that we once talked about? Well, now we're married, and I have some things I picked up to make sure I don't get pregnant, and by the time the sun sets we'll be in our private cabin on the ship taking us to Altis." Mari pulled back and gave him a worried look. "You did get a private cabin, didn't you?"

Alain felt his breathing stop and only got it going again with difficulty. "Y-yes."

"See, you are happy, aren't you?" she teased.

"Yes," Alain repeated. He swallowed, looking over at her. "Do we have to wait until sunset?"

Mari laughed. "Men. One thing at a time, love. Let's get to the pier before the boat to the ship casts off."

*White Wing*, when Mari and Alain passed a group of sailors trudging up from the harbor. One of the sailors glanced at them as they passed, then Alain heard a shocked exclamation. "It's her! She got away from them!"

Mari had turned toward the sound before Alain could warn her, and as he turned, too, Alain could see the entire group of sailors had come to a halt and were staring at Mari. "The daughter," a female sailor whispered in awed tones.

Another sailor pointed at Alain. "That's her friend, the one that went to help her. Her Mage."

Mari had that horrified look on her face again and seemed momentarily lost for words, so Alain spoke for them. "You are from the *Sun Runner*? It is important that no one know we escaped and arrived here."

The startled sailors all made noises of agreement, but as Alain saw the excitement in them he wondered how long their promises to keep quiet would hold.

Finally finding her own voice, Mari spoke quietly as she looked around for anyone else who might be close enough to hear. "Please do as my Mage says. I need to keep the Guild guessing as to where I went."

"Is there anything we can do for you?" one of the sailors asked eagerly, generating more agreement from his fellows. "It was terrible hard to let the Mechanics take you. But we did what you and your Mage said, and now we'll do anything you ask."

"Are you going back out to sea?" another asked. "Aren't you worried about that metal ship coming after you again?"

Mari shook her head. "That ship isn't going to be giving anyone else any problems for a long time to come."

"You stopped that ship?" All of the sailors looked at Mari in awe, which Alain could see startled her.

"When are you going to move against the Great Guilds?" the first sailor asked again.

"I don't know yet. There are things I have to do first," Mari said.

"How long?" the female sailor pleaded. "Years?"

Mari gazed back at her. "No. Months. Maybe a year."

"And then we'll be free?"

"Free." Mari looked down, then back up at the sailors. "I hope so. Nothing is certain. But I'm going to do my best. The Great Guilds are very powerful, and I need to be ready to confront them. Spread the word for everyone to... to stay calm, and wait to hear. They will hear when I start doing things. Change is coming. Now, thank you, but please, we have to hurry."

The sailors straightened up as if someone had commanded them, then the eldest brought his hand to his brow in a salute that the others copied. "May the stars shine on you, Lady Mari."

Mari blinked in surprise, then smiled quickly again and tugged at Alain. "Thank you. We have to go. Please say nothing." Pulling Alain along, Mari fled down toward the pier.

Once out of earshot of the sailors, Alain looked back to see them in a group talking together excitedly. "We must hope that no one else noticed them all saluting you, but by nightfall some of them will be drunk and speaking of seeing you here."

"I know," Mari groaned. "How did they know my name?"

"The Mechanics who arrested you used it, and the commons on the *Sun Runner* heard. Some of them spoke your name in my hearing before I was taken from the *Sun Runner*. Your mother told me that the rumors from the north have also carried the name Mari with them."

"Oh, great. Lady Mari." She sighed heavily as they rushed on toward the pier. "From you I like that, but if everyone is going to be using it as some sort of title I'd almost rather be called the daughter."

The conversation reminded Alain of something else. "Who is Mara?"

Mari turned a perplexed look on him. "Where did you hear that name?"

"On the *Sun Runner*. Someone said you might be Mara, whoever that is."

Mari was looking straight ahead. "I'm not Mara. That's all you have to know. And don't you ever, ever call me that. Understand?"

"Yes, but—"

"How did they know that you're a Mage?"

"I had to reveal that to keep them from charging the Mechanics after you went down the ladder."

"Lady Mari and her Mage," Mari sighed. "To think once I was just Master Mechanic Mari. What ship are we looking for again?"

"The *White Wing*." They were at the waterfront now and rushing toward a boat where the sailors were already untying the lines holding it to the pier.

"Hold on!" Mari cried, then she and Alain ran the last distance to the boat.

A ship's officer who wasn't trying to hide his annoyance looked at their tickets, then waved them aboard before shouting at his crew to get moving.

As Mari and Alain settled in on some seats, an older couple facing them nodded in greeting. "Good thing you made it," the man commented. "The sailors heard something a little while ago about the Imperials or one of the Great Guilds wanting to shut down this harbor. They wanted to be sure their ship got out before that happened."

Mari spoke in the puzzled voice of an innocent traveler. "Why would the Imperials or one of the Great Guilds want to close this harbor?"

"Who knows? There has been a lot strangeness going around these days. Rumors, you know." The older man glanced around for Mechanics or Mages within earshot, then nodded with grim satisfaction. "She has come at last. The masters know their days are numbered."

His wife smiled in anxious agreement, then bent a concerned look at Mari. "You look a bit like the descriptions we've heard of her," the woman whispered. "Best be careful of any Mages or Mechanics you see. They might mistake you for her."

Her husband frowned at Mari. "She doesn't look anything like her."

"I'm sure you're right, dear," his wife said with a conspiratorial wink to Mari.

Mari winked back, then smiled at Alain.

The wife smiled wider. "I know that look. Newlyweds?"

"As of about twenty minutes ago," Mari replied.

"There, you see?" the husband said. "She couldn't be the daughter. No one ever said the daughter would be married."

"No one ever said she wouldn't be," the wife rejoined. "Congratulations to you both. Perhaps your children will be free."

"They will be," Mari said with a calm certainty that drew looks of surprise from both man and woman.

The wife gazed at her with a sudden suspicion dawning, then smiled again, this time proudly. "I am very glad to have met you."

The boat had no sooner pulled alongside the *White Wing* than the passengers were hustled up the accommodation ladder and the boat itself hooked up to its davits and raised into position. Mari and Alain were still walking across the deck when a whistle sounded and sailors raced into the rigging above them to unfurl sails. The *White Wing* lived up to her name as brilliant expanses of white canvas filled in the breeze, catching the wind and bringing the ship around as the anchor was rapidly hauled in.

Mari brought Alain to the rail, where they watched as the ship bore across the harbor, tacking once to clear the breakwater, and out into the open sea. The sun was setting now, dropping in the west behind the mountains of the largest of the Sharr Isles. In the harbor some other merchant ships were also scrambling to get underway, but Mari pointed past them. "Look at the sailors going up into the rigging on those Imperial warships. They're getting ready to move. And those people on the breakwater, I bet you that they're preparing to raise the chain across the harbor mouth."

"This might have been the last ship to get out of the harbor," Alain observed.

Mari sighed. "Even though it almost caused us to be stuck here, I don't regret taking the time to marry you before we left. Do you think we'll ever be back here?"

"Perhaps not, since these islands are dominated by the Empire. But we can see your family again even if we never return here. They may need to leave for their own safety."

Her hand tightened on his. "*Our* family, Alain. Remember? It's official now that we're married."

"I have felt it was so since your mother spoke those words." Alain looked at her, trying to smile. "This day I have gained a wife and a family."

"Uh-huh." Mari's smile became wicked. "Speaking of which, the sun is setting, Alain. Maybe we should see what our cabin is like. You know, how comfortable it is. What the bed is like. Stuff like that."

He barely had time to ensure that the door to their cabin was locked behind them before she was in his arms, kissing him and pulling at his clothing.

# CHAPTER TWELVE

On the third day out from Caer Lyn, Mari had relaxed sufficiently to suggest that they mingle a little with the other passengers. "If my Guild hasn't intercepted this ship by now, we should be safe for the rest of the journey. We could try to find some commons our age and see what they're like. We can't spend the entire voyage in our cabin."

"I like being together in our cabin," Alain replied.

"You like being together in our bed in our cabin! Even on a honeymoon couples are supposed to get out and breathe fresh air every once in a while."

"Being on a honeymoon gives us the perfect excuse for staying in our cabin where no one can recognize you," Alain pointed out.

"Alain, I will suffocate if I don't get out a bit," Mari said. "As much as I love you and as much I'm enjoying getting physical with my new husband, I cannot endure being locked in a room for days on end. I need freedom."

He had finally understood, then, and agreed to try to mingle with others. Which was a big concession from someone who had been brought up as a Mage, Mari knew. She thanked him with a kiss, which led to another, which led to other things.

They managed to make it out of their cabin for dinner.

The dining room on the ship was fairly fancy, decked out with shining brass and gleaming woodwork. The dining room ran across the entire width of the ship, and portholes on both sides provided light and could be opened for air in good weather. Mari led Alain toward a table where five men and women about their age were already seated and eating, introducing herself and Alain using the false names on their current set of forged Imperial identification papers.

Two of the men and one of the women were in the Western Alliance military, the other man and woman friends of theirs, the entire group finishing up a trip to the Sharr Isles "while things are sort of quiet," as one of the soldiers put it.

Mari mostly listened, trying to get a better feel for these people who were like her and yet not like her. She had spent most of her childhood in a Mechanics Guild Hall, learning not only the science and technology of the Mechanic arts but also living within the closed society of the Mechanics Guild. Commons had lived very different lives. They represented diverse cultures, but all had been brought up in the shadow of the Great Guilds, whereas Mari had been taught to be one of their rulers. Never comfortable with that role, Mari had grown increasingly ashamed of what she had once believed to be the proper order of things.

Most of the conversation among the commons was about things they had done together and spots they had visited, but Mari's attention was caught when she heard a certain name. "Flyn's in command of part of the army of Ihris," one of the Western Alliance soldiers said. "They hired him away from Alexdria."

"After that mess on the last raid he commanded?" another one of the soldiers asked. "His force got cut to pieces."

Mari was thinking about whether or not to ask more about Flyn when she heard Alain speaking.

"That was not the fault of General Flyn," Alain said, betraying an unusual amount of emotion. Fortunately, an unusual amount of emotion for a Mage appeared just mildly upset to other people. "His force was betrayed, ambushed by a full legion backed by many Mages."

The others focused on Alain. "How do you know about it?" one asked.

Mari answered before Alain could. "His brother was up there."

One of the women leaned forward eagerly. "Did he see the daughter?"

"Oh, come on, Patila," one of her companions laughed.

"All of the soldiers with Flyn saw her," Patila insisted. "And a lot of Mechanics went through later looking for her. I have a friend who personally talked to them, or was interrogated by them I guess I should say, and those Mechanics were looking for a woman about our age."

"Yeah, I know, but that doesn't make her the daughter of Jules. The stories say she was wearing a Mechanics jacket."

"But she fixed things for free, and gave away stuff to help injured commons. Does that sound like any Mechanic you ever met?" Patila gazed at Alain again. "Did your brother see her?"

Alain nodded. "He did."

Mari watched the others, trying to judge their reactions.

"Did she seem like the daughter?" Patila asked excitedly.

Alain glanced at her, and Mari nodded ever so slightly.

"Yes," Alain said. "He was certain of it."

One of the men looked skeptical, but the others exchanged looks filled with emotion. "I hope you're right," the other woman said. "We need her. When we left home, everything felt…what's the word?"

"Tight as a drum," the skeptical man said. "And ready to snap from being pulled too tight. Like those civil disturbances near Genese."

"There was rioting in Palandur recently," Mari said.

"Really? In the Imperial capital?" The man shook his head. "This world is going to blazes like a raft going over a waterfall, and I don't see where anyone can stop it."

"Hey, lighten up," the second soldier said with a grin. "We're still on vacation for a few more days. Let's talk about something fun."

"Such as?"

"Uh…hey, that other story, the one we heard from some Imperials in Caer Lyn the night before we left."

"You mean Mara?" Patila asked with a roll of her eyes.

"Yeah. It really had them spooked," the soldier explained to Mari and Alain. "Have you heard about it?"

Mari shook her head wordlessly, aiming a warning look at Alain as she did so.

"Well," the soldier began, obviously relishing the chance to tell the story, "apparently there had been some worries about Mara before, just superstitious stuff. In most places Mara is just a creepy legend to tell stories about around the fire, but I guess you Imperials take her a lot more seriously. The Imperials told us that somebody got out of Marandur recently, which is supposed to be impossible. You know, the dead city?"

"We've heard of it," Mari replied dryly.

"Oh, yeah, of course you guys would know about it. According to the Imperials I talked to, there were a lot of funny noises in the city, where nobody is alive to make funny noises, and soon after footprints were found coming out, right through the area where there were legionaries guarding the city. Somebody snuck right through the Imperial sentries and then vanished completely."

"Mages can be invisible," one of his companions pointed out.

"Yeah, but they can't fly without a Roc, and legionaries couldn't miss a Roc. From all I hear, those guys are really sharp. Anyway, half the Empire has been trying to find whoever escaped and having no luck at all. So," the soldier leaned forward, grinning, "the Imperials are starting to say it was Mara who left Marandur, that she'd been at Maran's tomb, maybe trapped there for a long time, but now somebody let her out and she's running free." He laughed loudly. "I can't believe the Emperor would encourage that kind of superstition. Every young man in the Empire must be checking the teeth of every attractive girl he sees."

"If Mara leaves the Empire," the other woman suggested slyly, "maybe you guys will have to worry about that. You're just the right age for her appetite."

"See? That's what I mean! How can making guys nervous around good-looking women serve any good purpose?"

"Maybe it's a stratagem," Patila replied. "I'm serious. If the daughter really has appeared, that could create problems for more people than the Great Guilds. What's the Empire's first priority?"

Mari answered. "Control. Stability. Just like the Great Guilds."

The woman soldier nodded. "Right. Does the Emperor want the daughter running loose inside the Empire, stirring up the common folk?

Not on your life. But if the common folk of the Empire think she's really Mara, they'll be even more inclined to be good little citizens so the Emperor will protect them." She looked at Mari again, embarrassed. "Sorry I put it that way."

"No, that's probably a good way of saying it," Mari assured her.

Alain was nodding, too. "It is a possibility. The Emperor would want to be able to control the daughter as well as his own people."

"Then why feed the rumors at all?" the first male soldier asked. "That's what I can't figure out, why so many people are paying attention to them right now."

Patila tapped her finger on the table to emphasize her words. "Because this time it's different. I talked to my grandfather before I left, and he said there's never been so much talk about the daughter, or so many people claiming to have actually seen her. Grandfather said that in the past every once in a while somebody would say that the daughter was coming soon, but nobody ever said she was alive and getting ready to move against the Great Guilds, and nobody ever claimed to have seen her or what she had done. She killed a big dragon in the Northern Ramparts. Lots of people saw her do it and others hiked out to see the dead body before it finally dissolved. Before that there was Dorcastle. Nobody knows exactly what the Great Guilds tried to cover up there, but somebody killed a dragon there, too, and messed up a lot of Mechanic equipment."

"And there's rumors about what happened at Ringhmon," one of the men added.

"Maybe she did go to Marandur," the second woman suggested. "I mean, Jules was in the Imperial fleet before she headed west. Maybe Jules left something in Marandur centuries ago and her daughter had to go looking for it. Why else would anyone go to that city?"

Another of the men shrugged. "Whether the rumors are true or not, the Mechanics are in an uproar. One of the ship's officers told me several of them were supposed to sail with us but got yanked off at the last minute. He said they were complaining about a Guild emergency when they left."

Mari feigned only a small amount of interest, even though she was feeling intensely curious. "A Guild emergency?"

"Yeah, like they were needed back in Caer Lyn for something."

"I wonder if the Mages are upset, too?" another soldier asked.

"Who can tell? Though if the daughter really does have a Mage with her, that would be something, wouldn't it?"

The second male soldier grinned. "It would be for her. You know what they say about Mages."

Patila glowered at him. "Pig."

The other woman was looking out the nearest porthole. "How many people have lived and died under the control of the Great Guilds? But if the daughter really has come, maybe our kids will be free."

"Maybe we'll live to be free," one of the men agreed.

Mari finally spoke again, consumed by guilt as she thought about people like these risking themselves for her. "It might be hard to gain that freedom. There might be a war."

The soldier nodded in reply, unfazed. "Yes. There's certain to be a price. Maybe a big price. I can't imagine the Great Guilds giving up easily, and with apologies to present company, I don't think the Emperor is going to be thrilled at the idea of that much change, either. But we die as it is, don't we? Dying for that…well, it might make it a lot easier." The soldier raised his glass of wine. "To freedom, and to the daughter."

Mari, Alain and the others raised their glasses as well, Mari wondering what the others would say if they knew the daughter was sitting with them.

But as the toast ended, the skeptical man shook his head. "I'd be as happy as anyone if she really came," he said in a way that didn't sound sincere to Mari, "but listen to yourselves. You're putting your hope in someone who was wearing a Mechanics jacket and working with a Mage. Why would either of them care about what happens to us?"

"Maybe," said Mari, "they both know that everyone deserves freedom, and that everyone will suffer if the world doesn't change."

"There's nothing in the prophecy about any Mechanics, though," the skeptic objected.

"There is," Alain said. "The prophecy says that the daughter will unite Mages, Mechanics, and common folk to overthrow the Great Guilds."

Patila pointed at Alain. "Yes! That's what the guy with General Flyn said the Mage told him!"

"So," the skeptic continued, "we're going to base our hopes on the word of a Mage?"

"He wasn't a normal Mage," Patila said hotly. "All right, I know it's silly to say normal and Mage. But every soldier with Flyn in that action said that Mage was special, that he saved their butts from the Imperials and nearly died more than once doing it."

Alain spoke in a voice so calm that Mari feared he would give away that he was a Mage. "You are soldiers. Think of a battle, where the foot soldiers and the cavalry and the siege machines work together to achieve victory. Now think of a battle where Mages, Mechanics and soldiers of the common folk work together as allies in one cause."

Every eye stayed on Alain, then one of the male soldiers nodded. "That would be something. Tough to beat."

"And suppose," Mari added, "that the daughter used her Mechanic skills to get new weapons made, new kinds of rifles, and lots of ammunition for them."

"That would be awesome," Patila said. "New kinds of rifles? I've never heard anyone talk about different kinds of rifles. There are just the ones the Mechanics make." She peered at Mari, puzzled. "How did you even think of something like that?"

"I heard about it," Mari said, trying to think how to cover her tracks. "Somebody was talking and…who was that guy?" she asked Alain, hoping that he could come up with something.

Alain pretended to think. "We were not able to learn his name."

Patila looked from one of them to the other doubtfully. "Who would talk about that kind of stuff? Doesn't Mechanic equipment always stay the same?"

"And it doesn't matter anyway," the skeptic said. "Help some Mechanic overthrow the Great Guilds? A Mechanic who's working with a Mage? They'd just set themselves in charge as soon as we got rid of the old bosses. Just a couple of new Great Guilds, that's all. Count me out."

"Jorge," one of the other men began. "Anything is better than—"

"No," Jorge interrupted. "People going crazy and rioting because they think things can't worse? Attacking the Great Guilds because they think they can win? Everything going to blazes because people believe that some mythical daughter is going to make everything right? How is that better?" He stood up. "I need some air."

The others watched Jorge walk out of the dining room and toward the ladder up onto the deck.

The other woman sighed. "I can't blame him for being that way. A lot of people may feel like that. I bet the Western Alliance government will feel like that. It's scary. Cities are already starting to pop. When the people hear about the daughter, it could get a lot worse."

"Nobody should do anything until the daughter says it's time," Mari insisted.

The others nodded, but Patila eyed Mari. "Do you know when that will be?"

"No," Mari said.

"How would she know?" one of the male soldiers asked Patila.

❖   ❖   ❖

Once back in their cabin, Mari sat on the bed. "What do you think?"

"I think you are revealing yourself," Alain said.

"Not on purpose," Mari said. "That thing about the rifles was because I'm not used to talking to commons. A Mechanic would have understood. For the rest…it's just…they need hope. You told me that!"

"I did." Alain stood, his eyes hooded in thought. "The things they said about violence in their cities were worrisome. I have been uncertain about your decision not to announce the arrival of the daughter, but now I see the wisdom in it."

"*Now* you see the wisdom in it?" Mari asked. "So, you didn't think it was a wise decision before?"

Alain looked at her, plainly considering his words before replying. "It was your decision to make. I withheld judgment. I did not decide either way."

"You are my husband," Mari said. "You should assume wisdom on my part."

Alain's expression changed slightly, gaining a slightly puzzled air. "This is a rule of being married?"

"Yes," Mari said. "It's one of the rules. Assume your wife is being wise when she makes a decision or says something."

"I did not know this. Is there a place where all of these rules are written down?" Alain asked.

"Um...I'll tell them to you whenever you need to know one." Mari looked at him, feeling guilty for misleading Alain. "All right. I'll tell you the truth. There aren't actually any written rules for being married."

"There are not?" Alain asked, even more puzzled now. "But it is so important. You have told me the Mechanics have written rules for how to do everything."

"Yes," Mari admitted. "They do. Construction manuals. Operating manuals. Repair manuals. Maintenance manuals. Organizational manuals. Procedural manuals. You name it."

"But there is no marriage manual?"

Mari frowned. "No. There ought to be. Shouldn't there? I wish I'd thought to ask my mother about that."

"I will trust in your wisdom, then," Alain said.

She gave him a suspicious look. "Was that sarcasm? That better not have been sarcasm. What was that thing those commons said about Mages and women? All of the commons seemed to understand."

Alain shook his head. "I do not know. Commons know so little of Mages that they create stories. On the matter of the rumors about Mara, the soldier may have been right that this is being deliberately pushed by the Emperor, though it is also possible that the Emperor is as superstitious as some of his people."

Mari winced, looking down. "Mara! What did I do to deserve that?"

"At least the Mara story and the belief that the daughter has returned are serving to conceal the actual reason we went to Marandur," Alain pointed out. "The idea that the daughter of Jules sought something her ancestor left there may satisfy many."

"Jules didn't leave those texts," Mari muttered, her eyes going to their packs. "But maybe you're right and that story will help us. The Mara thing, though, is just so appalling."

Alain watched her, puzzled again. "Why does it bother you? You are not Mara."

Mari pressed her fingers against both sides of her head. "Alain, I don't want to seem ungrateful. I'm sure any woman would be happy to hear that her husband doesn't consider her to be an undead, blood-sucking fiend. But that still leaves a lot of people inside the Empire who are going to be worried about Mara—about me—coming through the window to devour their children."

"From what those men and women said," Alain pointed out, "the chosen prey of Mara is young men, not children. Mara would seek out a man about my age."

Mari felt her brow lowering as she glared at Alain. "And why did you feel it necessary to say that?" she growled.

Belatedly realizing that he had made a serious mistake, Alain was groping for words. "I did not…that is…what should I say now?"

"As little as possible."

He nodded silently.

"Do you have any idea how it feels to have people think you're some loathsome creature?" Mari demanded.

Alain did not respond immediately. "Yes."

"What?"

"I am a Mage."

She felt a burst of shame. "Of course you know how that feels. Mechanics and commons use a lot worse words to describe Mages. I'm sorry. I'm just feeling so much pressure. I don't understand why I couldn't have more time, a few years at least, to lay the groundwork for overthrowing the Great Guilds. Instead I have to worry about getting it done faster, without attracting too much notice from the Great Guilds before I assemble the strength needed to withstand the inevitable all-out attack."

"It may be that your presence has created the conditions for the storm," Alain suggested. "That is why it approaches swiftly."

"My— What?" Mari glared at him. "Are you saying it's my fault?"

"No." He paused, then spoke slowly, as if forming the thoughts behind his words as he talked. "Whenever the daughter appeared, whenever that happened, her presence would create the conditions for the commons to erupt into violence. Instead of waiting with patience for the one who would help free them, they would want to act."

"But you said this storm was threatening before anyone was talking about me being the daughter!" Mari objected.

"You existed," Alain said. "In getting to know me, a Mage, and in surviving the attack on the caravan, you had already taken the first steps on the road the daughter had to travel."

"Great." Mari slumped backwards. "So it's my fault just for existing. Just like so many Senior Mechanics have implied for years."

"That is not—"

"Speaking of my Guild, I've been thinking, Alain. This ship raced to get out of Caer Lyn because they'd heard the harbor was going to be closed, and those guys at dinner said some Mechanics were called off this ship for some Guild emergency. Even though the reaction was badly coordinated, doesn't that sound like my Guild had realized that I was in Caer Lyn after all?"

Alain considered her question, then nodded. "It does. Yet the two who went to your home betrayed no signs of worry or suspicion."

"But what else could have betrayed our presence? There is no way that the ship we sabotaged could have gotten that far-talker working again. We saw those sailors after my Guild had already started those measures to close down the port, so they couldn't have told anyone."

"You have told me that Mechanics cannot sense the presence of other Mechanics," Alain noted. "But something is revealing where you are."

Mari shook her head. "I wish I could figure out what it was. Maybe the Guild has hired lots of commons with orders to keep an eye out for me. How could we avoid being seen if the Guild had that many commons also searching for us?" She tried to think of anything else that might betray her presence, finally hauling out her far-talker and confirming that it was off. "If I was talking on this they could track the signal. I used to leave it on standby sometimes so I could hear what any nearby Mechanics might be saying to each other, but ever since Severun it has stayed off. I don't even know if the battery is still good. Probably, I guess, since I haven't been using it." She pushed the far-talker back into her pack, then looked at the watertight bundle holding the banned Mechanics Guild texts. "About another week and we'll be at Altis. I wonder what we'll find there? Answers? Or just more questions?"

"Perhaps both answers and more questions," Alain suggested.

She sealed her pack. "We'll know in a while, I guess. What do you want to do now?" Alain smiled at her. "I should have guessed," Mari laughed, then held out a restraining hand. "How do you feel? You've told me that being too close to someone else was supposed to make you lose your powers, and, well, we've gotten really, really close."

He regarded her with that serious look. "I feel stronger than ever. Still. I cannot actually test that, of course."

"Alain, if you lose your powers—"

"It will have been worth it. I told you that before this voyage began, and everything since then has only reinforced for me that I was right."

She smiled, reaching for him. "Come here, my Mage."

The city of Altis lay on the island of Altis in the far northwestern part of the Sea of Bakre. Mari stood at the railing of the sailing ship *White*

*Wing*, gazing up at the mountains rising steeply from the waters of the sea. The entrance to the great circular harbor was just coming into view as the *White Wing* swung past the southern headland of the island. The breeze sweeping past the island carried a brisk reminder of winter's cold, but also the promise of the spring which would soon warm the lands around the inland sea.

Mari looked at the white buildings of the city of Altis on its high tableland and wondered what awaited her there, her and Alain, what enemies might be lying in wait for them at this moment. After more than a week at sea marred only by the worry of another ship intercepting them as the Mechanic ship had, it was jarring to face the prospect of immediate danger once again.

She had been more careful and said less in subsequent conversations with commons on the ship, but had noticed the soldier Patila and the skeptical man both regarding her more than would be usual in the last several days.

Alain came to stand beside her, and Mari reached out to grip his hand tightly. "I've been wondering if the last week was a dream," she confessed. "Wondering if I'll wake up and find us still trapped in Marandur, or me locked in a cell someplace, all alone."

"If it was a dream," Alain noted, "I have shared it with you, and it has been a very good dream."

"Oh, yeah. No complaints there." Mari grinned. "But right now I'm trying to get back into the right state of mind for a couple of fugitives from the most powerful enemies in the world. Our honeymoon cruise is over. It's back to being constantly alert for people trying to kill or capture us."

"Yes," Alain agreed. "Our enemies, and your Guild in particular, have shown too much skill at anticipating our moves. No one should know that we have come here, though, so with any luck we will not have to worry about anyone waiting on the dock. Nor should anyone expect us to stay in Altis. Assuming we make it ashore without running into trouble, what do we do first?"

Mari looked down at her left hand. "One thing I regretted is that we didn't have time to get promise rings in Caer Lyn. We'll have to do that in Altis, first thing."

"Before trying to find the tower?" Alain asked, surprised.

"Yes." She spread her fingers, imagining a ring there. "I've made a great many sacrifices for the sake of others and I don't think it's unreasonable to want this one little thing to take priority. It won't take all that long. We can't afford anything really fancy, but then I don't want anything fancy. Just plain gold bands for both of us. Is that okay with you?"

"Yes." He paused. "Gold bands on our hands."

"That's right." Mari gave him a rueful smile. "Just like in that vision of yours back in Dorcastle. We did get married."

"What would you have done in Dorcastle if I had told you then about the gold bands? If I had known what they meant?"

She gasped a brief laugh. "That's hard to say. By the time you did mention them I had already made some decisions about committing to you, but back then...stars above, Alain. I might have run."

"It is well that I did not mention it, then."

"Sure is." Mari met his eyes, her face serious. "I need you in so many ways. What am I going to do if I lose you?"

"Keep trying. You must."

She exhaled heavily, then held him close and kissed Alain quickly. "I'll try, but I doubt that will be enough. There's no way I can do this alone. The daughter needs her Mage." Mari raised her free hand and rubbed the place under her coat where her pistol rested in its shoulder holster. She hadn't worn it for part of the time they had been at sea, but she might need the weapon again soon. "No more visions?"

"No."

"Have you been totally honest with me about your Mage powers? Are they really still strong?"

Alain nodded. "Yes. I sometimes feel that if should someone threaten you I could muster enough power to blow a hole the size of that harbor in a city."

Mari let him see how startled she was by that. "All right. Let's not blow up any cities on my account, if you don't mind." The *White Wing* tacked, swinging around toward the entrance to the harbor, Mari bracing herself against the railing as the deck tilted. "Now we need our minds on business. Let's get our packs and get ready for trouble, just in case." She kissed him again, longer this time, knowing they were probably getting more amused looks from the commons on board who knew they were newly married. "Welcome to Altis, my beloved Mage."

❀   ❀   ❀

The *White Wing* had anchored out from the quay, her boats shuttling passengers ashore. While most of the passengers had jostled for places to get on the first boats, Mari and Alain had held back. He kept an eye on things around them as Mari, from a position where she could not be easily seen, was using her far-seer to study the docks of the lower port without being obvious about it. "I can't see anything that looks too suspicious," Mari told him. "There are a few Mechanics visible down at one end, but they're obviously working on something. I don't see any Mages. Everybody in common clothing seems to have a good reason for being where they are, and when the first boat came in nobody jumped out of the shadows to arrest them all."

Alain let his own gaze roam over the dock area. "My foresight tells me nothing."

Mari sat back, chewing her lower lip as she put away her far-seer. "There is an Imperial warship in port, but there is no sign of trouble from that quarter, either. Do you think we finally got ahead of the reports and rumors and arrest orders?"

"No." Alain gestured toward the north and east, memories of the events there crowding into his mind. "The stories spread by General Flyn's soldiers in the Northern Ramparts will have found fertile ground here, there is no doubt. But we may have outrun the rumors of Mara for a while."

"That's one blessing, then."

"It could be useful some day," Alain suggested, "if we are confronted by superstitious Imperials."

Mari turned her glare on him. "You're crazy if you think for even one moment that I will ever play at being Mara." She stood up, adjusting her pack. "I'm not going to miss hauling these packs around, let me tell you. Shall we get in line to get ashore?" She looked at Alain again, her expression becoming concerned. "What's the matter?"

He was looking north, and only when she asked did Alain realize that he must have shown some feeling. "I was thinking of home. The home I had and lost."

"I'm sorry," Mari said, her voice full of apology. "I should have expected that would bother you and not have been so self-centered. Just remember that you've got another home now." She took his hand and placed it over her heart. "Right here, and you're always there. Now let's go change the world."

He smiled at her, feeling better. "Yes, Lady Mari."

The line to board the boats was still fairly long, but Alain did not mind spending a little more time on the ship. It held memories that would never fade. He saw some of the other passengers they had spoken with, the commons who were soldiers in the Western Alliance, and somewhat awkwardly returned their waves of farewell. He saw that the woman soldier Patila once again kept her eyes on Mari, and that the soldiers' skeptical friend Jorge avoided looking their way.

Mari held his arm as the line moved forward, until they reached the ladder to the boat and had to go down it single-file. She led him to seats near the stern of the boat, then as the boat cast off and the crew members began rowing it to the quay, Mari met his eyes, tapped the place under her arm where her weapon was kept, and sat alertly. The honeymoon was officially over.

Alain kept his eyes on the area ahead for any sign of trouble, but saw nothing suspicious as the boat came alongside the quay and tied up. Once ashore they joined another line for customs, eventually facing an official who looked relaxed and a little rumpled, a big contrast to the polished menace of the Imperial officers with whom Alain and Mari had been forced to deal for some time.

The customs officer held out a hand for their papers, and Mari handed over the false ones. "Imperials out of Emdin? What brings you to Altis?"

"Distant relatives," Mari explained. "They've been asking us to visit, and this is a quiet season on the farm."

"Well, you'll have to get back soon for the spring planting, won't you?" The official took another glance at the identification papers, shrugged, then began to hand back the papers.

He halted in mid-reach as another official hastened up and whispered to him, glancing toward Mari and Alain.

Mari's attention was centered on the officials. Alain let his gaze roam, seeing the man Jorge standing some distance away and watching nervously, then turning to walk off with a fast gait.

The seated customs official gave Mari and Alain an appraising look as his comrade gestured to some nearby local police. "I am afraid we will have to question you further and search your belongings," the customs official said.

# CHAPTER THIRTEEN

Mari had tensed, flicking a glance at Alain. He nodded to indicate that he was ready to follow her lead. "Is something wrong?" Mari asked, trying to sound plaintive and worried like the young rustic her identity papers claimed her to be.

"This way," the second official ordered, the two local police at his back.

Alain took another look around. They were very exposed here on the quay. Anything they did would be seen by many people, including the Mechanics working down at the end of the quay. But allowing the local officials to search their packs would not only reveal Mari's Mechanics jacket and equipment, but also Alain's robes, and the two packs of texts which they had brought from Marandur.

Escaping from the local officials would be difficult, but not impossible. However, it would create a huge commotion and brand him and Mari as criminals before they had any chance to look for the tower she sought.

Mari hesitated, giving Alain another glance that this time revealed she had no ideas and needed one from him.

He began to shake his head slightly in response.

The seated customs official began to stand up, frowning, as the two local police stepped closer.

The woman soldier Patila suddenly walked up next to the customs desk, smiling at Mari and Alain. "Is anything wrong, sir?" she asked the customs official, offering her identity papers.

The official turned his frown on Patila, looking down at her papers. His expression cleared. "We're just acting on a tip, Captain," he said respectfully.

"About these two?" she asked. "Why would anyone have tipped— Oh, wait." She leaned close, whispering to the official.

He frowned again, looked at Mari in an appraising way, then inclined his head toward Patila. "I see. Thank you, Captain. If you vouch for them, there is no need to inconvenience anyone."

The official waved away the police and handed Mari back her and Alain's identity papers. "Sorry about that. We're not the Empire here, or Mechanics, giving people trouble just because we can. Enjoy your stay in Altis."

Patila walked with them as they left the quay. "I saw Jorge talking to one of the customs officials," she told Mari. "He's not a bad person, but he's been on edge a lot lately. Worried about things at home. And he thinks you might make things worse. I thought he might cause some trouble for you."

"Thank you," Mari said. "You really saved us back there."

"It's the least I can do," Patila said, looking at Mari. "For the daughter." As Mari fumbled for a reply, the soldier switched her gaze to Alain. "It took me a while to be sure you were a Mage. When you're not careful, though, your face goes all expressionless instead of relaxed. You need to work on that still."

"I will," Alain said. "What did you tell the official?"

Patila grinned lopsidedly. "I told him that this one guy on the cruise had been hitting on her," she said with a nod toward Mari. "I said I had heard him threaten to cause trouble for her if she didn't show him a good time even though she was just this naïve kid from a farm who only wanted to be left alone. And then I'd just seen that guy talking to customs officials and I thought maybe he had made good on his threats. Since I'm an officer in the Western military, and Jorge wouldn't even give his name, they took my word for it."

"Captain Patila," Mari began.

"Look, you don't owe me anything," Patila said. "But I wanted to tell you something I couldn't when others were around. There are a lot of commons like Jorge. They're scared. Worried about their homes and families and all. They're unhappy with how things are but frightened of how much worse they could get."

"They're not the only ones worried about that," Mari said.

"Yeah. I could tell. So, you need to know, if the daughter starts raising an army, a lot of commons will want to join, but many of those won't be able to, because they'll be trying to keep the lid on things at home, trying to keep their cities from boiling over and protecting their own places and people from whatever the Great Guilds try to do to stop the daughter." Patila gave Mari a somber look. "Do you understand?"

"Yes," Mari said. "I wouldn't ask anyone to abandon their responsibilities."

"Are you a Mechanic?"

Mari grimaced. "Yes. And no. I'm not a member of the Guild anymore."

"Her Guild wants to arrest and kill her," Alain said.

"Yours, too?" Patila asked. "I thought so. The daughter is poison to them. Are you going to be in Altis long?"

"I don't think so," Mari said. "There's something I need to do and then we're leaving."

"That's good. Altis can be hard to get out of, so it's not a good place to be trapped if anybody happened to be hunting you. I don't need to know your business. You shouldn't have any more trouble in Altis. Not from common folk, anyway. I'm only here for a couple of days myself, then I'm heading back to my unit. I need to pass on word to some people, higher-ups, to let them know it's real, that *she's* for real, and that we had better brace ourselves for the blast when the world learns about it." She studied Mari again. "You know, if anybody had come strutting around, claiming to be the daughter and telling everybody what to do, I wouldn't have been happy. Somehow I always thought that the daughter would be about us, not about her, and that's how I'd know she was real. That's why I got involved back there, and I think that's why Jorge tried to trip you up. The people who meet you know that you're the real deal, and not all of them are going to be happy about that. Good luck, daughter."

Patila veered off, walking down the street without looking back.

"She did not lie," Alain told Mari.

"I already knew that," Mari said. "You and I are going to keep our heads down, talk to as few people as we can, say as little as we can, find that tower, and then get out of Altis."

"Where will we go?" Alain asked.

"I am really hoping that something we find at the tower will help us decide that," Mari said. "But at this moment, we need to get out of the low port and up to the city."

She stopped to ask directions of some commons while Alain kept an eye on the crowds around them. The low port felt as low-key and casual as the customs official they had dealt with, and Alain felt himself relaxing a little as well. He could see numerous taverns lining the waterfront and guessed that come evening there would be plenty of high-pressure activity here as sailors relieved themselves of their money and their worries. But for now the low port just showed the bustle of trade and the movement of cargos and passengers. There was no sign of the betrayer Jorge, and Alain's foresight offered no warning.

But then it had also offered no warning before their near-conflict with the local officials.

Alain followed as Mari led them through the streets of the low port, then up the long slope to Altis proper. "Some older and wiser Mechanics I knew at the academy told me that jewelers in ports are not to be trusted," she explained to Alain. A few moments later, as if invoked by Mari's mention, a trio of Mechanics came into view, swaggering down the street alongside each other so that everyone else was forced to move aside. Mari bent her head as if laboring under her pack while the Mechanics passed, unobtrusively putting Alain between herself and them. Alain saw one of the Mechanics give him a disinterested glance, then the group of Mechanics had passed.

Mari straightened, her face sad. "Why do I have to hide from my former comrades? That still hurts. We'll take pains to avoid the area around the Mechanics Guild Hall, though."

Alain nodded. "As well as the Mage Guild Hall. There are a good number of Mages here, though I can sense no sign of worry among them."

"Does worry show up somehow in what you can sense?"

"Not directly," Alain explained. "I sense what is happening. If Mages are trying to hide themselves, if many are practicing spells, or if there is a strange lack of any spell activity, these would all be signs that something is amiss."

"Can you tell if there are any Mages you know here at Altis?"

He shook his head. "I cannot feel the presence of anyone I know. That is not too surprising. Altis is a backwater. The harbor is magnificent, but the island itself offers little beyond spectacular scenery."

"And an ancient tower full of answers, we hope." They had reached the city after toiling up the rise. As the street leveled out, Mari's face brightened when she caught sight of a casually elegant storefront. "Aha! Shah Jewelers of Altis. Not too fancy and not too cheap. Just what we need."

"Should we take time for this?" Alain asked. "After the incident on the quay—"

"Alain," Mari whispered, her voice intense, "I am running for my life and liable to be killed at any time. I'm expected to save all of Dematr from your chaos storm and overthrow the Great Guilds. I don't think it's too much to ask if I take a very little time to get the rings that will show how proud we are to be each other's partner in life."

He considered possible responses before replying. "That is wise."

Mari stared at him, then muffled a laugh. She pulled out some coins and held them up before Alain. "I hadn't mentioned this before, but do you remember that bag of food my mother gave us?"

"I recall there were some cookies within it which I never saw," he said.

"Oh, yeah, the cookies. There weren't very many of them." She made a pleading gesture begging forgiveness. "It had been so long since I'd had my mother's cookies."

"Next time I would like some."

"You will. I promise. Anyway, Mother stuck a fair amount of money in with the food she gave us. I didn't realize it until we were out at sea, of course, or I'd have given it back. She knew that, which is why she hid it in the bottom. I'll pay her back someday, but since we're stuck with it, I can't think of a better use for some of it than paying for our rings, can you?"

"I am sure that would bring your parents joy," Alain agreed. He wondered if Eirene had gotten around to telling Mari's father that Mari intended to marry a Mage. That news might not have brought all that much joy.

A short time later, Alain made a fist of his left hand and contemplated the bright gold band on the third finger. He felt somehow very different. It seemed such a small thing to be able to make such a big change in his own world.

Mari came beside him and spread her own hand next to his so their rings lay side-by-side. "Like us," she whispered. "Next to each other. Isn't this great? This makes it official."

"I thought the ceremony at Caer Lyn made the marriage official," Alain said.

"Well, yes, it did, but the rings make it officially official," Mari explained, hoisting her pack onto her back once more.

"Officially official?" Alain asked.

"Yes. Now let's find that tower."

Unfortunately, finding the way to the tower proved frustrating. Mari insisted on going first to a large and neatly laid out map store, where young clerks tossed the question of the tower among themselves, then finally asked a middle-aged supervisor who shook his head. "Our maps show everything that's there. If it's not on the map, it's not there," he pronounced confidently, pointing to the same motto engraved over the doorway.

Asking passing citizens of Altis was also fruitless. "A big tower? Somewhere in the interior? Never heard of it. There aren't even any roads into the interior. Nothing's there."

Some members of the city guard they asked also had no idea what they meant. "If a tower like that could be found on the island, we'd know about it."

The clerks at the city records hall expressed total confidence that no such tower could really be on the island. "It's not on the property tax rolls, so it can't exist."

Alain finally suggested that they try another mapmaker. "Not one who makes maps for today only. If this tower is a thing of history, then those who map history might know of it."

Footsore by this time, and with the day well along, Mari agreed. She did seem skeptical of the place Alain selected, though, a small map-maker's establishment which appeared to be as ancient as the city, with maps and documents piled up inside the dusty windows. To Alain, this was just the place for finding memory, but Mari shook her head. "How about we find some place where things are filed and neat and clean?"

"We have tried one such place. I believe that the map which we seek will not be found in a drawer," Alain replied.

Mari made a defeated gesture and waved him inside.

"The old tower?" The mapmaker's shop which Alain had chosen proved to be a joint venture between an elderly man and his wife, both of whom had obviously been at their trade for a long time. The old man nodded in instant recognition. "I haven't been asked about that since…"

"The year of the current Emperor's inauguration," his wife finished.

"Yes! But that wasn't someone asking how to get there…"

"It was someone who had seen it in the distance and wondered what it was," his wife completed the sentence.

"We couldn't tell him that…" the man confessed.

"But we could tell where he had seen it," his wife added.

Mari hid a smile behind her hand, glancing at Alain. "Can you tell us how to get to it?"

The old couple dug through large, shallow drawers and piles of maps, searching for the drawing they needed, before eventually sur-facing with a map of a part of the island which was well inland. "This is the best map…" the man assured Mari.

"For anyone seeking the tower," his wife agreed.

"The tower is…"

"There," his wife noted, using her finger to point out a spot.

The man inked a quill and made a small notation. "Yes, there."

Alain studied the map, trying to understand what it showed. "What do all these lines around the tower mean?"

"Mountains, lad! Very rough terrain there. You see?" The man traced peaks with his fingers.

"The tower sits in a sort of bowl-shaped valley," his wife said.

"Not well mapped, that area," the husband added.

"No reason for it," his wife agreed.

"That's why so few know of the tower…"

"Because the heights around block any view of it."

Mari looked at the map as well. "No one climbs these heights?"

"Why would they?" the man said.

"There's nothing there," his wife added.

"Except the tower…"

"And the mountains."

Mari held out a coin for the map. "I don't suppose you have any idea whether or not anyone still lives in the tower?"

The old couple exchanged surprised looks. "No…" the husband said.

"No idea at all," the wife conceded. "Why are you interested in it?"

"I like old things," Mari answered with another smile.

"Except when it comes to men, eh?" the wife replied, pointing to the obviously new rings on Mari's and Alain's fingers. "My man is old and comfortable now, but he was as raw and young as this one, once."

"You were pretty raw and young yourself in those days," her husband noted. "But mainly pretty. Still are."

"Men take a while to train," his wife confided to Mari, "but I found it worth the effort." She handed Mari back the coin. "Take the map as your promise gift from us. We'll not have it otherwise."

"I couldn't—" Mari started to protest.

"It'll make us happy, girl," the woman suggested with a smile.

"You'd not deny us some happiness?" her husband asked.

"Would you?" his wife finished.

"No," Mari said in a very soft voice. "I would not. Thank you. Thank you very much."

Once outside the mapmakers' shop, Mari stared upward, toward the peaks rising inland. "Alain, those two were common folk. The sort of people you and I were taught by our Guilds to hold in contempt."

"That is true," Alain agreed. "For your Guild. Mine taught me that they did not even exist and so were not even worth contempt."

"I don't know what we'll find at this tower, what answers it might hold, but when I meet people like that I already know in my heart that neither Mechanics nor Mages are some sort of superior beings. They are taught to look down upon the common folk, and I think an unquestioned sense of entitlement and superiority is more likely to make someone inferior in spirit. No one should be certain that they are better than everyone else."

"Not all commons are good."

"No. Of course not." Mari took a look at the map, her lips spreading in a broad smile. "Do you think we'll ever be like that? Finishing each other's sentences? As comfortable together as a pair of trees which have grown into each other's embrace?"

"I hope so," Alain said.

"Me too. I'm going to keep this map safe all of my life, as a memento to remind me of them." She looked around. The number of people, horses and wagons on the streets of Altis had diminished, and shadows were filling the streets as the sun fell low. "It's late, and according to this we've got at least a few days' walk to get to that tower. Tonight we'll get some food, wine and water for the trip, but there's no sense in trying to start until morning."

❋   ❋   ❋

The mapmaker's shop was on the edge of town, so they had to backtrack into the city to find some accommodations for the night, then a little farther yet to get something to eat. Mari looked up the street as they finally located an eatery and was startled to see that they had come far too close for comfort to the Mechanics Guild Hall. Several long blocks still separated them from the open plaza around the Guild Hall, but that wasn't far enough for her peace of mind. "Let's get something and get out of here," she muttered to Alain as they walked into the restaurant. She stood checking the list of items on the menu. "Good. They sell things we can wrap up and take on our hike." Mari looked at Alain. "Do you—? What?"

Alain used one hand to gesture toward a female Mechanic who must have come in behind them and was now alone at a corner table and staring in their direction. Mari felt a momentary stab of panic, then recognized who was sitting there. "Alli! What's she doing here on Altis? Alain, I know her. She's my best friend."

"You have spoken of Alli."

"Yes." Mari looked around, running her hands nervously through her hair, grateful to see that no other Mechanics were in the café at the moment. "You'd better keep an eye out while I talk to her." Mari walked toward Alli's table.

As she got closer Alli's eyes widened and she waved Mari over. "Mari?" Alli breathed. "It is you. I couldn't believe it when I saw you walk in here. Do you have any idea how much trouble you're in?"

Mari sat down, shrugging. "Well, I know there's an arrest order out on me."

"That doesn't bother you?"

"Of course it bothers me. It also bothers me that the Guild intends to kill me after it questions me."

Alli stared at her. "Who told you that?"

"A very experienced professor, and a Senior Mechanic confirmed it when she thought I was safely under arrest." Mari smiled apologetically. "But I got away."

"Mari, you used to be sort of a rebel, but this…" Alli shook her head. "Why? What's going on?"

"Have you heard from Calu?"

"Yeah. He sent me a letter using a commons courier service instead of the Guild's postal system. I got the impression he still couldn't say much, though. I could barely work out between the lines that he'd met you and that there was some kind of big trouble."

"Really big trouble," Mari agreed, then gave Alli a curious look. "What are you doing in Altis? Why did you leave Danalee?"

Alli looked cross. "I left because I was ordered to leave. I've been internally exiled by the Guild. That's thanks to a certain Master Mechanic with an arrest order out for her."

"Oh, no. Alli, are you serious?"

"Not really." Alli dropped her annoyed look and smiled ruefully. "I mean, I did get sent here under a dark cloud, but it's not really your fault. Not completely, anyway. I kept digging into old designs. None of them were supposed to be off limits, none of them were restricted, but the Senior Mechanics kept complaining anyway about me trying to build things. None of them were new, but a lot of it hadn't been worked with for a while. I kept getting told I was innovating! Heavens forbid I should innovate, right? Like those weapons I gave you. I think that was the last straw that got me exiled here. What did you do with them, anyway? The way I got interrogated about them made me think you'd tried to blow up a Guild Hall or something."

"I never used them against the Guild," Mari denied. "I only used one, actually, and that was because I had to kill a dragon."

"What?" Taken aback, Alli peered at Mari. "You had to kill a what?"

"A dragon. And Alli, it worked great. It was a huge dragon and it never stood a chance. Your weapon nailed it with one hit."

Alli smiled proudly, then remembered what they were talking about. "You're serious? Please tell me you're not joking. Or crazy. There's been some talk about…you know."

"No." Mari shook her head. "I don't know. Do you mean that I'm supposedly irrational because I got hit on the head in Ringhmon?"

"Partly, yeah. The Senior Mechanics are oh-so-worried about poor Mari," Alli said with broad sarcasm.

"I told you about Ringhmon, but I've found out a little more since the last time we talked. I was set up by the Guild. Nice, huh? The Senior Mechanics wanted me dead, and they wanted to be able to pin it on commons."

"Who told you this?" Alli demanded.

"Mechanics who knew it for a fact."

"Why didn't Calu say something about that?"

"Are you kidding?" Mari asked. "How could he hide something that explosive in a letter without some snoop spotting it? Besides, I didn't find out the details until after I'd seen him."

Alli exhaled heavily, looking at the tabletop. "That's just sick. I've been more and more unhappy with the Senior Mechanics, but this… Mari, I can tell you're not whacked out. But there's another reason being given for why you need help. There's supposed to be some guy that you're traveling with," she paused and looked to where Alain was standing against a wall some distance from them, "who's controlling you with drugs or something."

Mari couldn't help laughing. "Oh, yeah. I've heard that, too. Don't they think I can behave badly on my own?"

Alli grinned. "They certainly ought to know that by now. But I think they're trying to get your friends to help catch you by making us think that we're helping you."

"Well, it's ridiculous. Nobody's controlling me."

"Nobody ever could," Alli agreed. "But then what's going on? Who is he?" Alli rested her chin on the palm of one hand, gazing at Alain. "He's not half-bad looking…"

"Hey, back off! He's mine."

"Yours?" Alli raised both of her eyebrows and smiled slyly. "That sounds interesting. What's up with you two? Just working partners, or…?"

"Or," Mari said, smiling back.

"Where's he from? What's his specialty? Where did he apprentice?" Alli demanded.

"He's not a Mechanic, Alli."

"He's not? But the Guild thinks…" Alli studied Alain again. "You took up with a common?"

"No…"

"Mari, if he's not a Mechanic and he's not a common, what is he? He's not a Mage."

Mari hesitated for only a moment. "Um, yes, he is."

Alli gave Mari a startled and skeptical look, then gazed at Alain again. "Stop messing with me. He's not a Mage."

"Yes, he is."

"No, he's not. They all look like their faces are dead."

"I've been working on him," Mari explained.

"But why? Why work on him if he's a Mage?" Alli must have seen something in her face. "You said you two weren't just working partners. Oh, Mari, tell me you haven't."

"Haven't what?"

"A Mage. Mari, that is so…you promised me that you'd only get with the right guy. You promised me, Mari!" Alli shook her finger at Mari.

"I know," Mari said. "And I did. He really is the right one."

Alli shook her head again, looking very worried now. "A Mage, Mari. How could he be right? Wait. Is this the guy Calu talked about? He was trying to tell me something about him, but I couldn't figure out what it was." Alli stared at Alain. "He said you were in really good hands, and the other hints…yeah, he knew this guy was a Mage. No wonder I couldn't figure it out. That was the one answer I didn't try to fit to Calu's vague clues. Calu said he liked— What's his name?"

"Alain," Mari said. "Yes, Calu did like him. Alli, I swear to you that Alain is the greatest. He respects me and he believes in me and he's risked his life for me more times than I can count." Mari raised her hands in a pleading position. "Please, Alli. You know me. You can see I'm still myself. Can you still believe me?"

Alli hesitated. "That's a big thing, Mari, but—" Her eyes suddenly focused on Mari's hands. "Oh. My. Stars."

"What?"

"Is that a promise ring?"

"Uh…this?" Mari held up her hand, spreading the fingers a bit. "Yes."

"You married him?" Alli just sat staring at Mari, then shook her head with a dazed expression. "If Calu hadn't already told me that this Alain was all right, I'd… Who proposed?"

"He did, first. Then later, I did."

"You got a Mage to propose to you? Wow." Alli's eyes were on Alain again. "He looks all right, and I can tell he's worried about you by the way he's watching us."

"Do you remember when I told you about the guy who saved me in the desert, and from the dungeon in Ringhmon and later in Dorcastle? That was Alain."

Alli made a helpless gesture. "All right, Mari. It's your heart, and you know it better than anyone else. I know Mages aren't frauds like the Guild told us. I've seen what they can do, too. I was told never to talk to anyone about it."

"That's what happened to me."

"But Mari, how do they do it?"

"I don't know yet," Mari admitted. "I mean, Alain has tried to explain it to me in Mage terms, but it doesn't make any sense in Mechanic terms. Though Calu gave me some ideas, based on some kind of physics he was taught. I was wondering if I'd find some more clues in Marandur but—"

"Marandur?"

"Yes." Mari leaned forward, delighted at the chance to finally share with another Mechanic. "You won't believe the stuff I found there. Things from the vaults inside the old Guild Headquarters."

Alli's eyes had widened. "Banned technology?"

"Oh, yeah. Alli, this stuff is so great. The things we could build with it!"

Alli's face lit up. "Really? I can't begin to imagine—"

"No! You really can't! It's astonishing."

"But, Mari, the penalty if you're caught with it—" Her expression sifted to shock. "Marandur? You got it from Marandur? If the Empire gets its hands on you it'll kill you."

"The Empire has already tried," Mari admitted. "Alli, don't tell anyone else about Marandur or what I found there. Not yet."

"Sure. I promise. As long as I get to see it someday." Alli frowned at Mari. "Have you heard some of what the commons are saying? About this young female Mechanic who's the daughter of Jules and traveling with a Mage? I thought it was crazy common talk, but you really are with Alain. You might get mistaken for the one the commons are talking about."

Mari sighed and spread her hands apologetically. "The commons are talking about me."

"You're telling people that you're the daughter of Jules? Mari, that's suicidal! If the Guild gets its hands on you now—"

"Alli...I..." Mari didn't know how to say it, so she finally just blurted it out. "I am the daughter."

"What?" If Alli had looked dazed before, it was nothing compared to now.

"The Mages have seen it. They say I'm the woman who will fulfill the prophecy. If I live that long."

"Oh my stars." Alli blinked, then stared at Mari. "If the Mages believe that you're her, why haven't they killed you?"

"They're trying," Mari said.

"And so are our Guild and the Empire."

"Well...yeah. A lot of people want to kill me."

Alli looked away, then mimicked Mari's spread-hand gesture. "All right. So, to summarize, everybody is trying to kill you, and you're married. To a Mage." She leaned forward and whispered. "Is it true what they say about Mages?"

Mari knew that she looked puzzled. "Is what true about Mages?"

"You know. Those things they know. In bed."

"Things?" Mari asked.

"Come on, Mari! Everybody's heard about that!"

Mari gave Alli a bewildered look. "I haven't. What are you talking about?"

"Like you don't know!" Alli said with a laugh. "Oh, wow. Mari of Caer Lyn, married." Alli shook her head suddenly, sobering. "We need to talk about the Guild. How much do you know about what's going on?"

"Not a lot. I haven't been able to talk to anyone since I saw Calu in Umburan and someone else in Severun. Well, I was talked *at* by a Senior Mechanic on the ship that captured me, but she didn't seem to be interested in giving me any information."

"Calu isn't at Umburan anymore." Alli saw Mari's expression. "It's not that bad. I'm sure he wasn't sent to Longfalls. But he was transferred somewhere else. There's a lot of that going on—Mechanics being sent to different Guild Halls, often a long way from their original Halls. Officially, it's all routine, which everyone knows is ridiculous because of how many transfers are being ordered right now. Unofficially, the Guild is trying to break up gangs."

"Gangs?" Mari asked.

"Uh-huh. The Senior Mechanics think that there is a traitor behind every tree. That's one reason they want you so badly. It's an open secret that they've been trying to find you for months with no luck, and after what you did to the *Queen of the Seas*—"

"Was that the ship that captured me?" Mari asked. "You've heard about that?"

"A report came in on our far-talker a few days ago. You didn't quite sink the ship, you know," Alli confided. "Which I guess means you weren't trying to sink it, because the Mari I know would have done that if she'd wanted to." Her face lit up with understanding. "The rumor mill was trying to figure out how you escaped. Was Alain with you? And the Guild doesn't know he's a Mage?"

"Right, and right," Mari confirmed.

"Cool. I want all the details someday. What the Guild thinks happened is that some of the Mechanics aboard must have helped you escape, so the whole crew is under suspicion. Anyway, everything you're doing is making you a symbol for disaffected Mechanics. And after word got around about the mess in Emdin, what the Senior

Mechanics were doing to the apprentices there and how the Guild leadership had been covering it up, there are a lot more disaffected Mechanics. And they look at Mari and see someone who is thumbing her nose at the Senior Mechanics and getting away with it." Alli bent a mock disapproving look on her. "You're encouraging rebellion by commons and Mechanics."

"Mages, too."

"Really?" Alli asked.

"Well, one other Mage besides Alain, at least." Mari sat back, deciding to tell Alli the rest. "There's a storm coming."

"No, the weather's supposed to be fine for a few days."

"Not that kind of storm, Alli." Mari mimed steam escaping from a valve. "Pressure has been building up in the commons for a long, long time. They're about to blow."

She nodded, eyes intent. "How bad?"

"Extremely bad. Think Tiae. Only worse, and everywhere."

"Are you serious?" Alli asked. "How…what's the relief valve? There has to be a relief valve."

Mari pointed to herself.

"Oh my stars." Alli twisted her mouth. "And with the Guild maybe about to blow up, too."

"What?" Mari demanded. "The Guild is about to blow?"

"Yeah." Alli leaned toward Mari. "I don't think this is the first time that's happened, but the other times the commons weren't about to blow as well. I have a friend who tried to go through the official Guild records, and he said there were strange gaps, places where lots of stuff had just been yanked out. Like about a century ago. The rosters of the Guild Mechanics suddenly disappear, and when they show up again years later they're a lot smaller, as though hundreds of Mechanics just vanished."

It was Mari's turn to stare at Alli. "Just like that Mechanic who disappeared from the Guild Hall in Caer Lyn when we were apprentices. Remember him? I wonder just how big the prison at Longfalls is?"

"Not that big, Mari," Alli said. "I was wondering whether my worst suspicions about what happened to all of those Mechanics who disappeared could actually be true, but with what you just told me about what the Guild tried to do to you at Ringhmon, now I think I know."

Mari found herself looking down at the table, studying the marks in it as if they held great meaning. "Alain told me that the elders in the Mage Guild, who are like their Senior Mechanics, are ruthless in dealing with anyone they think is an enemy of their Guild. I remember thinking, how horrible to just decide to kill people, to kill other Mages just because they are suspected of being disloyal. Maybe the Mage Guild isn't all that different from the Mechanics Guild that way, though."

"Maybe not," Alli agreed. "The Senior Mechanics control what little we learned about history, so it looks like they told us whatever they wanted and left out a lot of other stuff."

"I wonder…" Mari gave Alli a curious look. "The Guild's technology has been regressing for a long time. I wonder of purges like that are part of the reason. You can't kill that many trained people and not have some impact. Think of all the stuff that never got passed down from one generation to the next."

"I bet it is part of the problem. Remember how we used to complain about short-term solutions to long-term problems?" Alli leaned forward again, her elbows on the table. "So, speaking of long-term solutions, when do we start the revolution, o daughter of Jules?"

"We? Alli—"

"I'm in, Mari. Do you think I want to sit around pretending to be a good little girl until I disappear in some Guild loyalty sweep?" Alli looked to the side, frowning in thought. "Speaking of which, I heard late today that some special Mechanics are arriving here in about a week. The word came in just this afternoon to the Guild Hall by high-priority far-talker message."

"Special Mechanics? What's their specialty?" Mari asked, feeling uneasy.

"I don't know. Officially, they don't even exist, but the Guild had to make room for them at the Hall, so of course lots of us have heard that they're coming, and we were told not to talk about it, so of course everybody is talking about it. But no one who knows who they are will say why they're coming, or what the rush is about."

Mari took a deep breath. "Maybe you should get out now."

"No. If I hang in there a little longer I may be able to find out something about them."

"Alli—"

"You'd better not be getting ready to lecture me on careful behavior, Lady subject-of-arrest-order daughter of Jules who went to Marandur and married a Mage."

Mari couldn't help laughing. "You've got me there. Alli, I still don't know exactly what comes next. I'm here in Altis because I think there's a place that holds some answers I need before I can figure out what to do. The less I tell you about that, the better." Blinking back grateful tears, Mari reached over and grasped Alli's hands. "Thank you. I can't tell you how much it means to me that we're still on the same team. I'm going to be out of the city for several days at least, but when I get back I'll get in touch with you again."

"You'd better." Alli nodded toward Alain. "Now do I finally get to meet your promised husband?"

"Sure, but if you try to steal him from me you're a dead woman." Mari turned to gesture Alain over to them. He came quickly, yet without moving so fast it attracted attention. "Alain, this is Alli."

Alain bowed to her. "I have heard much of you. You are the Lady Mechanic who makes the dragon-killer weapons."

"Yeah, I guess I am." Alli grinned. "I love that title. Someday when I have my own weapons workshop I'll put Maker of Dragon-Killer Weapons over the front entrance. So, Alain, what attracted you to Mari?"

"Alli!"

Alain eyed Alli for a moment, then Mari saw his small smile. "I was attracted to Mari by her intelligence, her spirit, and her excellent taste in friends."

Alli stared at him for a moment, then covered her mouth to stifle laughter. "You are the right one for Mari," she finally said. "No wonder Calu liked you. Does he know about the marriage?"

"Not yet," Mari replied.

"Good. I would have killed him if he'd known and not told me." Alli stopped smiling, looking around. "You two had better get what you came for and get out of here. How do we meet again? You said several days. I'll wait five days and then come back here in the evening. After that I'll try to come every other day or so, as often as I can without arousing suspicion. Deal?"

"Deal." Mari reached to clasp Alli's hand again. "I am incredibly lucky when it comes to friends."

"You make that luck, Mari. There were a few times when we were apprentices when I had nowhere else to turn, but I knew Mari would be there for me, and you always were."

"Mari never leaves anyone behind," Alain said.

"Exactly!" Alli winked at Alain. "Nice meeting you. I always wondered who Mari's Mister Right would be."

Alain bowed toward her. "I am fortunate, though I believe that since Mechanic Calu is favored in your eyes he considers himself more fortunate than I am."

"He'd better," Alli said with a laugh.

Mari grinned. "Thanks, Alli."

"No problem. See you at the revolution." Alli gestured them away. "Stay safe."

"I'll try," Mari promised as she and Alain walked away.

They quickly bought enough food for dinner and for the trail, then left just as a batch of Mechanics came in and called greetings to Alli, who smiled back as if nothing unusual had happened recently. As Mari and Alain slipped out the door, Alli was focusing the attention of the other Mechanics on herself by asking some loud questions about contracts.

❖ ❖ ❖

Mari trusted Alli but still felt extra nervous until they left the city early the next day. There had been too many cases where the Mechanics Guild had managed to locate Mari without any obvious slip-up on her part or Alain's. Until she figured out what was betraying them, any period of time in one spot left her jumpy.

The first part of their travel wasn't too difficult: through the city of Altis, then through the outlying portions lying up against the slopes of the mountains rising behind the city. Mari was surprised at how rapidly the city dwindled as they moved inland, the road very quickly changing from a paved street lined with buildings to a dirt lane bordered by sheds and storage huts and then a narrow path lined only by a couple of small orchards before it vanished completely where it met the skirts of a mountain. As Mari and Alain climbed higher into the interior through territory unmarked by human artifacts, she looked back at the city beneath them. "If this tower does exist inland, it's no wonder nobody but those old mapmakers know about it. Everything on this island seems to be focused toward the sea."

Alain paused beside her, breathing deeply but evenly from their climb so far. "I thought the same from my study of the map. There are towns and villages elsewhere on the island, but all lie along the coast. The roads follow the coastline, but often end where cliffs going down to the water block their passage."

Mari looked upward, where the mountains rose amid steep slopes and deep chasms. "The interior of this island is the perfect place to hide something, isn't it? Even a long time ago people could have figured that out. How the blazes did anyone build a big tower in terrain like this, though?"

Their progress became slower and slower as they struggled through the rough landscape, and when night fell they had to sit wedged on a small shelf overlooking a sharp drop, taking turns sleeping while the one who was awake made sure neither of them slipped off. About midnight a sudden late-winter squall sent freezing rain to lash the mountains, further adding to the misery of the day.

In the morning the sun rose on a rough countryside glittering with an icy glaze. They had to wait for the ice to melt enough for their footing to be safe. Mari consulted the map often in search of landmarks as they went steadily higher and deeper into the island. Difficult climbs alternated with perilous descents, each complicated by scrub brush which all too often bore thorns instead of leaves. Measuring their apparent progress against the map, she felt despair. "It will take us a month at this rate."

"Perhaps it will get easier," Alain said.

"Right now I just wish one of those Mage Rocs would appear so we could fly to that blasted tower."

This time, darkness descended while they were halfway up a scree-covered slope. Unable to keep going in the uncertain footing and poor visibility, they found a patch of bushes they could lie against, hoping the roots would hold until morning. Neither got much rest that night, either.

Mari blinked at the sun as it finally rose over the rocky peaks around them on the third day. "I hate this island. If that tower is empty I'm going to be one unhappy Mechanic, let me tell you. This little hike better prove to have been worth it."

"We have had worse," Alain pointed out, looking as worn out as Mari felt.

"Thanks. That makes me feel so much better." Mari pulled out her far-seer and studied the ground around them, checking all directions. "Bad that way. That way's worse. Wow. A lot worse. Hey." She thought she saw something and blinked to clear her eyes, then took another look. "There's somebody moving over there."

"Where?" Alain asked, shading his eyes with one hand as he looked in the same direction.

"Along the side of that ridge there. He's gone now. No, wait, there he is again, on the side of that mountain. All I can see is his head and a bit of his shoulder. How is he moving so fast? There's got to be a path there even though we can't see it."

Alain shook his head. "Without your Mechanic device, I cannot see any sign of this traveler you are watching."

"Looks like he's disappeared for good." Mari lowered her far-seer, thinking. "Suppose the tower does exist, and suppose there are people living there, and those people need to get to the outside world every once in a while."

"They would need a path," Alain agreed.

"But since practically nobody knows about this tower, whoever lives there must be keeping it secret, so…"

"Their path would be secret as well." Alain looked at the ground ahead. "It will be difficult to reach wherever you saw this traveler, but it will be difficult to go in any other direction as well."

Mari grinned fiercely, coming carefully to her feet on the slope. "Let's go find us a path, my Mage. Down that way, up that slope, over that ridge and hope what's on the other side isn't too bad."

The other side wasn't great, but it wasn't impassable, either. Not quite impassable, anyway. Mari had determined certain landmarks on the way to where she had caught brief glimpses of the traveler: a large rock with an odd shape, a cluster of evil-looking scrub bushes, and a nearly vertical ravine in one cliff face as if a huge knife had sliced into the rock. She was able to stay headed in the direction of what was hopefully a hidden trail while they toiled down, up and around numerous obstacles. About noon, as Mari was struggling up another steep slope, she suddenly found herself stepping onto a very low ridge and looking down at a path heading inland. Stumbling down onto the surface of the path and resisting an urge to kneel and kiss it, she helped Alain step down as well. "That ridge is almost like a wall running alongside this path, completely hiding it." She looked up at an almost sheer cliff face. "You couldn't see the path except from overhead, and nobody is going to be walking up there. If I hadn't spotted that person, which I couldn't have without my far-seer, we would have never known this was here."

Alain sat down, relieved enough for the emotion to be obvious. "This is not a heavily used way, but it has clearly been here a long time."

"Like part of the landscape," Mari agreed. She studied what she could see of the path, puzzled. "It looks artificial, as if the path was cut through here, but I can't tell what did the cutting through so much rock and left such smooth surfaces." They took a break to eat, Mari hauling out the map and studying it again. "We haven't even come halfway, but on this path we can move a lot faster. I think we should push on today until sunset, get a decent night's sleep, then try to reach the tower tomorrow."

Alain nodded, standing up with a heavy sigh. "I miss the *White Wing*."

"I bet. Are you sure what you really miss isn't being in bed with me?"

"That, too." He looked back and forth along the path. "Perhaps tonight, on a level surface like this…"

"Do men ever stop thinking about that? And in any case, forget it. That's rock and gravel. I will not engage in any vigorous activity on that kind of surface."

Despite their weariness, the easier road lent Mari and Alain extra energy, and they covered a lot of ground before it grew too dark to travel. They slept on a level surface, hemmed in by the path's concealing barrier and the slope rising on the other side, so that even though they alternated watches through the night both got a decent amount of rest for the first time in days.

Mari felt a curious mix of elation and dread as they started off the next morning. What if the tower was not there? What if the "records of all things" it once held had long since crumbled to dust? What if the current inhabitants had no idea the tower had been a place to keep important information safe and could tell her nothing?

But what if the tower was there and the people in it could answer her questions? The possibility lent wings to her feet as they walked.

Mari's prediction from the map proved accurate. The sun was still just short of noon when they rounded a mountainous curve and found themselves gazing down into a pocket valley. It was bigger than Mari had expected from the map and greener, too. Meadows and cultivated fields covered a wide area beneath them, with stands of trees here and there as well as on the slopes of the valley. They could see the shapes of farm animals moving in some of the fields.

Rising against the back wall of the valley was the tower. Even though it was dwarfed by the mountains rising around them, Mari couldn't hold back a gasp of surprise at the tower's size. It soared upward for what she guessed must be a hundred lances, its surface some sort of smooth, shiny stone with no sign of break or seams except for windows and a large entry. On the tower's top, an unbroken expanse of dull black material not only roofed the structure but created the odd impression in Mari that the stuff was actually soaking up the sunlight. "Did they carve it out of the living rock?" Mari wondered out loud as she studied the tower through her far-seer.

She moved her head slowly, using the far-seer to view more of the valley. Near the base of the tremendous tower other, much smaller, buildings were clustered. Some of those looked as if they had been fashioned from the same mysterious substance as the tower, but most appeared to have been built of stone and timber in ways Mari was familiar with. "Looks like communal living areas, barns and structures like that. There are plenty of people down there. I'd guess maybe a hundred within view right now. It looks like they're all wearing plain robes of some kind."

"Robes?" Alain asked.

"Yeah, not like Mage robes, though," Mari said. "As far as I can tell, they're tending to animals, working the fields and doing other work. Wait." Mari spotted some smaller figures who weren't wearing robes. "Children. There are families down there."

Mari lowered her far-seer, glancing at Alain. "Families with children. And the children are playing. That's a good sign."

"It may be," he agreed cautiously. "If children are among them, and playing, they are definitely not Mages, despite the robes."

She raised the far-seer again. At the base of the tower, great doors stood open, with robed figures passing in and out. "The tower's definitely still occupied. I see no sign of defenses or weapons, unless you count the staves being carried by the people herding the flocks. No sentries, no guards."

Alain nodded. "These people depend for safety on not being known. They raise their own food, and must require little contact with the rest of the world."

"Yeah. But this path proves they send people in and out for something. I wonder what? Medicine? Mechanic devices? Do you want a look?"

Alain shook his head, eying the far-seers warily. "No. I would see nothing that you did not, and I do not know how to safely use that."

"They're just far-seers, Alain. They can't explode."

"Then they are unlike the other Mechanic devices I have experience with," Alain said firmly.

Reminding herself that Alain's Mage arts still seemed as perplexing to her as Mechanic devices were to a Mage, Mari put away her far-seer and looked to Alain. "What do you think? Sneak around and see what we can spy out? Or just walk down, introduce ourselves and see what they do?"

"If I lived as these people do," Alain suggested, "I would be highly suspicious of anyone acting suspicious."

"You mean someone sneaking around and spying, I take it."

"Yes. I think we would be best served by acting open and unthreatening."

Mari drew her pistol and checked it, then replaced it in her shoulder holster. "All right. I agree. But let's be ready in case they turn out to be a bunch of maniacs who consider outsiders to be the spawn of demons." She paused, thinking some more. "Yeah, let's be open and honest for once." Pulling off her coat, she stuffed it into her pack and drew out her Mechanics jacket, putting it on and settling it into place with a small smile. "I've missed wearing this, you know," she confessed to Alain.

"I could tell, every time you were able to put it on and every time you saw another Mechanic." Alain also bent to his pack, removing the Mage robes inside and donning them. "Here we are, once again openly the Mage and Mechanic, just as when we first met."

"That seems so long ago." Mari glanced at the ring on her hand.

This was the first time she had worn her Mechanics jacket and the ring at the same time. "You know, back when I was single."

"As I was."

Mari bit her lip, staring outward. "Your vision of us fighting in a battle at Dorcastle someday. We're obviously on the path to that. We're married now, just like in the vision. You have no idea who we were fighting?"

"No. Only you and I were clear."

"It looks more and more like we're going to be fighting the Great Guilds." Mari looked over at him, feeling somber. "Have you seen anything else? Anything that would tell whether or not we both survive that battle?"

Alain regarded her gravely. "No. I have seen nothing of us, together or alone, in any period after the battle."

"At least you haven't seen either of us dead." Mari swallowed, put her doubts and fears aside, then straightened her jacket and smiled at him. "Come on. Let's go visit the tower of Altis."

The path they were on switched back and forth twice as it descended into the valley, the obscuring barrier on its outside edge dwindling away to nothing so that there was no obstruction hiding their approach from everyone in the valley. "They have no need of sentries," Alain observed.

The path followed the rise and fall of gentle slopes as it headed for a stream cutting through the valley. Mari and Alain walked at an easy pace, approaching a bridge spanning the stream. As they got closer to the bridge, Mari could see that it was made of the same seamless rocklike material as the tower.

Alain pointed. "There is a small group coming this way. A dozen, I think."

Mari squinted, making out the figures. "Do we have a cover story this time, or do we just tell the truth?"

"You are asking a Mage about truth?"

"Yes, you clown." Mari couldn't help smiling, though. "I think we should try the truth. We're fighting people who lie. Let's be on the side of honesty regarding what we want and why we came."

"I agree with your wisdom," Alain said.

"And once again you affirm one of the many reasons I love you." She grasped his hand as they walked, using her free hand to check her pistol again. "But they could be hiding all kinds of weapons under those robes. You're still ready for trouble, right?"

"Of course."

# CHAPTER FOURTEEN

ari and Alain kept walking toward the robed figures, while the group who apparently made up a welcoming committee strode toward them. They met at the bridge, the robed group spreading out to block the span. One of their number stopped ahead of the rest.

"Good day," Mari said politely.

"Good day," the robed figure in the lead responded, throwing back a hood to reveal that she was a woman, tall, a bit thin, with sharp eyes. She managed to look both gracious and unwelcoming at the same time. "You are lost. We will give you directions back to Altis."

"We're not lost," Mari said.

"Then I regret to tell you that we do not welcome visitors here. Our people live apart from others. We must ask that you leave this valley and explore some other part of the island."

Mari raised her arm to point at the tower. "We're not exploring. We came here to visit that tower and those who live in it."

The woman conveyed puzzlement. "Why would you seek that? Our people have lived here for generations, and we have nothing in which the outside world would be interested."

Alain leaned close to Mari to speak in her ear. "The first part of her statement was true, the last part a lie."

Nodding, Mari smiled at the woman. "You can see that this man is a Mage. He can tell when someone speaks the truth. And when they don't."

"He wears the robes of a Mage," the woman agreed. "But Mages do not accompany Mechanics. One of you is false. Perhaps both of you are."

Mari smiled. "I wouldn't be so certain of that if I were you. I am

Master Mechanic Mari of Caer Lyn, and this is Mage Alain of Ihris." She noticed some of the robed figures reacting slightly when she said her name, and wondered what news the person they had seen on the path might have brought here. "We have questions which we hope you can answer."

"Then you will surely be disappointed," the woman replied, more severely this time. "I ask you again to go. You are not welcome in this valley and will not be permitted to go farther."

"There's nothing in that tower?" Mari asked.

"Our homes. Nothing more."

Mari glanced at Alain, who shook his head, then back at the woman. "But I have read that there is much more there," Mari said. She didn't need Alain's help to see the way the robed figures tensed after that statement.

But the robed woman recovered quickly, smiling sadly. "There are many stories with no basis in fact. Whatever you read of that tower is no more real than one of the tales of Mara the Undying."

That made Mari fix a cross look on the woman. "At the moment, Mara is kind of a sore subject with me. Do you want to know where I read about this tower? I'll show you." The robed figures all watched as Mari shrugged off her pack, kneeling to carefully unseal the watertight package holding her half of the banned Mechanic texts from Marandur.

She stood up slowly, holding one of the texts, then carefully opened it to the page with the drawing on the side. "It says here, 'The tower on Altis, where records of all things are kept,' and the drawing certainly resembles your tower."

The robed woman was staring not at Mari but at the book she held. "What is that?"

Mari turned it to read the cover. "Survival Technology Manual, Base Level Two, Volume Four, Wireless Communications, Second Edition, Revision Three, Demeter Projekt." She looked back at the men and women facing her. "Demeter. That sounds like our world. Dematr."

A ripple passed through the ranks of robed figures. "The tech manuals," a woman whispered. "Coleen, it's one of the tech manuals."

One of the men cried out in a much louder voice. "We cannot let this opportunity pass!"

"Silence, all of you," the woman ordered. "We know nothing of this, or of that book you hold," she insisted to Mari.

"Don't you want to know where I got it?" Mari asked.

"Such knowledge could be extremely dangerous to us," the woman named Coleen replied, but even Mari could see the yearning for answers in her.

"Not as dangerous as it is to me and my Mage. We got it in Marandur. It's from the vaults of the old Mechanics Guild Headquarters in that city." It hadn't come directly to her from those vaults, but the statement was still true.

She could see the people before her wavering. Mari held up the text. "This is only one of what we have. If you truly value knowledge, perhaps you would like to see the texts. All of them."

"What...what is you want?" Coleen asked.

"We are here seeking records of the past," Mari said. "Records which might tell us how our world came to be as it is. I need to know this."

The woman rallied. "We cannot help you."

Alain spoke to her for the first time. "You *choose* not to help us."

"I'm offering a trade," Mari said. "You answer my questions, and I let you look at the texts that are in our packs."

"Can you tell us about Marandur?" a man asked. "What it is like right now?"

Coleen turned to glare at the man as Mari answered. "Yes. And about the masters and students still occupying the university there."

"They still survive?" a woman cried. "Coleen, please, this is priceless."

"We have our mission," the leader said, but her resolve was clearly wavering. "What do you seek in our records?"

Mari met her eyes. "I need to know why the world is the way it is, why the Great Guilds control its fate. I need to know if there is a good reason for that, if the world's subjugation to the Great Guilds was in the name of some higher purpose or in response to some awful events. And I need to know anything about other ways that the world could be, ways that give more freedom than anyone has now."

"Why do you need to know this?"

Mari took a deep breath and then spoke steadily even though the words felt as if someone else were saying them. "Because I am the daughter of Jules, and our world will soon face a great crisis that will destroy everything. I can stop that, if I can unite Mechanics, Mages, and the common folk to overthrow the Great Guilds and bring freedom to this world."

Another of the robed men spoke. "It is her, and the Mage. The ones we were told of."

Coleen gazed at Mari. "Do you have any idea of the cost if we reveal ourselves to you, and if that information becomes known to the Great Guilds?"

"I swear to reveal nothing of this place, not unless you give me permission."

Her eyes went to Alain. "But what of the Mage? What oath can he give?"

Alain inclined his head toward the woman. "I vow also to say nothing."

"The word of a Mage means nothing."

Mari felt anger that she couldn't quite suppress. "That may be true of most Mages, but it is not true of my Mage. He is a man of honor." She held up her left hand so the promise ring shone in the sun. "He is also my husband, and I will not have his word questioned." She could see the eyes of the entire group focusing on her hand in disbelief, then shifting to see the identical ring on Alain's.

The woman leader stared at Alain. "Why did you marry this Mechanic?"

"Because I love her," Alain answered.

"But the wisdom of Mages says that all people are shadows, and no feelings must bind you to others."

"Lady Mari has shown me a new wisdom, one stronger than that which the elders of the Mage Guild teach. That is why we walk together, and why I have resolved with her to do the right thing."

Mari spoke into the silence which followed Alain's declaration. "We wish you no harm. Please. We need to know that what we are doing is the right thing."

The woman shook her head, looking down at the path. "We hold knowledge, Lady Mechanic, but the answers you seek may be beyond the wisdom of any man or woman. We can provide facts, but right and wrong are judgments, and only you can decide them."

"Then give me the facts to make such a decision wisely! That's why I came here, to have the data I need to make an informed decision!"

The woman turned to look at her fellows, and one by one they nodded back at her. She faced Mari and Alain again. "We cannot deny your request, for knowledge must have a purpose, and for too long our only purpose has been to protect it, not to assist in the use of it as our calling demands. I am Coleen, head librarian of the librarians of the tower. If you will come with us, we will try to answer your questions, and in exchange you must grant us access to the materials you carry. The knowledge in them will be a great gift to us and to the people of this world."

Mari nodded, smiling. "It's a deal."

❖   ❖   ❖

Coleen led the way to the tower, the rest of the librarians following behind Mari and Alain. People they passed stopped to look at the procession in amazement, but either Coleen or one of the other librarians always assured them that all was well. Mari endured the slow walk, wanting to run to the tower, but Alain's hand in hers helped hold her back.

When they reached the tower, Mari paused to run her fingers across its surface. Up close, the material was just as smooth as from a distance, but also very hard and apparently unmarked by time. "What is this? Mari asked.

"We don't know," one of the male librarians admitted. They had all dropped their hoods and seemed just as eager to talk now as they had formerly been reticent. "It was something our ancestors could make, a material which could be poured like water, yet would hold a shape and then harden into something stronger and more enduring than stone."

"Our ancestors." Mari glanced at Alain. "Did they come from the stars?"

"Yes. Very few people are still aware of that."

Mari felt her breath stop for a moment. "Our ancestors really did come from the stars?"

"Don't the Mechanics still boast of their lineage from the stars?"

"Yes, but most of them don't believe it anymore. It's true?"

Coleen gave Mari a wry smile. "If you truly wish to know how our world came to be as it is, that is where you'll have to start, with the ship that came from another star."

The ground floor of the tower was a vast room, with stairs leading upward and down. The interior was illuminated by some kind of electrical lighting, though Mari noted that a lot of the lights had failed. "Where's your power generator?" she asked.

A librarian waved around to encompass the tower. "The tower itself turns the sun's rays into power for us to use. But the amount of power has been slowly dwindling for generations for reasons we do not understand, and when lights now go out, we have no more replacements for them."

Coleen headed for one of the stairways down, leading Mari and Alain down three flights to what must be a level well beneath the surface. "It is very safe here," she said. "The safest storage space in all of Dematr. Not just because it's deeply buried in living rock, but because this part of the planet is very geologically stable. It is where we keep Original Equipment." From the way she pronounced the words, it was easy for Mari to hear the capital letters in them.

Coleen paused at the door at the bottom of the stairs, manipulating a lock and then standing aside as she opened the door to allow Mari and Alain to enter.

Lights came on as Mari walked into the room, apparently triggered automatically. She came to a halt, staring around at an assemblage of equipment which surpassed anything she had ever imagined. Mari knew her mouth had fallen open as she gazed at the smooth panels, at the devices whose functions she could only guess at. As Mari slowly turned to take in everything, she felt moisture running down her cheeks, and reached up to wipe away tears of joy and wonder. "Stars above. So many things in the banned texts are right here, truly existing. Oh, this is awesome." Her voice cracked and Mari had to close her eyes, more tears spilling out as she cried at the marvel of these devices which actually did exist, which were real and here in front of her. Things that the Mechanics Guild had kept from her world.

"Mari?" Alain's voice was concerned as his hand touched her gently.

"Oh, Alain." Mari shook her head, opening her eyes and turning around and around to look at everything over and over again. "This is so beyond belief. This is what the Mechanics Guild took from us. Am I right?" she asked Coleen, who had entered behind them and now watched Mari with shared joy.

"Yes," the librarian said. "All of these things came from the great ship, which means all of them came from a world warmed by another star. They were all built an unimaginable distance away, many, many years ago. We have had to keep them hidden to protect them from your Guild."

"Not my Guild," Mari denied violently. "I am a Mechanic, but that is not my Guild any longer. I could never belong to any organization that forced the suppression of such wonders."

Coleen had walked over to one wall, where a large diagram hung, the image on it faded but still legible. "This was the ship."

Mari came close, staring at the drawing. "What's the scale?"

"Here," the librarian said, indicating a marker in one corner of the diagram. "Our ancestors used something called a metr. A metr was about half a lance in length."

Checking that against the diagram, Mari felt her jaw drop again. "It was huge."

"It had to be. The voyage took hundreds of years." Coleen indicated a map on the wall next to the diagram of the ship. Even under its protective covering, the map had browned with age.

Mari and Alain studied the map, seeing huge continents of unfamiliar shape. "What does this show?" Alain asked.

"The home of our ancestors," Coleen said, her voice now worshipful. "The place from which the great ship came. Another world. Urth is its name."

Mari traced the outlines of the continents with her fingertip, carefully not touching even the covering of the map. "Urth. How far away is it?"

"We do not know anymore," another librarian answered. "We know only that the distance is so great that light itself takes many years for the journey." Her voice saddened. "One of the stars we see in the sky is the sun which warms Urth, but we no longer know which star that is."

Coleen, plainly enjoying sharing this information, pointed to one part of the ship. "This was where the crew lived and worked. Because the trip was so long, the original crew aged and died along the way, and their children continued in their stead, and so on until this world was reached."

Mari ran her finger under one large word, the text odd but readable. "*Demeter*. The name of our world. Just like on the texts. That's how it was originally spelled and pronounced?"

"Yes. It was also the name of the ship." The librarian indicated another portion of the diagram. "And this area was where the passengers were, along with all of the animals, fish, plants and other creatures the ship brought."

"There couldn't have been very many passengers," Mari said. "That area is a lot smaller than the crew area."

"There were thousands of passengers." Coleen's face lit with awe as she spoke. "Our ancestors knew how to take newly created children from the bodies of their mothers, then freeze them so that they would exist unchanging for many years, until thawed and allowed to grow into babies."

Mari stared at the other woman, shocked. "They took children newly created from the mothers?" Mari became aware that her hands had dropped down of their own accord, covering her own lower abdomen protectively. Alain had noticed her gesture as well and seemed unusually startled by it. But why should he be? Perhaps because he was a man he couldn't grasp why that would appall a woman. "That's horrible."

Coleen shook her head, speaking gently. "No. It harmed neither mother nor child, and every mother and father who gave their unborn children to this purpose did so by choice, so that their children could live here someday." She gestured to the equipment around them. "The ship also carried devices which could serve as mothers to bring the children to term."

"Machines?" Mari demanded. "Machines in which babies grew until they were birthed?" She had worked around machines most of her life, she loved machines in many ways, and yet the idea felt incredibly repulsive.

"Machines of a sort," the librarian agreed. "It was necessary. Upon arrival here the devices brought to birth a first generation of passengers, and when those were old enough to care for babies another generation, and so on until every passenger had been born. Since then," she added with a slight smile, "every birth has been in ways more familiar to us."

"The animals, too?" Alain asked. "This is how the first animals came here?"

Mari thought Alain was still rattled, but then she was used to spotting subtle signs of how he felt.

"Yes, the animals as well," Coleen replied, then turned a serious look on Mari. "And this is how the Mechanics Guild came to be and to control so much, and why so little of our history is truly known. When the great ship reached our world, most of the crew felt that they and their ancestors had done the work to reach here and deserved to be rewarded far more than the passengers. So they decided to violate the orders that had been given long ago on Urth. These crew members allowed only a small portion of the science and technology they had brought here to be made known to the passengers as they grew. The crew members also never told the passengers where we had all come from. Those who chose to create the Mechanics Guild claimed to be the only humans who could build and repair mechanical devices. The passengers knew only what they were told and were too busy laboring to build the first cities and scatter life through this world to dream of the truth."

Mari felt a sense of anger as well of relief. "Then the Mechanics Guild was always about power and wealth. It never had any higher purpose, never had any other justification."

"And what of the Mage Guild?" Alain asked. "Did the Mages on the great ship make an agreement with the Mechanics Guild in those days?"

Another librarian answered. "We have no records we can read and no memory passed down to us of any Mages being on the great ship," he said. "The first mention of Mages comes more than a generation after the ship arrived here."

"None of the ship's records we have been able to read speak of Mages as real beings," Coleen added. "We found only children's stories and fantasies and other fictions which feature humans able to do supernatural things."

Mari stared at Alain. "Mages didn't come on the ship along with everyone else?" She felt a sudden, awful, sinking sensation, wondering if she and Alain could ever have children.

But the librarian who had spoken before was shaking his head. "All people here came from the ship. There was no one on this world before its arrival. Something happened after people came here, or perhaps on the voyage itself. There are words which may hold the answers, though we no longer understand enough about them. Mutation. Genetic drift. Something called genetic engineering, which was able to change the very nature of a person's body, may have been involved. We don't know. All we do know is that a generation after the arrival of people here there began to be reports of people who had magelike powers, weak at first but growing in strength and variety. More and more of these Mages appeared, and eventually they were strong enough to form their Guild."

"And," Mari added, feeling some relief to know Alain was as human as she, "strong enough to be able to survive the attempts of the Mechanics Guild to destroy what it couldn't understand. But Mages are...like us? I mean, in all of the important ways?"

A woman librarian frowned slightly at Mari's question. Then her expression cleared as understanding came and she looked at Alain. "As far as we know, yes. You should not need to worry on that account."

"Thank you."

Alain was looking concerned again, but that was easy to appreciate given the topic. "From where did the librarians come?" he asked.

"Not all members of the crew agreed with the decision of the majority," Coleen explained. "Some of the crew were what were called..."

Another librarian spoke up. "Data Storage and Media Retrieval Technicians."

"Yes. It meant librarian, in part, and so our ancestors reverted to the simpler and more complete name." Coleen gestured around to include the entire tower. "The plan for settling this world included the construction of this tower in a safe place, as a refuge in the event of disaster and a secure location to keep records and equipment of value. When those who established the Mechanics Guild made their decisions, the ancestors of we librarians were forced to agree to their terms. In order to prevent the Mechanics Guild from destroying these records and devices, our ancestors agreed to remain silent about them. In exchange, the Guild knew all of this remained available to them if it was ever needed."

The librarian sighed, she and the others looking guilty. "It was a bargain with demons, but necessary. The alternative would have been the loss forever of everything here and all we knew. For century after century the librarians have remained hidden here, protecting the past but unable to share it, hoping for the day when the Mechanics Guild would fall and we could once again give our knowledge to the world."

Mari grasped Coleen's arm. "I can't fault your ancestors or you for that decision. I know just how ruthless the leaders of the Mechanics Guild can be." She took a step toward one case, gazing at some of the small devices within it. "I saw something like these in the Mechanics Guild Headquarters. A very old far-talker that looked like this." She bent to read the labels. "Rah-dee-oh. What does that mean?"

"It was what our ancestors called far-talkers."

"Why? What does it mean?"

The librarian looked embarrassed. "We don't know. Much of this equipment no longer works. Other devices still work, but we no longer know how to operate them safely." Coleen gestured toward another small device. "This is a mass data storage reader. According to our information, it can hold thousands of books within it and display all of the knowledge, but how it did this we cannot remember."

Mari stared at the racks near the device, which were filled with what looked like coins. "That's not money?"

"No. Each of those coins holds a tremendous amount of information. Perhaps. Once they did so, but we do not know if the information on them has deteriorated over time, as the pages of a book will crumble with age."

"How could something this small hold so much?" Mari wondered, peering at the coins. "And how could the information be read?"

Another librarian spoke up. "I believe something called a lass-er was used for that."

"A lass-er?" Mari knelt down, digging in her pack and surfacing with one of the texts. "Like this?" She offered the ancient text to the librarian, who took it with trembling hands.

"Yes," he breathed. "Yes. Just so. Somehow this light could be used to do things which normal light cannot."

Mari looked at Coleen. "You don't have copies of these Mechanics Guild texts?"

"No," Coleen said, leaning to look at the one held by her fellow librarian. "The Guild kept anything designed for easy use and understanding. We have heard of those texts but thought them forever out of our reach. They were supposed to aid the people who came here if they lost more complex equipment or suffered a loss of knowledge. Those texts were designed to provide easy instructions and knowledge for regaining technology that might have been lost in a disaster. The texts are of incredible value now, literally priceless because no sum of money could replace them."

Mari looked at the text she held, its pages made of some very tough and durable material instead of paper, but which were nonetheless showing signs of age. "You mean if something happens to these, there are no others?"

"Perhaps in the vaults of the Mechanics Guild headquarters in Palandur, where none will ever see them," the librarian replied. She hesitated, then spoke with great care. "Lady Mari, we are skilled at making exact copies of what records we have. It has been one of our major occupations in the last few centuries, to preserve things whose originals were fading or crumbling. It would be a great service to all the people of this world if you allowed us not just to view the texts you have, but to make copies of them as well."

"Copies?" Mari turned the text in her hand, thinking of the vast distances it must have come, the hands which must have first held it. Thinking of the perils which she and Alain had faced on the journey from Marandur to here, the times when the texts might have been lost forever. "This came from Urth? This very text? All that way, and it was held by our ancestors?"

"Yes."

Mari took a deep breath and looked to Alain. He nodded back in agreement.

Another deep breath, and then Mari held the text carefully in both hands as she looked back at the librarians. "Exact copies? You can make exact copies? No errors? Every line, every drawing, perfect and correct?"

"That is our calling and our often-practiced skill," Coleen confirmed eagerly.

"Then I do wish that you would make copies." Mari swallowed

nervously, then rushed out the rest of her words. "As long as they are exact copies, I would like to take the copies, and leave the originals with you, where they will be safe."

An extended silence followed her words, then all of the librarians bowed to her, embarrassing Mari. Coleen straightened, fighting back tears. "You may be the daughter of Jules in truth, but you also have the soul of a librarian, Lady Mari. There is no way in which we can adequately repay you for a gift of this magnitude."

"The texts aren't mine," Mari insisted. "They belong to everyone in this world. I'm not giving you anything that you don't already have a right to." She looked around, feeling very awkward, trying to find something else to talk about, and her eyes came to rest on the map of Urth and beside it the diagram of the *Demeter*. "What became of the great ship?" Mari asked. "It was so huge. Surely its remains must lie somewhere, or was it completely taken apart?"

"The ship was stripped of all it held and much of its structure." Coleen pointed upwards. "The bones of the ship remain to this day, far above the sky we know, floating like the moon above this world."

Mari jerked in surprise. "It's still there above us? But we can't see it?"

"Even the remains of the great ship are small compared to, say, the moon," another librarian explained. "If we trained powerful far-seers on it, we could see the remains, but—"

"But," Mari continued, "the Mechanics Guild has discouraged or banned anything to do with the study of the skies and the stars. Of course. They didn't want anyone figuring out where we came from, or seeing the ship." She shook her head, feeling her jaw tighten. "What incredible selfishness and arrogance."

Alain had gone back to study the map of Urth. "Why did the ship come here? It must have been a tremendous undertaking."

"We are no longer certain," Coleen admitted. "I'm sure the truth lies somewhere in there," she added, with a wave at the drawers full of shiny information coins. "But we no longer know which of the possible reasons we recall are true. Some say that it was simply adventure and exploration. Some that it was an attempt to spread humanity's seed to the stars. Others think that such an expensive and enormous undertaking meant that they had no choice, that some disaster loomed which would cripple or even kill all who remained on Urth."

Mari stared at Coleen. "Like a terrible storm?"

"We do not know," she replied.

"If what we remember is true," a male librarian said, "worlds can suffer enough variation in climate to cause serious problems. Then there are said to be huge stones floating in the vastness between stars, and sometimes these fall to a world, as if a mass equal to the entire island of Altis became a projectile to strike Dematr. You can imagine the damage. It is also said stars such our sun and the sun that warms Urth can change, becoming hotter, larger, or even exploding when their fuel is exhausted."

"What?" Mari shook her head firmly. "I don't know about the rest, but that last can't be right. How can something explode after it runs out of fuel? An explosion needs something to feed it."

"We do not know," the librarian said with equal firmness, "but what remains to us says this can happen."

"I don't see how. What kind of fuel does a sun use, anyway?"

The librarian made a helpless gesture. "That knowledge was withheld from us by the Mechanics Guild's founders."

Alain was looking at another map. "This is Dematr, our world. But it looks more like a painting than a drawing."

"It is an image," Coleen explained. "Made from what were called orbital surveys when the great ship first arrived here."

"I have been told how the world appears to one riding a Roc high in the sky," Alain said. "This seems the same, but as if from a height no Roc could reach." He pointed to the map. "There is the Dematr we know, the lands around the Sea of Bakre. But what is this far to the west across the Umbari Ocean?"

Mari answered before the librarians could. "The western continent? It's real?"

"Yes," Coleen said. "Far enough distant to be difficult to reach with the ships we have. Needless to say, the Great Guilds have not permitted any expeditions in search of it. As far as we know, no ship has ever gone there, and no people live there. Perhaps it has plants and animals such as those we know, or perhaps it is still like this world was before the great ship came."

"You know so much," Mari said softly. "You have kept so much knowledge safe. And yet there is still so much more to learn."

Coleen smiled. "Those things are the definition of happiness for a librarian. That and sharing the knowledge we have."

Mari walked carefully through the room, not quite touching the devices, noting that all had been kept clean and free of dust. The Mechanic in her admired the care with which the librarians had tried to maintain these things. "When I saw the texts in Marandur, and saw all of the amazing things they described, I knew it had to have come from somewhere. All of that technology had to have developed over many years, building on advance after advance." Her gaze went to the maps again. "And now I know where it came from. Urth. Where our ancestors lived and hopefully our brothers and sisters still live. And now I also know how much was taken from us, and why, by those who founded the Mechanics Guild."

She stopped in front of a very large box which rose slightly higher than her height and was about three times her width. Mari read the label on the device, which had words stamped into metal. "'Transmitter.' This is the largest far-talker I've ever seen. Why is it so big?"

The voice of the librarian who answered Mari was hushed. "It is designed to talk not to anyone on Dematr, but to the stars. This device is supposed to be able to send a message to Urth itself, and receive replies."

Mari stared at the librarian, then back at the transmitter. "It has enough range to reach across a distance that took centuries to cover? Does it still work?"

"We don't know. It should. It has never been activated."

"Why not?"

Coleen answered this time, her voice resigned. "The Mechanics Guild forbade our ancestors to activate it. The librarians of the tower have survived these many years because the Guild wanted to have these devices and knowledge still available if they were needed to maintain control of this world. But we have always existed at the sufferance of the Mechanics Guild, for we have neither weapons nor defenses. Over time, knowledge of us may have faded in the Guild, a loss of memory probably aggravated by the purges which have occasionally resulted in the deaths of numerous Mechanics."

"Purges?" Mari asked. "Was the last one of those about a century ago?"

"It was." Coleen made a helpless gesture. "We have had no inspectors from the Mechanics Guild visit for many decades, and when you first appeared we feared that the Guild had remembered our presence here. But it appears the Guild has forgotten us. However, if we activate the transmitter, it might alert the Guild. We don't know. We have never dared try it, for if the Guild learned we had done so then everything here could be lost."

Another librarian spoke gruffly. "It's questionable whether we still can activate the transmitter. We told you earlier that the power we receive from the tower has slowly lessened. It may no longer be enough."

Mari ran one hand very gently across the surface of the transmitter. "Maybe someday I can get another generator here. I saw that your stream is fed by a waterfall, so a simple water turbine might be all you need." She bent to look at the transmitter's label again. " 'Feyn-man. Feynman Transmitter.' What does Feynman mean?" The librarians shook their heads in reply. "I didn't see an antenna."

"The tower contains the antenna—*is* the antenna, if what we have remembered is true."

Once more Mari touched the device reverently. "We'll speak to the stars. Someday we'll speak to the stars."

Coleen spoke with sadness this time. "We can offer you no aid in your task, Lady Mari. We must remain hidden while the Mechanics Guild retains power, and we have no weapons to offer you."

Mari gazed back at the librarian. "My friends and I can make weapons, with the help of those texts. I don't want to have to use them, but we may have no choice. If the Great Guilds remain in control of this world, everywhere will end up like Tiae and eventually Marandur—because the founders of the Mechanics Guild wanted the wealth and power of Dematr for themselves."

Alain nodded. "And because the Mage Guild will not care what is happening to everyone else as long as its elders stay in control. They do not wish change, because they do not believe the suffering of others is real. They would not believe this is real, even as they die at the hands of mobs of commons."

"You said most of the crew of the great ship disobeyed the orders they had been given long ago," Mari said to Coleen. "Do you know what those orders were?"

Coleen looked at the other librarians, who made various gestures of ignorance. "All that we know," she told Mari, "is that what they did—take control of all technology and power for themselves—was in violation of those orders."

"Then whatever they were told to do involved sharing their knowledge with everyone," Mari said. "And sharing power with everyone. Those people who built the great ship, who knew so much more than we did, intended that this world be free of the control of anything like the Great Guilds. They intended that the commons have more control over their own lives."

"That is safe to say," Coleen agreed.

"Then I know what my job entails," Mari said. "In order to fix things, I need to correct the errors made long ago. I need to break the power of the Great Guilds, and I need to give the common folk the right to rule themselves."

"Do you truly believe that you can do that?" Coleen asked.

"I don't know," Mari said, looking toward Alain. "But we're either going to succeed, or die trying."

❖ ❖ ❖

The librarians had given them a comfortable room to stay in while the librarians worked through the days and nights copying everything Mari had brought. Night had fallen, and from their bed Mari and Alain could look through a window at the stars shining above the valley where the tower sat.

"Can you believe it, Alain?" Mari asked him. "It's so astounding. What must that voyage have been like? What is Urth like? Think how it must have felt when those people got here and first set foot on this world."

"And then decided to enslave all the others who would live here," Alain could not help adding.

She turned and gave him a narrow-eyed look. "I'm trying to focus on the romance here. What are you thinking? All of this Mechanic stuff in the tower and all, and finding out the Mages began appearing after people got here. How does that all feel for you?"

Alain did not answer for a little while, trying to put his thoughts together. "I thought at first that you were very unhappy, distressed when you saw all of those Mechanic devices. I wondered if you were jealous of those who had created such things. But then I saw that it was joy that moved you. And I felt some of that, through you. There is much to learn. We share that, you and I. In many ways our thoughts are different, but both of us want to learn new things. In that we are alike."

Perhaps Mari sensed that he had more to say, because she waited until he spoke again.

Alain gestured at the stars. "You know that I was taught that all we see is false, an illusion. Those stars, this world. And so I can change the illusion, for a little while. But people make the illusions, and this has been puzzling me more and more. Mage teaching says that people are but shadows moving across the world illusion. Even I would be but a shadow in someone else's mind. But I do not believe that any more, not of you and increasingly not of others. If we create the illusions by what we believe, then how can we be illusions as well?"

Mari made a baffled gesture. "I'm not quite following you, but I would think that to create something you'd have to be real."

"Yes," Alain said in a low but intense voice. "The people are real. That surely is the explanation for why the Mage arts cannot directly alter a person as they can anything else."

"You told me about that. It is kind of odd. I mean, people are made of the same elements as other things in the world."

"People are not those things. They are different somehow. But they are not illusions. No Mage can alter that which is real, and I now believe that each person is a reality, and a truth."

Mari reached over and grasped his hand. "I'd sure like to believe that's true."

"I think it is. Why has not my connection to other people harmed my ability to change the world illusion? Because it is a totally different thing. I can love you and it harms my art not at all. Indeed, I believe my love is somehow leading me to a new level of art. I have told you this, that I have found new strength. I do not understand it all, yet, but I feel things I did not feel before, and I sense possibilities beyond anything my elders promised."

"Because you love me?" Mari sounded uncomfortable. "I'm not that special."

"You are a truth, Mari. Everyone is. More importantly, you are my truth."

"You're really embarrassing me."

"I am sorry," Alain said.

She laughed and held him close. "Wait'll I get you someplace safe and private again."

"Must we wait?"

"You'll have to. The librarians said there is some sort of ancient recording device in each of these rooms and they never know when one will kick on for a little while. They may be willing to live with that possibility, but I'm not." Mari lay back, then spoke tentatively. "Alain? That reminds me. Is there something about being married that Mages know that nobody else does?"

Alain frowned up at the dark, puzzled by the question. "Not that I know of."

"But somebody told me that everybody knows Mages know something nobody else knows. I didn't know that, but everybody else knows it."

"What?"

"You heard me."

"Um." Alain tried to work his way through her last statement. "How could it be something only Mages know if everybody knows it?"

"No," Mari said, exasperated. "You're trying to confuse me."

"I am trying to confuse you?"

"It's something that Mages know that everybody knows Mages know but nobody else knows," Mari said.

"Mari, I really have no idea—"

"About being married, Alain!"

Alain tried to remember every reference to marriage he had heard from other Mages. There were not many, and they were all the same. "The only thing I was ever told about marriage by Mage elders was to avoid it all costs, because it weakened you."

"That's not it. And I'd like to have a talk with those Mage elders someday."

"That probably would not be a good idea," Alain suggested. "What is this thing Mages know about marriage supposed to be about?"

"You know."

"Uh, no."

"People," Mari said. "In bed together. Something special about that."

"Are you serious?" Alain thought, then again shook his head. "No. Nothing. No one ever said anything about that. We were told that sex was but a physical act and no emotion must connect to it."

"Really?" Mari asked. "Maybe a female Mage would know. I'll ask Asha the next time we see her."

"Mari, I must ask again if you are serious?"

"Yes. Alain, I'm afraid this is something you just don't understand."

Alain lay back again, staring at the ceiling. "I am certainly not going to argue that," he murmured under his breath.

"I heard that!"

Alain raised his hand to gaze at the ring there. It had not caused any physical changes in him that he knew of, but Mari's ring seemed to have given her extraordinarily good hearing. He wondered if they only had that effect on Mechanics, or if all women gained that ability along with their rings.

"Alain?"

"Yes, Mari?"

"Would you have done it?"

Alain took a moment to ponder what that could refer to. "What do you mean?"

"What those people did, the ones who gave their unborn children to the ship." He heard her sigh. "They would never see those children, and those children would never know their parents. They would grow up so unimaginably far away, and they wouldn't even be born until long after their parents had died. That would be so hard. But those children would someday walk the soil of another world, one warmed by a different sun, and they'd see and experience things their parents couldn't even imagine. And those people knew that someday their children and grandchildren and so on would live on that world and make it their own. So I can't decide."

Alain lay silent for a little while, thinking about it. "I do not know. As you say, it would not be an easy choice."

"No. It would be very, very hard. I guess I'm lucky we'll never face that choice. I have a feeling that having children will require enough difficult decisions as it is."

Alain felt a curious blend of wonder and fear fill him. He could not see her expression well in the dark, but Mari's comments reminded him of her statements about children earlier that day, her actions when she had heard about the passengers on the great ship, as if she were protecting something inside her. "Mari? Are you trying to tell me something?"

"What do you think I'm trying to tell you?"

"This talk of children…"

"Well, we have to think about it, Alain."

"But…"

"You seemed upset when the librarians and I were talking about the passengers on the ship." Mari rose up on one elbow and gazed at him. "Does having children scare you? Do you not want children? You never said that before."

Alain stared back at her, feeling his questions crystallize into near certainty at the upset sound in her voice. "I want children. I do. But I thought that would be later, when the risks to us were much lower."

"That's right," Mari said.

"But, you keep talking about…acting as if…" Alain was having trouble getting the words to come out, something that he found perplexing. "Mari, are you…?"

"Am I what? Am I sure?"

"No." Neither his Mage training nor his time with Mari had prepared him for this. "Are you expecting a child?"

"Am I what? Stars above, no! I need a few more years of life under my belt before I'll be ready to handle raising children, especially if ours have any combination of your personality and mine. I'd also like a little better assurance that I'll even be alive a few years from now before I take on responsibility for a new life." Mari suddenly laughed. "Was I trying to tell you something! I had you worried, didn't I?"

"A little," Alain admitted.

" 'A little'? I'll bet you were terrified! Oh, now I understand! No wonder you got so nervous! You thought—!" Mari laughed some more, and even after she fell asleep Alain suspected Mari still had a smile on her face.

But he lay awake a while longer, gazing up through the window at the stars filling the night sky, feeling relieved but also, in some strange way, disappointed.

❖ ❖ ❖

The next few days passed slowly. Mari kept fidgeting, knowing that Alli would have begun looking for them to return to the city but would be waiting in vain each evening. The mysterious special Mechanics would have arrived in Altis by now. What would they be doing? Had either the Mechanics Guild or the Mage Guild figured out that Mari and Alain were on this island? As Captain Patila had warned, there was only one good way out of Altis, via the city and the port, and Mari wanted to be gone before that path was blocked. Her most important questions had been answered, but the librarians needed time to copy the texts she had brought even with all of them working at full speed on the project. She couldn't complain about the food, since the librarians kept offering the best their small farms could provide, and the sleeping room was quite comfortable except for the ever-present possibility that some kind of device would begin making a record of her actions without her knowledge.

But there was so much to do, and she had no way of knowing how much time was left to do it. "I'm worried about Alli," Mari informed Alain.

"She seemed very capable," he commented.

"Of course she is! But so am I, and I wouldn't have lasted nearly this long if not for having you around." Mari frowned, looking out the window and down across the valley. "You know, that's important."

"I am glad you think so."

"Stop it. I'm serious." She turned to look at him. "It's like we found out at Ringhmon. Something that would have trapped or killed one of us, the other could get through. Working together, we could overcome any threat. That's personally important to us, but I'm wondering about these purges in the Mechanics Guild that have happened every now and then, according to what Alli's friend found out and what the librarians say. There must have been Mechanics like me before, people who were willing to risk themselves for what was right. But they always must have failed."

"They were not the daughter," Alain said.

"How do we know that?" Mari asked. "How do we know that I'm not just the latest daughter? That there haven't been others, now and then in the centuries since Jules died, but those others never made it this far?"

Alain considered her words before replying. "That is possible. A daughter of Jules, the prophecy says. Not *the* daughter. It could be read to mean that there would be more than one, though eventually only one would succeed. You think the others, if they were fated for the same role, failed because they had only Mechanic skills?"

"Yes." Mari sat down next to Alain. "I've asked the librarians if they have any record of people who could have been earlier daughters, but they can't find anything. If those daughters died right away, as I would have at Ringhmon, who would have heard about them? They would have been gone before they could accomplish anything, just like I would have if not for you. You're the wild card, the random variable that Mechanic traps can't hold. And because you're with me, I've been able to escape that fate. That's what may be different this time. You. It's not just the daughter."

He shook his head. "What is different is you and me, because I would not have survived alone, either. Yes, with my help you escaped the Mechanic ship, but I would have died in the Northern Ramparts long before that if not for you."

"You and me." She thought about that and liked it. "A team. Individually, we'd both be long dead. Together, maybe we can finally change the world. Maybe that's what the world has been waiting for, what the prophecy really required. A Mechanic and a Mage who would work together to make things right."

❊ ❊ ❊

They stood at the point in the valley where the path back toward Altis began.

Coleen the librarian hesitated, then offered her hand. "We're not supposed to take sides, but good luck anyway. May you find success in your efforts and may your life be a good one."

"Thank you." Mari gave her most sincere smile back. "But we'll meet again. Alain and I will return some day, just like I said." She swung her arm and pointed toward the base of the tower. "Some day

I'll come back with a generator, and we'll power up that far-talker you've got, the one that talks to the stars, and we'll see who answers when we call."

Coleen's eyes shone. "That would be a marvelous thing. What would we say, Lady Mari? What would we say to them?"

Mari grinned. "First off, we'd have to apologize for taking so long to get in touch."

❀ ❀ ❀

The journey back was much easier; they took the librarians' path the entire way. The path proved to be cleverly routed, not only concealed but also containing a couple of breaks where it seemed to come to a halt. In each case, only the guidance they had received from the librarians allowed Mari and Alain to spot the relatively easy but difficult-looking route to meet up with the next stretch of the path. At its end, the path let out through a maze of broken stone into a pass which in turn led to one of the finger valleys that led into the city of Altis.

By the time they reached the city proper on their second day after leaving the librarians' tower, the sun had long since sunk behind the mountains to the west and the streets of Altis were dark. "Let's eat something fast and find a place to sleep," Mari suggested. "It's too late to meet Alli tonight."

Alain agreed, and after cramming down a meal from a street cart which was about to shut down for the night, they found a decent though far from fancy hostel. The only room available was on the second floor, but that suited them. Once inside the room, Mari sighed and hugged Alain. "Hey, nice room, nice bed, no ancient recording devices. It's really late, and I'm really tired, but we can still try to have some fun tonight."

Alain held her tightly. "That would be nice. I wish we were not so tired."

"If wishes were horses…what's the rest of that saying, anyway? There'd be a lot more horses around?"

Alain didn't answer, his grip tightening on her.

Mari winced. "Ouch. Careful, lover. I've got a lot of sore muscles."

"Danger," Alain murmured.

She got it then, stepping silently from Alain's grasp and gliding over to the room's window to look out and down. The scene outside was mostly of the alley beside the hostel, but a strip of the street could be seen past the crates stacked near the alley's entrance. The street was dimly lit this late in the evening. She saw a couple of people walking by in the weary manner of those just trying to get home for the night. A horse-drawn wagon rolled past slowly, the hollow clopping of hooves sounding strangely threatening. "I don't see anything out here," Mari whispered.

Alain shook his head. "My foresight warns of danger outside the window." He pointed toward the door. "And there. I do not know what."

Mari drew her pistol, carefully and quietly chambering a round and letting off the safety, then walking on cat's feet to the door. Kneeling, she peered under it and saw nothing. Standing again, Mari listened intently. She heard nothing, and yet that very silence felt dangerous in some inexplicable way. Mari reached for the door handle, turning it carefully, then with infinite care eased the door open very cautiously, her pistol aimed at the gap as it opened. Nothing was visible in the barely lit hallway outside the room. Mari waited, breathing shallowly, then suddenly swung out as fast as she could and stared toward the stairs.

Easily half a dozen people were stealthily coming down the hall, carrying rifles, their Mechanics jackets a deeper dark against the night. They froze as they saw Mari, then charged toward her, raising their weapons as they came.

# CHAPTER FIFTEEN

Mari swung herself back inside with haste borne of panic and slammed the door shut, locking it. "Mechanics!" she hissed at Alain.

Alain had his pack on and tossed hers to Mari. She was backing toward the window, her pistol pointed at the door, as Alain threw the shutters open wide.

Thunder sounded in the hall outside and holes appeared in the door. If she had been standing at the door, those holes would be in her now. Mari stumbled back, hitting the window sill with her thighs and falling backwards out the window. She bumped into Alain, who had reached the fire escape ladder and grabbed at her to keep Mari from falling to the alley below.

The door to their room crashed open. "Go!" Mari yelled, getting her feet under her and pushing Alain. He jumped, grasping at the ladder as he fell, but missed a hold and dropped too far too fast, hitting hard and lying unmoving on the floor of the alley.

Mari, feeling tears of rage starting, stood in the window and emptied her pistol, firing as fast as possible into the figures crowding through the door. Some fell and others scuttled backwards under the furious barrage. Mari ejected the spent clip, her mind numb, and loaded another. She jumped to the ladder and dropped down it so fast her stomach knotted.

She landed near Alain and scrambled to his side, kneeling to check him with her heart in her mouth. He was breathing but seemed to have been knocked out by the fall.

A bullet snapped by so close that the wind of its passage ruffled her hair. Snarling, Mari spun and fired back, holding her ground with Alain lying helpless beside her.

Bullets kept coming at her. The crates and boxes at the entrance to the alley were masking several Mechanics with rifles, and those Mechanics were far better fighters than the usual Mechanic who had been handed a weapon and pushed into using it. These Mechanics used cover well, constantly popping up to snap dismayingly well-aimed shots at her.

Mari knelt on one knee next to Alain, using both hands to steady her pistol, aiming carefully despite her growing fear, aiming and firing at an arm behind that crate, aiming and firing at a flicker of clothing behind that wall, aiming and firing at a muzzle flash as a rifle fired. A shot struck the wall near her, spraying her with fragments of brick dust, and Mari felt a thrill of pure terror. She had only a few shots left in this clip, and she knew with ugly certainty that the instant she stopped firing those Mechanics at the end of the alley would rise up and aim carefully and she would feel their bullets slamming into her and all of her running and planning would be over and the daughter would have failed and the world would fall into chaos. But Alain was lying there helpless so there was nothing else she could do, absolutely nothing else she would do, and so Mari knelt and aimed and fired and waited for that last bullet which was surely only one or two away now.

Her latest shot knocked splinters from a crate. She heard a howl of pain from someone hidden behind it, then the slide on Mari's pistol stayed back, signaling the clip was empty. Everything felt as if it were happening in very slow motion as Mari began to scramble up and backwards, trying to draw fire away from Alain and fumbling for a new clip as she saw Mechanics standing up and raising their rifles toward her.

The crates between Mari and the Mechanics exploded into flame, dazzling her sight and that of the attacking Mechanics, and Alain was standing up beside her and pulling her to one side and through a hole where a solid wall had been.

Mari lay in the semi-darkness of a large room, quivering with reaction, unable to move. Her mind kept insisting that she had to be dead now, even though she could hear the muffled sound of shots on the other side of the wall as the Mechanics at the end of the alley blindly fired into the area where she had been only a moment before.

Alain, staggering with exhaustion from the effort of deploying the two spells close together, was trying to pull her up. "Mari! We have to run!"

Mari stared blankly up at him for a moment as she slowly absorbed the fact that Alain had recovered in time to save both of them. Her mind suddenly kicked into gear and she got her feet under her, wavering under the weight of her pack for a moment and wishing for the umpteenth time that she could just dump the thing but knowing that she couldn't. "I love you," she gasped. "Remind me to tell my mother how nice it is to have a husband who can hurl fire and walk through walls."

Alain urged her forward, stumbling as he went. "I need time to recover from that and from whatever knocked me out."

"You'll get it," Mari vowed, ramming another clip into her pistol and letting the slide rock forward to load a round. "I don't care what happens to me. They don't get you."

"You should have run and left me. I would be angry, except for the fact that I know you are even more stubborn than I am."

Mari fought down a wave of giddiness born of her unexpected survival. "You're only allowed to be stubborn when I say so, Mage. Remember that."

"Is this another rule of marriage?" Alain reached a doorway and leaning against it while he peered into the darkened room ahead, his Mage knife ready in one hand.

"Yes. I'll try to keep you informed as I come up with them. You pulled me to the right, didn't you? We must be in the building across the alley from the hostel." Mari crouched and went past Alain into the room, holding her pistol at ready. The room stretched a short distance, ending in large windows facing the street. Shelves packed with clothing and other goods could be dimly seen. "It's a store of some kind." She paused. "All right. We're fighting Mechanics. They don't believe

Mages can actually walk through solid walls, and they would have been temporarily blinded when you set fire to those crates. So they've got to believe that we somehow made it down the alley and over the fence at the back end. They'll be searching for us in that direction. If my orientation is right, those windows we see face on a street to the front, the opposite from that."

Alain nodded heavily, his tiredness showing in his movements. "Can you get us out to the street?"

"Probably." They scuttled through the store, keeping below the level of the shelves, until they were close enough for Mari to see through the windows. She crawled carefully forward, peering out. "Lots of lights to our left. That'd be at the hostel. People out there, some obviously city guard. I see some Mechanics jackets moving through the crowd. Most of the people seem to be bystanders, though, commons attracted by the noise."

Alain came up next to her. "Can we get out without being spotted?"

"If we're lucky." Mari edged her way to the main door. As she expected, it was locked, but the lock wasn't keyed from this side. Breathing a silent prayer of thanks, Mari slowly turned the latch until it clicked open with a sound that seemed to fill the silent store. The noise outside had probably covered the sound from being heard by anyone out there. Mari pushed down on the lever. "We walk out smooth and calm, like everything's normal and we've every right to be here. Clerks working late or something. Got it?"

"Got it," Alain agreed.

Mari put her pistol into the shoulder holster under her coat, closed the coat to hide the weapon and holster, then stood up, pushed open the door and stepped out onto the street, Alain right behind her. Some of the nearest bystanders gave them curious looks, but Mari calmly closed the door, then turned to Alain and pointed away from the hostel. They started walking steadily through the crowd, trying not to seem fearful or in a special hurry.

Mari caught a glimpse of a Mechanics jacket to one side, but the owner was fighting his way through the crowd toward the hostel, yelling insults at the commons who were too caught up in trying to find out what was happening to be aware that an exalted Mechanic was demanding they make way for him.

They reached the end of the street and crossed quickly, heading up into the city and walking into the relative sanctuary of a quieter cross street, where they could still hear echoes of Mechanic rifle shots bouncing from building to building. Behind them the sound of fire bells was resounding, and a faint flickering against low clouds told of a spreading fire. The fire in the crates must have spread to the surrounding buildings.

Mari realized that her hands were shaking again and hastily gripped Alain's arm. "That was too close."

Alain nodded. "How do you suppose they found us?"

"I can't imagine. I haven't talked to anyone since we got back to the city. No one knew we were there. We didn't even know we'd be there until we picked the place. Could Mages somehow be helping my Guild and detecting you?"

He shook his head. "Had Mages been present, they would have attacked us as well. They would not have any confidence in the ability of Mechanics to kill me."

"I guess you're right." Mari felt a prickling of alarm as she realized something. "Hey, the shots have stopped. They've already figured out where we aren't."

Alain just nodded and began walking faster. They dodged from corner to corner, crossing streets and changing direction as they put more distance between themselves and the hostel. The crowds had long since been left behind; they saw only an occasional other person on the darkened streets. Finally Mari pointed to a small bar on a street corner, still open this late in the evening. "Let's go in there, rest a little and figure out what to do next."

The dimly lit bar had only a few patrons, all of them drinking with the grim efficiency of those for whom alcohol was not a diversion but a constant companion. Mari and Alain took a table against one wall, gazing at each other and catching their breath. Before she could say anything, Alain frowned. "I have tried to sense the amount of power available here. It is very small. There is not enough power to support even a single spell, even if I put all of my own strength into it as well."

"Then we'd better get the blazes—" Mari broke off in mid-sentence as she turned, staring at the small window next to the door. A shadow had flickered across it, as if someone had moved quickly and stealthily there.

Alain caught Mari's worried look and turned to stare that way. "There is danger," he announced. "Darkness lies that way."

Alain's foresight had kicked in again, but perhaps too late. Mari turned toward the back of the bar, getting out of her chair only to have Alain grab her arm. "That way as well."

"Alain," Mari hissed, "you can't get us through a wall here, can you?" He shook his head. "That means front and back are the only directions we've got!"

"Both are deadly," Alain repeated, his face worried.

Mari looked around. Aside from the flimsy tables, the only cover in the place was offered by the actual bar itself, a fairly substantial-looking piece of furniture anchored to the outside wall and with a sturdy load-bearing brick interior wall behind it, extending most of the way across the room. The brick of the wall next to them, which must be shared with the next building over, went all of the way up to the ceiling. Opposite them, the outside wall was made of brick up to about waist high, but above that were thick wood planking and beams, hinting that this place had once had a far grander occupant. It also had no windows at all except the small one near the front door, no way of getting out through.

With nowhere else to go, Mari tugged Alain toward the bar, coming around the end to confront the bartender, a wiry elderly woman who would have looked grandmotherly if not for the aura she carried of having spent a good portion of her life in prisons. The woman scowled at Mari. "No one behind the bar but me."

Mari whipped out her pistol and pointed it at the woman. "Can't you make an exception in my case?"

The old woman stared, then rolled over the top of the bar with surprising agility, dropping off the other side to the floor. Before the bartender could scramble to her feet, the front door exploded open, fragments spraying the room. Mari brought her pistol around, squeezing off a couple of shots as dark-jacketed figures burst into the room, themselves firing rifles into the gloom of the bar. The few patrons hurled themselves to the floor.

Mari tried to aim at one of the attackers, but a volley of shots shattered bottles and glasses behind her, spraying fragments of glass in all directions. She dropped behind the bar, shoving Alain down against the outside wall and crouching between him and the opening at the end of the bar. More bullets hit the top of the bar, sending splinters flying, as others thudded into the front of the bar. From the other side, Mari could hear the thunking noise of bullets plowing into the brick wall behind her, sending out spurts of pulverized brick dust to drift downward. Armed Mechanics must have burst through the back door as well.

Some of the lanterns in the room had been knocked over, their flames now catching on the floor and tables to brighten the dimness and give Mari a decent view of the open end of the bar. Someone in a dark jacket appeared at the opening and Mari aimed and fired in one motion, making the figure jerk back and away.

*We're trapped. No way out this time. It's over.* Mari felt fear filling her again, but along with that fear was a powerful certainty that overrode everything. "Stay down," she said to Alain over the sounds of gunshots and the impacts of the bullets. "They won't get to you while I still live." The conviction she felt was an odd thing, separate from her terror and utterly unyielding. She might soon die, but all that mattered, the only thing that mattered in all the world, was trying to save Alain even though she knew it was hopeless.

Mari felt a sudden rush of fatigue and her arm drooped. She was raising her weapon again when Alain's hand grabbed her shoulder and pulled backwards. Off-balance and surprised, Mari yielded to his tug even as she wondered where he had found room to get farther back.

An instant later she was stumbling onto the street outside, staring at a once-again solid wall and at another Mechanic who was staring back at her with a dumbfounded expression. Mari recovered first, swinging her pistol to club her opponent senseless. A shout from the corner drew her attention and she saw another Mechanic there, yelling and pointing at her. Mari brought her weapon up again and fired, sending splinters flying as the shot hit the wall near him. He dodged behind the corner, still yelling.

Mari looked around, seeing Alain propping himself up against the wall, ashen-faced with fatigue. She put one arm around him. "Lean on me!" Moving as fast as possible while supporting Alain, she staggered across the street. Shots rang out behind them and bullets went snapping past. Mari hit the corner of the next street and swung them behind it as another volley tore holes in the bricks and wood of the structure there. She leaned out and fired, sending Mechanics diving for cover, then waited despite the shots still coming her way and fired again to discourage pursuit for a few more seconds before swinging back and supporting Alain once more.

"Run, blast you!" she urged Alain, who was still having trouble getting his feet under him. Mari supported as much of his weight as she could. She would carry him if she had to, but she knew they had to move faster if they were to get away again. They reached the next street and Mari crossed immediately, then went down the next side street and took the next corner as another shot took a chunk out of a window frame near her.

She staggered with Alain down a short side street, her heart pounding with fear and fatigue, her legs wobbly with effort, and saw an open-top horse-drawn cab there, the driver looking with a puzzled and worried expression toward the sound of the gunshots growing closer. Seeing Mari, he shook his head. "I'm not taking any fares. I'm leaving."

"Not without us." Mari tossed Alain into the cab with a strength she hadn't known she possessed, then jumped in as well and stuck her pistol in the driver's face. "Go!"

Mari wondered just how deadly her expression must have looked as the driver paled and whipped his horse into motion. The cab thundered down the street, scattering a few pedestrians who stopped to hurl insults their way. Mari rested her free hand on Alain, rising up enough to look back and see Mechanics running out onto the street, then leveling their rifles at the fleeing cab. More shots rang out and the pedestrians scattered again, this time not stopping in their flight.

"Turn, you idiot!" Mari yelled, pivoting to stick the muzzle of her pistol against the driver's back. The cab swung wildly, tilting onto two wheels as it took the next corner going full out. The cab settled back onto four wheels with a jarring crash while Mari tried to figure out where to go next.

"Left," Alain mumbled from the seat where Mari's free hand was holding him in place.

"Turn left at the next corner!" Mari commanded the driver. "And slow down a little or I'll blow your head off!"

They took the corner with less danger that time and the cab rumbled down a long straight stretch before Mari ordered it to turn left again. As it settled onto the new street, she saw a city park to the right and pulled back her weapon. "Stop the cab." The driver reined in his foam-flecked horse. It was hard to tell which one was staring with wider eyes, the horse or the driver. Mari hopped out, pulling Alain with her. Before she could say a word, the driver whipped his tired horse back into motion. By the time Mari had dragged Alain into the cover of the park, the cab had vanished.

She kept going until they reached a bench well concealed by bushes from the street they had left, then dropped Alain onto it and collapsed beside him. Cursing her trembling hands, she pulled out some bullets and refilled the clip in her pistol, fumbling with the rounds as she tried to force them into place.

"Where are we?" Alain looked around wearily.

"I think we're at the boundary of the industrial areas," Mari guessed, angered by the way her voice wavered from stress. "That's where the parks are. What happened back there? You told me you couldn't get us through a wall because there wasn't enough power."

"There was not," Alain confirmed, breathing deeply and staring upward. "There definitely was not. But then, while we were behind the bar, the power was suddenly there."

"Why didn't you tell me that could happen?" Mari asked crossly. It didn't make sense to be angry at Alain, but her nerves were jumping crazily.

"It cannot happen. Power can be drawn down by the work of Mages, but then can be renewed only slowly. It cannot spike as the power did there. It came from somewhere, Mari." Alain's expression suddenly shifted and he stared at her. "It came from you."

"What? Alain, that's totally ridiculous."

"But it happened. I do not understand it at all, but it came from you. With what you provided and my own strength, I was able to get us through the wall."

Mari stared back at him, remembering the strange burst of tiredness she had felt. "No. It must've been something else. Not me."

"Mari, I have been noticing this for a while. I am becoming more aware of a power that people carry, that strong emotions can create."

"I didn't give you power! Knock it off, Alain!" She didn't know why, but the idea frightened her. On top of other events so far this night, it was simply too much to handle.

He seemed surprised by her reaction. "I will not speak of it again for a while then."

"How about not speaking of it ever again?" Mari growled. She looked around them. "How did they find us at that bar? First the hostel, then the bar. What's going on?"

"I have no idea."

Mari stood up, offering Alain her hand. "Let's go. I've got a bad feeling."

Alain stood up, nodding. "I can walk now." Then he turned his head toward the street.

Mari did, too, hearing the sounds of horse hooves, of carriages rattling to a halt, then of boots hitting the pavement. *No. It's impossible.* But she grabbed Alain's hand and they both took off through the park, running as fast as Alain's tiredness would permit. Mari heard a command shouted and saw the flash of light from a rifle shot, then heard the shot and its passage through nearby bushes. They dodged to one side, then dodged again, hitting a slope and almost falling down it before reaching another patch of shrubbery and racing through it.

They stumbled out onto a wide street which looked deserted, stretching off in both directions with no cover. On the other side of the street was a wall easily half again as tall as Alain. Mari spotted a gate in the wall and urged them that way. It was locked, of course, but with a big lock, easy to pick for someone skilled. Mari hurriedly pulled out a lock pick and quickly clicked the lock open. Pushing the gate ajar, Mari pulled Alain inside and pushed the gate closed again, relocking the gate as she did so, then leading them into a warren of large buildings that loomed high on all sides. "The warehouse compound," Alain got out between breaths. "I remember it from the city maps."

Mari nodded wordlessly. She was feeling more and more like a hunted animal, chased from place to place, running out of endurance and options while the hunters closed in relentlessly. High, narrow windows with heavy bars on them stared down at the fugitives as they raced down the alleys between warehouses. Finally they reached a dark corner and collapsed next to each other. *Please, please, don't let them find us again. The other gates out must be locked, too, and they're too easily guarded. Alain's too tired to take us through another wall. This looked like a good place to hide but I've trapped us in here.*

She heard boots running toward them and almost groaned with despair. It sounded like only one Mechanic, but even one Mechanic would force her to fire her weapon and bring the others down on her.

"Mari! Don't shoot!"

She was swinging her pistol around to bear on the person who had called her name, her finger quivering on the trigger. Somehow Mari managed to control her overstressed nerves and kept from squeezing off a shot. "Alli?"

Alli came closer, her Mechanics jacket making it hard to see her clearly in the dark. "Yeah, it's me." A moment later Alli dropped down next to them, breathing heavily from her run. "Thank the stars I found you! They know you're in here somewhere but I managed to get away from the others and sneak in ahead of them. Mari, listen, you've got—"

"What are you doing here?" Mari cried. "They'll kill you, too."

"Will you please shut up, Mari?" Alli demanded. "Listen. The Guild is tracking you."

"What? How?"

Alli fumbled at Mari's pack. "Your far-talker. You've got a far-talker with you."

"Yeah. I thought I should hang on to it." Mari hastily began aiding Alli, digging for the far-talker she had faithfully lugged across half the world despite the frequent temptation to drop the heavy object down a deep hole. "How did you—? What about—?"

Alli seized the far-talker. "We've got to rid of this! Fast!"

"Why?"

"A friend helped me plant a far-listener in the office of the Guild Hall supervisor so I could hear what they were saying. Yeah, I know how illegal it is to bug a supervisor's office, and you're in no position to be lecturing me about it anyway. I was worried about you and about me. And do you know what I heard them talking about? Portable far-talkers send out a low-powered signal even when they're off, Mari. The Guild can use that signal to find you. That's how they're locating you. That's how they knew you were on that ship when the *Queen of the Seas* captured you, and that's how they realized you were in Caer Lyn and that you had come here."

"A homing signal?" Mari stared at the far-talker. "But I know the Guild lost track of me at times."

"I told you it's low-powered, Mari, so no one would suspect their far-talker was operating even when supposedly powered down. They could only find you if you were close enough for them to pick up the signal. Whenever you got close enough to a Guild Hall with the far-talker, they could tell where you were. These killers they sent to get you have several portable devices that give them bearings on your signal, so they're able to locate you pretty precisely and pretty fast no matter where you are."

"Blast!" Mari pointed her pistol at the treacherous far-talker, feeling an irrational urge to execute the traitorous device, then restrained herself with an effort. "Alain, this is how they've been able to find us! When a far-talker is sending out a signal it isn't directional, but by using different timed bearings or multiple intercept stations they can—"

"Mari," Alain interrupted. "I appreciate your attempt to keep me informed, but since I am not understanding a single thing you are saying to me, is it really wise to spend time doing this?"

"I guess not. We can pull the battery...no, let's use this to misdirect them. The blasted thing has betrayed me many times. I'll let it betray the Guild for once." Mari stared around, focusing on a window in one of the warehouses nearby. "Can you boost me up, Alain?"

She had to climb on his shoulders, balancing against the warehouse wall to keep from falling, but that was high enough to be able to look into the warehouse through the barred window. Mari shoved the far-talker between the bars, then one-handedly tossed it to fall down between several large crates. "Catch me," she warned, then dropped into Alain's arms.

Alli actually grinned at them. "That looked really romantic. You guys must have done this kind of thing a lot."

"Alli! This isn't the time! We need to—" Mari raised her pistol again as another figure appeared.

"Alli!" a new voice called.

"Here," she answered, pushing down Mari's gun hand. "It's okay, Mari."

The new person ran to them, his open Mechanics jacket flapping. "They're localizing on the new location right now. We've got to move."

"All right," Alli agreed. "Mari, this is Dav. He helped me get in here, and he's the guy who helped me bug the supervisor's office. We can trust him."

Mari returned the other Mechanic's handshake, noting that he seemed to be in his mid-twenties. "Dav?"

"Yes. Dav of Midan."

Mari stared at him, causing Alli to give her a worried look. "Mari, you look like you've seen a ghost."

"Maybe I have. Dav, did one of your ancestors die in the siege of Marandur?"

"Yes. How did you know?" Dav asked, astounded by the question.

"I can't tell you yet." Mari turned to Alain. "I've made a lot of bad choices tonight. Where do you think we should go now?"

Alain pointed east and led the way toward one wall of the compound, the small group running across open spaces as they tried to put as much distance as they could between themselves and the telltale far-talker. But when they reached the warehouse nearest the east gate they ran up against a barrier of lights outside. Crouching in the shadows of the last warehouse, Mari tried to make out what was beyond the lights. "They've got to have people there."

"Yes," Dav agreed. "That's the plan. They opened the gates to encourage you to try to run out, but they've got the lights set up to blind you as you come and sharpshooters with rifles behind the lights. I was hoping they hadn't gotten things ready yet, but that's why they've taken a little while to come in here after you. You kept getting away every time they had you, so this time they were going to have every exit covered before they went in. They've got orders to shoot on sight," he added.

"We've noticed." Mari sighed heavily. "How do we get past them? Anybody? Any ideas?"

Alain studied the lights. "I can muster enough power to blow one of the lights if placing a small fireball there would do it."

"One light wouldn't be enough," Alli replied in a grim tone. "Besides, if they figure out we're here they'll come charging in and nail us all." She gripped her rifle. "I could shoot out some lights here and hold them off while you guys run—"

"No, Alli!" Mari snapped. "Your chance of surviving would be zero." She slumped against the warehouse wall. "Too bad we can't just walk through walls until we get past them."

The other two Mechanics exchanged puzzled glances as Alain shook his head. "One small hole, perhaps," he said, "but then I would be unable to do another. There has been too much effort tonight."

A new voice spoke then, one which Mari recognized instantly.

"Then perhaps a friend can help."

Mari stared at the robed figure standing in the shadows nearby. "Asha?"

Alain was on his feet, too. "Mage Asha. You have found us. I did not sense you near."

Amid the blood and fire of the night, Asha's cool Mage voice sounded even more bizarre than usual. "I have worked hard to improve my ability to hide myself, a necessary thing when the Mage Guild seeks my death as well as that of my friends. As to finding you, how could I not? Even if the fires and destruction on your track were not easily seen, the being of my friend Mari has been blazing in my mind for the past few weeks as if to blind me."

Mari rounded on Alain, all thought of their desperate straits momentarily forgotten in her sense of humiliation. "You said she couldn't tell!"

"I said she could not tell what we were doing! If your feelings were more intense—"

"It's the same thing!"

"Uh," Alli interjected hesitantly. "I don't really understand what this argument is about, but if this Mage can help us escape I really think we ought to get going as fast as possible."

Mari took a deep breath. "You're right. The first priority is to get under cover so we have time for more planning without worrying about being surprised." She eyed the warehouse next to them. "Where's the door to this thing? Nobody knows? We can't go running around looking for it and maybe running into assassins on the way." She looked at Asha. "Alain is exhausted from helping us get this far. Can you get us though this wall? Please?"

Asha raised one eyebrow the barest fraction. "You need only ask, friend Mari." She turned and beckoned. Another robed shape appeared and that Mage turned to face the warehouse wall. A moment later that solid wall showed an opening large enough for each of them to scramble through in turn. Inside, the darkness of the warehouse was dimly lit by reflections through high windows of the Mechanic lights outside the gate.

Mechanic Dav shook his head as the hole vanished. "I wouldn't have believed it."

"Believe it," Mari muttered. She leveled a finger at Alain. "You and I have some things to discuss later. Alone."

Alain held up his hands to signify defeat. "Whatever you wish. If we survive."

Asha came close, staring at Alain's left hand. "What is that ring you now wear? A promise ring? I know of them. You have wed her. Now I understand the intensity of friend Mari's bonfire."

Alli stared at her. "Mari has a bonfire?"

"Will everybody stop talking about my bonfire?" Mari gazed threateningly at the small group. Even Asha's eyes widened slightly as she stared back. Mari focused on the third Mage. "Who are you? A friend of Asha's?"

The hood on the robes came back to reveal the expressionless face of a middle-aged man. "We have met before," he said, the lack of emotion in his voice giving no clue as to how that meeting had gone.

"We have?" Mari stared at the Mage, trying to remember where she had seen him.

"Yes," the Mage said calmly. "You tried to kill me."

Mari gave Alain a startled look. "Did I have a reason? I must have had a reason."

"I was trying to kill you."

"Well, there you are." Something finally clicked in her memory. "In the alley in Palandur. You're the Mage I shot."

The male Mage nodded. "And, when you could have slain me, refrained. Then you gave me a bandage and instructions on how to use it until a healer could preserve my life. I did not understand why any shadow would do such a thing. I did not understand how a shadow could save something that is real. The Mage Asha and I spoke of that and many other things, for she is my niece." Mari looked from the tall, gorgeous female Mage to the dumpy male Mage, wondering how they possibly could be that closely related. "In speaking with her, I came to realize that I could give my loyalty where I choose, and that the feelings I had been fighting for so many years were to be welcomed instead. When I learned that my Guild sought Mage Asha's death, I did not hesitate to renounce the authority of our elders."

Asha gestured toward the male Mage. "This is my uncle. In Palandur I sensed that he was injured, and would not leave without him. This I learned from friend Mari. Do not leave anyone behind."

"Well…yeah," Mari said, embarrassed. She smiled reassuringly at Asha's uncle. "I'm honored by your trust and grateful that you chose to help Asha. I'm not always this stressed, by the way. What's your name?"

"I am Mage Dav."

Two Davs in their small group. Nothing was going to be easy this night. "All right, Mage Dav. I'm glad to meet you. This is Mechanic Alli and Mechanic Dav, and Mage Alain, of course."

Mage Dav looked at each of them, not showing any trace of gladness or other expression.

Mari glanced at Alli and the other Dav. "I know it doesn't look it, but he's being very polite by acknowledging that you exist."

"I've known Senior Mechanics who acted like I didn't exist," Alli remarked. "Hey, Mage Dav. Welcome to the revolution."

Asha indicated her uncle. "In the confusion as the Mages attacked you in Palandur, I was able to reach my uncle and take him to a healer. It did not surprise me to learn that Mari had aided him even while fighting for her life. Mage Dav and I had to hide while the healer worked his art, but my uncle is strong and quickly recovered enough to travel. I said we would find you and join you, and we have. Our timing appears to be fortunate."

"You might say that." Mari gazed around the group again, surprised to realize that there were now six people total. Mechanic Dav, getting his first good look at Mage Asha, appeared to be in a state of stunned nirvana.

Mari was easily the youngest person in the group, except for Alain who was only a little younger than she, but all were looking to her for leadership. *How did that happen? When did I become the leader in a situation like this? Me, the crazy woman with the bonfire that has now reached blinding levels of intensity. They're probably picking it up back on Urth and wondering who I am. All right. The daughter of Jules has to figure a way out of this mess or the revolution ends here.* "Mechanic Dav, what are the Mechanic assassins going to do once they have all of the exits covered?" It had finally occurred to her that these were the Guild assassins Professor S'san had warned her of back in Severun.

Mechanic Dav jerked his attention away from Asha with obvious difficulty. "They'll come in and quarter the area until they find you and kill you."

"Nice. Are they guarding the walls between the gates?"

"Yes. But that's a lot of territory to cover, so between the gates there's just a screen of armed apprentices posted at intervals. I'm supposed to be supervising some of them. A lot of them are way too young to be doing that kind of thing, but their main role is to sound an alarm if they see you."

Mari gave Alain an anguished look. "I don't want to shoot at apprentices. I don't want to hurt them at all. A lot of them are just kids."

Before he could answer, a deep boom sounded outside and the floor and walls of the warehouse shook. Dust filtered down from the high ceiling and a shock wave rippled through the floor beneath them. Alli scrambled up onto some crates until she could see out of one of the windows. "I think that warehouse where we left the far-talker is gone."

"Gone?" Mari demanded. "They blew it up? The whole warehouse?"

"Looks like it. Boy, Mari, they really want you dead." Loud thumps

sounded on the roof over their heads. "That's debris from the explosion coming down. Wow, I wish I could've set that charge. It must've
been great putting something that big together."

"Alli! Focus! We're trying to survive here!" Mari closed her eyes,
trying to pull up a mental map of the area they were in. "Walls. Warehouses. The outer wall of this warehouse is also one of the outside
walls. We're in a trap, but every trap has a weak point because everything has a weak point. That's simple engineering. What's the weak
point in this trap? The apprentices."

"They're the youngest and the weakest and the least experienced,"
Mechanic Dav agreed. "But like you said, a lot of them are just kids."

"That's all right," Mari said. "Thanks to these Mages, we've got some
non-lethal ways of dealing with the apprentices. Alain, that thing you
did when they tried to kidnap me in Dorcastle, where you made it
really bright for a moment? Can you do that again?"

He nodded. "Yes. I have that much remaining in me. I cannot hold
it long."

"You won't have to. Just a flash in a small area. But we have to do
something to keep the assassins from noticing when we do that."

Alli brightened. "How about an explosion?"

"An explosion?" Mari grinned. "Do you know where we can get
some explosives?" she asked, already guessing the answer.

"I've got some with me," Alli said. "And some fuses. Don't look at
me like that, Mari. I packed some tonight because I thought we might
need to blow up something."

"You were right about that," Mari admitted. "Do you have enough
to blow a small hole in one of these warehouse walls?"

"Oh, yeah. I don't know if it would be a big enough hole for us to
get through, though, and the sound of the explosion would attract the
assassins for sure."

"That's the idea! It'll be a... what do they call that, Alain? A
distraction?"

"A diversion," Alain said.

"Right. Alli, we'll need an explosion going off near that closest gate outside, to divert the attention of the assassins and everyone else. Do you have a timer?"

Alli shook her head. "I have a fuse I can cut to the right length, though."

"Good enough." Mari looked at the two other Mages. "Mage Asha and Mage Dav, I don't know how much you had to go through to get here. How tired are you? Do you have many spells left in you? Is there enough power in this area for you to use?"

Both Mages nodded. "We are fairly well rested. The journey to find you was not difficult," Asha explained. "Our main concern was staying hidden from the senses of other Mages. We did not have to search for you, since as I said earlier I had no trouble sensing your bonfire. At one point its intensity was almost painful."

Mari winced, looking daggers at Alain, who took a sudden interest in the far side of the warehouse. "Can we just not bring up that bonfire thing again for as long as possible? I'm a little sensitive about that."

Mage Dav gave Mari what passed for an intrigued look from a Mage. "You know a great deal about Mages."

"Well, yeah." She pointed at Alain. "I'm married to one. Can either of you throw fire like Alain?" To Mari's surprise, both shook their heads.

"The use of fire is a very difficult art," Asha explained. "Few Mages can master it."

"Alain never told me that," Mari said, giving him a different kind of look. "All right. Here's what we're going to do," she announced. "Alli, you're going to lay a charge against this warehouse wall as close to that nearest gate as you can. Use a short fuse."

"I've got enough fuse for a longer burn if you need that," Alli said.

"Of course you do. We want a short burn, Alli, because we need to get out of here before the assassins figure out where we are, but give yourself enough time to get back here. After Alli has lit the fuse, she'll join us along the wall of this warehouse. That's part of the outside wall, too. We'll get as far from the nearest gate as we can. Just before the charge blows, Alli lets us know so Mage Dav can open a hole in the wall, giving us access to the street, and as the explosion goes off Alain sets off his flash spell thing through the hole to dazzle the eyes of any apprentices nearby. It has to be at the exact same time, Alain. While the Mechanics watching the gate are diverted by the explosion and watching for us to charge out the gate, and the nearby apprentices are temporarily night-blinded, we all run across the street and head for, uh…"

"The entertainment district," Mechanic Dav suggested. "There'll still be crowds there so we won't be the only people on the streets, and it's only a few blocks east of the warehouse district."

"Great. Mage Asha, you're our…um…spare," Mari said.

"Reserve," Alain corrected her.

"Reserve. Right," Mari said. "Be ready to cast a spell if we need it right after Alain and Mage Dav have cast theirs and can't do another quickly. Has everybody got that?"

Mechanic Dav shook his head. "I get the hole in the wall thing, because I just saw it even though that seems impossible, but what's the flash-spell thing?"

"Just keep your eyes averted when I tell you," Mari said.

"What are explosives?" Asha asked.

Alli stared at her. "Somebody has really neglected your education, Lady Mage! Explosives are mixtures of ingredients that have been processed in a way that allows them to either oxidize extremely quickly or to instantaneously release large amounts of energy when triggered by a detonator employing chemical, mechanical or electrical—"

"Alli," Mari interrupted. "Mage Asha is a smart person, but she is not understanding one word of that because she has been taught very different things than you and I have."

"Really?" Alli frowned. "Um…explosives make a lot of noise and blow up things."

"Like a Mechanic boiler," Alain said.

"No," Mari said. "Not like a boiler. A boiler can explode but it is not an explosive." That sounded a little odd even to her. "Listen, we'll have time to explain things to each other later. For now, just each do your part." Mari looked at the motley group, amazed that she suddenly had five Mechanics and Mages following her instructions. Alli seemed perfectly happy with that, Alain was used to working with her in a crisis, the other Mages weren't giving any clues as to what they thought, and if Mechanic Dav didn't stop drooling over Mage Asha he would walk straight into a wall and knock himself out.

"Alli," Mari said, "do your stuff and get back to us fast. We won't go if you're not with us when the charge goes off." As Alli dashed off, Mari pointed toward the wall facing the street. "Let's get in position. Asha, does your Guild have any idea that Alain is here?"

The female Mage shook her head as they ran to the wall, making her long blond hair shimmer and causing Mechanic Dav to trip over something. "I do not know. However, before the Mechanics began destroying this city we did not notice any unusual behavior among the Mages here."

"That's one piece of good news."

They wove through a maze of crates of varying heights and finally reached the wall. Mari leaned against it, trying to calm herself, running through her plan in her mind to see if she could spot any flaws in the time they had left. "Having more than one Mage to use is very handy," she said to Alain.

"Having extra Mechanics around is useful as well," he replied.

"Yeah," Mari agreed. "The bad part of all that, though, is that if I mess up I won't be the only one who pays the price. It's been that way for a while for both of us, hasn't it?"

Alain nodded, his expression revealing tension to her even though others probably would have thought it calm. "A mistake would harm both of us. It has been like that for some time."

"Hey." Mari spoke in a quieter voice as he looked at her. "I'm a little crazy about that bonfire thing, but I do love you. Remember, if I fall, you—"

"Will stay with you."

"Alain, you're the only other person who knows all the things I know! The only other person who has a chance of fixing things if something happens to me!"

"I cannot bring the new day. You are the daughter. It is your fate."

"I need you to stay alive." Mari insisted. "We both have to make it back to Dorcastle, right? That's what your vision showed."

He shook his head. "The vision showed what might be, not what will be."

"I say it will be, Alain!" She held his hand tightly. "We've made it this far."

Mari heard the sound of running boots and dropped her grip on Alain to draw her pistol and ready it again. "Alli! Over here!" A moment later Alli appeared, one extended forefinger moving in a steady beat as she counted. Alli gave Mari a warning look. "All right, everyone. Stand by." Alli's forefinger came down one last time and she gave Mari a thumbs-up. "Now, Mage Dav. Go, Alain."

# CHAPTER SIXTEEN

The solid wall of the warehouse now held a hole the size and shape of a narrow door, through which pale light from the nearby Mechanic searchlights filtered into the warehouse. Alain took two steps and stood in the opening Mage Dav had created, one hand extended, the other arm covering his eyes. A loud explosion erupted at the far end of the warehouse as Alli's charge went off, blowing out part of the wall down near the gate, and at almost the same moment Alain's spell caused bright light to flare for an instant right outside, then vanish.

Mari blinked away spots. Even though she had been screened from most of Alain's light, it had still been bright enough to dazzle her a little. "Let's go!" She rolled around the corner of the opening, her pistol held ready, and sprinted across the street, coming even with Alain. In the middle of the street an apprentice was staring around, his young face panicky. "Kris? Fathima? Who's there?"

Mari swung close to the boy, who she thought couldn't be older than ten. "Guild business," she snapped with the most attitude she could muster, mimicking a Senior Mechanic. "Don't worry about us."

The boy nodded in confusion, blinking around as the other Mages and Mechanics ran past. The Mage-created opening in the warehouse wall had already vanished as if it had never been. Mari heard a girl's nervous voice call from down the street. "Kyl? What happened down there? Are you all right?"

"Guild business!" the boy called back. "Yeah, I'm all right."

In the other direction, shots rang out. Mari pivoted that way, bringing her pistol up as a heavy lump formed in her guts, but the shots weren't followed by the sounds of bullets striking nearby or going past. She stared down the street at the bright lights around the gate, able from this angle to see the figures of Mechanics behind the lights, some of them aiming into the cloud of dust raised by Alli's explosive charge. More shots rang out as the Mechanics fired into the dust and the small opening the charge had made in the warehouse wall.

A hand grabbed her arm. Mari spun again, seeing Alain even as her pistol came around. He pulled at her urgently and Mari realized she had been standing still instead of fleeing. She ran with Alain after the rest of her tiny army, none of them stopping until the group had reached the minimal shelter of a side street. "Your plan worked!" Alli exulted. "Those guys are professional killers and you outsmarted them!"

"Yeah," Mechanic Dav agreed, giving Mari the sort of look he had previously reserved for Mage Asha. "Alli was right. You're brilliant."

Mari stared at them, unsettled by the praise. "Oh, please. We're not out of this yet. How do we get out of Altis alive?"

"There is a boat down at the landing," Asha said with her unnaturally calm voice even though her eyes were glittering with excitement. "It will take us to a small ship in the harbor."

"A small ship?" Mari asked. "What small ship?"

"My small ship," Mage Dav answered. "The common members of my family are traders out of Gullhaven. I discovered that I had inherited a trading vessel, the *Gray Lady* by name, from one of them. The ship and crew await us."

"We've got a ship," Mari exulted. "If we can get to it. Alli, Mechanic Dav, you guys know Altis better than I do. How do we get to the landing?"

The other Mechanics exchanged glances. "The Guild's got a ship in the harbor, too," Alli told her.

"A ship? One of the steam ships?"

"Yes, but not one of the all-metal cruisers. There's only one of those left right now since you crippled the *Queen*," Alli explained.

"You really did almost sink the *Queen*, all by yourself?" Mechanic Dav asked with an awed expression.

"Alain helped a lot. Is this Mechanic ship in the harbor armed?"

"Yeah. A medium-caliber deck gun."

"Is that bad?" Alain asked.

"That's bad," Mari confirmed. "All right. Fine. We'll deal with that when we get there." Mari led the way down the street at a fast walk, putting away her pistol. "First thing, we head for the entertainment district." A few more shots rang out behind them, muffled by distance. Mari could hear more fire bells ringing, and when she looked back she could see at least two columns of smoke rising into the night sky, illuminated by the fires beneath the smoke, fires that had been caused by the fights near the hostel and the bar. Mari suspected that the Mechanics Guild and crowds drawn by the sounds of battle had prevented the local fire wardens from getting to the blazes and putting them out before the fires spread. Nearer at hand, a wide and growing pillar of smoke was rising from the warehouse area, this one lit up by the lights of the Mechanic assassins and from more flickering flames beneath it. As she watched, another explosion resounded from among the warehouses and a fountain of smoke and debris flowered skyward as tremors rippled through the street underfoot. "This is going to be a tough night for the city and citizens of Altis," Mari said.

Alli squinted back the way they had come. "From what I can see, I'm guessing that marks the end of the warehouse we were inside. Good idea to use a short fuse and get us out of there fast, Mari."

"Thanks," Mari said. "Hopefully, now that I'm not hauling around that far-talker, the Mechanics Guild assassins will keep shooting at and blowing up warehouses for a while before they notice we've gone." She glanced back at her group, Mage robes and Mechanic jackets intermingled. "Guys, this looks weird. Really, really weird. Alli and Dav, Mechanic Dav that is, get in front so the commons will clear a path for you. Alain and I will go next, because we still look like commons, then Asha and Mage Dav. That way we won't look like we're all together."

They walked, trying to keep up a good pace but not so fast as to look like fugitives. Not for the first time, Mari envied the Mages' ability to look totally emotionless no matter what was happening.

Alli turned her head to talk to Mari. "So, you've already got a plan for dealing with the Mechanic ship?"

"Uh…"

Alain's hand came to rest comfortingly on Mari's shoulder as he answered for her. "Yes, Mari has a plan."

"Good." Alli and Mechanic Dav both seemed reassured.

Mari leaned close to Alain. "I have a plan?" she whispered.

"Yes, you do. The same plan we used on the Mechanic ship."

Mari gave him a baffled look. "The make-it-up-as-we-go-along plan?"

"I thought you preferred to call it improvising." Alain indicated the others with them. "They have confidence in you, but still need the comfort of feeling that you have the situation under control."

"Alain, tonight I wouldn't even be able to recognize a situation that was under control," Mari confessed.

"They only need to believe you can lead them and they will follow you anywhere."

"Is that supposed to be comforting? Because it isn't. It was bad enough when your life was my responsibility, Alain, but now there were four more riding on my decisions."

Alli dropped back a little again, nodding her head in Asha's direction, her voice a whisper that only Mari could hear. "Where did you find her?"

"She's an old friend of Alain's," Mari replied.

"Oh."

"What does that mean?"

"Nothing! If you're comfortable with that, then—"

"Comfortable with what?" Mari demanded.

Alli gave her a doubtful look. "You have noticed how beautiful she is, haven't you?"

"Duh. She's got a great butt, too, in case you haven't noticed that."

"I haven't had the chance, but I'm sure Dav of Midan has drooled over the sight of it." Alli rolled her eyes. "You're not worried about her and, uh…"

"No." Mari turned a baffled look on Alli. "Alain thinks I'm better-looking than she is."

"No way!" Alli grinned. "Maybe he's seeing the inner you."

Mari couldn't help smiling, too, grateful for the distraction from her worries. "Oh, yeah, the inner me has to be one incredibly hot female, huh? If Alain could see the real inner Mari he'd have run away a long time ago."

"I don't think so. Why does Asha keep calling you 'friend Mari'?"

"She is my friend," Mari explained. "And that's pretty special to her. She hasn't had any friends, Alli. Not like you and me. Not ever. Asha can't really show it, but she keeps calling me that because it means so much to Asha to have a friend."

"Really?" Alli shook her head. "No friends. That must have been rough. Were you Alain's first friend, too?"

"Uh, yeah, I guess so."

"That's our Mari." Alli laughed, checked her rifle, then walked faster for a moment to catch up with Mechanic Dav.

Well-lit streets were visible ahead, a fair number of people still upon them despite the late hour, but many of those people were now ignoring the bars and nightclubs which tried to lure them in. Instead, most were staring to the west, where lights flared, the not-too-distant crack of Mechanic rifles sounded off and on, and an occasional deeper boom marked large explosions going off. The faint sound of fire bells ringing deeper in the city carried between the closer and louder noises of destruction.

Mari guessed that the Mechanic assassins were methodically blowing open warehouse after warehouse in search of her and Alain, while shooting at anything that moved. The rodent population of the warehouse compound was certain to be taking a serious hit tonight. It felt odd to know that the battle sounds Mari was hearing were aimed at her when she was outside the area of battle and trying to get farther away by the moment.

"This is the high-class district," Mechanic Dav looked back to announce as they entered the crowded streets. "Most of the people here are citizens of the city. They don't usually go down to the entertainment district by the port."

"What's the difference between the entertainment district in Altis and the one down by the port?" Mari asked.

Alli gave Mari an incredulous look. "Mari, don't you know anything about sailors?"

"Not much, no."

"Cheap booze, cheap entertainment, cheap food," Mechanic Dav summed up. "Back home they've got nice families and nice houses. In a foreign port they've got good times."

"But we need to get down to the port," Mari said, exasperated. "Are you saying there's not much traffic between here and there at this hour?"

"Not much, no. During the day we'd blend in. But at night we'll stand out."

Their group cut through a swarm of commons that split like a frightened school of fish to make way for the Mechanics in front and the Mages behind them. "At least all of the other Mechanics are busy trying to catch us and we don't have to worry about being spotted," Mari remarked.

"Unfortunately for that idea, one approaches even now," Alain warned.

Mari turned to see a Mechanic hurrying toward them, her jacket easy to spot in the crowd. "I had to open my big mouth. Does anybody know her?" The Mechanic looked young, about Mari's age.

"It's Bev." Alli waved in greeting. "I think she'll be all right, but act casual, Dav."

"Casual? We're both armed and the city is being blown apart back there."

"Just try."

"Bev's a little…high-strung, Alli," Dav protested. "Are you sure she won't blow her circuit breaker when she sees us?"

"I think she deserves a chance," Alli said firmly.

The other Mechanic came running up, breathing heavily. "Alli,

Dav? What're you doing? They sent me to find you guys. The Guild needs every—" Bev's eyes had been wandering across the group as she spoke and now came to rest on Mari. "Oh, no." Bev's hand went for her waist, where a holstered revolver was visible.

Dav was the closest and grabbed her arm. "Bev, it's all right."

"All right? Don't you know who she is? That's her!"

"I know." Dav shrugged apologetically. "I'm with her now. Me and these others."

"Dav, that's crazy! Let go of me. If the Guild finds out, they'll kill you!"

*Told you,* Dav mouthed at Alli.

"Bev," Alli insisted, "you can trust Mari."

"We have to follow orders, Alli!" Bev pleaded.

Mari stepped forward, eyeing Bev. "Why are you working for people who want to kill your friends?"

Bev froze, staring at Mari like a bird viewing a snake that was ready to strike. "Don't talk to me."

"Mechanic Bev, you—"

"Don't talk to me! I don't know how you managed to get your hooks into Dav and Alli, but you won't mess up my mind!" Bev struggled harder and Dav had to use both arms to restrain her. Commons walking past were averting their eyes, trying to avoid any involvement with this strange Mechanic altercation.

Alli came closer, her voice and face pleading. "Bev, you can trust Mari," she repeated. "Mari is not like what the Guild says. I've known her almost all my life."

"Trust her? And not trust the Guild? You're turned inside out, Alli. We have to trust the Guild! The Guild is our only family, remember?"

Something broke inside Mari as those words tore the still-thin skin off a deep wound that had only lately begun to heal. "The Guild stole our families, our mothers and our fathers," she almost shouted. "They did it to me and I'm sure they did it to you. You never heard from your common family after you went to Mechanics schools, did you? Nei-ther did I, and our oh-so-nice Senior Mechanics told us that's what commons did. Let me tell you, they lied. Your parents, my parents, tried to stay in touch, and the Guild destroyed every letter and package they sent and destroyed everything we tried to send. And all of you, like me, were too ashamed to admit that hurt and too brainwashed to realize that the Guild was lying to us. Is that who you want us to trust, Mechanic Bev? The Guild that stole our true parents so it could become a false parent that would use us as it saw fit?" She stopped speaking, her heart pounding with pent-up rage now released again. "Go to your true parents. They'll tell you. They still love you."

Alli and Bev were staring at Mari, their faces pale with shock. Dav, who Mari suspected had Mechanic parents, seemed both shocked and ashamed. Bev glared at Mari for a long moment before she could speak. "No! You're lying! That can't be true!" She suddenly collapsed in Dav's grip. Dav pulled the pistol from her holster and let her slump to the ground. "It can't be true," Bev whispered. "It's all I have left."

"What do we do with her?" Alain asked. "We cannot stay here."

Mari looked to Alli. "I don't want to hurt her."

Alli was still apparently stunned. "Hurt her? Stars above, Mari. If what you say is true…" Alli swallowed. "Oh, no."

Mari knew just how they felt, but she could also feel the looming threat of their pursuers. "Snap out of it, people! I know what this feels like. Believe me. It's not too late to reconcile with your real families. But we can't stand around discussing it right now!"

Bev had fallen to a sitting position, her knees up and her face in her hands, sobbing. Mari knelt beside her. "I'm sorry."

The other Mechanic raised her face enough to look at Mari, her expression angry and torn. "What?"

"I'm sorry. You can come with us, or you can stay. We'll tie you up so you can say you fought us."

"And if I want to tell the Guild where you are?" she asked in a strained voice.

Mari stood up, sighing. "Go ahead."

"What?"

"Go ahead. I've hurt you enough."

The others came forward in a group. "Mari—" Alain began.

"No! We let her go if that's what she wants." Mari knew her voice was torn with emotion and the strain of all they had been through recently. "I've hurt her enough today and I'm sorry, Mechanic Bev."

Alli knelt this time. "Bev, please. At least don't tell the Guild where we are. For Dav and me."

Bev stood up slowly, wiping her face roughly. "That person, that Mari, she said she was sorry." Bev glared at Mari. "No one in the Guild has ever apologized to me. Ever."

Alli hung her head. "Bev was an apprentice in Emdin," she murmured, as if that explained everything.

Bev took a step to stand close to Mari, staring directly into her eyes. "If you betray me, I swear I'll kill you. I swore I'd kill the next person who betrayed me. I thought the Guild was all I had left. Will you give me something else?"

Mari nodded, her face solemn, for once feeling no doubt about what to say. "I will if you will let me. You can help me on the biggest and most important repair job ever. You can help me fix this world."

Bev inhaled deeply, as if she had stopped breathing and only now remembered to do it. "The Guild has barricades on all of the roads to the lower port. They're checking anyone passing through. They've told the city authorities that two mass murderers are trying to escape them, and they're forcing the city guard to provide assistance."

"How do we get past that?" Mechanic Dav asked in despairing tones.

"We could head into the mountains," Mage Asha suggested, her placid voice sounding strange amid all the emotion.

"We?" Bev glared at Asha. "Mages?" Asha gazed back, her expression unchanging.

"They're different than we've been told," Mechanic Dav told her.

"I'll take your word for that," Bev stated in a rush, as if now that she was committed she didn't want anything to make her doubt that decision. "We can't go inland, either. The paths into the mountains are also being blocked."

"How can they occupy so many barricades? How many Mechanics are there on this island?" Mari erupted.

"I told you, they've got the city guard helping, and the island militia." Bev pointed toward the warehouse district. "Did you hear the biggest explosion back there a while ago? I heard Senior Mechanics telling city officials that you did it, that you intended doing the same to schools and hospitals."

"Schools and hospitals?" Mari knew her revulsion was showing. "That is so sick even to suggest."

"But it means the commons on Altis want to help capture you!"

"We could change that," Alain suggested. "If they knew you were actually the daughter—"

"Alain, if I tell the commons of this city that, they'll try to rise up right now!" Mari whispered angrily. "Just like those commons on the *Sun Runner* almost did. And all of these Mechanic professional killers will murder them in huge numbers. We can't start the rebellion here. Even if the commons here won, Altis isn't big enough or isolated enough for us to build up the power we need to confront the Great Guilds! They'd isolate the island and kill everyone on it!"

Alain thought, then nodded. "You are correct. But it may be necessary to tell the commons in order for us to escape this city. We may have to…trust in their ability to act wisely."

"You may be right, and sooner or later we will have to do that, but we're not at that point yet." Mari paused to think, feeling the stares of six other people on her. Time was working against them. Every moment spent thinking, spent cautiously making their way to safety, was a moment for their enemies to concentrate force against them. "All right, then." She pulled out her pistol and checked the clip, ignoring the passing commons who were trying not to notice the weapon. Making sure she had plenty of bullets still in the pistol, Mari returned it to its holster. "Here's what we'll do. It's already past midnight, and the city is crawling with people looking for us. If we try to sneak out it'll take forever and we'll likely run into barriers anyway."

"Then how do we get out?" Mechanic Dav asked.

Mari pulled out her Mechanics jacket and put it on. "We're four Mechanics and three Mages. We're done sneaking around. We're going to walk down toward the low port like we own this city, and we're going to walk right up to whatever barricade they've put up across this street, and if anyone tries to stop us we start breaking stuff. If we absolutely need to, we'll let the common troops know who I am rather than kill them." She gave her followers a confident look, settling the jacket on her shoulders and trying to ignore the knots in her stomach. "What do you say?"

"That's crazy," Alli replied. Then she grinned. "I like it."

Asha and Mage Dav nodded to each other. "The plan is acceptable," Asha advised.

Mechanic Dav shrugged. "I'm not staying behind if the rest of you are going."

Mari gave Bev a look. "You?"

Bev stared back. "Who's in the lead? Who takes the first bullet?"

"I'm in the lead. I take the first bullet."

"Unless I take it first," Alain added.

"Fine." Bev nodded. "What're we waiting for?"

Mari glanced unobtrusively at Alain, who nodded slightly to indicate that Bev was not lying, then gestured to Mechanic Dav. "Give her back her weapon."

They headed out, Mari and Alain in front, the three other Mechanics right behind, and the other two Mages trailing. Mari let herself adopt the Mechanic attitude she had once used as a matter of course, even though she had never been able to affect a swagger. The commons on the street made way for them, though some couldn't help staring at how closely a pair of Mages was following some Mechanics.

Mari nudged Alain. "Do you want to put on your robes?"

"No. That would make it too hard for me to walk alongside you without attracting too much attention."

"You don't need to walk alongside me. I'll be fine." He shook his head, so Mari continued. "Alain, you'd better not mean what you said about taking a bullet for me. I told you the first time we met that I don't let other people die if I can help it, and the man I love is very high on my list of people I won't let die. At the top, actually."

"Mari." Alain looked down for a moment, his face composed. "The worst may happen. As you said once, it may happen at any time. If that occurs, you must move on without me."

She stared straight ahead. "No."

"There would someday be another man you could love."

"Are you saying I should hang out around Mage Guild Halls until another Mage exactly like you walks out? Alain, if you die, my bonfire goes out and there'll be nothing but ashes left inside me. Sorry. That's just the way it is." They walked in silence for a few more steps. "But if something happens to me, you find yourself someone else."

His voice sounded openly incredulous. "You do realize you are being a little inconsistent?"

"So what's your point?" She saw the barricade ahead. "Here we go." Mari turned her head to speak to those behind her. "Remember, everybody. We own this city."

The street down here, roughly midway between the city of Altis proper and the port, wasn't well lit, and the partial moon didn't help much. The two dots in the sky which marked the Twins that perpetually chased the moon provided little light. Mari felt confident that she wouldn't be recognized until she reached the other Mechanics. At least, she hoped that would be the case. She walked briskly up to the barricade, remembering to set her face in the arrogant lines of some of the other Master Mechanics she had known. The two Mechanics at the barricade, both with rifles cradled in their arms, watched the approach of Mari and the three other Mechanics with no sign of alarm. That wasn't surprising, Mari realized, since they had undoubtedly been told to watch for one or two, not four. "You've got new orders," Mari called out as she reached the barricade. "We'll take this post. You're to report back to the Guild Hall."

The older Mechanic, a woman with a hard face, held out her hand. "You know the rules for this operation. All orders in writing."

Alli called out a greeting, her voice thick with sarcasm. "Senior Mechanic Larissa. Just my luck that I'd see you tonight."

The Senior Mechanic glared at Alli. "What are you doing here? I told you that one more screw-up and you'd be—"

"Excuse me," Mari interrupted, cued by Alli that this Senior Mechanic needed to be dealt with, not negotiated with. "I've got your orders right here." She reached casually into her jacket, then drew her pistol with one smooth motion, leveling the barrel a hand's-width from the woman's nose. "Any questions?"

Senior Mechanic Larissa was still gaping at Mari when Alli, Mechanic Dav and Bev rushed in to seize the rifles and pistols that she and the other Mechanic at the barricade were carrying. "Tie them up," Mari ordered, then turned to point at the unit of Altis city guard members who were watching the scene with confusion. "This operation has been canceled by order of the Guild Master. Return to your normal duties."

The city guard members shuffled their feet, looking uncertain. Then their leader spoke hesitantly. "Our orders are from the city, Lady Mechanic. We can't leave unless they tell us."

The older female Mechanic had finally found her voice. "It's them, you fools!" A moment later Alli stuffed a gag in her mouth.

"Them?" The city guard's leader hefted his short sword. "You mean—?"

Mari brought her pistol up to aim at him, her arm fully extended, then lowered it again as she decided that a threat wasn't the right approach. "You don't want to do that. We intend no harm to anyone here. We're on your side, and we're leaving this city to prevent the Guild from doing any more damage. Please don't get in the way."

The guard leader hesitated again.

Alain came to stand beside Mari, wearing his Mage robes now. "Do you need assistance, Lady Mari?" he asked her.

The militia and their leader gaped at Alain, then at Mari. "A Mechanic with a Mage?" the leader said in strained tones. He looked closely at Mari. "Young. Dark hair. Are you the daughter? Is this your Mage?"

Mari realized at that moment that this was the first time she would be making such a declaration in public, and found herself reluctant to say the words. "I am Lady Master Mechanic Mari."

"But are you…?"

"I am the daughter," Mari said, feeling as if she had just stepped off the edge of a high cliff.

"No wonder the Guild wants us to believe that you are a danger!" the unit leader cried, beginning to sheath his sword. But then he paused and looked at the bound Mechanics, the sword poised in his hand.

"No!" Mari ordered, and all of the common soldiers straightened to attention to listen to her. "Not here, not now, and I will not ever have mass killing or revenge killing of anyone!" She swung an arm back to indicate Alli, Dav and Bev. "Some Mechanics are my friends and allies. You can't tell which are which. Just as important, right now the Mechanics Guild has a heavily armed unit of assassins here, hunting me. They are causing a lot of the destruction, and if they turn their guns on the people of this city there is no telling how many would die. You must hold back a little longer, wait for me to build up strength. You'll hear of it, I promise you. You must keep control, maintain order among yourselves, and protect your people and your homes. When the time is right, the Great Guilds will be overthrown and all will be free to rule themselves."

She wondered where that speech had come from, the words appearing in her mind as if from deep inside her. But Mari saw the effect those words had on the commons, and was grateful for whatever inspiration had provided them.

The leader of the militia saluted. "Yes, Lady Mari. What are your wishes now?"

"Go and tell the leaders of Altis what is really happening, and of my wishes in the matter. A new day will come for this world, but you must wait for your own protection and not act against the Great Guilds tonight. I deeply regret the damage done here by the Mechanics Guild's attempts to kill me, but I am going now and the wrath of my former Guild will follow me."

The leader saluted again, then turned to his militia unit. "You heard Lady Mari! Let's go!" The militia raced off into the night, every common waving at or saluting Mari as they left.

Alli shook her head. "You're riding a locomotive downhill with the throttle full-out and trying to slow it down with just the brakes. But if anybody can do it, it's you." She pointed to the two bound Mechanics. "We've got all of their weapons and they're tied up. Doesn't your pistol use this same ammunition?"

"Yes!" Mari stuffed bullets into the pocket of her jacket. "I resupplied myself on the *Queen*, but I was afraid I'd never get another chance at more ammo, and I burned through a lot tonight." Then she knelt before the two Mechanics. "If you cause harm to any common in this city, I'll be back for you. The assassins of the Guild couldn't kill me, so if you harm anyone, no one will stop me from making sure you personally pay the price." She glanced at Alli, Dav and Bev, indicating the Mechanic with the Senior Mechanic. "What about this guy?"

Bev shook her head. "Total careerist and backstabber. On his way to Senior Mechanic status himself." Dav and Alli nodded in agreement.

Mari focused on the Senior Mechanic and the Mechanic again. "Remember what I told you," she said in as menacing a tone as she could manage, then stood up to gaze down the street. "It's all downhill to the landing, right? Let's see what kind of pace we can maintain." She began walking quickly down the hill, a feeling of urgency growing within her.

The road down to the low port was as unused at this hour as Mechanic Dav had predicted. Mari felt her hopes rising, but unexpectedly another barricade loomed out of the dark just short of the port. Mari slowed her walk, grateful for the chance to rest a little and knowing her companions also needed the break. "Bev, Dav, Alli, what is this? Any idea?"

"No." Bev came up beside Mari, her breathing coming fast. "I'll find out."

"Wait! You could get killed!"

Bev smiled humorlessly at Mari. "There are worse things than death." Bev spun and started jogging ahead, running right up to the barricade. As she reached it, a bright light flared. A portable electric light, spotlighting Bev. She held up both hands. "I'm from the city! The Guild sent me down with a message!"

Three figures appeared, all holding Mechanic weapons. One aimed at Bev, while the others pointed toward Mari and the rest of her followers. "Anyone coming down this road is to be disarmed and held for inspection," someone at the barricade called out.

"Asha, Mage Dav," Mari said in a low voice. "Can you destroy that light somehow?"

Mari had expected a Mage spell, but to her shock a long Mage knife was thrown from behind her, spinning end over end overhead. The knife slammed into the light, which went out with a loud popping sound.

"That worked," she heard Alli say as they all broke into a run.

One of the Mechanics at the second barricade fired at Mari, his shot whipping past her. Bev had grabbed the weapon of the man facing her, and as they struggled Mari and her friends arrived. Mari kept running. She ducked as her closest opponent awkwardly swung her rifle like a club, then came in under the swing and rammed her elbow into the other's stomach. Her foe doubled over and fell back, dropping her rifle, as Mari staggered to one side. A moment later Mechanic Dav had that Mechanic's arms pinned behind her.

Mari looked around. Between her Mechanics and her Mages, all of the Mechanics at the barricade had been disarmed and restrained. "Is anybody hurt?"

"Do you mean us or them?" Bev asked, her voice gleeful.

"Us. Is anyone hurt?" No one answered, and Mari counted six others standing beside herself. "These certainly aren't the trained killers we fought up in the city. Where did these guys come from?"

"They're not anyone I've seen around the Guild Hall. Who are you guys?" Mechanic Dav asked.

The three captured Mechanics stared back at him with mingled hostility and confusion. "We're—" one began.

"Don't say anything!" another interrupted.

"They must be from the ship in the harbor," Alli guessed. "Just the three of them. I guess they were supposed to be a last-ditch defense against Mari getting away."

"No," Alain corrected. "Their ship will fill that role."

"Oh, right."

Mari looked at the three Mechanics, brushing back her hair in worry. "I don't like fighting other Mechanics."

Alli nodded. "I know, Mari. But in some ways we've been fighting other Mechanics all of our lives."

"I guess." She addressed the three Mechanics. "We don't know you so we don't know if we can trust you, but we won't hurt you. You'll be tied up, but you won't be harmed."

Mage Asha had pried her knife free of the broken light as if the task were an everyday occurrence.She and Mage Dav began walking down to the landing. Mari stayed at the barricade for a moment, watching as the three Mechanic crew members were tied up as quickly and efficiently as possible. She finally went down to the landing proper, where the lapping of the small swells in the harbor sounded peaceful and relaxing after all the chaos she had endured so far this night. This far from the city, the destruction still being wreaked in the warehouse area sounded as muffled rumbles and echoes. The Mages were waiting at the landing alongside a skiff that looked like it just might carry everyone. Two commons wearing the clothing of sailors stood to one side, watching everything with wide eyes.

"These shadows brought us here and will return us to my ship," Mage Dav said.

"Hi," Mari said, knowing that Mage Dav and Asha would not offer any other introduction or acknowledgement of the two sailors. "We're in a big hurry."

The other Mechanics joined her and Mari gestured for everyone to board, though Alain insisted on waiting beside her. Finally she got in, too, worried as she saw how heavily laden the boat appeared. Alain followed, the boat wallowing in the water as the sailors cast off with worried looks and cautiously began rowing out into the harbor. Even though an occasional boom still echoed from the city, the port remained dark except for a scattering of lights in what Mari assumed was the entertainment district for sailors. "Where's the Mechanic ship?" she asked the sailors. "Steam and sails, deck gun, arrived within the last few days."

One of the sailors nodded. "Aye, Lady Mechanic. That ship lies off to starboard there. Is that where you wish to be taken instead of to the *Gray Lady*?"

"No. Thank you," Mari answered in a dry voice. Mage Dav, though the owner of the ship, didn't seem interested in telling anyone what to do. "We need the *Gray Lady*. Then we need to get out of this port as fast and quietly as possible."

The sailors grinned knowingly. "Trouble with the authorities?"

"Right," Mari assured them. She pointed back to where the sounds of destruction still rumbled. "That's going on because they're after us."

The sailors exchanged looks and then bent to their oars, driving the boat ahead at a faster rate.

Despite Mari's fears and an occasional larger swell that slopped a small amount of water over the side of the skiff, they made the *Gray Lady* without sinking. Mari climbed aboard the small clipper-rigged ship, delighting in the trim shape it showed in the starlight. Some machines were clunky and some were sleek. This particular sailing machine was a thing of beauty.

A man with a nicely trimmed beard approached Mari and Mage Dav, his manner deferential but not servile. "Sir Mage, we've been watching and hearing the events up in the city. Where and when do we sail?"

Mage Dav simply indicated Mari.

"I guess I'm still in charge," she said. "You're the captain? We need to leave port now without anyone noticing."

"We can do that. The harbor guard won't know we're gone."

"I'm more worried about the Mechanic ship." Mari pointed out the silhouette of the much larger Mechanic vessel.

"Mechanics fear a Mechanic ship?" The captain rubbed his chin, eyeing her, then the other Mechanics and the Mages. "You wouldn't be the daughter, would you?"

"Yes," Mari admitted. It was easier to say this time. "But call me Lady Mari. Is there anybody on Dematr who hasn't heard about me?"

"Not on this ship, anyway. Some months ago every tavern on the waterfront of Marida had men and women telling how they'd seen you in the Northern Ramparts and what you'd done there." The captain bowed. "It's an honor to sail with you, daughter. But that Mechanic ship has a big weapon on her deck."

"I know. If they open fire, try not to get hit by it."

The captain grinned. "I never thought to meet a Lady Mechanic after my own heart. You heard Lady Mari, you tars," he ordered his crew. "Get anyone still sleeping up here now. It'll be dawn soon and we need to be gone before then even though we'll have to fight the tide."

Alain had remained amidships at the rail, leaning on it and looking weary. Mari came back to stand by him. "We're almost out of here."

"Yes," he agreed, then frowned noticeably, a sign of how tired he was. "Something is missing."

"What?" Mari had learned not to question Alain's judgment in a crisis.

Alain looked back and up. "The city lies silent. There is no more sound of Mechanic warfare."

Mari followed his gaze, trying to fight off another wave of anxiety. "Then they've figured out that we're not where they've been blowing up stuff. Or maybe they think we're there, but dead and buried under rubble."

"Or they have found or heard from the Mechanics at the first barricade we went through—which means they will soon find the second barricade we took."

"Which means they'll know we're on the water," Mari finished. "Captain! Get this thing moving!"

The clanking of the capstan announced the anchor coming up and other sailors rushed upward to spread and trim the sails. The *Gray Lady* wore round under her sails, gently gathering headway under the soft breeze which was all they had to work with. "We won't be going anywhere fast fighting that tide," the captain announced.

Mari met the gazes of her followers: Alli grinning, confident beyond reason; Mechanic Dav chewing his lip as he stared at the dark shape of the Mechanic ship; Bev standing by the rail with a worried expression; the Mages Asha and Dav as apparently unworried and unemotional as ever; and Alain right beside her. Mari felt totally worn out as she swayed slightly with the movement of the ship and wondered how Alain was able even to stand after his exertions earlier in the evening and then the long trek down to the harbor. "We've got four rifles. Alli, Mechanic Dav and Bev take three of them and line up at the rail with me facing the Mechanic ship so we can shoot if we have to."

"Rifles against that?" Mechanic Dav asked, pointing to the Mechanic ship. The tide was forcing the *Gray Lady* closer to the Mechanic vessel as she tried to beat her way out to sea, so that the shape of the deck gun was now possible to make out as a dark, deadly silhouette between the masts of the large sailing ship.

"It's what we've got," Mari said, trying to sound firm and confident.

"They've got a far-talker on board. Once they hear we were at the landing..."

"They've already heard," Alli interrupted, pointing.

Mari stared through the nigh, seeing the dim, distant shapes of sailors rushing along the deck of the Mechanics Guild ship to the big deck gun, pulling off its canvas covering. The *Gray Lady* had been borne by the tide so far to starboard that they were within hailing distance of the Mechanic ship, and a moment later a voice came to them faintly over the water, magnified by a speaking trumpet. "Ahoy the ship! Heave to and await our boat!"

The captain gave Mari a questioning look. "Tell him we're on official business for the Mechanics Guild," Mari suggested.

Shrugging in a why-not way, the captain hoisted his own speaking trumpet. "Ahoy the Mechanic ship! We're on official business for the Mechanics Guild, and the Mechanics aboard will not allow me to heave to."

Unfortunately, that bought far less time than Mari had hoped. A reply came almost immediately. "That is a lie! Heave to in the name of the Mechanics Guild! No ships are allowed to leave this harbor by order of the Guild!"

The captain lowered his speaking trumpet. "Any more suggestions, Lady Mari? If I announce that the daughter is aboard, every other ship in the harbor will likely come to our aid."

"And be sunk," Mari added grimly. "They couldn't get here in time to help us, anyway."

The big deck gun on the Mechanic ship was training around to point at the *Gray Lady*. The sky was beginning to brighten in the east, making the Mechanic ship a little easier to discern but making the *Gray Lady* an easier target as well. "We'll dodge, as you suggested, Lady, but we're making little headway and our turns will have more in common with the sway of an old drunk than with the swerve of the barmaid evading his grasp," the *Gray Lady*'s captain advised.

Alli was shaking her head. "Do you realize there's no action around their boat at all? They're just planning on blowing us away and hope we'll stop so we'll make an easier target for that cannon. Oh, I wish I could build a gun like that."

Mari found herself momentarily struck by the absurdity of the comment after Alli's all-too-likely assessment of the Mechanic ship's intentions. "Alli, if we get out of this, I'll let you build guns a lot better than that one. Heavy artillery that will fire over the horizon."

"Really? That'll be so cool. I can't wait." Alli shook her head again as she looked at the Mechanic ship. "I hope we survive."

"Me, too," Mari said. "Everybody, rifles up." She pumped the lever on the rifle she had acquired at the barricades, then brought it to her shoulder, aiming at the figures of Mechanics on the other ship. Mechanics wearing the same jacket she wore, maybe people she had known in other places, studied beside as an apprentice, worked beside as a Mechanic. "I don't want to do this," she whispered to Alain.

"You may not have to." Alain was standing at the railing, facing the Mechanic ship. "Is it made of wood?"

"Is what made of wood?" Mari asked, sighting toward the person aiming the deck gun.

"The Mechanic ship," Alain explained patiently.

"Yes, sure. That ship has a boiler, you can see the stack, but it also depends on sails. Only two of the remaining steam-powered ships are made of metal, and they don't have masts like that, and you and I almost sank one of those a few weeks ago anyway. Even though this one probably has some metal hull plating for armor, the decks and the hull underneath are all wood."

The voice from the Mechanic ship called again. "This is your final warning! Heave to now or we will fire upon you! There will be no warning shots!"

Bev stood at the rail to one side of Mari, face set, her rifle steady. "Thanks," she whispered to Mari. "Even if we die in the next few minutes, you gave me something worthwhile to fight for."

Mari blinked sweat from her eyes, wishing that she weren't so tired, trying to hold a good aim at the crew of the deck gun and knowing the *Gray Lady* was well within range of the big gun but that the Mechanic ship was outside the effective range of their rifles.

"Do not let me fall," Alain said in that same calm voice.

As soon as Alain's words registered in her brain, Mari forgot about aiming. She jerked around to stare at him. Alain was standing very still, his gaze locked on the Mechanic ship, hands held at waist height and spread well apart. Something glowed there as enough heat radiated for Mari to feel it easily where she stood. Then the glow was gone and Alain was falling toward the rail, gone limp and possibly unconscious. Mari dropped her rifle onto the deck, grabbing Alain and yanking him back onto the deck before he could go overboard.

"Wow!" Mari heard Alli exclaim as a crash and roar sounded. Thinking the deck gun had fired, Mari crouched down over Alain to shield him with her body even though her mind knew that small amount of protection would do no good at all against the destruction that would be wrought by the deck gun's shell.

But no shell came to shatter the *Gray Lady* and her passengers. Asha was kneeling beside her, offering with a gesture to hold Alain safe and pointing toward the Mechanic ship. Mari stood, turning to look back and stopping in mid-turn.

The deck of the Mechanic ship was ablaze between the mainmast and the deck gun, flames leaping upward to devour the rigging and spreading outward along the railings. Figures were running frantically from the deck gun. Mari stared, trying to figure out why they weren't rushing to fight the fire.

"Mari!" she heard Alli yell. "The ready ammunition! Get down!"

Suddenly she realized what Alli was talking about. The big shells stacked next to the deck gun, the flames licking about them as she watched. "Everybody!" Mari shouted. "Hit the deck! As fast as you can!" Disregarding Asha, she dropped down next to Alain and pulled herself over his unconscious body again. "You put everything into that fire to try to save us," Mari whispered in Alain's ear, "and if it doesn't work you're helpless. I'm going to give you an incredibly hard time for taking that risk once you wake up. But until then I'm going to keep you as safe as I can."

A titanic roar born of multiple explosions merging into one sounded from the direction of the Mechanic ship. Mari buried her head next to Alain's, her arm over his face, as pieces of shrapnel tore past overhead, then waited as more fragments of metal and wood rained down upon them. Finally she rose up to look at the Mechanic ship.

A giant had taken a huge bite out of the Mechanic ship where the deck gun had been. The gun itself had fallen through the main deck and lay canted at a crazy angle, barrel pointed almost straight up. Flames had completely engulfed the forward part of the ship, the mainmast had already fallen and, as Mari watched, the foremast toppled slowly sideways like a tree falling to the axe, the top half crashing into the water of the bay and the bottom part lying across the deck of the doomed ship. Mechanics and apprentices were jumping off the ship and into the water, where chunks of wood that once had been part of the ship now served as improvised life preservers and rafts.

Overhead, the sails of the *Gray Lady* were pocked with small holes caused by debris hurled from the blast, and here and there pieces of the rigging hung limp where they had been sliced through.

Alain blinked, looking up with eyes bleary with exhaustion. Mari met his gaze. "That was stupid," she told him angrily. Then she kissed him. "Thank you. I love you." Alain's lips curved into a barely visible smile as he passed out again.

Alli was back on her feet, gazing at the devastated Mechanic ship. "Wow," she repeated. "Alain has got to show me how to do that."

Mari laughed. "Alli, stick to regular explosives." She staggered to her own feet. "Is everyone all right?" Mari saw the captain watching her with an awed expression. "Captain, let's get out of here!"

"Yes, Lady Mari!" he cried. "And thanks to your Mage for our salvation this day!"

Though they saw some harbor guard vessels veering in to rescue the crew of the Mechanic ship, which was now on fire from stem to stern and lighting up the entire harbor with its death throes, none of the guard boats made any move to intercept the *Gray Lady*. Instead, they all took care to avoid the ship with four Mechanics and two Mages visible at the rail. One harbor guard craft armed with a small ballista on the bow angled past the *Gray Lady* close enough that the crew was clearly visible, all of them gazing fixedly toward the wreck of the Mechanic ship as if the *Gray Lady* did not exist.

"They must have heard what you told those commons," Mechanic Dav said in a wondering voice. "We've got commons helping us because they want to, not because they have to. That's so weird. I didn't think anybody could do that, Mari."

They cleared the harbor, past fortifications which remained silent as the *Gray Lady* passed, as the blazing wreck of the Mechanic ship finally sank to settle on the harbor bottom. In the growing light of day it was easy to see a huge cloud of dust and smoke rising over the city of Altis, illuminated from within here and there by fires still raging in various places.

Alli shook her head. "Mari? You really did it this time. I mean, you totally trashed a city, and this harbor is kind of messed up, too."

Mari laughed, though with no immediate crisis to face she was starting to feel the total exhaustion brought on by the labors of the night before. "I didn't do that. It was the Mechanics trying to kill me. Do you think the commons will believe that?"

"You already told them, remember? By now the entire city probably knows that the Mechanics Guild tried to murder Lady Mari, the daughter of Jules herself, and that she got away again." Alli looked at Alain where he still lay on the deck. "She and her Mage. That guy is really handy in an emergency, isn't he?"

"He's nice to have around at other times, too." Mari blinked but couldn't dispel a haziness in her vision despite the growing light as the sun rose in a blaze of glory. Her mind felt full of fog and her legs wobbled unsteadily. She tried to remember how many hours she had been running and fighting and escaping with barely any pause, but her fatigue blurred recent events into a cloud of disjointed images. "Alli, please take command for a while. Tell the Captain to get us away from Altis, whatever course lets us make the best speed and avoids any pursuers."

"Sure. What are you going to do?"

Mari looked down at Alain, chest falling and rising as he slept, Asha kneeling nearby. "I'm going to pass out now." She took a couple of uncertain steps to stand near Asha. "Thanks for everything, Lady Mage. I'll take it from here." Dropping down beside Alain on the deck, she rolled next to him and lost consciousness.

# CHAPTER SEVENTEEN

The *Gray Lady* was running almost due south, coasting before the spring winds, bow slicing through the long swells before her with a rhythmic pounding that Mari found oddly soothing. The white spray occasionally being tossed over the bow shone under the light of the half-moon.

Mari sat on the deck, leaning her back against the railing, staring up at the sails and beyond them the stars. Mage Asha came by, looking down impassively at Mari. "Please join me," Mari offered.

Asha nodded and sat carefully, then uttered a most unmagelike sigh. "We are all so weary, even after a day's rest."

"Tell me about it."

"I did," Asha replied. "You wish me to say it again?"

Mari grinned. "That's just an expression, Lady Mage."

"I see. Why do we go to Julesport?"

"We'll need to take on food and water. The Captain believes that's our safest destination even though the Great Guilds will lean heavily on the Confederation to attack us. He's also worried about the Syndaris, who he says would sell out their own mothers if the price was right."

"If they find we are there," Asha said tonelessly, "the Great Guilds will not depend on commons but mount their own attacks as well. Can we...? I do not know the word. How do we know the shadows in Julesport will not betray us?"

"Can we trust the common people there, you mean?" Mari shrugged. "I think so. I only passed through there once, so I don't know much about the place personally, but the captain told me that Julesport still takes after the person who founded the city."

Asha nodded. "Jules?"

"Herself. Explorer, pirate and hero of the Confederation. She didn't exactly live by the rules."

"My uncle has told me that sailors hold her name in awe to this day," Asha said.

Mari remembered the way the sailors from the *Sun Runner* had reacted to her when they believed she was the daughter of Jules, and the way the sailors on this ship looked at her. She didn't look forward to seeing those gazes constantly aimed at her. "That may be true. Anyway, the captain says that Julesport has never strayed all that far from its origin as her home. They have a fairly lax attitude toward laws and don't ask a lot of inconvenient questions. At the least we can resupply ourselves there and decide on the next destination."

Asha gazed across the dark waters. "If the leaders of Julesport learn that the daughter of Jules is among our number, perhaps they will greet her as a long-lost and long-sought-for relation."

Mari stared up at the stars, wondering which of them was the sun that warmed Urth. "We'll tell them if we have to. It's…uncomfortable for me to call myself that."

"Why?"

"Because it's as if I'm suddenly someone else," Mari explained. "As if Mari of Caer Lyn was never real, that who I always was is just…"

"An illusion?" Asha asked.

"Yes. Exactly. And, really, I don't feel like I'm all that special. On top of which, the daughter has got the biggest job in the world, and if she screws up the entire world goes to blazes, and we don't know how much time we have to work with, but we do know it's very limited." Mari sat quietly for a while longer, wondering at the way she could feel companionship with a female Mage who betrayed no feelings. Maybe it was because Mari's association with Alain had taught her how to see the woman beneath the mask. "Asha, there's something I have to know. About me."

"You have a question about yourself that I can answer?"

"Yes." Mari steeled herself. "About my bonfire."

"Ah. It is remarkable."

Mari gritted her teeth. "You said it had gotten brighter."

"Very much so."

"I just…" Mari buried her face in her knees. "How much can you tell from it?"

"I can tell where you are."

"No. I mean, about other things."

"Other things?" Asha asked.

"What I'm…what Alain and I…are doing."

"Nothing."

Mari jerked her head up, turning to stare at Asha. "Still? Nothing at all?"

"Nothing," Asha repeated.

"But you said it got brighter after Alain and I got married and started, uh…"

"You need not give me details. I know what passes between men and women." Asha's lip twitched in what passed for a Mage smile. "Lady Mechanic Mari, I must explain. The bonfire represents the feelings you hold at the core of your being. They do not change by the day or the week or the month, they do not change based on what your body experiences, but only when there has been a great alteration in your thoughts. Or, if you had taken great harm, then it would weaken. Nothing else affects it."

"So my bonfire only got blinding because I married Alain? Not because of anything we were doing after that? Anything we did that night?"

"When you married him, yes, and committed yourself truly and completely to him, as Alain tells me he has also to you. I believe that is what brightened your feelings. Perhaps the physical sharing you have enjoyed has contributed to the fire within, but if so even that, I think, was fed by the feelings you share. I have seen those who shared their bodies and nothing else. There is no brightness there, nothing that lasts. What I have seen in you was one of the things which caused me to see the importance of the emotions I was taught to deny."

Mari closed her eyes, feeling a wave of relief wash over her. "That is so good to hear. You have no idea how good that is to hear."

Asha nodded. "I can guess now that you have shared your worry. I am a woman, beneath these Mage robes."

"Asha, there is no man in the world who needs to be told that, and I'm pretty such most of the women can figure it out, too."

The female Mage seemed to be trying to smile again. "You and Alain have given much to each other."

Mari grinned. "I think I get more than he does, but he's been nice enough not to complain much."

"A Mage and a Mechanic," Asha mused. "The Mechanic Dav seems interested in me."

"Oh, you've noticed that, have you?"

Even under the starlight Mari could see the humor dancing in Asha's eyes. "Yes. It is nothing I have not seen many times before. But…he feels oddly appealing, this Mechanic, and he acts very nice toward me. He took a great risk to aid you and Alain, even when he did not know you, and he acts brave. Are he and the Mechanic Alli close?"

"No. Alli's got a guy back in Umburan. Well, he was in Umburan. Neither of us is sure where he is right now."

"And the Mechanic Bev has not gone to him for companionship. So perhaps I will see."

Mari grinned again, thinking that Mechanic Dav might soon be happy beyond his wildest dreams for at least a little while. She heard Alain's voice and looked over to see him speak briefly to Bev, who was sitting a little way off on the quarterdeck gazing out to sea. Then Alain came down the deck, pausing before her. "Am I welcome?"

"Why wouldn't you be?" Mari said, patting the deck next to her on the side opposite Asha.

Alain sat down, but still looked cautious. "There was something you wanted to discuss with me once things calmed down."

Mari frowned at him. "There was?"

"In the warehouse. You said we must speak later."

"Oh, yeah. The bonfire thing." Mari waved it off. "Never mind."

"Never mind?" Alain had the look of a man facing a firing squad who had just received a reprieve and had no idea why.

"Right. That's all taken care of. I forgive you."

Alain nodded cautiously. "I am still not sure why I needed forgiveness."

"I'll fill you in some day. How's Bev doing?"

"She is moody." Alain looked back at the quarterdeck. "I think that one bears a deep wound."

Asha nodded in agreement. "She tries to hide it as a Mage would, but she hurts greatly inside."

"Alli said Bev had been an apprentice in Emdin," Mari noted. "Something happened in Emdin, but I don't know what. Something the Guild covered up. I need to corner Alli in some private spot and find out just what sort of things were done to the apprentices in Emdin at the hands of the Senior Mechanics there. There's some very ugly possibilities that I hope didn't happen."

"But," Alain replied, "that you fear did happen?"

"Exactly. Especially given the way Bev is acting. Like you say, the girl's been hurt badly." Mari looked up at the stars again. "What now, Alain? We're going to Julesport, but we can't stay there. You're our best long-term planner. What does the daughter do now? Where do we go next?"

Alain nodded toward the south. "I have given it some thought. I recommend we keep going south."

"What, to Edinton? I've been there, and let me tell you, it's an end-of-the-world sort of city. They even call it that now. End-of-the-world Edinton."

"But Edinton is not the end of the world. I suggest that we go farther south."

Mari puzzled for a moment. "Tiae? Are you serious?"

"Yes." Alain pointed east this time. "We want to be as far from the resources of the Empire as possible. Our Guilds will surely try to enlist the Empire's aid if your strength grows too much, and the Empire itself seeks us because of our visit to Marandur. Yet I think even the Confederation and the Western Alliance could be forced by the Great Guilds to aid action against us, though they would surely be sympathetic to your goals. Syndari is too mercenary to trust. That leaves Tiae or the Free Cities, and the Free Cities are far too close to the Empire despite the protection offered by the Northern Ramparts."

"If there is any place that needs fixing in this world," Asha observed coolly, "it is certainly Tiae, the Broken Kingdom."

Mari looked from Alain to Asha. "A place with no central authority? A place with no armies to muster against us? The Great Guilds have pulled out of Tiae because it wasn't safe even for them, so it's the one place in the world where neither the Mechanics Guild nor the Mage Guild has a presence. Nobody goes to Tiae. It's been that way for years. It would take a while for the Great Guilds to hear we were there, and even longer for them to figure out what we were doing. Valuable breathing space to use those banned texts to start manufacturing things that will give us advantages over the Mechanics Guild and any army of commons. We could find someone decent, some commons trying to rebuild a bulwark of civilization against the anarchy in Tiae, and help them."

"This was my thought," Alain agreed.

"But it's more than that," Mari said, as new ideas came to her. She stared into the darkness. "The unraveling of this world started at Tiae. The authorities in Edinton were scared of it spreading into the Confederation, and you tell me that's just what will happen."

"The storm of chaos," Alain said, nodding.

"So we stop the break there, at the origin," Mari said. "We start fixing Tiae, and the rot won't spread as fast elsewhere. People everywhere will hear that Tiae is rebuilding itself, regaining order and…and freedom, because the Great Guilds aren't there to try to reassume control as soon as that is possible. We'll hit that storm where it's strongest, and we'll beat it."

Mari wrapped her arms around Alain. "My darling, brilliant Mage. The second smartest thing I ever did was not to shoot you in the waste outside of Ringhmon."

Asha had been looking south, but now turned her head to gaze at Mari, her long hair rippling like liquid silver in the starlight. "Not shooting Alain was the second smartest thing you ever did, friend Mari? What was the smartest thing?"

"Marrying him, of course!"

"I see." Asha nodded, her voice still betraying no emotion. "Though you could not have married Alain if you had shot him earlier."

"At the least, it would have made me think carefully about doing such a thing," Alain agreed. Then he gazed at Mari. "Tiae will hold many dangers. I have advised going there, but what you say is true. That is where the storm has begun, and where it is strongest."

"It's not as though anywhere is safe for me," Mari pointed out. "For the first time since you told me about being...the daughter, I really believe I can...*we* can...do this. But it's going to be hard getting to Tiae and building a foothold there. We'll need a lot more Mechanics, and I wouldn't mind some more Mages, and commons, lots of them willing to learn and fight for us, and the Great Guilds are going to be after you and me as soon as they figure out where we are and...have I forgotten anything?"

"It will be a dangerous road and a hard road," Alain said. "It is fortunate that you always prefer the harder road."

She punched his arm, surprised that she had that much energy. "Don't forget that you'll be walking that road too, my Mage. Thank the stars above that we'll be together. The daughter isn't going to be able to do this without your brains, your courage, your skill, and your love. Alain, I'm glad we're not going to Dorcastle. I'm not ready to face the possibility of that big battle your foresight showed you." Mari looked up again as Alli walked over.

"Hey, Mari, you got anything to read?" Alli asked.

"How about some banned technology manuals?" Mari said.

"Oh, yeah! Give me some of that!" Alli's grin faded into a questioning look. "So, how long will this trip be? What's our next move after Julesport?"

"We're going to Tiae."

"Tiae!"

"That's right."

Alli shrugged, then nodded, sitting down to join the group. "Sure. We're Mechanics. We fix things, and Tiae needs to be fixed."

Mari nodded as well, feeling better than she had since boarding the caravan for Ringhmon a year ago. "That's what we're going to do. We've got a world to change, a storm to stop, and some Great Guilds to overthrow, and we're starting there."

# ABOUT THE AUTHOR

"Jack Campbell" is the pseudonym for John G. Hemry, a retired Naval officer who graduated from the U.S. Naval Academy in Annapolis before serving with the surface fleet and in a variety of other assignments. He is the author of The Lost Fleet military science fiction series, as well as the Stark's War series, and the Paul Sinclair series. His short fiction appears frequently in Analog magazine, and many have been collected in ebook anthologies Ad Astra, Borrowed Time, and Swords and Saddles. The Pillars of Reality is his first epic fantasy series. He lives with his indomitable wife and three children in Maryland.

*CONTINUE THE STORY
IN...*

# THE PIRATES
# OF PACTA SERVANDA

PILLARS OF REALITY

BOOK 4

COMING SOON!